A CHIP AND A CHAIR

SEVEN OF SPAD

CORDELIA
KINGSBRIDGE

RIPTIDE
PUBLISHING

Riptide Publishing
PO Box 1537
Burnsville, NC 28714
www.riptidepublishing.com

This is a work of fiction. Names, characters, places, and incidents are either the product of the author's imagination or are used fictitiously. Any resemblance to actual persons living or dead, business establishments, events, or locales is entirely coincidental. All person(s) depicted on the cover are model(s) used for illustrative purposes only.

A Chip and a Chair
Copyright © 2019 by Cordelia Kingsbridge

Cover art: Garrett Leigh, blackjazzdesign.com
Editors: Rachel Haimowitz, Veronica Vega
Layout: L.C. Chase, lcchase.com

All rights reserved. No part of this book may be reproduced or transmitted in any form or by any means, electronic or mechanical, including photocopying, recording, or by any information storage and retrieval system without the written permission of the publisher, and where permitted by law. Reviewers may quote brief passages in a review. To request permission and all other inquiries, contact Riptide Publishing at the mailing address above, at Riptidepublishing.com, or at marketing@riptidepublishing.com.

ISBN: 978-1-62649-642-2

First edition
March, 2019

Also available in ebook:
ISBN: 978-1-62649-641-5

A CHIP AND A CHAIR

SEVEN OF SPADES #5

CORDELIA KINGSBRIDGE

RIPTIDE
PUBLISHING

For my parents, Michael and Victoria, who changed the entire course of my life with one generous offer five years ago. I wouldn't be here without you.

TABLE OF CONTENTS

CHAPTER 1 ♠

"**S**hame you gotta ruin the view," Martine said.

Levi turned from the heavy mesh grating Dominic had installed over the glass door to their new balcony. "It's only temporary. The minute the Seven of Spades is in cuffs, this thing is coming down."

She grinned. "That's what I like to hear."

He meant it, too. Although the Seven of Spades had been inactive in the month following Carolyn Royce's live-streamed murder, he knew the investigation was closing in. He felt the inevitability of the killer's capture in his bones—it was only a matter of time.

Two men came through the apartment's front door, carrying a couch between them—Antoine Valcourt, Martine's tall, laconic husband, and Ezra Stone, husband to Levi's friend Natasha. They almost tripped over the four-year-old boy who barreled around the corner of the island in the center of the room, screaming and laughing at the top of his lungs.

"Jack!" Natasha exclaimed from the kitchen, where she was unpacking boxes of plates and silverware. "What did Mommy say about running inside?"

"It's okay, Natasha, I've got him." Adriana scooped a giggling Jack off the floor, tossed him in the air, and then swung him around with the easy strength built by almost a year of rigorous training with Levi. She'd spent most of the afternoon playing with Jack instead of moving anything, but that was just as helpful.

Trusting Martine's judgment, Levi left her to direct the placement of the couch while he headed out to grab another load from the moving van. Right in the doorway, however, he had to quickly sidestep another couple carting boxes—Carlos and Jasmine, Dominic's now former next-door neighbors.

"It's a good thing *one* of you is so organized." Carlos nodded to his box's neatly printed label, which read *LIVING ROOM* in bold type above a detailed list of the contents. "Dom would have just thrown his crap into random boxes and marked them all 'Stuff.'"

Levi chuckled, took the box Jasmine was holding, and followed them into the living room.

Planting her hands on her hips, Jasmine stood in the center of the open floor plan and looked around with an artist's critical eye. "This is a nice place. Tons of natural light, and I love these hardwood floors."

"Levi, you want this in the spare room, right?" Dominic said behind them.

Any response Levi might have made died when he turned around. Dominic was standing in the entryway, holding one end of a bulky armoire. Underneath its weight, the brawny muscles of his shoulders and arms stood out in sharp relief, glistening with sweat and straining against the sleeves of his T-shirt. Beneath that, basketball shorts clung to the rock-hard ass and massive thighs that gave him the thrusting power of a jackhammer.

The other end of the armoire was supported by Dominic's brother Vinnie, who was similar to Dominic in height and build. But Vinnie and everyone else in the room might as well have ceased to exist for all Levi was aware of them. His mind went blank.

Dominic cleared his throat. "Baby, this is kind of heavy," he said, his warm eyes crinkling at the corners.

"Sorry." Levi snapped himself out of it, his face flushing. "The spare room, yeah."

He and Dominic had chosen a two-bedroom apartment so Levi could use one room as an office—and, honestly, an escape route for when he needed to be alone. He was far more introverted than Dominic, who thrived on personal connections with everyone from the mailman to passing strangers.

As Dominic and Vinnie carried the armoire away, Dominic flinched and subtly shifted more of its weight to his right arm. Levi's eyes narrowed. Dominic had been fine when they'd gone their separate ways this morning, but since they'd reconnected in the afternoon, Levi had noticed him favoring his left side three times now.

Levi's thoughts were interrupted by the entrance of the last member of their moving party, Leila. "What about these?" she asked. "They're the only things that aren't labeled."

His breath caught when he saw the two file boxes she was holding, one stacked atop the other. They were locked, but if Leila of all people somehow got a glimpse of what was inside—

"I'll take those." He snatched the boxes out of her arms so fast he almost knocked them to the floor. "Actually, I'll deal with all the boxes that look like this. Don't worry about it."

She gave him an odd look. "Okay," she said slowly, before returning the way she'd come, accompanying Carlos and Jasmine on another run to the truck.

Martine appeared at Levi's side. "You need to get your shit together," she hissed so that only he could hear. "If you keep acting so weird around Leila, she's gonna figure out something's up."

"I'm not good at hiding things."

"Try harder."

Levi sighed. Given their recently aroused misgivings about Leila, he probably shouldn't have asked her to help today, but that would have been just as suspicious.

He brought the file boxes into the spare room. They were the first two of more than a dozen identical containers; each was crammed full of his and Dominic's independent investigation into the Seven of Spades, which properly belonged in the armoire Dominic and Vinnie were placing against the wall. Most of the work in these boxes had never been seen by eyes other than Dominic's, Martine's, and his own, and he planned on keeping it that way.

After Vinnie left the room, Dominic lingered behind with Levi. "Have you seen Rebel?"

"She's in the master bedroom. She's been moping in there all afternoon—it's not like her at all."

"I know," Dominic said glumly. "I think she's upset we're moving."

"She'll adjust, especially once she sees that great dog park."

Dominic leaned down to kiss Levi, then brushed his lips over the jagged diagonal scar that slashed across Levi's forehead. Levi's eyes drifted shut.

After the Seven of Spades had murdered a man in Levi's last apartment, he'd only returned to remove his belongings. He'd been staying at Dominic's place since the day they'd gotten back together five weeks ago, but they'd both known that wasn't a sustainable solution. Dominic's apartment was too small, and while the closeness had helped solidify their reunion, it wasn't practical over the long term. They'd started apartment-hunting right away.

At first, they'd had trouble finding a building that was willing to even show them around. Everyone in the goddamn country knew a serial killer was prone to dropping bodies around Levi, and Levi himself was a notorious public figure—though now that he'd been cleared of suspicion in the Seven of Spades's crimes, public sentiment once more skewed heavily in his favor.

He and Dominic had finally found a building more intrigued by the cachet of housing the famous Detective Levi Abrams than they were worried about the Seven of Spades striking again. The place also met his and Dominic's stringent security requirements—gated grounds, in-unit alarm system, and a management company that would let them install increased security measures on all the doors and windows—so Levi hadn't hesitated to sign the lease.

Dominic's name wasn't on it. Even after Levi's ex, Stanton, had paid off Dominic's mountain of gambling debts, Dominic's rock-bottom credit would have had their application rejected out of hand, cachet or no. The lease was an extremely touchy subject for Dominic, so although they were making a conscious effort to keep the lines of communication open and honest, that was one topic they always skirted around.

"So are you gonna help me move some of the furniture," Dominic said, "or were you just planning to ogle me lifting heavy objects all day?"

Levi smacked his ass. "I'll ogle you later," he said, and led the way out of the room.

Within two hours, the moving truck was empty, and while dozens of unpacked boxes littered every room, all of the basics were in place. Levi ordered enough pizza to feed everyone, and they spread out around the living room and dining nook to devour the food with the kind of hunger only inspired by manual labor.

When Levi was with his friends, talk usually turned to work, because they were all in law enforcement. Even Ezra had chosen a career of service similar to his wife's, spending the past eight years as a public defender. But Dominic's friends and family were civilians—not to mention Adriana and little Jack—so the conversation remained lighthearted, never straying toward topics of blood and death.

Balancing his paper plate on his lap, Levi curled up next to Dominic on the couch—*their* couch—and basked in the warmth of being surrounded by love and friendship. The Seven of Spades had tried to take this away from him. They'd failed, and they would keep failing as long as he had breath in his lungs.

Everyone departed gradually after dinner. Natasha and Ezra left first, wanting to get an overtired Jack home before a tantrum; Martine and Antoine followed, needing to pick up their teenage daughters. When Leila left, Levi managed to behave normally as he said goodbye.

"See you guys at brunch tomorrow?" Vinnie asked at the door.

"We'll be there," said Dominic.

Vinnie shook Levi's hand, then pulled Dominic into a brief hug and slapped his back. As Vinnie walked away, Levi rubbed the spot between Dominic's shoulder blades.

The relapse of Dominic's gambling addiction had strained all of his relationships, including those with his large, tight-knit family. He was doing his best to rebuild them now, starting with regular attendance at their weekly Sunday lunches. He and Levi hadn't missed one since he'd quit gambling again.

The last people remaining were Carlos, Jasmine, and Adriana. Trying not to be too obvious, Levi pulled Adriana off to the side to give Dominic some privacy with his friends. They'd lived next door to each other for years, and this parting was going to be difficult all around.

Levi watched from the corner of his eye as Dominic faced Carlos and Jasmine. The three of them stood in silence for a moment before Jasmine burst into tears.

"Hey, come on," Dominic said, though he didn't look far from the verge of tears himself.

"I'm sorry, it's just . . ." She swiped at her cheeks. "It's going to be so *weird* not having you right next door. We'll go from seeing you multiple times a day to, what, once a week?"

"I didn't move that far; we'll still see each other all the time." Dominic embraced her and dropped a kiss on top of her head. "Things were changing anyway. I mean, fuck, you guys are getting married next weekend. You wouldn't want me around after that."

Jasmine laughed against his chest. Dominic reached out to rest one hand on Carlos's shoulder.

"Leaving you guys is the only thing that sucks about moving," he said, his voice cracking.

Carlos joined them, his eyes glistening, turning it into a three-way hug. Levi retreated farther, uncomfortable with the display of emotion, and he could tell Adriana felt the same way.

He threw a punch at her face.

She had her hands down, not ready for it, and she reacted exactly the way a Krav Maga practitioner at her early level should—she leaned back out of the range of his strike even as her hands came up, one to redirect his fist and the other to protect her face. Her foot lashed out, stopping just short of what would have been a solid kick to the groin, and then she disengaged.

"Nice." Pride warmed Levi's chest. "Just passed your P1 test, and you've already got some of your P2 curriculum down."

She grinned, turned in profile, and sent a side kick toward his knee. He swept her leg aside with one arm.

They played around like that, trading light blows back and forth, until Carlos and Jasmine were ready to go. As everyone said their goodbyes by the front door, Levi hugged Adriana gently, mindful of her need to not feel restrained. "See you at the rehearsal dinner."

She surprised him by kissing his cheek, something she'd never done before. "See ya." She gave Dominic a stiffer smile—she still wasn't comfortable around him. "Bye, Dominic."

The door closed behind them, leaving Levi and Dominic alone in their new apartment for the first time. Well, except for Rebel, who was still sulking in the bedroom.

The apartment was quiet, the vibe strangely awkward. Levi looked at Dominic, struck by the reality of the situation: this was their home now. They would go to bed together tonight, wake up together tomorrow morning, and after they went about their respective days, they'd return here, to their shared haven from the outside world. And that would happen every single day for the foreseeable future.

Dominic was the first to break the silence. "This is weird, right?"

"Yes," Levi said, relieved he wasn't alone. "But I don't know why. We've already been living together for more than a month."

"Not really. You were crashing at my place; now we live together in *our* place. It's not the same."

He was right. And for Levi, it wasn't even the same as the two years he'd lived with Stanton, because this carried a sense of permanency he'd never felt before. Dominic was his *bashert*, his soul mate, his partner fated by God. This . . . this was it. The beginning of the rest of his life.

Dominic rubbed the back of his neck. "Do you think we rushed into this?"

"No." Levi closed the distance between them, settling his hands on Dominic's waist. "It was the right decision for us. That doesn't mean there won't be an adjustment period."

He tilted his face up, and Dominic answered his unspoken request, kissing him deep and slow. Levi melted into it with a sigh, sliding his hands up Dominic's chest—and then broke the kiss when Dominic flinched.

"I knew it," he said. "You're injured."

"I'm not—"

Levi tapped the left side of Dominic's chest, right where he judged the injury to be. Dominic grimaced, cursed, and stumbled backward, his shoulders hunching in an instinctive pain response before he straightened himself out.

"You said you wouldn't lie to me anymore, Dominic." Fear was bitter in the back of Levi's throat. He didn't know how a chest injury could be connected to gambling, but they'd been apart all morning. If Dominic had relapsed and was lying about it again, hiding it *again*, after he'd promised he wouldn't—

"I'm not lying!" Dominic raised both hands. "It's nothing bad, I swear. I just . . . It was supposed to be a surprise."

Giving him the side-eye, Levi said, "You wanted to surprise your homicide-detective boyfriend whose paranoia is at an all-time high after being stalked by a serial killer for a year?"

"...Yes?"

Levi snorted and gestured for Dominic to proceed, curious despite himself. Dominic stripped off his T-shirt.

There was a fresh tattoo on Dominic's left pectoral muscle, right over his heart—two lines of simple black Hebrew script. It was still raw, dotted with blood, and covered with a clear bandage. Levi's mouth fell open, but no sound came out.

"Jasmine did it this morning," Dominic said. "It was the only open slot in her schedule. Can you read it?"

Levi brushed his fingertips just below the tattoo. He'd forgotten most of the Hebrew he'd learned decades ago for his bar mitzvah, of course, but he would have recognized this quote anywhere because it was so iconic.

"'*Ani l'dodi v'dodi li*,'" he murmured. "'I am my beloved's and my beloved is mine.' Song of Songs 6:3."

"One of Jasmine's foster brothers is a cantor now. He wrote it down for us so we could be sure it was right."

Levi's throat was so swollen with emotion he wasn't sure he could speak. He coughed, swallowed hard, and managed, "You understand the irony in getting a tattoo to honor your Jewish boyfriend, right?"

Dominic laughed. "Oh, please. Plenty of Jews have tattoos these days. I crossed paths with the IDF a few times while I was with the Rangers, and lots of those guys are tatted up six ways from Sunday."

Smiling, Levi studied the tattoo a few seconds longer. He leaned forward and very carefully grazed his lips against the bandage. Dominic shivered, exhaling one shuddering breath.

Levi looked up at him. "I am."

Dominic raised an eyebrow.

"My beloved's," Levi said softly.

"So am I," said Dominic, brushing his fingers along Levi's cheekbone.

They kissed again, more urgently this time, twining around each other as if they couldn't get close enough. In that moment, everything in Levi's life was perfect, his happiness complete.

He pulled back just enough to speak against Dominic's mouth. "Take me to our bedroom."

CHAPTER 2

"Uh-oh, Big Man on Campus alert," Justine Aubrey said as Dominic entered the break room at McBride Investigations later that week.

The half-dozen people in the room exploded into whistles and catcalls. Waving them off, Dominic set his mug beneath the single-cup coffeemaker and dropped in a pod of dark roast. "All right, guys, take it down a notch."

"Seriously, Dom," said one of the firm's receptionists. "Hammond & Cochran has been searching for Gary Booker for six months, and you found him in four *days*. How'd you do it?"

He gave her a sly wink that had her blushing down at her sandwich. "Trade secret."

It wasn't, really. But flushing out Booker—a missing witness in a multimillion-dollar class action lawsuit—had required an exhausting, complicated scheme involving a flower shop, a Persian rug, and a speedboat, and he was *not* getting into that before he'd even had lunch.

Aubrey bumped her shoulder against his arm. She'd supervised his first time in the field with McBride, and he had the sense that she took his success or failure personally. "You've been on a real hot streak lately. Cases are toppling like dominos."

Yeah, it's amazing what I can accomplish when I focus my time and energy on work instead of gambling.

"Just having a run of good luck, I guess," he said.

His coffee had finished brewing when Kate McBride herself popped her head into the break room. "Heard you were in here, Russo," she said in her hoarse smoker's voice. "You ready for another case?"

He poured a generous helping of cream into his coffee. "Sure."

"I'll send the client your way at two. Big payout with this one, but it's a sensitive case that needs to be handled delicately."

"Understood." Dominic dumped three packets of sugar into his mug, followed by some hazelnut syrup for good measure.

"You're going to end up with diabetes," said McBride.

He grinned and took a long, exaggerated sip.

Once alone in his office, Dominic stripped out of his jacket and loosened the knot in his tie. He reached for the sandwich he'd bought for lunch, only to clench his hands into fists when he noticed them shaking. He bowed his head and took several deep breaths.

His gambling cravings were usually triggered by feelings of worthlessness and guilt—something he was unpacking with the therapist Natasha had referred him to—but he also felt the urge when in a celebratory mood. Right now, he was flush with the adrenaline and triumph of having tricked Booker into revealing himself, elated by his colleagues' admiration and his boss's trust. All he wanted was to keep that high going in any way possible.

Lifting his head, he thought through the situation logically. He was safe at work. The software installed on his computer blocked all gambling-related websites, and he wouldn't leave when he was expecting a client in an hour. Besides, he only had sixty dollars in his wallet. He'd destroyed his debit card and all his credit cards, along with his personal checks. The only way for him to access his bank account was through electronic transfer or by withdrawing cash in person, which threw another obstacle in his path to gambling.

It didn't make it impossible, though. He was fine now, but what about when he left the office?

He glanced at the locked drawer in the bottom of his desk. Levi and Martine were expecting him for dinner tonight, during which they'd discuss the troubling research he'd hidden inside—research Levi had asked *him* to do because some of it wasn't precisely legal. Dominic couldn't miss that conversation, but he also didn't want to jeopardize his recovery.

He tapped out a quick text to Levi. *Going to be late for dinner. I need to go to a meeting after work.*

Levi's reply came less than a minute later. *No problem. Call me if you need me.*

Dominic smiled. It was always painful for him to admit to Levi when he was struggling, but that was his own hang-up. Levi never failed to offer immediate reassurance, and his support was consistently unwavering.

After ensuring that his sponsor, Judd, was planning to attend the Gamblers Anonymous meeting as well, Dominic was able to return his attention to where it belonged. He ate lunch while he wrapped up his report on the Booker case, and by the time his new client arrived, he was much steadier.

McBride had emailed him the basics, and a quick assessment of Miranda Cassidy confirmed his expectations. White, late thirties, attractive, and well put-together with an old-money aura.

He showed her into a chair and offered her a drink before settling behind his desk. As he smoothed out his tie, he caught her giving him a strange look.

"I'm sorry, you seem so familiar," she said. "Have we met?"

This was happening more and more often lately. "No, but you may have seen me on the news. I'm Detective Levi Abrams's partner."

Recognition sparked in her eyes, followed by a flash of distaste that she wasn't quite quick enough to suppress.

"Is that a problem?" he asked neutrally.

"Of course not," she said with a thin-lipped smile. "I'm sure it has no bearing on your effectiveness as an investigator."

Wow, thanks. Maintaining his pleasant expression, Dominic poised his pen over his notepad. "Ms. McBride told me you're interested in having your ex-husband Conrad Bishop placed under surveillance?"

"Yes. I believe he's using drugs again."

"That was a problem during your marriage?"

"It's why we divorced." Cassidy crossed her legs primly at the knee. "The damage Conrad was doing to himself and his career was bad enough, but when he started getting high around our children, I was done."

McBride's email had mentioned the kids—two of them, ages nine and seven. "Does Mr. Bishop have any custody?"

She nodded. "While we were divorcing, he went to rehab and got clean, so the judge awarded him every other weekend. But if he *is* using again, that would violate the agreement—"

"Giving you sole custody?"

"Yes."

Dominic tapped his pen against the desk. He preferred to keep an open mind until he had all the facts, but Cassidy's poorly veiled homophobia had already biased him. He couldn't help wondering if this was retribution on her part, a ploy to snatch her kids away from their dad as payback for the failed marriage. People with addiction problems made easy targets for witch hunts.

"What makes you think Mr. Bishop has relapsed?"

"I was married to the man for almost a decade. I know when he's hiding something. Plus, his friends and coworkers have all told me he's been acting oddly for months—ducking their calls, canceling plans at the last minute without explanation. The last three weekends that he had the children, he hired a babysitter in the evenings and didn't come home until the middle of the night. It's the same pattern of behavior I noticed when we were married."

She'd done some investigating on her own, then. "I'll need a lot more information from you to set up a feasible surveillance operation," Dominic said. "But before we dive into that, I want to make sure you understand that it's impossible to prove a negative. If your ex-husband is abusing drugs again, I'll be able to find hard evidence of that. But if he isn't . . ." Dominic shrugged. The lack of proof drove some clients crazy, as they refused to accept that their target wasn't guilty.

"He is," Cassidy said with total confidence.

"All right. Let's get started."

"Police!" Levi flashed his badge as his suspect exited the 7-Eleven. "Hands up."

The man, a Utopia gangbanger by the name of Lonnie Hale, took off running. Levi smiled—he'd been hoping the scumbag would give him a chance to stretch his legs.

Hale darted around the side of the building, parallel to the street, and through the back lot. He tossed his plastic shopping bag at Levi's face as he ran; Levi dodged, gaining ground with every step.

The car wash behind the 7-Eleven was built on a slight incline. Hale leapt the guardrail, but lost his footing and rolled down the slope on the other side, right into the road. A horn blared as a car slammed to a halt, missing him by inches before he sprang back up and continued running.

Levi vaulted the guardrail smoothly and landed without a problem. He didn't bother drawing his gun as he chased Hale across the road—he wouldn't have fired even if there'd been nobody else around for miles, let alone in a civilian-populated area.

Besides, he didn't need a gun to bring this asshole down. Hale was already flagging, winded by the sprint and limping from the tumble he'd taken. Levi caught up as they hopped a low wall into a derelict shopping plaza, and tackled Hale to the asphalt.

Hale swung at him, wild punches that Levi easily countered before flipping the man onto his stomach and pinning his skinny, tattooed arms at the small of his back. "Lonnie Hale, you're under arrest for the murders of Victor Nuñez and Javier Ibarra. You have the right to remain silent. Anything you say can and will be used against you in a court of law."

Levi stood, hauling Hale upright.

"You have the right to an attorney. If you cannot afford an attorney, one will be provided for you. Do you understand these rights as I have read them to you?"

Hale scowled at Levi over his shoulder. "I don't take orders from Jews," he said, and spat in Levi's face.

Levi's hands tightened on Hale's arm. Rage clawed at his heart and lungs, crashing against his rib cage like a feral animal desperate to be set free. It would be so satisfying to smash his fist into Hale's face, feel the bones break, watch the blood spurt—

STOP.

He replaced the violent fantasy with the image of a stop sign. *He* was in control of his anger; it wasn't in control of him.

Levi wiped the saliva off his face with the sleeve of his suit jacket, then smiled coldly. Hale looked disappointed—little wonder, because a police brutality charge could have gone a long way toward having his case thrown out.

"Maybe you'll enjoy taking orders from your cellmate," Levi said. Hale blanched.

"Sorry I'm late," Levi said as he hurried into the conference room at the substation. "I got a hit on the gun used in that double homicide and traced it back to a Utopia foot soldier."

Martine made a disgusted noise in the back of her throat. "Those freaks need to be shut down *yesterday*."

Her assessment was met with murmured agreement throughout the room. Utopia, a neo-Nazi street gang turned private militia, grew larger and more brazen every week. Intent on spreading their venomous message while grabbing up resources, territory, and fresh recruits wherever they could, they were responsible for a string of violent hate crimes across the Las Vegas Valley. The two men Hale had killed had been members of Los Avispones, a Latino gang that was Utopia's fiercest rival.

But while Utopia was a huge problem for the city, Levi's involvement was limited to picking up their members when their murders crossed his desk. In the larger organizational sense, Utopia was the responsibility of either Gang Crimes or Organized Crime, depending on who was winning that turf war on any given day.

Levi's focus belonged here, with the official task force created to address the city's other largest threat—the Seven of Spades.

He'd been reinstated to the task force after being cleared of suspicion in the Seven of Spades's crimes. The group was run by Dean Birndorf, captain of the Homicide Bureau; in addition to Levi and Martine, it included their sergeant James Wen and a cross-departmental selection of detectives, uniformed officers, and technical support staff. Leila Rashid and Special Agent Denise Marshall served as their liaisons to the DA's office and the FBI, respectively.

Levi took the empty seat beside Martine. "What did I miss?" He couldn't quite meet Leila's eyes as he sat, but he felt her heavy gaze.

"Not much," said Wen, who was as impeccably dressed and well-groomed as always. "We were just discussing the killer's radio silence—no new murders, no phone calls, no messages, no contact of any kind for over a month now. It's the longest the Seven of Spades has remained inactive since framing Keith Chapman."

"And it's all thanks to Levi's epic bitch-slap." Martine elbowed his side.

Levi agreed that his reaction to Carolyn Royce's murder had rattled the Seven of Spades—but whether they'd withdrawn simply to lick their wounds or to gear up for some sensational vengeful return, he couldn't say. He remained on high alert regardless.

"How are things proceeding with the ketamine angle?" Denise asked.

"No developments," said Levi. "But it's kind of like looking for one specific drop of water in a lake."

The Seven of Spades used ketamine to drug their victims into a dissociative paralysis before slitting their throats. From the beginning, Levi had believed the killer obtained the drug from a legitimate source. For one thing, illicit sales of ketamine were small-scale, not the kind of operations that would allow for stockpiling. Legal channels were more reliable, involved far less risk of exposure, and carried no need to tangle with criminal elements.

The problem was the sheer number of people who had legitimate access to ketamine. In addition to countless individual practitioners, the drug flowed from manufacturers and distributors to pharmacies, hospitals, clinics, teaching institutions, and laboratories. The Seven of Spades could be getting their hands on it anywhere along that supply chain.

Levi's gut told him the Seven of Spades would prefer the end of the chain, where there were fewer moving parts and they'd have greater control over their access. With the cooperation of the DEA's Diversion Control Division, he'd spent the past year reviewing the licenses of every practitioner registered to dispense Schedule III controlled substances, beginning within the Las Vegas city limits and expanding outward in a circular geographic pattern. One by one, he'd researched every individual for criminal backgrounds, ties to personnel in the LVMPD and DA's office, unusual business practices, and other red flags.

In the process, he'd discovered several small, unrelated diversion operations, and he'd passed that information along to the appreciative DEA. But as far as the Seven of Spades was concerned, he'd had no luck.

"Do you need more personnel on it?" Birndorf asked.

Levi nodded. "That would be helpful. It's time-consuming work, and pretty tedious."

"Sounds like it'd be right up your alley," said Jonah Gibbs, a ruddy-faced officer with a hot temper that rivaled Levi at his worst.

"Thank you for volunteering, Officer," Wen said.

As Gibbs spluttered indignantly, Levi tried to hide his dismay. Having Gibbs on this would only slow him down, because he'd have to double-check every single thing Gibbs did.

"You can have all the people you need." Birndorf gestured to the massive board on the wall, which held brief profiles of the task force's top suspects. "Make sure you're cross-referencing all your results with the suspect pool."

"Of course, sir." Levi exchanged a quick sideways glance with Martine, but broke the eye contact before he could give anything away.

The task force's suspect pool was based on FBI agent Rohan Chaudhary's criminal profile of the Seven of Spades, further culled through personal histories, interviews, tips from the Seven of Spades hotline, and other investigative techniques. But Levi and Martine both knew that cross-referencing the ketamine investigation with that list would be a waste of time—the *real* top suspects weren't anywhere on the board.

In fact, half of them were sitting in this very room.

CHAPTER 3 ♠

"I'm glad you called," Judd said to Dominic. All around them, the room was filled with quiet chatter, rustling, and scraping chairs as the GA meeting broke up.

"I'm glad you could make it," said Dominic.

"That's what I'm here for." Judd was a big guy, as broad across as Dominic though not quite as tall, with a wild black beard and a taste for leather vests. "Did you tell Levi you were struggling today?"

"Yeah."

"How'd he take it?"

"Same as always—calm, supportive."

Judd eyed Dominic shrewdly. "But you still hated telling him, right?"

Dominic heaved himself out of his chair, folded it up, and carried it over to stack with the rest against the wall of the church rec room. "You don't understand. I know he loves me, and I know he supports my recovery. We broke up because I lied and manipulated him, not because I relapsed. But Levi is the strongest person I've ever met, and it's embarrassing to have to expose this weakness to him over and over. There's always a part of me that's worried *this* will be the time he gets sick of it and decides he's had enough."

"Addiction is a disease, not a weakness," Judd reminded him. "From what you've told me, Levi understands that better than you do. And you said he's got his own issues with anger management. There are some similarities there, so he's in a better position to empathize than most people. All he wants to see is that you're putting in the work—which you have been."

"I know all of that intellectually," Dominic said. "But I don't *feel* it yet."

Judd clapped his shoulder. "You'll get there. Just keep working the steps."

They parted a few minutes later, and Dominic headed home with his gambling cravings in check. He slung his messenger bag over one shoulder as he jumped out of his pickup truck and then climbed the stairs to the new apartment.

Rebel rushed to greet him the moment he stepped inside, her wagging tail swaying her hundred-pound body as she butted up against his legs. Dominic knelt to scruff her ears and kiss the tip of her nose.

"Hey, sweetheart. Did you miss me?"

He laughed when she licked his face. After her despondent behavior that first day, he'd worried about how the move would affect her—but she'd bounced back the very next day, returning to her usual cheerful, energetic self without a hint of distress. She'd been loving her explorations of the new complex, immediately taking to the agility course in the fancy on-site dog park.

"We're in the spare room!" Levi called out.

Dominic walked through the open door to find Levi stretched out on the carpet and Martine sitting at the desk chair, both of them surrounded by take-out containers of Thai food. His heart swelled with the same warmth he'd felt every night this week upon seeing Levi safe and comfortable in *their* home. He was sure the novelty would wear off eventually, but he'd never lived with a romantic partner before, and he was enjoying every moment of this honeymoon phase.

The room's double-door armoire stood open to its full extension, exposing walls papered with photographs, maps, and newspaper articles, as well as a shelf of overflowing folders crammed with their Seven of Spades research. Levi had been conducting this independent investigation on his own last year until Dominic discovered it over the summer and offered his help; they'd looped in Martine after Carolyn Royce's murder.

Once Dominic had greeted them both, Levi said, "I put your food in the refrigerator."

"Thanks, but I'm good for now." Dominic dropped his bag on the floor and settled next to Levi; Rebel cuddled up to him, and he slung an arm around her. "I had a few too many doughnuts at the meeting."

He left it at that. Martine was like a sister to Levi, and well aware of Dominic's compulsive gambling—but Dominic found the issue difficult enough to discuss with Levi, let alone anyone else.

"How's your side project coming along?" Martine asked.

"Finished, actually." Dominic watched as Levi stiffened and dropped his fork into his panang curry. There was a reason Dominic hadn't shared that news in advance—Levi would have stewed in his anxiety about it all day.

Dominic withdrew a thick stack of folders from his messenger bag and passed them to Levi, who hurriedly wiped his hands on a paper towel before accepting them.

"You were right," said Dominic. "Leila doesn't have a concrete alibi for a single one of the Seven of Spades murders. There are a few where she has a vague alibi, but those could all go either way. And during the week in December when Grant Sheppard was murdered in Philadelphia, she was out of town—ostensibly with her family in St. Louis."

Levi closed his eyes for a second, then leapt to his feet, shoved the folders into Martine's hands, and began pacing the room. Martine and Dominic looked at each other.

She and Levi had asked Dominic to investigate Leila's movements and behavior over the past year because legal access to much of that information would have required warrants—which would have alerted Leila to their suspicions. Thanks to his years as a bounty hunter, Dominic knew how to subtly break the rules, and didn't mind doing so when necessary.

"In Leila's defense, she wouldn't have an alibi for most things," Martine said. "Her job has little oversight, she lives alone, and she has few social ties."

Levi turned around. "You're not making her sound *less* like a serial killer."

"You were the one who raised her as a suspect in the first place!"

"I—"

"Levi," Dominic interrupted gently. "The reason you had to start your own investigation last year was because the LVMPD has never been on the right track when it comes to the Seven of Spades. That's still true today. You've said yourself that the task force is concentrating on all the wrong suspects because they're ignoring one of the most vital parts of the profile—the killer's personal connection to you."

Levi pressed his lips together. "The profile says the killer respects and admires me. That doesn't necessarily mean I have a relationship with them."

"But it's the likeliest scenario." Martine had spread the folders out on the desk, and she leafed through them as she spoke. "The intensity of their focus on you, the personal details they know, the way they've repeatedly risked exposure to help you—that's not the behavior of a person who only knows you from afar."

"I didn't even meet Leila until months after the Seven of Spades's first round of murders."

"It doesn't matter. I consulted with Rohan about this—he says that even if the Seven of Spades was only initially drawn to you because you were one of the lead detectives on the first murders, the connection they formed with you during the case would have driven them to establish a relationship with you under their real identity."

Expelling a noisy breath, Levi slumped against the wall. Dominic wanted to hug him, but he knew Levi wouldn't want to be touched in this mood, so he stayed on the floor and stroked his hand through Rebel's fur instead. He couldn't begin to imagine how painful it must be for Levi to put his friends and colleagues under a microscope like this.

Dominic pointed to one of the armoire's doors, which held the paper listing their top five suspects for the Seven of Spades, none of whom the task force had considered. They all fit the official profile, though: able-bodied adults, intelligent and well educated, working in law enforcement or related fields in positions which allowed freedom of movement throughout the day, each with a personal connection to Levi, and all but one with a history of significant trauma. Further, none of them had been present for any of the Seven of Spades's phone calls, nor the live murder of Carolyn Royce.

"We put together our own suspect pool weeks ago because we knew the LVMPD was going about it all wrong. Maybe we should go through the top suspects again, break them down individually."

Levi nodded, pushed himself off the wall, and resumed pacing. "Going from least to most likely, then. Kelly Marin."

Martine swallowed a mouthful of pad thai. "She was positioning herself as your protégé when the first murders occurred. She was involved with and interested in the Seven of Spades case from the beginning, and most importantly, she leaked the story to the *Review-Journal* after being explicitly ordered not to."

"She's also remained loyal to you ever since, including harassing me at your request." Dominic couldn't quite keep a sour note out of his tone.

Levi shot him a weary glance. "You said you forgave me for that."

"*Plus*," Martine said, "she was the responding officer when you found Quintana's body in your apartment, even though we found out later that there was another unit closer at the time."

"Counterarguments?" Dominic asked.

"She's too young," Levi said immediately. "I don't buy that she's had enough experience to leave flawless crime scenes or know her way around the surveillance equipment used to spy on us, let alone how to finesse security systems or hire a contract killer like Nick Bryce. And do we really think she has the emotional maturity to be so smoothly manipulative?"

Dominic agreed that it *was* kind of a reach. The primary reasons Kelly was under consideration were the news leak and Levi's mentorship. "She's also the only one on the list who never experienced a traumatic event, at least as far as we know. That means no trigger to become the Seven of Spades, according to Rohan."

They knew far more about their suspects' histories with trauma than they should have, thanks to Internal Affairs detective Valeria Montoya. She'd done extensive background research on personnel throughout the LVMPD and DA's office before turning the information—most of which had been well-guarded secrets—over to Levi. That insider knowledge was one of the things that gave Levi and Martine a leg up on the task force.

"Moving on, then." Martine pushed her food aside and scrubbed her napkin over her mouth. "Sergeant Wen."

Still striding restlessly around the room, Levi said, "He's been uncharacteristically heavy-handed about the Seven of Spades from the start. He refused to hear me out when I argued that Keith had been framed, he dismissed the card the killer left in my hotel room as a practical joke, and he suspended me when he found out about my side investigation, all without ever giving me a fair chance to state my case. Then, when the Seven of Spades was trying to isolate me from everyone last month, Wen was the one who kicked me off the task force and later suspended me again."

Dominic kept the ball rolling. "We know for a fact he was aware of the assault on Sergei Volkov's compound in advance, which means he would have had plenty of time to set up the Seven of Spades's intervention. And after that whole clusterfuck, he put in a good word for me with McBride, which ended up saving my job."

"He was shot by friendly fire while serving with the Marines, and a superior officer betrayed him by trying to cover it up," Martine said. "Could speak to motive."

Levi shook his head. "Not really. That officer was later discovered and court-martialed, so justice was served in that case. And honestly, Sergeant Wen? I just can't see it."

Dominic sighed; Levi had said that about every suspect they'd considered at one point or another. "Levi . . ."

"I'm serious. Wen is too neat. I don't think he's obsessed with cleanliness to the point of mental illness, but he hates messes and he always needs to have everything just so. The way the Seven of Spades kills people results in a ton of messy blood splatter. This may sound weird, but I think Wen would be too grossed out to murder people that way."

"That's . . ." Martine paused, her brow furrowing. "A good point, actually."

Deferring to their greater familiarity with Wen, Dominic said, "Okay. How about Montoya?"

"She was one of the IA detectives investigating Keith for police brutality," Levi said. "She would have known he'd make a perfect fall guy."

Martine hummed agreement. "She attended Rohan's briefing on the Seven of Spades's profile even though the department hadn't requested an IA presence, and she took it upon herself to get involved in the case for reasons she hasn't fully explained. Giving you her research could have been a mind game or a way of connecting to you—or both."

"Plus, we know from the things she uncovered that she has suspicious access to some highly protected information, including your assault in college," Dominic pointed out. "If she's the Seven of Spades, researching that could have been how she realized there was more to the story and discovered the bribe that kept your attackers from being identified."

Levi made a face, his shoulders twitching like he was physically shrugging off the memories. "Most damning, she was assigned to *my* IA investigation when I was suspended, and the afternoon of my hearing—the afternoon Carolyn Royce was murdered—Montoya was held up on another case. She knew exactly when I would be at the substation, and she managed to be conveniently absent."

"Arguments against?" Martine asked.

"We've never had much of a relationship. Before the murders, we were distant colleagues at best. Now, I consider her an ally, but we're definitely not friends. I can't believe that she has strong feelings about me one way or the other."

"Let's table her for now, then," said Dominic. "That brings us to Jonah Gibbs."

"Fuck, where to start? He's been lurking around the fringes of this case since day one." Levi counted his points off on his fingers while he spoke. "Gibbs is the one who *named* the Seven of Spades, for God's sake. He's been present at multiple Seven of Spades crime scenes. He was the first responder when Drew Barton attacked me, even though my hotel was nowhere near his usual beat. And he was outside the Regional Justice Center when Barton was shot, because *somehow*, his schedule always seems to line up with mine."

Martine picked up the thread from there. "He's expressed empathy with the Seven of Spades on numerous occasions. He was relieved when Carmen Rivera escaped custody after being revealed as a mole.

And the day after the Seven of Spades mass-murdered those Slavic Collective human traffickers—the only time their victims put up serious resistance—he came to work with significant facial injuries."

"His explanation for that was legitimate, though," Dominic said. "I checked it out myself. He *was* assaulted during a domestic disturbance call."

"He could have gone into that call already injured and deliberately provoked the guy into hitting him."

"Hmm. I can find out." Dominic made a note for himself on his phone. Rebel, annoyed he'd stopped petting her, bumped her head into his shoulder and then leaned her considerable weight against his side.

"As far as motive," Martine continued, "we know from Montoya's research that Gibbs and his mother were physically abused by his father throughout his childhood. He was arrested as a juvenile for assaulting his father with a deadly weapon in her defense. And as a police officer, he's been reprimanded many times for using excessive force in the line of duty."

Levi's pacing had slowed to more of an idle walk as he sank deeper into thought. "My biggest misgiving about Gibbs is his personality. He's impulsive and tactless with no self-control—the antithesis of the Seven of Spades, at least under normal circumstances."

"We've discussed the possibility of that being an act." Dominic absently rubbed his new tattoo through his shirt. It was healing well, but it itched like a bastard.

"Okay, but that's pure speculation. We don't have any evidence to support it."

"I'm also doubtful that he'd be so publicly empathetic to the Seven of Spades if he were the killer," said Martine. "Although . . . maybe that's part of the fun? Or a way to throw us off the scent?"

Levi came to a full stop, rocking back and forth on the balls of his feet. "Besides, Gibbs doesn't even like me, so why would he have focused on me like this?"

Dominic and Martine both stared at him.

"What?" he said, blinking back at them.

"Levi," Martine said slowly, "Gibbs *worships* you. It's why he's always hanging around you, getting in your face, deliberately annoying you so you'll pay attention to him. You're his hero, his role model; you always have been. In fact, if he were at all inclined toward guys, I'd think he has a massive crush on you."

Levi looked to Dominic for confirmation.

"She's right. Gibbs's attitude toward you is one of the strongest arguments in *favor* of him being the Seven of Spades, not against it." And while Dominic had never gotten the vibe that Gibbs was sexually attracted to Levi, he wouldn't have been shocked to learn otherwise.

His eyebrows drawing together, Levi opened his mouth—but closed it a few seconds later without saying anything and began pacing again, his movements even more agitated this time.

Dominic frowned, watching the way Levi's shoulders were creeping up toward his ears and his hands were flexing open and shut. Escalating stress could result in a rage-fueled outburst if Levi lost control of himself.

Martine hesitated before saying, "Finally, we have Leila."

"I can't," said Levi, his voice tight.

"Then I will." Martine's tone was calm and matter-of-fact. "Leila moved to Las Vegas last March, one month before the murders began, right after losing her father to a horrific hate crime. Her position in the DA's office gives her access to all of the information needed for victim selection, as well as the knowledge required to leave pristine crime scenes. She's one of the most intelligent people I've ever met, more than capable of pulling off every single one of the Seven of Spades's feats."

Though Dominic hated to add to Levi's distress, this needed to be discussed. "She's also a highly trained fighter, by far the most proficient of everyone on the list. She's no stranger to violence, and she knows how to handle herself."

"She's misanthropic, perpetually bored, and totally lacking in empathy for the Seven of Spades's victims," Martine said. "She stood with us at Judge Harding's crime scene, looked right at the gruesome way he'd been set up, and didn't even blink. She actually *gave* us the reason the killer had targeted him. And her essential personality—"

Levi spun around. "Is a lot like mine?"

"That's not—"

"Let's just say it. Rohan theorized that the Seven of Spades doesn't just admire me, but that they identify with me on a deep level. And after—"

Levi cut himself off as Dominic's pulse slammed into overdrive. *Don't look at me*, Dominic thought as he continued petting Rebel casually. *Whatever you do, do not look at me.*

Although deception had never been Levi's strong suit, he managed to keep his eyes off Dominic, dropping his gaze to the ground instead and clearing his throat. Martine raised her eyebrows.

Dominic and Levi both knew the full extent of how profoundly the Seven of Spades identified with Levi. The killer had recently lured him into a trap in an attempt to force him into murdering Scott West, one of the men who'd attacked him in college, under the belief that such an act would cement their connection and bring them closer together. But Martine was in the dark about the entire incident—because in the end, it'd been Dominic who'd killed West.

"Well, let's just say I believe it." Levi lifted his head as he recovered from his near slip, and Dominic's heart rate returned to normal. "Of all the people on the list, Leila is the one I have the most in common with, the one most likely to identify with me."

Martine shrugged. "She *does* identify with you. She insinuated herself into your life right before Barton was murdered—"

"She was assigned to a case we were working!"

"How do we know she didn't *ask* for that case? She created a connection with you by telling you she believed Keith had been framed. She initiated a friendship, spent months bonding with you, and came to your rescue in Boulder City when you were arrested."

"I've been delving deep into Leila's life the past couple of weeks," Dominic said. "She's lived here for a year now, and you are the *only* person she has a significant emotional attachment to outside her family."

Levi clenched his jaw and looked away, shoving his hands into his pockets.

"What's your counterpoint, Levi?" Martine asked.

"She's my friend," he said quietly.

Martine lowered her head. Dominic gave Rebel one final pat, got to his feet, and tugged Levi's hands free of his pockets, squeezing them until Levi met his eyes.

"Any way this turns out is going to suck," he said. "Big-time. There's no answer to the Seven of Spades's identity that isn't going to hurt."

"I know." Levi stepped closer to Dominic and laced their fingers together. "So what's our next move? All of our evidence is circumstantial; it's not anywhere near enough to make an arrest. If Leila *is* the Seven of Spades and she figures out we're on to her before we have all our ducks in a row, that's game over."

"I can put her under surveillance. Home, car, office, the whole nine yards."

"Ah, ah!" Martine said, clapping her hands over her ears.

Dominic raised his eyebrows. "You're sitting in front of folders full of information I obtained illegally."

She grimaced. "I'd like to maintain at least the illusion of plausible deniability."

"A lot of the surveillance you'd obtain would be illegal, too," said Levi. "It couldn't provide the basis for a warrant and wouldn't be admissible in court."

"It doesn't need to. It just has to point us in the right direction."

Releasing Dominic's hands, Levi moved a few feet away and chewed on his lower lip. Dominic could see the war waging inside him as clearly as if he'd asked the question aloud: Did these drastic, unprecedented circumstances make it acceptable for him to violate his oath to uphold the law?

Dominic, who was always in favor of rule-breaking in the interests of protecting innocent lives, kept his mouth shut. He wasn't a cop, and he didn't think like one. Levi's and Martine's perspective on this was vastly different from his own.

"All right," Levi said at length. "I don't see any other way. This has to end."

Dominic nodded. "I'll put everything in place tomorrow. And I'll start checking Gibbs's history for alibis for the murders as well."

"I'll focus part of the ketamine investigation on Leila. There's a chance she could be getting the drugs in St. Louis instead of here."

The conversation turned to technical matters as the three of them planned the next steps in their rogue investigation. Levi held himself together well, but Dominic could see the stress in the lines around his mouth and eyes, in the stiff set of his muscles that was sure to leave him with a terrible backache later. Though Dominic would do anything he could to help Levi through this, the only thing that would truly solve the problem was having the Seven of Spades behind bars.

Levi was right. This had to end.

CHAPTER 4

Saturday morning, Levi was sitting in the dining nook, paging through the local news on his tablet while he ate breakfast. Rebel was sitting beside him, watching intently; she knew he would let her lick the remnants of his eggs off the plate when he was finished.

The headlines were grim and getting worse every day. *Plummeting Tourism Panics Mayor, Local Businesses. Utopia Militia Claims Credit for Church Fire. City Council Seats in Danger as Angry Citizens Demand Change.*

He pinched the bridge of his nose. After college, he'd moved to Las Vegas because it was about as far away from suburban New Jersey as he could get, both physically and culturally. From the start, he'd fallen in love with the city's vibrancy, its nonstop energy, the sense of change and possibility that hovered around every corner. But now the city he'd adopted as his own was teetering on the razor's edge of self-destruction.

Levi dropped his hand at the sound of shuffling footsteps. Carlos trudged into the kitchen from the spare room, rumpled and bleary-eyed, his shoulders hunched. He stopped when he saw Levi.

"I didn't think anyone would be up this early," he said, bending over to pet Rebel as she rushed over to greet him.

"I'm always up early." Levi eyed Carlos critically. Jasmine and Carlos had gone the traditional route of spending the night before their wedding apart, so after last night's rehearsal dinner, Carlos had come home with Levi and Dominic while Jasmine had gone to her parents' horse farm in Henderson.

Carlos looked like he'd slept two or three hours, max.

Levi pushed back his chair and stood. "There's coffee in the French press. I'll make you some breakfast—scrambled eggs and turkey sausage okay?"

"I can make—"

"You're a guest. Besides, it's your wedding day."

Carlos smiled. "Okay, thanks."

Levi put together a quick meal, then rejoined Carlos at the table. He picked up his own fork again, but paused when he noticed the gray tinge to Carlos's golden-brown skin and the way Carlos was just pushing his eggs around on the plate.

"Are you all right?" Levi asked.

"I had trouble sleeping. I'm so nervous—happy nervous, but still. I hate being the center of attention, and a hundred people are going to be watching my every move all day." Carlos chewed and swallowed a mouthful of sausage before continuing. "You know, for most of my life, I never imagined this day would even be possible."

Levi nodded. Their experiences weren't the same, Carlos being trans, but he could empathize. He'd never been confused about his sexual orientation, so he'd grown up believing that an experience his peers took for granted—that they could get legally married one day—would always be out of his reach. Sometimes it was still surreal to realize that he and Dominic could get married tomorrow if they wanted to.

"And it's stupid, but it sucks that my family won't be there." Carlos scraped his fork through his eggs. "I know I don't owe them anything after the way they treated me, and actually having them there would make things worse, but . . . it hurts."

"Of course it hurts. And that's not stupid." Levi hesitated, considering, then made up his mind and said, "Did you know I have an older sister?"

"No. You've never mentioned her."

"Because we don't speak. After I was attacked in college, she never said the words 'It was your fault,' but she may as well have. She believed I'd brought it on myself—whether because I was gay, or because I was too weak to defend myself, I'm not sure." Levi leaned back in his chair. "I've never understood it, because that's not the way our parents raised us. Natasha says that some people blame the victim so they can deny the reality that terrible things can happen to anyone—could happen to *them*. Whatever the reason, it ruined our relationship forever."

Carlos's expression was soft with sympathy. "I'm sorry."

"I have a niece and nephew who are practically strangers to me. I saw them when I visited over the holidays, and I barely recognized them." Stretching an arm across the corner of the table, Levi rested his hand on Carlos's. "It hurts when your family rejects you. It probably always will. But family is also something you *choose*. And you couldn't have chosen better than Jasmine and the Andersons."

A small smile broke across Carlos's face, giving him an unmistakable glow. "Yeah, you're right."

"You might feel better if you talked to Jasmine."

"We said we wouldn't until the wedding, but . . . maybe a text wouldn't hurt." Carlos pulled his phone out of the pocket of his sweatpants. "Thanks, Levi."

Levi inclined his head, returning to his tablet as Carlos became absorbed in a text exchange with Jasmine. They finished their breakfasts in companionable silence.

Dominic finally emerged from the bedroom while Levi was doing the dishes and Carlos was nursing a second coffee. This was much earlier than he preferred to get up on the weekends, and he looked half-asleep as he stumbled over to kiss Levi good morning.

"Hey, Carlos," he said, dropping a hand on Carlos's shoulder as he rounded the table. "Ready for the big day?"

Carlos flinched. Touching base with Jasmine seemed to have mellowed him a bit, but he was still vibrating with anxiety, his hands clenched tightly around his mug and his foot tapping against the floor.

Dominic looked him up and down, then met Levi's eyes over Carlos's shoulder. Levi shrugged.

"Why don't we all go for a run after I eat?" Dominic said.

Rebel perked up immediately, leaping to her feet and spinning around once in a happy circle.

Carlos was far less enthusiastic. "I don't know, Dom. I don't think I'm up for that."

"Come on. Our brunch reservations aren't until eleven; what else are we gonna do until then? A good hard run will get your blood racing, your endorphins pumping—it's the best way to psych yourself up." Dominic gestured to Rebel, who was listening with bright eyes and a wagging tail. "And you don't want to disappoint Rebel, do you?"

Carlos raised his hands in surrender. "All right, all right. I'll go get changed."

Levi shook his head fondly as Carlos headed for the spare room and Dominic returned to his side in the kitchen. Manipulating people was as natural to Dominic as breathing, but Levi didn't mind so much when it was done for the greater good.

"How are *you* doing?" Dominic asked, his voice pitched low.

"I'm fine." Levi knew what he meant without needing to hear the words. Dominic had put surveillance measures into place around Leila a few days ago, but they hadn't turned up anything yet. "Today is about Carlos and Jasmine, not me or the Seven of Spades. I can set all that aside for twenty-four hours."

Resting his hands on Levi's hips, Dominic pressed him up against the counter. "Good. Because when we get home tonight, I plan on making up for everything we didn't get to do *last* night."

Although they'd both been very much in the mood, they hadn't been able to fool around; Levi was too loud during sex, and they hadn't wanted to subject Carlos to that.

Levi kissed the hollow of Dominic's throat. "Promises, promises," he said, and twisted away with a laugh when Dominic pinched his side.

"Do you have the rings?"

"For the fourteenth time, yes, I have them right here," Dominic said gently.

Carlos stared at his reflection in the full-length mirror in the groomsmen's room at the Las Vegas Paiute Golf Resort. His eyes went wide, and he began frantically patting himself down. "The vows! I don't have the copy of my vows—"

"They're in your breast pocket." Dominic took Carlos by the shoulders and turned him around, concerned by his shallow breathing.

It was still a couple of hours before the wedding itself—Carlos and Jasmine had opted for a first look, so they could be together before the ceremony and get the formal pictures out of the way. The rest of Carlos's wedding party was already milling the grounds, along with Jasmine's closest family members.

The run earlier had relaxed Carlos a little, but in the hours since, he'd gotten himself all worked up again. Dominic squeezed his shoulders.

"Everything is going to be fine," he said, stressing every syllable. "You're about to marry the woman you love, and I promise, the moment you see her, nothing else is going to matter. You're going to have the best day of your life." He straightened Carlos's tie. "And you're going to look great doing it."

Carlos laughed. He *did* look handsome, his floppy brown hair falling roguishly into his eyes, his lanky body clad in a dove-gray suit ornamented with a boutonniere of succulents and aromatic herbs. As the best man, Dominic had a similar arrangement pinned to his own lapel.

"Thanks." Carlos took a deep breath. "I mean it, Dom. Thank you, for—for everything. You've been an amazing friend."

Dominic glanced away. "Not always."

"Yes," Carlos said firmly. "Always."

He pulled Dominic into a hug. Smiling, Dominic slapped his back.

They broke apart when the door opened, and the photographer poked her head into the room. "Carlos, we're almost ready for the first look. Why don't you go ahead to the spot you and Jasmine picked out?"

Carlos nodded, checked himself out one last time in the mirror, and left the room with Dominic by his side.

The golf resort was an oasis of lush, rolling lawns in the middle of the desert, glowing under the rays of the afternoon sun. In early May, the day was hot but not stifling, and a light breeze cooled things off further.

Dominic and Carlos greeted the various friends and family members they passed on the way, all of whom were dressed to the nines. Dominic waved to Levi, who was standing with Adriana and the Andersons' two other current teenage foster kids, Josh and Rima.

The location for the first look was at the edge of the golf course's lake, with a stunning view of the stark desert mountains in the background. After a few more words of encouragement, Dominic withdrew, leaving Carlos facing the lake and fidgeting like a kid on the first day of school.

Less than a minute later, Jasmine approached, accompanied by her parents, a couple of her bridesmaids, and the photographer.

Dominic sucked in a breath. Jasmine had always been one of the most beautiful women he'd ever seen, but today she was *radiant*. She was wearing a flowing, sleeveless white gown that showed off the elaborate tattoos on her arms and chest; her dozens of rainbow braids cascaded down her back, with only a few on each side pinned back to keep them out of her face. Instead of a traditional veil, a wreath of greenery crowned her head.

Like Dominic, Jasmine's family and friends hung back a bit to give the couple some privacy. Carlos was standing stock-still now. Jasmine walked up to him from behind and tapped his shoulder.

When Carlos turned around, his jaw dropped. A brilliant smile crossed Jasmine's face. They gazed at each other for a wordless moment before they pressed their foreheads together, then embraced and kissed while the photographer discreetly snapped pictures.

A lump lodged in Dominic's throat as he watched them. Few things in life were better than seeing people you loved have their dreams come true.

As Dominic had anticipated, every ounce of tension drained from Carlos's body. He and Jasmine were completely wrapped up in their love bubble, murmuring to each other, oblivious to everything and everyone around them.

Dominic glanced back toward Levi. Adriana was saying something that involved a lot of wild hand gestures, and Levi was listening to her with a half smile on his usually solemn face, his posture open and relaxed as he gave her his full attention. He didn't seem to notice Dominic watching him.

Would he and Dominic ever find themselves in this position, gathering their families for pictures in the hours before their own wedding?

Dominic froze at the unexpected thought, the first one of its kind he'd ever had. This was the only serious relationship he'd been in, and marriage had never so much as crossed his mind before.

He and Levi hadn't even been together that long—their recent breakup had been nearly the length of the first phase of their relationship. Maybe he was just getting carried away by the romance of the wedding.

Or maybe not. His love for Levi was like nothing else he'd ever known. He imagined them spending the rest of their lives together, and instead of making him feel anxious or trapped, the thought filled him with a sense of excited wonder.

Levi finally caught on to Dominic's regard and sent him a puzzled glance. Feeling mischievous, Dominic blew him a kiss. Levi rolled his eyes, blushing as he turned away, and Dominic's heart seized with a swell of emotion.

No matter what their future held, he would love Levi Abrams until his last moment on Earth.

Levi didn't like to dance, but he wasn't surprised that Dominic did. After the reception dinner, Levi was happy to stay behind at their table, chatting to a few of Carlos and Dominic's friends from the club where they both bartended.

Every now and then, Levi looked over to where Dominic was cutting a rug on the dance floor, his exuberant energy drawing people to him like planets orbiting the sun. As always, Dominic was the life of the party. Even as Levi watched, Dominic twirled the laughing woman nearest him and spun her into a neat dip.

Levi's attention was diverted by Carlos and Jasmine, who were making the rounds table by table. They hadn't strayed more than two feet from each other since the ceremony; they both walked like they were floating, and the looks they kept sending each other redefined the word *sappy*. It was sweet.

"Mazel tov," Levi said, standing to hug them. "That was the most beautiful ceremony I've ever seen."

Her eyes sparkling, Jasmine said, "I'm surprised you even noticed, the way you and Dominic were staring at each other the whole time."

Levi flushed. "I— That wasn't—"

Dominic had been standing beside Carlos during the ceremony, of course, with Levi seated in the audience a few rows back. And all right, maybe their eye contact had gotten particularly intense at moments, but he hadn't thought it had been so obvious.

She laughed, touching his arm. "It was cute. We're really happy for you guys."

"Yeah, man." Carlos was glowing, utterly changed from the nervous wreck he'd been this morning. "We're glad you're here."

They were drawn away by their other friends at the table just as the music changed, the high-energy dance track fading into the mellower strains of "Never Let Me Go" by Florence + The Machine. Dominic left the dance floor, breathing hard and glazed with a light sheen of sweat. He'd long ago shed his jacket and tie, and his shirtsleeves were rolled up to the elbows.

"Come on," he said with an outstretched hand.

"I don't dance," said Levi, but he took Dominic's hand anyway.

"It's a slow song. All you have to do is sway."

Dominic pulled Levi onto the floor, his right arm around Levi's waist and his left hand clasping Levi's right. Levi sighed and slid his free arm around Dominic's waist as well.

They'd never danced together before. The act was startlingly intimate, their bodies pressed close as they rocked in time to the soaring notes of the song. They fit together perfectly, even if Levi had to tip his head back to meet Dominic's eyes.

"You seem like you're having a good time," Levi said.

"The best. You?"

"Yes."

Gazing down at Levi's face, Dominic said, "Do you think . . ." He stopped there, though, and cleared his throat.

"What?"

"Nothing." Dominic kissed him softly. "I love you."

"I love you too." Levi rested his head on Dominic's shoulder, closed his eyes, and surrendered to the moment, letting the music sweep him away.

After that dance, Dominic didn't leave Levi's side for the rest of the reception, stealing kisses and sneaking touches that grew increasingly bolder as the night wore on. Levi couldn't help responding in kind. By the time they sent Carlos and Jasmine off in a shower of rose petals at the end of the party, they were both in a giddy, frisky mood, as drunk on each other as the other guests were on champagne.

Out in the parking lot, Dominic shoved Levi up against Levi's new car and kissed him ferociously. Levi cupped Dominic's face with both hands and returned his aggression threefold, biting at Dominic's lower lip and hooking one leg around Dominic's thigh.

"Fuck, I need to be inside you," Dominic said when they broke for air. "It's too bad we took your car instead of mine. I could have fucked you in the bed right here."

"No, you could *not*," Levi said, though he was secretly thrilled by the idea of Dominic fucking him in public in the back of his pickup.

They kissed a few seconds longer, until Dominic retreated with a reluctant groan. "Actually, it's a good thing you're the one driving. The way I feel right now, I'd probably run us off the road."

Levi shooed him into the car, feeling a bit frantic himself. That mood only became more urgent as they turned onto the dark desert highway that would take them back into Las Vegas. Levi kept his eyes on the road, but he could feel the heat of Dominic's gaze, and his peripheral vision caught the movement when Dominic dropped a hand into his lap and began rubbing himself through his pants.

"Maybe I should just jerk off here," Dominic said hoarsely. "That way, when we get home, I can really take care of you. Last as long as you need, make you come all over yourself as many times as you want—"

"Oh my God." Levi was going to have to pull over. He was going to have to actually pull the car off to the side of the road and engage in public indecency, because otherwise they were going to crash.

His dashboard lit up then, displaying a phone call from Martine through its Bluetooth connection with his cell phone. Levi was relieved by the distraction until he realized that Martine would never call him this late unless something was wrong, especially when she'd known the wedding was tonight.

Dominic seemed to arrive at the same conclusion; he stopped touching himself and fell silent. Levi answered the call.

"What's wrong?"

"Is the wedding over?" Martine asked.

"Yes, we're on our way home now. What happened?"

"I told nobody to call you until I could be sure you'd left. I didn't want to ruin—"

"*Martine.*" Levi's hands tightened on the steering wheel.

"A construction crew was building a new access road in the desert north of the city," she said. "They—they found bodies. Over a dozen corpses, in various stages of decomposition, buried in the sand. It's hard to tell what killed the older ones, but the more recent bodies had their throats slit."

Levi couldn't breathe. Rohan had raised a theory about the Seven of Spades's origins, but it was one they'd set aside for lack of proof. Until now.

"Levi," Martine said, "I think these are the Seven of Spades's first victims."

CHAPTER 5 ♠

Martine had to text Levi the GPS coordinates to the site because it wasn't near any real address. As they drove, Levi found himself wishing they *were* in Dominic's truck, after all—the pickup could have handled this off-road desert terrain far better than his small Honda.

He and Dominic didn't speak on the way; the silence in the car was tense and anticipatory. The only sound Levi was aware of was the roaring of his own pulse.

When they arrived, he realized Martine hadn't been exaggerating about forbidding anyone from disturbing him all evening—this scene had been in process for hours. Portable floodlights were set up in a large, rough circle, with yellow tape strung around them. He could make out the hulking shape of construction equipment on the far side. The site was swarming with people in jackets identifying them as the LVMPD, the FBI, and the Clark County Coroner's Office.

There were also a few vans from local news outlets parked nearby, and a gaggle of reporters and cameras clustered as close to the tape as they could get.

"Oh, no." Levi stopped his car a fair distance from the tape. "Not *now*."

He and Dominic got out, the slam of the doors vanishing into the empty expanse of desert. Levi shivered as he buttoned his suit jacket. Once the sun set out here, the temperature plummeted.

It only took a few seconds for the reporters to catch sight of him. They rushed over en masse, clamoring to be heard over one another, their cameramen jogging behind.

"Detective Abrams!" One voice rose above the babble. "Is it true that the bodies being dug up here are previously undiscovered victims of the Seven of Spades?"

"No comment," Levi said without breaking stride. He didn't wonder how they'd found out so quickly. It was common knowledge that the media would pay top dollar for tips on the Seven of Spades case, and not every public servant was immune to bribery.

"Detective Abrams, do you—"

Dominic stepped smoothly between them, blocking Levi with his large body. "You heard him," he said in a mild tone that nevertheless brooked no argument.

The reporters fell back as Levi and Dominic reached the tape, and a uniformed officer came forward to shoo the jackals even farther away. Levi showed his ID to the officer maintaining the crime scene log, then gestured for Dominic to do the same. "He's consulting on the case," Levi said when the officer gave him a puzzled look.

She didn't argue. Dominic signed into the scene as well, and he and Levi donned gloves and booties from the supply provided before ducking under the tape to join Martine on the other side.

Levi's mouth fell open as he finally got a good look. Three rows of open graves scarred the gritty sand, outlined with wooden frames, next to which the unearthed corpses had been laid on tarps marked with plastic numbers. The crime scene technicians had to navigate carefully around the bodies and graves while they photographed the area and combed it for evidence.

"Jesus Christ," Dominic breathed beside him.

"How many?" Levi asked Martine, his eyes fixed on the corpses.

"Thirteen, so far. Luckily, they were each in individual graves instead of one mass burial pit, so the remains didn't get all jumbled together."

A burst of barking sounded to their right. At the far end of one of the rows, a cadaver dog scrabbled frantically at a patch of as-yet undisturbed sand.

"Make that fourteen," said Martine.

Levi stepped closer to the leathery, desiccated bodies. After years buried in the arid desert, most of them resembled beef jerky more than human remains. Many of the corpses had been partially skeletonized; one was simply a pile of disarticulated bones.

Seeing the direction of his gaze, Martine said, "That grave was shallower than the others. Looks like coyotes got to it. It's what drew the construction crew's attention in the first place."

Levi skirted the edges of the open graves, careful to stay out of the technicians' way. "Rohan was right. The Seven of Spades practiced killing people before they made their public debut. That's how all of their murders have been flawless since Billy Campbell."

"This is a hell of a lot of practice," Dominic muttered. His face had been drained of color under the sallow floodlights.

"*If* this was the Seven of Spades," Martine said. "It seems the likeliest explanation, but it hasn't been confirmed."

Levi swept out an arm, a poor way to encompass the nightmarish scene and all the horrors it implied. "Who else would have done this?"

"Detectives," said a new voice.

It was Dr. Maldonado, one of the county's medical examiners, an older woman with graying hair who wore her cat-eye glasses on a jeweled chain. Levi was surprised to see her—in the normal course of things, the MEs didn't visit crime scenes, which were the responsibility of the coroner investigators.

Then again, this was far from the normal course of things.

After introducing her to Dominic, Levi asked, "Do you have anything?"

"Not much. The victims seem to have been buried without any clothing or personal effects, and given the state of the bodies, identification will be challenging, to say the least."

Martine nodded. "How long do you think they've been here?"

"The more recent ones, a year at the minimum. And I won't be able to offer anything definitive until we get them to the morgue, but some of these bodies could have been buried here for five years, or even longer."

Years. The Seven of Spades had been slinking around Las Vegas, dragging away their victims, murdering them, and burying the bodies in the desert, for *years*, with nobody ever the wiser.

Levi suppressed a shudder. "Martine mentioned that several of the victims were killed with the Seven of Spades's usual MO?"

"There are some with enough tissue left intact to exhibit incised wounds across the throat, yes. Again, for most of the victims, it'll be impossible to determine anything of value without in-depth examination." Maldonado sighed, her tired eyes roving over the corpses. "But to be honest, there's nobody in the coroner's office experienced in working with these states of advanced decay and mummification."

"We can bring in a forensic anthropologist. I'll talk to Agent Marshall about it."

"I'd suggest a forensic entomologist as well. I've noticed a great deal of insect activity on many of the bodies."

"We can pretty much guarantee you'll get anything you need, Doctor," said Martine.

Maldonado was called away then by one of the technicians. Dominic came to stand by Levi's side, gazing at the bodies.

"This is . . ."

"Sickening," Levi finished for him. "These people weren't even human to the Seven of Spades. They were practice dummies who were dumped like trash once they'd served their purpose."

Levi didn't need forensic evidence to confirm the truth he knew in his gut. This was the work of the Seven of Spades; there wasn't an ounce of doubt in his mind.

"Levi." Martine waited for him to look at her before continuing, her expression troubled. "If this *was* the Seven of Spades . . . these bodies have been here for years. Years in which Leila was living in St. Louis, fifteen hundred miles away. It couldn't have been her."

Dominic woke to a cold, empty bed—which in itself wasn't unusual, even on a weekend, but it troubled him after the events of last night. He dragged himself away from the lure of the blankets and pulled on a pair of sweatpants before going in search of Levi, noting how weird it felt to not have Rebel in the apartment. He'd dropped her off at his mother's house before the wedding yesterday, and wasn't planning to pick her up until their family brunch.

Levi was standing in the living room, looking out through the mesh grating on their balcony door, a coffee mug clutched in both hands. Dominic's eyes flicked toward the kitchen, and he grimaced when he saw that the French press was already empty.

"Levi," Dominic said softly from a fair distance away. It was never a good idea to catch him by surprise.

Levi turned around. He managed a weak smile, but there was a pale cast to his skin and purple hollows beneath his eyes.

Dominic recognized the aftermath of Levi's recurring nightmare. "You're supposed to wake me up when you have the dream," he said, closing the distance between them and cupping the side of Levi's face.

"You needed sleep."

"I need to know you're okay more than I need sleep."

Levi laid one hand atop Dominic's, pressing it more firmly against his face for a moment. He turned his head and kissed Dominic's palm before pulling away.

"Same as usual?" Dominic asked.

"Every time. The setting changes, but the dream itself doesn't." Levi blew out a harsh breath, his attention returning to the grated door. "You know, I never catch up with whoever it is I'm chasing. Maybe that's a good thing."

Levi had been plagued by nightmares of being hunted by an unseen enemy for most of his life. When he and Dominic had gotten back together, though, he'd confessed that the roles in the dream had recently flipped: now *Levi* was the hunter, bloodthirsty and relentless, running down his hapless prey. These nightmares wreaked more havoc on him than the old ones had, especially after he'd put out Ramon Acosta's eye.

After watching the way Levi's hand shook as he sipped his coffee, Dominic snagged a banana from the fruit bowl on the dining table. He gently tugged the cup away from Levi and pushed the banana into his hands instead. Levi grunted an objection but then cooperated and peeled the banana.

Though Dominic was tempted to drink from the cup himself, he'd probably go into cardiac arrest if he drank the jet fuel Levi called coffee. He set it aside. "I know what triggered the dream this time, but there's no point in stressing yourself out over what happened last night. It's gonna take a while for those bodies to be identified, and there's nothing else you can do about it until then."

"That's what I'm worried about. When the Seven of Spades finds out that their early victims have been discovered, they might just vanish, and then we'll never catch them."

Dominic shrugged. "It's a possibility. But if someone from your life suddenly disappeared, at least you'd know the Seven of Spades's identity for sure."

Levi nodded thoughtfully and took a bite of his banana. Dominic squeezed his shoulder, then headed into the kitchen to make himself breakfast. Unlike Levi, he never voluntarily skipped meals; maintaining his muscle mass required a significant caloric intake.

Levi followed him, swallowing his mouthful. "Whatever surveillance measures you put in place to monitor Leila, you need to remove them as soon as possible. If she finds out—"

"I know. It'll have to wait until tomorrow, though. She's too likely to be home today." Dominic pulled a saucepan out of the cabinet beside the stove. "Do you want to skip brunch at my mom's later?"

"No. I like being around your family. They always distract me from whatever I'm worried about."

"Because they're the loudest, most opinionated human beings on Earth?"

Levi raised his eyebrows. "You really *haven't* spent much time around Jewish families."

Dominic laughed, leaning over to kiss Levi before he turned to the refrigerator.

They took separate cars to Dominic's childhood home, as they were headed for different destinations after brunch. Levi did seem to relax during the leisurely meal, plied with rich comfort food by Dominic's mother and grandmother and quality wine by his sisters. Dominic was less concerned about him when they went their separate ways—Levi to Counterstrike to train with Adriana, Dominic and Rebel to follow Miranda Cassidy's ex-husband.

Dominic had spent a good chunk of last week thoroughly researching Conrad Bishop's background, learning every detail about the man that he could obtain through legal means. He'd even arranged to run into Bishop's assistant and babysitter—the former at her gym, the latter at a bar—and cozy up to them for insider info.

Which was how he knew that, on the weekends Bishop had his kids, he took them to the same park every Sunday afternoon.

It was a gorgeous spring day, hot but not unbearably so, and the park was packed. Kids and dogs chased each other across the wide-open lawns; bicyclists zipped down the paths around couples pushing strollers. There was a birthday party in progress at a cluster of picnic tables, and a mouthwatering smell wafted from their grill.

Dominic and Rebel ambled through the park until he spotted Bishop kicking a soccer ball around with his two kids. They continued walking until Dominic judged they were at the right distance for him to observe Bishop without raising suspicions.

He unclipped Rebel's leash, then pulled a tennis ball from the pocket of the windbreaker he had to wear to conceal his shoulder holster. Rebel snapped to attention, her body quivering with the intensity of her focus. She raced after the ball the second he let it fly.

Their game of fetch provided the perfect way to keep an eye on Bishop. The information Dominic had gathered so far confirmed Miranda Cassidy's claims that Bishop's behavior had been erratic recently, but he saw no evidence of that in the current moment. Bishop appeared physically healthy, tanned and fit, and he was clearly enjoying himself as he laughed and ran around with his kids.

Still, Dominic knew from personal experience how easy it could be to hide an addiction—at least at first—so he would reserve judgment for now.

As he tossed the ball for Rebel, he planned how he would continue his surveillance once Bishop left the park. He'd follow, though he'd need to be cautious. If Bishop was restraining himself from getting high around his kids, then he'd probably go straight for a fix as soon as he dropped them off at their mom's house tonight. Dominic might be able to catch him in the act and wrap this case up in record time.

All of a sudden, Bishop stiffened, missing the ball his daughter had kicked to him as he jerked around to his left. He gestured to his kids, spoke a few words to them, and then jogged over to an ice cream cart on the footpath nearby.

There was a young white guy standing to the side of the line, average height and build for someone barely out of their teens. More interesting than the guy himself was the change to Bishop's body language as the two of them began talking.

In a complete reversal from his earlier behavior, Bishop became twitchy, darting glances from side to side. His hands were in constant motion: smoothing through his hair, rubbing over his face, tugging at his clothing. The young guy, by contrast, was as relaxed as everyone else in the park.

Pulling out his small digital camera, Dominic angled himself and Rebel so he could pretend to take pictures of her while photographing Bishop and his friend. He used the high-quality zoom to get a closer look.

The two men conducted a short, whispered conversation before Bishop withdrew what was clearly an envelope full of cash from his jacket pocket and handed it over.

Dominic almost dropped the camera in his shock. Did Bishop have the balls to engage in a drug deal in a public park, fifty feet from his own children?

The young guy didn't give Bishop anything in return, though. He just shoved the envelope into his own pocket, nonchalantly bumped his fist into Bishop's shoulder, and sauntered away.

Still flustered, Bishop joined the line for the ice cream cart. By the time he returned to his kids with ice cream sandwiches, he was back to normal.

Dominic watched the unknown man walking away at the far edge of the park, listened to his gut, and made a split-second decision. Whistling to Rebel, he set off in pursuit of Bishop's mystery contact.

They caught up with the guy in the parking lot, where he got into a car not far from Dominic's truck. Dominic jotted down the license plate, noting the car's UNLV Rebels bumper sticker with interest.

He followed at a prudent distance as they drove away from the park, eventually finding themselves in a middle-class neighborhood in

Enterprise. The car pulled into the driveway of a bland Southwestern house with two other cars out front, and the kid strolled inside like he owned the place.

Frowning, Dominic parked half a block away on the other side of the street. This didn't *look* like somewhere a drug dealer would find himself, but maybe that was the point.

There was no telling how long Dominic would have to wait until something interesting happened—if it ever did—so he'd use the time wisely. He retrieved his laptop from the passenger footwell and booted it up.

His truck's mobile hotspot provided access to the internet, and it was the work of minutes to run the car's plates and learn the driver's identity through DMV records: Jim Watts, age 22. From there, a simple switch of databases was all it took to run a basic background check.

Dominic blinked and leaned back in his seat. Watts, who was indeed a senior at UNLV, had a handful of arrests on his record—vandalism and similar petty crimes, nothing bad enough to get him kicked out of school. But it was one particular field on his rap sheet that caught and held Dominic's attention.

Known Affiliations: Utopia [far-right militia].

Dominic shot a startled glance toward the house. Sensing his tension, Rebel whined and turned to look out the window as well.

"Settle." He stroked her head, scratching the sweet spot behind her ear, and refocused on his laptop.

His next step was to research the house's property information. It belonged not to Watts's family, but to a man named Roger Carson. A cursory background check proved Carson to be clean—ostensibly, anyway. Dominic could think of no good reason for an upstanding citizen to have a neo-Nazi college student in their home, especially when the two men weren't related by either blood or marriage as far as he could tell.

He ran the other two cars in the driveway. One belonged to Carson, while the other was registered to a woman named Maggie Spencer, who shared Watts's known Utopia affiliation but was much older.

There was no way that handoff in the park had been a drug payment. Even if Watts or Spencer had drug offenses on their records—which they didn't—Utopia only dealt in meth and diverted narcotics, neither of which were Bishop's drug of choice.

So why was a wealthy real estate developer like Conrad Bishop passing envelopes full of cash to a college kid with Utopia connections? And why had that kid brought the money straight to the home of a man who seemed to have no connection to Utopia at all?

A short while later, Watts emerged from the house and drove away. Dominic let him go, more interested in the house itself. Roger Carson might have evaded suspicion until today, but Dominic knew there was something shady going on in there.

Though he was itching with curiosity, his options were limited while there were people inside, and nothing happened after Watts left. As the evening wound down uneventfully, he had no choice but to let the matter rest—for now.

He started his truck and headed back to the city, his mind racing with possibilities.

Dominic met Levi for dinner at a restaurant with outdoor seating, where Rebel lay perfectly well-mannered beneath their table. Training with Adriana had done wonders for Levi, even more than brunch. His cheeks had regained their color, he was leaned back in his chair instead of perching at the very edge, and he actually ate his meal rather than pushing it around his plate.

When they arrived home in the late evening, walking up the path to their building side by side, Dominic caught Levi's hand and pressed a kiss to the back. Levi gave him the small, private smile that he treasured.

Rebel stopped short, pricked her ears forward, and let out two sharp barks—her "stranger danger" warning.

Dominic's hand flew to the butt of his gun under his jacket, and he crouched to unclip Rebel's leash so she was free to attack. Levi shifted his grip on his keys so he was holding them like a weapon, even though he was armed as well.

They advanced up the path, Dominic comforted by the weight of his second gun in his ankle holster, as well as the sense of Levi's lethal strength beside him.

And then he saw Leila sitting on the staircase of their building, her legs crossed and her arms folded.

God, we were wrong, and she's here to kill us.

He heard Levi's strangled gasp and knew they were thinking the same thing. Fighting the urge to put himself between Levi and possible danger, he firmed his hold on his gun, ready to draw and fire in seconds if Leila made one threatening move.

All she did was sit there, regarding them coolly.

Logic reasserted itself. Leila couldn't be the Seven of Spades. The fact that she'd lived in St. Louis for years before moving to Vegas was beyond doubt; she'd never have been able to kill all those people and bury them in the desert.

Unless they'd been mistaken, and those bodies weren't the Seven of Spades's victims at all—

"Leila." Levi's voice was unsteady. "What are you doing here?"

"I think I'll be asking the questions, thanks." She placed a plastic bag in her lap and dug out a handful of small electronic devices, letting Levi and Dominic get a good look before she dumped them back into the bag.

When Dominic had set up his surveillance of Leila, he'd taken his cue from when the Seven of Spades had spied on him and Levi, figuring turnabout was fair play. He'd bugged her home, office, and car in multiple places, and had planted a GPS tracker in her car as well.

It looked like she'd found everything.

Dominic released his gun, his face blank. Levi, however, had never been skilled at repressing strong emotional reactions.

"How did you—" He cut himself off too late, and Leila laughed without humor.

"You've been acting weird around me for weeks. I had my suspicions as to why, but I didn't want to believe it." She rose to her feet and descended the last few steps.

Dominic and Levi both tensed. Leila was a proficient fighter, a master of the Filipino discipline Arnis, and highly dangerous even without her batons in hand. Neither of them retreated, but it was a near thing. Dominic had to clench his fist to keep from going for his gun again; that would only escalate the situation.

"Still, I know the kind of tricks the two of you get up to." She glared at Levi. "So once you started behaving so strangely, I hired a specialist to regularly sweep my home and office for surveillance devices. Imagine my surprise when he came up with all of *this*."

She shook the bag for emphasis, then pulled out the GPS device.

"A GPS tracker in my car?" she said to Dominic. "Really?"

Before either he or Levi could respond, she dropped the device on the ground and smashed it with the heel of her boot. He winced.

"Sorry. I hope that wasn't expensive."

Levi stepped forward. "Leila . . ."

She whirled on him. "How could you believe I was the Seven of Spades?"

"I didn't want to!" Levi held both hands palm-up in a supplicating gesture. "But we had to take a hard look at everyone connected to me and the case, and you—"

"Just screamed *serial killer*?"

"It was more complicated than that. And I know now that it wasn't you."

She scoffed. "Because you found victims killed and buried in the desert while I was living in another state. Not because you changed your mind about me."

Levi had no response for that. Dominic put a hand on his back, lending silent support as best he could. Rebel watched the confrontation anxiously—she'd been trained to regard Leila as a friend, but she must have sensed Leila's hostility from the start, or she wouldn't have barked to warn them.

"Honestly, I don't care that you think I'm capable of murder," said Leila. "What kills me is that you could think I'd *torture* you the way the Seven of Spades has." She clenched her jaw, and when she spoke again, her voice cracked. "I know I'm not the kindest person in the world, or the most empathetic, but for you to believe that I'd stalk and harass and torment *you*, of all people? How could you have so little faith in me? In our friendship?"

Dominic stared. He'd *never* seen Leila display emotion like this; he thought he even caught the sheen of tears in her eyes before she blinked them away. The only emotions he'd seen her express before were boredom, irritation, and mild amusement—which, admittedly, had played a role in their suspicions. But there was no faking the deep hurt on her face.

Levi bowed his head. "I'm sorry. Whoever the Seven of Spades is, it's probably someone I trust. I didn't know what to do."

Leila visibly reined herself in, inhaling through her nose and exhaling through her mouth, before she switched her focus to Dominic. "I know you two didn't get warrants for any of this, which means most of it was illegal. From now on, both of you stay the hell away from me."

She threw the bag at Levi's face. He barely caught it in time.

"I mean it, Levi. You come near me again, and your boyfriend is going to jail."

She stalked past them and down the path. Dominic and Levi stood in place, unmoving and unspeaking, until they heard a car start up.

Levi tilted his face toward the sky and closed his eyes. "Nailed it."

CHAPTER 6

"One of those days, huh, Detective?" said the corrections officer at the front desk of the CCDC. "I think we've had five of those Utopia creeps dragged in today alone."

"Don't get me started," Levi grumbled as he signed out. Earlier, he'd responded to a hot call regarding a shooting outside Planned Parenthood, and had joined the hunt for the skinheads responsible. It had eaten up most of his afternoon, on a day when he already had to leave work early for an appointment with Dominic. "I'd like to know where they keep finding all these fresh recruits."

The CO shrugged. "Well, outside the Valley, we're surrounded on all sides by rural Nevada. And . . . you know how some people are these days."

That was a diplomatic way of saying that a good chunk of the country had gone batshit insane. Levi just wished that the LVMPD's other bureaus could handle their business, so that he wasn't continually distracted from the Seven of Spades case by chasing radicalized white supremacists all over Las Vegas.

"Detective Abrams," said a familiar, unwanted voice behind him.

Levi took a deep breath before he turned to face Jay Sawyer. He refused to notice Sawyer's preppy, clean-cut good looks, focusing instead on the arrogant swagger that irritated him so much—though ever since their one-night stand a couple of months ago, Sawyer seemed to rein in the worst of his smugness when he and Levi crossed paths.

"Sawyer," he said evenly. "What are you doing here?"

"Visiting a client." Sawyer signed out as well, flashing the CO a dazzling smile full of bright white teeth. "You know him, actually— Lonnie Hale?"

That was the man who'd spit in Levi's face while being arrested. Levi grimaced and took a step back. "You're representing Nazis now?"

"Sixth Amendment, Detective. All citizens have the constitutional right to counsel." Sawyer paused, then added, "No matter how much said counsel might personally like to throw them out a window."

Levi snorted, somewhat appeased. He'd never understood how defense attorneys could stomach their jobs, but somebody had to do it.

"How can a punk like that even afford you?" he asked. Sawyer's time billed at a cool grand per hour. "Hatfield, Park, and McKenzie at least has the PR sense not to do pro bono work for white supremacists."

"You know I can't tell you that." Sawyer moved out of the intrigued CO's earshot and lowered his voice to a more intimate tone. "I heard about the bodies you found in the desert. Were they really left there by the Seven of Spades?"

They were indeed. Targeted preliminary lab tests of the most recent corpses had confirmed the presence of ketamine, though more extensive, in-depth testing was required. Still, the combination of ketamine with a slit throat was too unique an MO to be credited to anyone else.

Due to the case's worldwide notoriety, the FBI had been able to fly in a respected forensic anthropologist and her team immediately. They'd started this morning on determining times and causes of death; positive IDs would take much longer.

"Yes," Levi said, giving the simplest response to Sawyer's question he could. It would become public knowledge anyway. "And you know that I can't tell *you* any more than that."

"Fair enough." Before they'd slept together, Sawyer would have ended with some kind of sly innuendo, or even an outright proposition. Now he only ran his gaze once over Levi's body and smirked before walking away. "Good luck with the investigation, Detective. Give my best to Mr. Russo."

Levi sighed. It was too much to expect that Sawyer would give up being a douchebag altogether.

"Thanks for coming in again, Ms. Cassidy," Dominic said as he ushered her into his office. He gestured toward a chair and sat behind his own desk, where he had Bishop's file ready and waiting.

"What's this about?" she asked. "Did you already find evidence I can use against Conrad?"

"Not exactly. I wanted to ask you a few follow-up questions." He'd decided that directness would be the best tack, so he didn't fuck around with euphemisms and leading questions. "Does Mr. Bishop have any connection to Utopia?"

Her face screwed up in unfeigned disgust. "The *gang*? No, of course not. What kind of people do you think we are?"

"Utopia is much more than a street gang these days. And the reason I ask is that I saw Mr. Bishop hand an envelope full of cash to this man—a known member of the organization."

Dominic slid several blown-up photographs of the park handoff across his desk. He watched Cassidy closely, but didn't catch so much as a flicker of recognition as she studied the pictures.

"So?" Still frowning, she sat back. "Passing money to a criminal looks like a drug deal to me. That's your evidence right there."

"Except this man didn't give Mr. Bishop anything in return for the cash." Dominic tilted his head. "When Mr. Bishop was using drugs, did he ever take methamphetamines?"

"No. He may be an addict, but he's not white trash."

Charming. "How about prescription painkillers?" Dominic asked, maintaining a blandly pleasant demeanor.

"No. Conrad uses cocaine because he wants to speed things up, not slow them down." She narrowed her eyes. "What does this have to do with anything?"

"The only drugs Utopia deals are meth and prescription narcotics," said Dominic. "The cocaine trade in Las Vegas is entirely controlled by Los Avispones, and Utopia hasn't been able to make any inroads there. Los Avispones is the only criminal organization that's been able to hold strong against them." That was due in large part to the Seven of Spades, who had long ago allied with Los Avispones and continued to lend subtle assistance.

Cassidy shrugged. "I'm afraid I still don't see your point."

He looked her straight in the eye. "Then let me rephrase my question. Is there any reason your ex-husband would sympathize with white supremacists?"

After a moment of contemplative silence, she said, "Conrad would never deliberately hurt anyone. But if you're asking if he has strong values—real *American* values—then yes. Regardless of his personal issues, he's always been a patriot."

Dominic was so flabbergasted that he just stared at her, at a loss for words. Even when he found his voice, it was faint. "An American patriot . . . financing Nazis?"

"Oh, please," she said, wrinkling her nose. "That term is so overwrought. People always rush to scream *Nazi* to discredit real Americans who are just trying to defend their country."

Dominic's blood pressure skyrocketed as if she'd drawn a gun on him. Every muscle in his body went rigid, and a vicious internal heat swept through his limbs, making them tremble with barely repressed rage. He had to clamp his hands on both his thighs to prevent himself from leaping out of his chair.

God. If this was how Levi felt all the time, it was no wonder he had trouble controlling his anger.

"Let me tell you something about defending this country, Ms. Cassidy." It was a struggle for Dominic to speak calmly. Though he didn't anger easily, this bullshit was one thing that made him see red. "I was an Army Ranger for eight years. I served multiple tours in Afghanistan. I watched friends die in service to this country. I took a *bullet* for this country. You don't get to sit there and lecture *me* about patriotism."

Despite his best intentions, by the time he finished, his body was thrumming with the fury he'd tried to conceal. Cassidy had shrunk back in her chair and was eyeing him with clear anxiety.

He took a deep breath. No matter the provocation, it was *not* okay for a man his size to lose his temper, especially in a closed room with a much smaller woman.

"Get out," he said.

She blinked. "I beg your pardon?"

"You can ask Ms. McBride to reassign your case to a different investigator, but I won't work with you. Please leave."

She hesitated for a moment, as if he might be joking. When he glared at her in stony silence, she huffed, tossed her hair over her shoulder, and swept out of the room like a disdainful queen.

Slumping in his chair, he pressed his hands to his face. He didn't care if McBride chewed him out for this. He wouldn't work for a Nazi sympathizer under any circumstances.

After gulping down half of the bottle of water he kept on his desk, he closed his eyes and focused on the physical sensations created by the sudden spike in his gambling cravings: the quivering in his muscles, the warm and wriggling excitement in his belly. Breathing slowly, he let those sensations wash through him, picturing them as literal waves—rising and falling, peaking and subsiding. He "surfed" the urge, neither fighting it nor giving in, just riding it out.

The technique settled him down enough to make it through the rest of the day. Fortunately, he already had a therapy appointment scheduled after work, one that Levi would be joining.

He decided not to tell Levi about Cassidy and Bishop until afterward. Levi was stressed out enough about the appointment as it was.

Dominic's email to McBride summarizing the situation was answered an hour later with a terse response, stating that she'd spoken to Cassidy herself and had decided to terminate the contract due to incompatibility with the firm's principles. That was an enormous relief, and he was able to concentrate on his other cases without further distraction.

In the early evening, he drove to the tidy office park that housed his therapist's office, along with several other independent medical practices. Levi was waiting in the lot, leaning against his car and absorbed in his phone. He was still dressed in his entire prim charcoal suit—unlike Dominic, who'd stripped out of his jacket and tie in the elevator on the way out of work.

Dominic parked his truck next to Levi, then hopped out and kissed him in greeting. "You could have gone inside, you know. It's hot out here."

He laughed at the arch look Levi gave him. It could have been 110 degrees in the parking lot, and Levi wouldn't have gone into the office alone.

Levi was always awkward around strangers and in unfamiliar situations, unless he was in the thick of a case, but he was more tense than usual as they settled onto a couch in Roberta Caruso's waiting room. He held his hands in his lap, rubbing his thumb repeatedly over the fingers of his other hand.

Dominic leaned over to whisper in his ear. "You don't have to do this. If you're too uncomfortable, it's okay for you to leave."

"No. Your therapist thinks I should come to a session, so that's what I'm doing."

Dominic kissed Levi's cheek and squeezed his hand. Then he smiled broadly at the startled man watching them from across the room.

Roberta came to fetch them a few minutes later. She was an older woman, the grooves around her eyes and mouth attesting to good humor and a life well-lived. Dominic had immediately responded to her air of maternal warmth, which reminded him of his grandmother.

Once they'd entered her cozy office and exchanged introductions and pleasantries, she waved them to a love seat. Levi sat painfully upright next to Dominic, like a man on trial.

"How has your week been, Dominic?" she asked.

"Uh . . ." He glanced sideways at Levi. "Stressful." He left it at that, knowing Roberta would be well-aware of current events, and unwilling to get into it further when Levi was already on edge.

"And how has that affected your gambling cravings?"

"It's definitely made them worse. I haven't gambled, though."

Briefly, he filled her in on how he'd handled his gambling urges over the past week while she gave him her full attention and took the occasional note. As the minutes passed with neither of them focusing on Levi's presence, Dominic sensed him slowly relaxing.

"How's it going, living together?" Roberta asked.

"It's great." Dominic smiled at Levi, who gave him a smaller but no less genuine smile in return.

"Has it put any pressure on your recovery?"

"No. If anything, it's made things easier. I feel more . . . accountable now, I guess."

"And you, Levi? How do you feel about the change?"

Seeming surprised at being addressed, Levi said, "Oh, um, I think we made the right decision."

"I'm happy to hear that." Roberta looked to Dominic, who nodded. "Levi, the reason Dominic and I wanted you to join us today was because we've been discussing the possibility of getting you more involved in his recovery."

Levi leaned forward slightly, his expression solemn. "I'll help any way I can."

"I know you already provide a great deal of emotional support, which is excellent. But it may also help for you to take a more practical role as well."

"Like what?"

"With gambling disorders, one of the most important treatment measures is limiting the individual's access to money." She straightened her pad on her knee. "Of course, Dominic's case is a little unusual, as he'd already taken some of the recommended measures before entering treatment, and his debts had been cleared by Mr. Barclay."

A subtle wince crossed Levi's face. He was even more uncomfortable with the fact that his ex-boyfriend had paid off Dominic's debts than Dominic was himself.

"Dominic and I have discussed additional measures he could put in place, though, and that's what we'd like to talk to you about." Roberta gestured for Dominic to take over.

Turning on the love seat, Dominic focused fully on Levi. "I'm going to give notice at Stingray. I only work there once or twice a week these days, and between the job at McBride and Stanton paying off my debt, I don't need it anyway. I've been giving my cash tips to my manager at the end of the night to add to my paycheck, like we talked about—but now that my access to money is so limited, that cash is more tempting than ever before."

He wet his lips, steeling his nerves.

"And it's not just my own tips; it's the cash people pay with too. I've never stolen money to gamble with, but I've come close. I think it would be best not to put myself in a situation where that's a possibility."

A couple of quick blinks were the only indication Levi gave that this was news to him. "Okay. That makes sense. And you're right, we don't need that money."

We. Dominic always got a little thrill when Levi said that. And it made a nice segue into what he was going to say next.

"I also want to move all of my money into a joint account with you, one that requires both of our signatures to withdraw funds."

Levi's forehead creased. "That's not really practical, is it? You'd have to have me with you every time you needed money."

"I know." Dominic took a deep breath. Levi *really* wasn't going to like this. "That's why I want us to take out a certain amount of money once a week, and have you give me a set amount of cash every day."

It took Levi a few seconds to process that, and once he did, he recoiled on the love seat. "You want me to give you an *allowance?*"

"We don't have to call it that."

"But that's what it would be!"

Roberta cut in gently. "For people in recovery from gambling disorders, it can be very helpful to have a partner or other trusted family member take as much control of their finances as possible—not just in the logistical sense of making gambling more difficult, but also as a source of emotional reassurance. I'd also suggest that you be the one to pay all of the household bills, though I understand from Dominic that you two more or less have that arrangement already."

"Because I'm more organized! Not because I'm . . . *in charge.*" Levi made a face. "I don't want to be in a parental role to my own boyfriend."

Dominic couldn't resist a setup like that. "You mean you don't want me to call you 'daddy'?"

Levi's answering glare could have flayed the flesh right off his bones.

"Sorry." Dominic took both of Levi's hands, looking deep into his eyes. "Levi, I trust you way more than I trust myself. I'd be comfortable giving this kind of control to you because I know you'd take it seriously and never abuse it. It would make me feel more secure to have that safety net."

"I just . . ." Levi hesitated, his eyes flicking sideways, but he soldiered on at an encouraging nod from Roberta. "You may feel that way now, but I'm worried you'd start resenting me later. This kind of thing could put a huge strain on our relationship if we weren't careful."

"That's a good point," said Roberta. "When you make a decision like this, you need to be aware of how it could potentially impact your power dynamic. We can discuss some ways to address that, if you want."

Dominic maintained a carefully neutral expression. He didn't want to influence Levi's decision one way or the other, beyond the honest statements he'd already made. He'd promised that he wouldn't manipulate Levi anymore, and he was sticking to that.

"All right," Levi said briskly. "What would you recommend?"

They spent the rest of the session reviewing ways to navigate both the emotional and logistical aspects of the proposed changes. By the time Dominic and Levi left the office, Dominic was more at ease, and Levi's usual reserved aura was contemplative rather than anxious.

"Why didn't you tell me you were thinking about quitting Stingray?" Levi asked when they reached their cars.

"I wanted to be sure first."

"You didn't tell me you were struggling so much with handling cash, either."

Dominic knew where he was going with this. "I wasn't hiding it. If it had gotten really bad, I would have told you." He fiddled with his keys. "I'm still not sure you understand how embarrassing it is for me to tell you this stuff."

Levi shook his head. "Why?"

"I don't like you seeing me weak." Dominic raised his hand, cutting off Levi's protests as soon as they began. "I *know* you don't think of it like that, and that I shouldn't either, but I do. Maybe I always will."

"Even if it *was* a weakness, you wouldn't have to be embarrassed to show me." Putting a hand on Dominic's arm, Levi gazed up at him with serious eyes. "You've seen me at my worst, and it only made me feel safer with you."

Dominic melted and pulled him into a tight embrace. "I want to get to that point," he murmured. "I really do."

Levi tilted his face for a kiss. "I'll help you."

CHAPTER 7

"**H**ow long have you been here?" Martine asked.

Levi raised bleary eyes from his computer to blink at her and Natasha, who were standing side by side next to his desk. They must have walked in from the parking lot together.

He'd been immersed in the mind-numbing tedium of his ketamine investigation for a while, so he had to check the time before he could answer—a few minutes before 9 a.m. "About two hours."

Martine set down her coffee mug and slung her giant purse onto her desk, which adjoined his. "Your shift doesn't start for another five minutes."

"I woke up early and couldn't fall back to sleep. Figured I might as well get a head start."

He turned his attention to Natasha. She had a large Tupperware container tucked under one arm—which wasn't unusual, because she often brought in home-baked goods to set people at ease during their counseling sessions. But she was also juggling a few small bags with her other arm.

"I was just telling Martine that I experimented with a new cookie recipe last night, and I ended up making way too many," she said. "I was hoping you guys could take some off my hands so I don't eat them all myself."

Martine eagerly accepted the bag Natasha handed her, opening it right there and snagging a cookie. Levi put his own bag in the lower drawer of his desk.

"Thanks. Dominic goes crazy for everything you make."

"I have something for you too, since I know you're probably not interested in cookies." She placed half of a wrapped loaf of banana bread on his desk and grinned.

He smiled back, touched by her thoughtfulness. It was true that he didn't have a sweet tooth, something that baffled all of his friends. "Thank you."

"You're welcome, weirdo." She tugged one of his curls affectionately. "Have a good day, guys."

After Natasha headed for her office, Levi returned to his task, comforted by the familiar sounds of the bullpen's increasing activity and Martine settling in across from him. He'd vetted a handful of controlled substances licenses this morning, but his progress was as slow as ever, and the pair of uniforms Birndorf had assigned to the project wasn't faring any better. He was beginning to despair of ever seeing results from this painstaking investigation. Maybe his time would be best spent doing something else—

"Hey, did you read this report from Dr. Paquin yet?" Martine asked.

"No. What does it say?" Even as Levi spoke, he clicked through to his own email and opened the report from the forensic anthropologist working the Seven of Spades case.

"Mm . . ." Her eyes flicked back and forth across her computer screen. "Preliminary profiles for the victims: age, sex, stature, approximate time of death. Looks like Dr. Maldonado was right about the time frame. Most recent body's been dead about one year, oldest five or six."

When Paquin had first arrived, she'd briefly met with the task force to caution them on the difficulties of identifying human remains against an open population. Without a list of known victims to compare the bodies to, identification would be lengthy, complicated, and potentially impossible.

Several factors were in their favor, however. If the Seven of Spades had chosen mostly criminals as their original victims, the way they did now, the victims' biological information might be on file with the LVMPD. There was also a possibility that the victims could be identified from local missing persons reports or the NCIC's Missing Persons database.

Levi scanned Paquin's other progress updates. Fingerprints were mostly a bust, as she'd warned; the majority of the bodies either didn't have skin left on their hands, or the friction ridges on the fingertips were too degraded. But she was optimistic about her chances of rehydrating a couple of the corpses' fingers enough to get decent prints.

Dental records and X-rays would only be helpful with something to compare them to. One of the X-rays had revealed traumatic fixation plates on the radius and ulna of J. Doe #2's arm, though. Paquin suspected she'd be able to trace the plates to their manufacturer and then to the surgeon who'd implanted them, once she was able to remove the mummified skin to get a better look—ugh, gross.

All in all, it seemed DNA would be their best bet, even if the only usable samples could be obtained from bone marrow. But that kind of analysis would take weeks.

He and Martine took startled breaths at the same time, and he guessed she'd reached the same part of the report he had.

She looked at him with raised eyebrows. "Some of the earlier bodies were *stabbed*?"

"The Seven of Spades doesn't stab." According to Paquin, though, several of the older corpses displayed indications of stabbing wounds to the trunk of the body, delivered from the front.

"They stabbed Grant Sheppard."

"That was because they had to conceal their identity so his murder wouldn't ruin their plan to lure my attackers here." Levi narrowed his eyes at his computer. "The stabbings were earlier in the timeline. The later victims all had their throats slit, at least the ones with enough tissue remaining for Dr. Paquin to be sure."

"So . . . the Seven of Spades started out stabbing people, but realized along the way that they preferred slitting throats?"

"Could be. Rohan did say that one of the defining features of slitting someone's throat from behind is that it allows the killer to avoid eye contact with the victim. That's not the case when you stab someone head-on." Levi continued reading as he spoke, until he reached a section that made him bolt upright. "Paquin says two of the bodies show signs of *torture*."

"Okay, that's weird," Martine said. "Again, the only person the Seven of Spades has ever physically tortured was Sheppard, and that was only to get a confession out of him. Even when they mutilated those human traffickers from the Collective, the damage was all done postmortem."

"The first tortured victim was from the beginning of the timeline, the one with the plates in his arm," Levi muttered. "The other from the middle. So this can't be a case of growth or evolution. The Seven of Spades tortured Sheppard to obtain something specific from him—they must have tortured these other two men for the same reason. There was something the killer wanted from these particular individuals that they couldn't get from their other victims." He met Martine's gaze across their desks, his stomach clenching with a sudden thrill. "If we find out who *these* victims were, that could be the key to everything."

Her eyes were wide and excited. "Shit."

He reached for his desk phone. "I'll tell Dr. Paquin that she needs to prioritize identifying those two J. Does right away."

"Uh . . ." Martine rose to her feet. "Actually, why don't I go down to the coroner's office and speak to her in person? I can pick her brain while I'm there."

Levi knew exactly why she was suggesting that, and he scowled. "I wasn't going to be rude."

"Dr. Paquin hasn't had time to get used to your personality yet. Let's not push her into the deep end right off the bat."

Annoyingly, Martine had a point. Like Dominic, her charisma was a force to be reckoned with, and having her handle their requests for Dr. Paquin would be more productive. He backed down, and Martine hurried off.

Once she left, however, he was too restless to settle. A few minutes of unproductive fidgeting later, he gave up, walking all the way to the nearest coffee shop and back to burn off his nervous energy. By the time he returned to the substation, he was able to focus on his ketamine investigation again.

After the intrigue of his discussion with Martine, this research was even more dull than before. His eyes were all but bleeding as he processed page after page of the same dry minutiae, to the point where the words started blurring together on his computer screen.

When they'd suspected Leila, he'd shifted the investigation to controlled substances licenses in and around St. Louis, but once she'd been ruled out, he'd returned to Nevada. After a year of sorting through DEA licenses in geographic circles expanding from the heart of Las Vegas, he'd gotten as far as Mesquite. He finished vetting the person he'd been working on when Martine arrived—Dr. Erica Flores—and moved on to the next license on the list, a veterinarian named Seth Fowler.

He felt a brief spark of interest when he learned that Dr. Fowler had been charged with suspected negligence with two animals who'd died under his care, but both of those charges had been dropped without prosecution. In every other respect, Dr. Fowler lived a boring, ordinary life, just like almost every person Levi had investigated this way.

God, this was a waste of time. He'd been so sure when he'd started that he was on the right track, and he'd never been wrong to trust his gut before. But now he could only regret all the dozens if not hundreds of hours he'd spent on this wild-goose chase—

Levi blinked and then frowned at his computer. He'd been operating on autopilot, running Fowler through every local, regional, and national database he had access to—which was a long list these days, thanks to the Seven of Spades's notoriety—and he'd been about to call it quits. All of Fowler's licenses and registrations were in proper order, there'd been no recent criminal activity, and he had no ties to anyone in the suspect pool.

But this year, he'd been flagged for an audit by the IRS.

Levi chewed his lip for a moment before deciding he might as well look deeper. He'd already invested his time and energy into this. If it didn't pan out, he'd consider wrapping up the ketamine investigation altogether, or at least surrendering it to the uniforms so he could concentrate on more relevant aspects of the case.

Dr. Fowler owned a small, private practice that he ran out of his suburban home. Levi wasn't well-versed in finance or accounting, but from what he could gather from the IRS, Fowler filed an appropriate tax return every year; he scrupulously reported his income and paid every dollar owed on time, never claiming any business losses or even deductions.

Accordingly, it had taken the IRS a while to catch on to the fact that they couldn't account for the *source* of said income for the past several years—unless all of Fowler's patients were paying in cash, which was suspicious in and of itself. Even fishier, Fowler hadn't paid payroll taxes for the same period of time, because apparently his practice didn't have any employees.

There was no way a vet could run a practice without at least a vet tech, even if that person did double duty as a receptionist. So either Fowler was paying his employees under the table . . . or his practice was a front.

Pulse pounding, Levi reached for his phone.

After three hours of long, frustrating conversations, chasing paper trails, and arguing with the officials of various institutions until he stubbornly got his way, Levi hung up and stared at the papers he'd covered with notes. His heart was lodged firmly in his throat.

Several years ago, Fowler had owned a home and a veterinary practice in Summerlin. Then he'd sold both without warning, moved to Mesquite, and opened his current practice.

Fowler wasn't married, and had no children or other close family, so there had been nothing tying him to Summerlin. His new practice was properly licensed, and as Levi already knew, he'd maintained his veterinary license and DEA registration without problems.

But the timing of his move coincided with the suddenly mysterious origins of his reported income, as well as the point at which he'd no longer had employees. The office phone number went straight to an automated answering service. Further, Levi couldn't find a single record of anyone claiming to be a patient of the new practice. Fowler didn't even have a page on Yelp.

The mortgage and utilities for Fowler's home were always paid in full and on time—by cashier's check. His personal bank accounts hadn't been touched since the move, and there hadn't been any activity on his personal credit cards in the same time frame.

The business credit card *had* been regularly used, but only to pay for insurance and regular orders of ketamine. His new practice hadn't purchased any other medical supplies since it had first been established, nor had it ever purchased any other controlled substances.

Levi would bet everything he owned that Seth Fowler had been dead for years.

His hands trembled, and he closed his eyes, taking a few shaky breaths. He couldn't get ahead of himself, not yet. Not until he went to Mesquite and saw the situation in person.

He texted Martine, who promised to meet him there, and then dialed a different number.

"Agent Marshall," said Denise's sunny voice.

"It's Levi." He jumped out of his chair, grabbing his bag from his desk drawer and slinging it over his shoulder. "Do you have time for a road trip?"

The local police were happy to cooperate, sending some uniformed officers to assist but otherwise conceding authority to Levi, Martine, and the FBI. Fowler's split-level building was located on a picturesque suburban street; the door on the ground floor bore a discreet sign advertising the practice, and an exterior staircase led to the private home's entrance on the second floor.

They canvassed the neighborhood while they waited for the search warrant. As Levi expected, none of the neighbors could recall ever seeing anyone go in or out of the house or office. Not one had ever met Dr. Fowler in person or could even describe what he looked like.

Levi grew increasingly agitated as the afternoon wore on, his body thrumming with caffeine and adrenaline—until Martine drew him aside, shoved a bottle of water at him, and glared with folded arms until he drank the entire thing.

The backyard of Fowler's house was screened with tall brick walls that could easily conceal a person coming and going through the back door. That entrance looked easiest to force, so when the warrant came through, they climbed the rear staircase to the second floor in a single-file line. Two uniforms rammed the door open, then moved aside on the landing so Levi could go in first.

He stepped cautiously over the threshold, his gun drawn and his senses on high alert. "Police! We have a warrant to search the premises."

There was no response, but he hadn't anticipated one. He ventured further into the gloomy interior and immediately sneezed. Wrinkling his nose, he fumbled for the nearest light switch.

The house was *blanketed* in dust. As he took a few more steps, every footfall sent up another cloud. There was a dining table to his left covered in an undisturbed layer of dust that looked to be two inches thick.

He gestured for the people behind him to enter. The local uniforms and the FBI agents Denise had brought fanned out to clear the house, but Denise and Martine stayed with him in the main room.

Martine went into a coughing fit the moment she entered. "Damn," she said once she recovered. "Nobody's lived here for *years*."

Levi agreed. The house was furnished, but in the bland, impersonal style of a rental unit. The blinds were drawn, there were no personal effects in sight, and a search confirmed that all of the cabinets, drawers, and even the refrigerator were empty. This wasn't a home, just a facsimile of one.

He was reminded of a similar set piece, a house the Seven of Spades had designed to lure him and Dominic into a harrowing trap. He couldn't mention that, though, because not even Martine knew the truth of what had happened that day.

As they poked around the house, his attention was caught by a faint disturbance in the dust on the floor—difficult to see on the beige carpet, and nothing so distinct as individual footprints, but unmistakable nonetheless. The path led roughly from the back door to another door with a dust-free handle in an interior wall.

"Check this out," he called to Martine and Denise. "It may be true that nobody's lived here in years, but somebody's *been* here."

He was sure the door led to the office downstairs, and he was proven right when he eased it open to reveal a narrow staircase. He descended slowly, with the two women right behind him, and opened the second door at the bottom.

Like the house above it, the office was fully furnished and looked normal at first glance—until you noticed the thick layers of dust and the complete lack of personal touches. It was more like someone had done a Google Image search for "veterinary office" and popped in all of the necessary equipment and furniture like they were staging a play.

The flooring down here was hardwood, which made the path trodden through the dust much more obvious. They cleared the level before they followed that path down a side hallway and into a tiny office, where it terminated in front of an enormous, two-door metal safe with a keypad lock.

Levi's lungs constricted; his stomach cramped. He rested his gloved hand on the safe and saw it trembling as if he were in caffeine withdrawal.

"Any of your guys know how to crack safes?" he asked Denise.

She examined the keypad for a moment before shaking her head. "No need. This brand is built with an internal failsafe code the manufacturer can provide to law enforcement with the proper warrant—which we have. Give me ten minutes." She pulled out her phone and walked away.

Those ten minutes were the longest of Levi's life. He stood rooted to the spot, staring at the safe like he could will it open with the force of pure unleaded desire.

He knew what was in there. He *knew*.

An eternity later, Denise returned, cheerfully punched in the code, and swung both metal doors open.

All of Levi's breath left him in a rush. He sagged, grabbing Martine's arm for support; she slid her arm around his waist to help hold him upright.

The safe contained racks upon racks of neatly organized ketamine vials, and nothing else. There were dozens of them. *Hundreds.*

"God, Levi, you were right," Martine whispered. "You've been right all along. The Seven of Spades found a way to obtain their ketamine legitimately, and they've been storing it here."

Levi made an embarrassing noise, a strangled cross between a gasp and a laugh.

"This is incredible." Beaming, Denise clasped her hands, looking like she was about to start bouncing up and down. "And this is now officially a crime scene. I'll get the techs and photographer out here stat."

She hustled out of the room again. Levi swallowed, trying to work up some saliva in his parched mouth.

"One of the bodies from the desert must be Fowler," he said. "Probably one of the two that were tortured, since the Seven of Spades managed to get all of his personal information and access to his accounts. That might help Dr. Paquin make a positive ID."

"I'll call her." Martine released him, then arched an eyebrow. "Maybe take a minute to get your shit together before you let anyone else see you like this, okay?"

After he nodded, she left the office, already dialing her phone.

He pressed both hands to his face and shuddered. When he lowered them, he scanned the room, picking up the details he hadn't noticed when he'd been preoccupied by the safe.

There was a small desk along one wall, its surface adorned with tidy stacks of office supplies that had clearly never been used. An ergonomic office chair was pushed up to it. Against the other wall stood a bookcase full of veterinary reference texts.

And high in the corner where the wall met the ceiling was a security camera with a blinking red light, aimed directly at the safe.

Levi stiffened. The Seven of Spades might be watching now, or they would see this later, but either way, this office couldn't be used to stage an ambush. The killer would know not to return here.

It didn't matter, though. Their access to the stash had been cut off. Any other way they tried to get their hands on ketamine would be risky, given that the entire country knew it was the Seven of Spades's drug of choice. The noose was tightening around their neck.

Vicious glee ripped through Levi, making him light-headed. He tore a blank page from the notepad he kept in his jacket, grabbed a Sharpie from the desk, and scribbled a message in all capital letters, underlining it twice. Helping himself to a strip of tape, he shut the safe doors and slapped the note on them in plain view of the camera.

FOUND YOU

He turned around, smirked at the camera, and gave it the finger.

CHAPTER 8

Dominic had stopped trying to argue himself out of things he was going to end up doing anyway; it saved a lot of mental energy. And as an additional benefit, staking out Roger Carson's house was a great distraction from his gambling cravings.

He sat in his pickup half a block down the street from said house. Magnetic decals on either side of his truck bore the name of a fake landscaping company—although that company had a seemingly legitimate website if anyone happened to Google it—and an assortment of landscaping equipment had been thrown into the bed for good measure.

Honestly, he might not have even needed the cover. This wasn't the kind of neighborhood where people walked around outside on a weekday, especially not in the heat of encroaching summer.

One of the things he loved most about being a PI was the autonomy. He'd told McBride he'd be working in the field today—which was true, because he could easily manage his other cases from his laptop in the car while keeping an eye on his target.

He'd also been able to swing home to pick up Rebel, who was delighted by a mission so reminiscent of their bounty hunting days. He scratched under her chin, smiling as she thumped her tail lazily against the bench seat, and then looked back up the street to what he was becoming increasingly certain was a Utopia safe house.

After his therapy appointment last night, he'd detoured on his way home to set up a surveillance camera on a lamppost across the street from Carson's house. The camera was legal, since it didn't record audio and was directed at the driveway and front yard, where there was no reasonable expectation of privacy.

Between a review of the footage and today's stakeout, Dominic had established that people came and went from the house at all hours of the day and night—though never in large groups, so it wouldn't draw anyone's attention unless they were already watching. He'd used the various cars' license plates to ID more than a dozen of the visitors.

Of those he'd identified, about half had no criminal records and no remarkable details in their background checks, while the other half were either known or suspected members of Utopia. A good chunk of both groups were students at UNLV.

A Utopia safe house, no doubt about it. People came and went so frequently that they couldn't be using it as a temporary residence; given the number of students among the visitors, he suspected it served more as some combination of meeting place and recruitment center.

Most troubling was how many people entered the house carrying bags and packages, then left empty-handed. He couldn't shake the feeling that something much worse than bureaucracy was lurking behind that ordinary façade, and he was consumed by a yearning to see what was inside. That would be all kinds of illegal, of course, but what really held him back was the fact that the house was never empty.

The afternoon was fading into twilight when Levi called. Dominic answered without taking his eyes off the house. "Hey, baby. What's up?"

"I found it," Levi said, his voice thin with what could have been either stress or excitement.

Rebel cocked her head, eyeing the phone. Dominic rubbed her ear reassuringly. "Found what?"

"The ketamine!" Levi continued, speaking faster and faster, stumbling over his words as they poured out. "There was a veterinarian, and I *knew* something wasn't right, and he's dead and his house and office are fake, and there was a safe full of ketamine, *full* of it—"

"Levi!" When Levi came to a panting halt, Dominic said, "I have no idea what you're talking about. Slow down."

Levi started over and told him the story of his day from the beginning. Dominic's mouth fell open while he listened, relief and elation blossoming in his chest, the Utopia safe house all but forgotten.

"Oh my God," he said once Levi had finished. "This is—this is huge."

"I know. I'm almost home; are you going to be finished with work soon?"

Dominic recognized the edge in Levi's voice. It was the same way he sounded after he'd been in a fight—that hint of wildness, of frantic, triumphant desire that could only be gratified one way.

"I can leave now if you want me to." Dominic was already turning the key in the ignition. Carson and his merry band of Nazis could wait.

"Yes. Please."

"I'm on my way."

"Hurry," Levi said, and hung up.

Levi must have been waiting for him by the door, because no sooner had Dominic reengaged the locks than Levi jumped into his arms. Dominic caught him with a startled grunt, clasping his hands securely beneath Levi's ass. Levi had *never* done that before.

He was vaguely aware of Rebel scampering deeper into the apartment, but most of his focus was commanded by the arms Levi had locked around his neck and the aggressive kiss Levi was ravishing him with. Walking as best he could with an armful of sexy detective kissing the fuck out of him, he lurched into the kitchen and then dropped Levi on the island in the center of the room. Levi bumped the spice rack, knocking it over and sending little jars rolling everywhere.

Dominic tore his mouth away from Levi's to cover his throat with kisses instead. "You're amazing, baby. I knew you'd do it. You're unstoppable."

"I almost gave up." Levi tilted his head to one side, giving Dominic more room to work.

Dominic scoffed against his skin. "No, you didn't. You never, ever give up, even when you probably should. I love that about you."

Moaning, Levi scrabbled at the hem of Dominic's shirt and tugged it up. Dominic had dressed for his landscaping cover in an old T-shirt and jeans, so it was the work of seconds to strip the shirt off and toss it aside. He paused for a moment, processing his surge of arousal at the way Levi was ogling his bare chest, before he gave Levi's T-shirt the same treatment.

Wait . . . T-shirt? Dominic blinked at Levi's sweatpants. "Did you change when you got home?"

"I wanted to make it easier for you to fuck me."

Dominic hooked his fingers in Levi's waistband. Levi pushed himself up on his hands, holding his body in midair with only the strength of his arms while Dominic got rid of the pants and revealed nothing underneath them.

"You could have waited for me naked," Dominic teased.

"Oh my God, stop talking." Levi raked his fingers reprovingly through Dominic's chest hair and then wrenched at his fly. "I need your cock."

Dominic loved that Levi was such a hungry, assertive bottom, rarely shy about demanding what he wanted during sex—and what he usually wanted was to be fucked deep and hard by a big cock, the size queen.

Moving swiftly, Dominic yanked Levi off the island, spun him around, and shoved him face-first over the marble edge. Levi was still gasping when Dominic sank to his knees and buried his face in Levi's ass.

"*Ah!*" Levi spread his legs, canting his hips to push his ass against Dominic's face. "Fuck, Dominic . . ."

Dominic spread Levi's ass cheeks with both hands and ate him out sloppily, ravenously, holding nothing back in his worship of that perfect hole. It wasn't long before he had to drop one of his hands into his own lap to finish what Levi had started, pulling his zipper down the rest of the way and freeing his erection. He jerked himself off while he fucked Levi with his tongue, delighting in the soft moans and cries above him.

When he had to take a break to catch his breath, he kept a hand on Levi's ass, massaging his thumb in circles around Levi's rim. Goddamn, he wanted inside. But he didn't have any lube on him, and the thought of leaving Levi to fetch some was physically painful.

As he knelt on the kitchen floor, stretching his aching jaw, his eyes fell on the low, open shelving in the island—more specifically, on the decanter of pure artisanal olive oil he kept there. Nothing but the best for a Russo.

He considered it for a moment, then shrugged. If olive oil had been good enough for the ancient Greeks, it was good enough for them.

Grabbing the bottle, Dominic rose to his feet. Levi's chest and open palms were pressed to the island's surface, his face turned to one side, his eyes shut. Bent over with Dominic standing behind him, he was terribly vulnerable, but his body was relaxed. Trusting.

He felt safe.

Overcome, Dominic leaned forward and laid a line of kisses along Levi's spine. Levi hummed and arched his back, never opening his eyes.

Dominic poured a few drops of olive oil onto the fingers of his right hand. He smoothed his clean hand over Levi's back, then abruptly plunged his slick fingers into Levi's hole, filling Levi the way he'd been begging for.

Levi groaned and bucked against the island. Dominic showed no mercy, pumping his fingers in and out, twisting and corkscrewing them, working Levi open. The oil had a nice slippery slide to it, and he wondered how long it would take Levi to notice—

A frisson of tension rippled through Levi's body—nothing so intense as anxiety, more like confusion. Sure enough, he propped himself on his forearms and looked over his shoulder with a furrowed brow. "What is—"

Dominic grasped Levi's nape, forced him flat on his belly again, and thrust his fingers in deep. "Stay down and take it," he growled.

Levi let out a shuddering gasp, his legs shifting wider and his body opening up further. The change was so profound that Dominic was able to get a third finger inside without any resistance. He held Levi down and finger-fucked him roughly, almost brutally; he couldn't help but rut his throbbing cock against Levi's hip at the way Levi squirmed and cried out.

Every element of Levi's body language screamed pleasure, and they had a safeword besides, but Dominic still draped himself over Levi to whisper in his ear. "Is this okay?"

"*Yes.* Don't stop."

Dominic nipped the shell of Levi's ear before he straightened up and got back to business. He changed tack, returning to two fingers, seeking Levi's prostate, and then rapidly pulsing his fingertips against it in a way he knew drove Levi insane. This time, however, he didn't let up, not even when Levi was straining onto the balls of his feet and clawing at the island, shouts ringing off the kitchen walls.

Dominic didn't stop until he saw that Levi was about to come, frotting against the marble even though that must have been uncomfortable. He withdrew his fingers, and Levi slumped onto the island, his back heaving. Though Dominic couldn't see Levi's erection where it was trapped between his stomach and the counter, he was sure there was a *lake* of pre-come under there by now.

Staring at Levi's flushed, glistening hole, he stroked his oiled hand along his own swollen cock. God, that felt good, and it would feel even better once he was inside.

Only then did he realize the mistake he'd made in his lust-addled state: They couldn't use a condom now. Olive oil would destroy the latex.

He stilled. *Fuck.* They'd both been tested when they'd gotten back together, and all of the results had been negative, but technically, *technically*, they were supposed to wait for the three-month retest before having unprotected sex again.

He didn't care. Really, truly, did not give a shit. Any risk was negligible at this point, and he needed to bury himself in Levi's body so badly he was shaking.

Levi looked back again, no doubt puzzled by the delay. His eyes flicked from Dominic to the bottle on the island, and he blinked as he came to the same realization Dominic had.

"You can do it," he said quietly. "It's okay with me if it's okay with you."

Well, nobody had ever accused Dominic of being risk-*averse*.

Gripping Levi's hip with one hand, he guided himself to Levi's hole and pushed inside. Between the rimjob and the aggressive finger-fucking, Levi had been so well-prepared that Dominic was able to get halfway in before Levi's habitual internal tension halted his progress.

He was glad for the excuse to start off slowly, because it felt like *years* since the last time he'd fucked Levi bareback, rather than a couple of months. Sex with a condom just didn't compare. The scorching heat, the shiver-inducing slide of the oil, the way he could feel every twitch and clench of those tight muscles around his cock . . .

He pulled all the way back, then pushed inside again, a long, drawn-out penetration that Levi always responded to well. Levi was needier than usual today; a few rolls of the hips, and Dominic was bottoming out in no time.

As soon as Dominic knew Levi could take it, he picked up the pace, driving in harder and harder until his balls were smacking loudly against Levi's ass and they were both grunting on every thrust. Levi had his forehead pressed to the island now instead of his cheek, his restless hands roaming the surface and finding no purchase on the marble.

Dominic grasped Levi's nape, since Levi had enjoyed that so much before. He used that and his hold on Levi's hip to yank Levi's body backward onto his cock with as much force as he was slamming forward into it. Levi greeted the rough treatment with an urgent, approving cry, his hips bucking.

"That's it." Dominic squeezed Levi's ass hard. "You like that?"

"*Nngh.*"

Dominic closed his eyes and licked his dry lips. He was *not* going to come before Levi. Condom or no condom, he had better stamina than that.

He opened his eyes when he felt he could control himself. And suddenly, although this position gave him a delicious view, it wasn't what he wanted anymore. He wanted, *needed*, to see Levi's face. Plus, neither of them could easily reach Levi's cock like this.

When he pulled out, he almost came at Levi's angry noise of protest. He gripped his balls, breathed deeply, and then stroked a hand down Levi's side.

"C'mere." He turned Levi around and picked him up again. Levi let himself be manhandled, all but dead weight as Dominic carried him to the dining table, kicked a chair aside, and laid him on his back with his ass at the edge. Once Dominic had eased himself inside, he grabbed the backs of Levi's knees, spread Levi's legs wide, and resumed his earlier savage pace.

Levi's response was immediate and intense. His eyes fell shut, his head tipping back as his spine arched right off the table; both of his hands shot out to clutch at the edge. His cock jutted up furiously, twitching and dripping a steady stream of pre-come.

Oh, yes. Dominic could give Levi everything he needed in this position, pound into him deep and hard with absolute freedom of movement, and have the privilege of watching Levi's beautiful face while he did so.

He drank in the sight before him: the hectic flush splashed across cut-glass cheekbones, slender lips bitten to a deep rose, unruly curls plastered to Levi's forehead with sweat. Levi's eyes fluttered open every now and then, and the flashes of gray Dominic caught were entirely glazed over.

Levi wasn't making as much noise as he usually did, though. Under normal circumstances, Levi's shouts and screams during sex were loud enough to disturb the neighbors. They *had* been, earlier, but since the move to the table, Levi had gone uncharacteristically quiet. His jaw was clenched, allowing only the occasional deep grunt or ragged gasp to escape his pressed lips.

He hadn't touched his cock, either; both of his hands were still clinging for dear life to the edge of the table on either side of his hips. But that could just be to keep Dominic's forceful thrusts from sending him halfway across the surface.

Curious, Dominic reached for Levi's erection. Levi batted him away, shook his head without opening his eyes, and returned his hand to its previous position.

"God." Dominic's heart raced faster, his hips speeding up as well. "Are you gonna . . ."

Levi nodded, his face strained, his eyes screwed tightly shut.

"*Fuck.*" Dominic had only seen Levi do this twice before, and it had blown his mind both times.

He could help, too. Hooking his arms around Levi's thighs, he lifted Levi's ass off the table and changed angles, searching . . . *there*, if Levi's choked cry and seizing muscles were any indication.

Dominic hammered Levi's prostate, drowning in the pleasure of it, transfixed by the miracle of Levi's body. Levi grew quieter and quieter, until he was barely even breathing. The cords in his neck stood out sharply; his defined abdominal muscles quivered and rippled and clenched. In Dominic's peripheral vision, he could see Levi's toes curled up tight.

They hovered there for a moment, suspended right on the edge.

"Come on, baby," Dominic panted through his own harsh breaths. "Let me see you, come on—"

Levi *screamed*, the shattered, endless wail of pent-up pressure abruptly released. His body snapped into a rigid arc, his hands, shoulders, and head the only parts of him still touching the table. His cock jerked violently as he came untouched, pulse after creamy pulse spurting onto his stomach, his chest. A particularly ambitious jet made it all the way to the hollow of his throat.

That was it for Dominic. He dropped Levi's legs, fell forward onto his hands, and thrust wildly through his own climax while Levi's spasming muscles milked him dry.

After he'd come, Dominic couldn't stop rocking his hips—slow, gentle thrusts into the mess he'd made of Levi's body. Levi was quaking and gasping beneath him, shuddering viciously with sporadic aftershocks. He looked like he'd taken several hard blows to the head.

Careful to support most of his own weight, Dominic showered Levi's face with light kisses. "God, Levi, you're perfect," he murmured. He lapped up the come from Levi's throat, then nuzzled his jaw. "I love you so much."

"I love you." Levi lifted Dominic's face and kissed him, though he was too out of breath to maintain that for long. He pressed a hand to the tattoo on Dominic's chest. "I love you."

Eventually, they had to separate. Dominic pulled out, grimacing in sympathy at the sound of discomfort Levi made, and then lifted Levi's legs so he could see that wrecked, come-drenched hole.

"You really like seeing your come inside me, don't you?" Levi said with drowsy amusement.

Like was way too mild a word to describe how this made Dominic feel. "Yeah."

"I like feeling it."

Smiling, Dominic gently lowered Levi's legs. As his brain cleared, he realized that he'd never undressed himself beyond his shirt; his open jeans were smeared with oil stains that would probably never come out.

Oh, well. They were an old pair anyway. He tucked his cock into his boxers and zipped himself up. "I'll get a towel."

The kitchen was a bigger mess than he remembered making, but he'd been pretty distracted at the time. He grabbed a couple of clean dishtowels and turned around.

Levi was sitting up on the dining table, glaring at Dominic— although with his curls all tousled and his face pink, the expression was more adorable than anything else.

"What?" Dominic asked.

Levi raised his eyebrows. "Do you have *any* idea how long it's going to take to get this olive oil out of me?"

CHAPTER 9

"**B**y comparing J. Doe #7's dental X-rays to records on file with Dr. Fowler's former dentist here in Las Vegas, I have positively confirmed the body as that of Seth Fowler," Dr. Paquin announced to the task force during their next meeting. "Much easier to do when there's a likely victim in mind, so thank you for that, Detectives."

Catcalls rang out in the conference room. Levi snorted, but heat built in his cheeks. Next to him, Martine was grinning broadly.

Denise was also full of excited energy, but that was nothing unusual for her. "Fowler had never been reported missing. We located his next of kin, an aunt in Seattle, and she hadn't spoken to him in over a decade." Denise's smile dimmed a bit. "She didn't seem too upset to find out he was dead, either."

Across the table from Levi, Leila was staring at him. He could feel the searing weight of her gaze, although he couldn't quite bring himself to meet her eyes.

He cleared his throat, returning his focus to the matter at hand. "Our theory is that the Seven of Spades targeted Fowler for both his suspected history of negligence and his legitimate access to ketamine, then tortured him to obtain the information they needed to make it appear that he was still alive."

"I have a slightly different theory, if I may," said Paquin.

Intrigued, he gestured for her to continue.

"The tests are still coming in, but from what I can tell, the Seven of Spades didn't start using ketamine *until* they killed Dr. Fowler." She tapped the photos spread out in the center of the table—photos that made Levi glad he'd had a light lunch. "None of J. Does 1 through 6 exhibit any traces of ketamine, while almost every J. Doe after

Fowler does. The only ones who don't are those without enough tissue or organs left to test for it."

Levi leaned forward, his forehead creasing. This was the first he'd heard of this.

"You think choosing Fowler as a victim is what gave the Seven of Spades the *idea* to use ketamine?" Martine asked.

Paquin nodded. "I think the timing would be far too coincidental otherwise."

Musing aloud, Levi said, "So the Seven of Spades initially targeted Fowler for his professional negligence, and while they were planning the kill, it occurred to them how much easier it would be to murder someone zoned out on ketamine—a clear, tasteless liquid that could be easily slipped into a victim's drink."

"Isn't this around the same point in the timeline that the cause of death changed from stabbing wounds to incised wounds?" Wen asked Paquin.

"I can't be one hundred percent certain, because I haven't been able to determine exact cause of death for all fourteen bodies. But the general pattern does trend that way."

"A lot easier to slit someone's throat from behind when they're high as balls," Gibbs said.

A pained expression crossed Wen's face. "Yes, Officer, thank you."

Levi had been watching both Wen and Gibbs since he'd entered the room, and neither of them showed the slightest hint of anxiety. He'd also seen Kelly Marin and Valeria Montoya in the bullpen earlier, going about their days like it was business as usual. If any of those four remaining suspects were the Seven of Spades, they were either playing it cool or massively overestimating their own cleverness.

Martine was still studying the photographs. "So the earlier stabbings were more likely a matter of necessity than preference." Turning to Levi, she added, "This is growth, just like Rohan hypothesized—the Seven of Spades learned a better way to kill people through practice and experience."

He nodded slowly; everything seemed to fit together. "We know why the killer tortured Fowler. What was the purpose behind torturing J. Doe #2?"

"We won't know until we identify him, but there's good news on that front." Paquin swiped her fingers across her tablet, then turned it around to show another photo to the room at large. "The traumatic fixation plates on his radius and ulna are clearly stamped with serial numbers and the manufacturer's logo. We hit a snag when it turned out that the manufacturer has since been acquired by another company, but my assistant is working on tracking down the information."

They spent the rest of the meeting discussing other incremental progress: DNA analysis was underway, dental records and other biological data on the victims were being submitted to the NCIC one by one, and partial prints had been obtained from rehydrating the fingers of two of the most recent corpses. Paquin also had a specialist working on 3-D facial reconstructions of the victims that could be run through facial recognition databases.

Still, all of those methods would take a long time, if they panned out at all. For now, their best leads were Dr. Fowler and the other tortured victim. The meeting broke up with Levi and Martine set to thoroughly investigate Fowler's life in Las Vegas and any possible connection that could lead them to the Seven of Spades.

They were so close. Levi felt it as an itch in his back teeth, a restless squirming in his gut. It had been too long since he'd been this motivated on the job.

The one fly in the ointment was the contempt radiating from Leila as she swept past him on her way out of the room.

Dominic's phone rang while his hands were covered in Doritos dust. He hastily wiped them off on his jeans, then grabbed his phone off the truck's dashboard and smiled at the caller ID.

"Hey, baby," he said, pushing Rebel away with his free hand as she tried to lick the orange powder off his jeans. "How was the meeting?"

"Good. Some interesting developments, actually, but I'll fill you in tonight." Levi paused. "Are you staking out that house again?"

"Yep." Dominic had shared the whole story with Levi a couple of days ago.

"You've been there all week. What are you going to do if McBride finds out?"

"Hey, I can multitask. As long as I'm getting my officially assigned work done, she won't care where I'm physically located while I do it."

A put-upon sigh gusted over the phone line. "Why don't you let me send a couple of uniforms to check out the house?"

"Oh yeah? And what are you going to base the warrant request on?"

Silence.

"That's what I thought." Dominic glanced up the block at Carson's house. He knew Carson was home, and that Maggie Spencer had been in there for a couple of hours, but all was quiet.

"Just be careful," Levi said. "And *don't* do anything illegal."

"I make no promises."

"Ugh." Levi hung up on him.

Dominic grinned and tossed his phone back onto the dashboard. God, he loved that man.

In all honesty, he wouldn't be able to continue this stakeout much longer. Not all of his work could be done via computer, and the more time he spent parked on this street, the likelier he was to raise suspicions. He'd give it one more day, and then he'd have to rely solely on the camera he'd planted across from Carson's house.

He passed another hour splitting his focus between his target and the asset research on his laptop. Bored with the sleepy neighborhood, Rebel curled up on the seat with her head on her paws and watched him work.

They both snapped to attention when a car drove by—an event worthy of notice on a street as quiet as this one. Dominic narrowed his eyes as the car turned into Carson's driveway. He reached for his camera, a higher quality model than the one he'd used to spy on Bishop in the park, and zoomed in for a clearer view.

The car wasn't one he'd seen here before, and neither was the man who got out. But Dominic could swear he knew this man from *somewhere* . . .

It took a few moments, but when the recognition clicked, he realized the delay had been because he'd never seen this man out of uniform. The guy was a beat cop from Levi's substation—Officer Daley.

Dominic frowned. Was the LVMPD already working an undercover op here? It would make sense, and Levi wouldn't know anything about it. Gang Crimes and Organized Crime weren't just separate bureaus from Homicide; they belonged to a different division altogether.

Daley didn't go inside the house. He remained in the driveway, leaning against his car, cell phone in hand. Within a minute, Roger Carson came out the front door, and the two men fell into a quiet but clearly intense argument right where they stood.

As Dominic watched and snapped pictures, his unease increased. The vibe of this encounter wasn't what he'd expect from a cop working undercover. Daley's clenched jaw and thunderous glare spoke of genuine anger, while Carson's body language came off as more placating than anything else.

The men were still deep in conversation when Maggie Spencer emerged from the house, lugging two full garbage bags that she tossed into the can by the curb.

Daley whirled on her with several emphatic hand gestures. She threw her head back like an exasperated teenager, then wheeled the can around the side of the house to the backyard.

All sorts of alarms were going off in Dominic's head now.

Daley left shortly thereafter. Spencer returned from the backyard and exchanged a few words with Carson, and then they both got into her car and drove off as well.

For the first time since Dominic had begun his stakeout, the house was empty—at least, as far as he knew. But since he'd had the place under video surveillance 24/7 for days, he was as confident of that as he could be.

Wasting no time, he grabbed a pair of heavy work gloves, pulled a baseball cap low over his eyes, and transferred Rebel to the truck bed so she could act as lookout. He headed for the house with the confident, casual stride of a person who had every right to be there.

The backyard was well screened from the neighbors, so he didn't hesitate to throw back the lid of the trash can. With a flick of his keys, he sliced open the first bag.

Underneath an unremarkable layer of junk mail and discarded food, the bag was crammed with dozens of empty bottles of hydrogen peroxide.

Dominic froze, hunched over the can. Based on Daley's reaction, he'd assumed there was something incriminating in here. But this—this was so much worse than anything he'd imagined.

The second bag had the same contents as the first. He straightened up, shut the lid, and stood still for a moment as a sense of calm purpose smoothed out his thoughts. There was only one course of action he could take, and it had to be done quickly.

He hustled back to the truck, though never moving fast enough to arouse the suspicions of anyone who might be watching. A few soft words settled Rebel down while he rummaged through his supplies until he came up with a screwdriver and a ring of bump keys. He left her in the truck when he returned to the house; if his assumptions were correct, he didn't want her anywhere near it.

There was no evidence of a home security system that he could see. It stood to reason that if the house was hosting illegal activities, Carson wouldn't want the police or neighbors alerted to an intruder. Still, Dominic would need to be efficient. Infiltrate, confirm, retreat. If he got caught breaking and entering, Levi would have an aneurysm.

He matched the lock to the correct bump key, slipped the key in one notch short of full insertion, and smacked it with the handle of the screwdriver a couple of times while applying lateral pressure. The lock popped open in seconds.

Lock bumping was fast, but it was also loud—so if there *was* anyone inside, they'd know he was here. He stashed his tools in the pockets of his windbreaker and drew his gun before easing the door open.

As soon as he stepped inside, he was overpowered by an acrid chemical smell that triggered a cascade of unexpected sense memories. Coughing, he staggered against the wall and fell to one knee.

The last time he'd smelled this odor had been in the moments before he'd been shot.

He'd never had flashbacks to his service with the Rangers before, but there was no other explanation for the fugue he dropped into. The pain that ripped through his right shoulder was like being shot all over again. He could practically hear the shouts of his ambushed squad ringing off the walls.

Gritting his teeth, he shook his head and pushed himself upright. He didn't have *time* for this.

Luckily, he was right about the house being empty, because otherwise he would have been a sitting duck. In the interests of thoroughness, he cleared the house anyway before following the smell to a room in the back.

"Goddamn it," he muttered as he stood on the threshold. He knew a home explosives lab when he saw one, but even if he hadn't, the stacked bottles of acetone and hydrogen peroxide would have tipped him off. Carson and his buddies were using this house to manufacture triacetone triperoxide, a dangerously unstable homemade explosive used in IEDs.

The blinds were drawn over the one window, casting the corners of the room into shadow. A free-standing exhaust fan against the wall wasn't doing much to dissipate the smell—basically just blowing it out of the room into the rest of the house. Dominic flicked the light switch and took a few cautious steps inside, getting a better look.

All of the right supplies and equipment were here, but he didn't see the finished product. Maybe Utopia had already moved it, or they might be hiding it elsewhere in the house.

The closet seemed a logical place to start. He crossed the room and gingerly opened the door, every movement as smooth and slow as he could manage. TATP was prone to detonating itself at the slightest vibration or temperature increase.

There were no explosives in the closet, but it wasn't empty, either.

"What the fucking fuck," he said, staring at the massive bulletin board on the wall. A map of the Las Vegas Valley covered the entire board, and the map itself was plastered with photographs, sticky notes, foil stars, colored pushpins, floor plans, and a web of handwritten circles and arrows he couldn't make sense of.

Targets. These are potential targets and a plan of attack.

Jesus Christ. He shoved his gun into his holster and fumbled his camera out of his pocket, eyes still roaming over the board. The Stratosphere Tower, the Regional Justice Center, Masjid As-Sabur . . .

As he was lifting the camera, preparing to snap the first photo, his gaze reached the far right edge of the board. His train of thought sputtered and died.

There was a blown-up photograph of Levi pinned there, taken at a distance, the background blurry and indistinct. A targeting reticule was painted over his face, and a dart had been jabbed viciously through his neck. Beside the photograph, someone had scrawled a few stomach-turning homophobic and anti-Semitic epithets, along with the words *HIGH PRIORITY*.

Every other concern was knocked clean out of Dominic's head. He gaped at the photograph, his body unmoving except for the shallow jerking of his chest as he struggled to breathe.

No. No. No.

It was the only thought in his mind, bouncing around his skull in shrieking, mindless patterns. Before this very moment, he could never have imagined that this level of pure terror existed.

The sound of a dog barking broke him out of his stupor. He flinched, his throat aching as he sucked in badly needed air, and awareness of his surroundings rushed back.

That wasn't just any dog. It was Rebel, barking continuously in a way she *never* did, the sound escalating in volume and anxiety with each passing second.

He traded his camera for his gun, quietly shut the closet, and pressed himself into the corner behind the room's open door just in time to hear several sets of footsteps enter the house.

"I'm telling you, there's nobody here," said a man.

A female voice said, "The motion sensors wouldn't have gone off for no reason."

Dominic winced. So no *legitimate* security system, but they had their own private defensive measures in place. This was what he got for being impulsive.

"We've gotten false alarms before. Besides, who'd want to break in here? This house isn't exactly a prime target for burglary, and Daley's positive the cops don't know anything about the mission."

Seemed like Daley was Utopia's mole in the LVMPD, rather than the other way around. That wasn't going to go down well.

"I told you not to ever leave this house empty," said another man.

"Yeah, well—"

"Would you two shut up?" the woman snapped. "If there *is* somebody here, they're gonna hear you."

A little late to worry about that.

There was nowhere for Dominic to hide, so he'd have to fight his way out of the house. But he found himself facing a dilemma: use his gun or not? He was breaking the law here; did he want to compound the offense by committing assault with a deadly weapon or possibly homicide? If he killed someone while committing a crime, it would be considered murder, not self-defense.

Better in trouble with the law than dead.

The footsteps were approaching the room. Dominic readied himself, and the moment he heard them cross the threshold, he shoved the door forward with all his strength. It collided hard with whoever had entered the room first, drawing startled shouts, and rebounded as Dominic slipped out from behind it with his gun in a two-handed grip.

He found himself facing Carson and Spencer, as well as a man he didn't recognize. Both Carson and Spencer were holding guns, but the shock of being hit with the door had knocked them off-balance and made them lower their weapons.

"Ah, ah," Dominic said. "Guns on the ground, hands in the air."

They complied with poor grace. Spencer was still holding her car keys, and he was about to tell her to drop those as well when Carson spoke.

"I know you." Carson's eyes were narrowed, and the seething hatred pouring off him was so tangible Dominic felt it like oily fingers crawling over his skin. "Dominic Russo. You fuck that Jew cop."

Dominic remained calm, refusing to take the bait. "That's me. I'm also a veteran Army Ranger, so I'd suggest getting out of my way before I have to teach you what that means."

The man behind Carson spat on the carpet. "Letting perverts like you serve in the military is a disgrace to the entire country."

Dominic couldn't help it; he tensed, distracted for a single moment—and that moment was all it took for Spencer to throw her keys at his face.

He recoiled. Carson leapt forward with a savage yell, smashing into him, and struggled with him for the gun until it clattered to the floor.

Fine. Grabbing Carson's shoulder with one hand, Dominic drove his other fist into Carson's stomach so hard he lifted the bastard right off his feet. Carson made a horrible choking noise that cut off when Dominic's brutal right hook knocked him unconscious.

Even with Carson limp and insensate, it was no problem for Dominic to support the man's weight. He used Carson's body as a human shield while he glared at Spencer and the other guy. They both had guns trained on him, but they were clearly unwilling to shoot their friend, and there was a healthy amount of fear in their eyes now.

"You gonna fire those guns in here?" Dominic asked. "Probably bring every cop in the area right to your cute little home laboratory."

Spencer's eyes darted toward the second man. "Boyd?"

"Get a stun gun," Boyd said tensely.

She hurried out of the room. Boyd didn't make the mistake of watching her leave, but it didn't matter. As soon as she was in the hallway, Dominic heaved Carson's body at him. Boyd went down with a yelp, and Dominic lunged forward to slam the door shut and throw the lock while Boyd flailed out from underneath Carson's dead weight.

Spencer started pounding on the other side of the door, but Dominic was more concerned with Boyd, who was reaching for his dropped gun as he freed himself. Dominic flung himself atop Boyd from the side, sprawling his upper body over Boyd's torso in a way that crushed Boyd's arms beneath his chest and put most of his considerable weight on Boyd's rib cage. He trapped Boyd's head in the pincer of his elbow and knee.

Boyd thrashed like a beached dolphin, gasping for air—but because Dominic wasn't sitting on his hips, he had no leverage to buck Dominic off. It also helped that Dominic outweighed him by at least seventy pounds.

Dominic smashed his elbow into Boyd's face, breaking his nose. Boyd screamed, and *now* Dominic swung astride his hips, landing a couple of clean follow-up strikes that sent Boyd into dreamland with his buddy.

Spencer was shouting obscenities from the hallway as she kicked the door over and over. Dominic jumped to his feet, and just in time, because the next thing she did was shoot the lock off and charge inside.

He swept her arm aside, stripped the gun from her hand, and cocked his fist. But then, although he *knew* that in this situation it was patronizing at best, he hesitated. The taboo against hitting a woman was too deeply ingrained in him.

So, of course, she hit him first.

She had a solid right cross, almost as good as Levi's. It split his lip, making him stagger backward, but he managed to block her next strike and get in a punch of his own—though still not as hard as he'd hit either of the men. She crumpled to the floor, dazed but conscious.

Dominic snatched up his gun and ran.

He bolted through the front door and down the street. Rebel barked again when she saw him, her front paws up on the side of the truck bed. But he was only halfway there when her body stiffened and her lips peeled away from her teeth in a vicious growl.

He whirled around, raising his gun, to see that Spencer had chased him out of the house. She was weaving like a drunk as she ran, apparently not recovered from the blow to the head.

Before he'd decided whether or not to shoot, Rebel leapt out of the truck and bounded toward Spencer, loosing a ferocious snarl that would have done her lupine ancestors proud.

Dominic had yet to encounter a human being who could stand their ground in the face of that threat. Spencer shrieked and sprinted back to the house, tripping over her own feet in her haste to escape.

He whistled, yanked the truck door open, and dove into the cab. Rebel followed him, and he burned rubber as they hightailed it out of there.

"What do you mean, Utopia is making TATP?" Denise asked. Her skeptical expression implied that she wasn't asking Dominic to repeat himself so much as wondering *how* he'd obtained that information in the first place.

Levi was sitting next to Dominic in stony silence, his arms folded across his chest. He'd dragged Dominic and Rebel into this tiny conference room the moment they'd arrived at the substation, shoved Dominic into a chair and snapped at him to wait, then returned a few minutes later with Denise and Martine in tow. But he'd also brought an ice pack for Dominic's face, so he couldn't be *too* furious.

Dominic lowered the ice pack from his throbbing mouth. "There's a Utopia safe house in Enterprise, owned by a man named Roger Carson. They're using it to manufacture TATP."

"And you know this how?"

"Oh, Dominic," said Martine, who knew him a lot better than Denise. "Tell me you didn't."

"Oh yes, he did," Levi said. He'd already heard the full story during the frantic phone call Dominic had made to him on the drive over.

Denise frowned. "You're not saying that you . . . broke into the house?" Her tone was one of polite disbelief, like there must be some misunderstanding and she was sorry she even had to ask. God, she was almost too nice to be a cop.

"Let's say that, hypothetically, a concerned citizen found a ton of empty hydrogen peroxide bottles in the house's trash." Dominic reached down to pet Rebel, who was sitting quietly beside his chair. "And that concerned citizen hypothetically entered the house to check it out, and hypothetically found unmistakable evidence of a TATP lab, plus what looked like a plan for a series of attacks. Then the owner of the house came back with some friends, and the concerned citizen had to fight their way out. Hypothetically."

Martine palmed her face. Levi was glaring at Dominic in a way that promised serious consequences—and not the fun kind.

Denise, though, seemed more concerned by the news itself than Dominic's method of acquiring it. She got up to pace the small room, more grave than he'd ever seen her. "You're *sure* it was a TATP lab?"

"Positive. I've seen a few of them, in Afghanistan. My squad was ambushed while locking one down; it's how I got shot."

He rolled his shoulder as he spoke, grimacing. Damn thing still ached, which was ridiculous. There was no lingering damage there.

Some of the ice surrounding Levi melted, and concern flickered through his eyes.

"What *is* TATP, exactly?" Martine asked. "Levi and I never deal with explosives beyond the occasional department-wide briefing."

"It's a homemade explosive, easy to make but very unstable. Dangerous to store and transport, because it's highly sensitive to temperature and friction."

Levi cocked his head. "Then why risk it? We know Utopia has the resources to afford more stable explosives—C4 or TNT."

"You can make TATP with common household materials without raising any red flags," Dominic said. "Plus, it's a nonnitrogenous compound, so a lot of detection devices don't pick up on it, including dogs."

"It can also be used as a detonator as well as a primary explosive," Denise added. "So they could be planning to use it *with* a more stable compound."

Dominic nodded agreement.

"The question is where." Martine turned to Dominic. "You said you got a look at their potential targets?"

"Yeah, but they came back before I could take any pictures."

"Still, you're one of the most observant people I've ever met. You must remember what you saw."

"Some of it. But . . ." Though Dominic wasn't usually a blusher, heat crept up the back of his neck. "There was a picture of Levi on the board, with a target painted on his face and the words 'high priority.' It distracted me, threw me off my game. Most of the rest is a blur."

Levi rested a hand on his arm, and when Dominic dared to glance at him, he saw no reproach on Levi's face. No fear, either—but after everything the Seven of Spades had put Levi through, his tolerance for being stalked by homicidal maniacs was pretty high.

Denise put her hands on her hips, worrying her bottom lip between her teeth. "This situation needs to be contained immediately. But without legally obtained evidence, we have no grounds on which to enter that house."

"It doesn't matter," said Dominic. "They would have burned that place the second I left—not literally, but you know what I mean. By the time you get there, they'll be long gone."

Levi squeezed his arm. "We still have to try."

"You can, if you're willing to fudge the truth a little." Dominic sighed as all three of them pinned him with narrowed eyes. *Cops.* "If you report that you've received complaints from neighbors about an acrid chemical smell coming from Carson's house, and that raccoons got into his garbage and spilled hydrogen peroxide bottles all over his yard, that'll scream TATP lab with enough certainty to get a search warrant. And I have a legal surveillance camera that's been documenting everyone who's gone in and out the front door for almost a week. At the very least, you can round up all of those people for questioning."

"I don't see that we have any other choice," Denise said. "We can't have neo-Nazis running around Las Vegas with unstable improvised explosives. Do you have access to that video feed here?"

"On my laptop, yeah. And I'll write down everything I can remember from their murder board."

"Thank you. I'll get the ball rolling; I need to notify my superiors that we have an elevated threat level." Denise hurried out of the room.

Once she was gone, Dominic could bring up the sensitive detail that Levi and Martine wouldn't have wanted to learn in front of an outsider. "We have another problem. One of your uniforms, Officer Daley, was at Carson's house right before I broke in. I guess it's possible he's working some kind of undercover angle, but from what I saw and heard, it's a lot more likely he's on Utopia's side."

Martine clenched her jaw, her nostrils flaring. Levi made a low growling noise that did not bode well for Daley's future.

"You might want to loop in Internal Affairs. Though if Utopia has one guy inside the LVMPD, they may have more."

Martine stood. "I'll get Freeman and Montoya on it. I think we can trust that neither of them are working with white supremacists."

A safe assumption, given that Freeman was black and Montoya Mexican American. If Montoya really was the Seven of Spades, that might be even better.

Once Martine left, Dominic swiveled his chair to face Levi. "I can't apologize for breaking into the house. I wouldn't mean it."

"I know." Levi hesitated, his mouth still open, and then huffed out a breath. "Dominic, I've been in life-threatening danger right in front of you multiple times, and you've been able to stay focused. What about seeing my picture on a board made you lose your cool?"

This was something Dominic had thought about on the drive over. "It wasn't just the threat to your life. It was the premeditation behind it, the *hatred*. These people don't even see you as human; they're tracking and hunting you like an animal."

Levi's lips quirked. "I'm a gay Jewish cop. That would tick a lot of boxes on the neo-Nazi kill list even if I weren't notoriously linked to an active serial killer."

"I know. And it's not like it was a secret that Utopia has serious beef with you. But *seeing* that hatred in all its ugliness . . ." Dominic swallowed hard. "I've never been so terrified."

Levi leaned forward and took Dominic's hands, his eyes soft with understanding. "Not even the day you were shot?"

Dominic should have known Levi wasn't going to let that pass unremarked. "No. There's a big difference between being scared for you and being scared for myself. Until today, I didn't even think that day had left mental scars with the physical ones. I've never even had nightmares about it. But that *smell* . . ." He grimaced, cracking his neck from side to side.

"Olfactory triggers can be powerful."

"Yeah. And this is gonna sound stupid, but my shoulder hurts."

"That doesn't sound stupid at all." Levi brushed his fingertips against the scar through Dominic's shirt.

The intimacy of that action, of Levi knowing exactly where his scar was without being able to see it, made Dominic feel better. He laced their fingers together and pressed a chaste kiss to Levi's mouth before they released each other.

Back to business, Levi said, "You described TATP as unstable. I'm assuming it also degrades quickly?"

"Very."

"So if Utopia made a batch, how long a window do they have to use it?"

Dominic met his eyes grimly. "Ten days at the most."

CHAPTER 10

ominic ended up being right, of course, although Levi had never doubted him. By the time the FBI obtained a warrant to search Carson's house, the place had been emptied out and scrubbed as clean as an operating room.

They tracked down most of the people identified in Dominic's surveillance feed and brought them in for questioning—including Daley, who was dragged in by Freeman and Montoya—but each one lawyered up and refused to say a word. Because Utopia was being bankrolled by the likes of Conrad Bishop, its members could afford excellent legal representation. In retrospect, Levi realized that was how a lowlife like Lonnie Hale had been able to hire Sawyer.

Without hard evidence of a crime, they had no choice but to release everyone eventually. At least they had enough to suspend Daley pending an IA investigation, and Freeman and Montoya were on the hunt for any other Utopia moles inside the LVMPD.

The silver lining of everyone refusing to talk was that neither Carson, Spencer, nor Boyd implicated Dominic in anything illegal. Still, there was no guarantee that wouldn't change.

So, as Levi and Dominic were standing behind two-way glass watching yet another punk smugly demand an attorney, Levi turned to Dominic and said, "I think you should talk to Sawyer."

He could have said that Dominic should hop on the next shuttle to Mars, and Dominic wouldn't have looked more surprised. "You want me to what?"

"You broke the law. What if one of the people who were there tries to leverage that to cut themselves a deal?"

"They won't."

"They *might*." Levi felt sick at the thought. "I think you should have a legal strategy prepared, just in case."

Dominic crossed his arms, a move that made his giant biceps bulge even more. "And you want me to get that legal advice from your one-night stand?"

"I *want* you to get it from Leila," Levi retorted. "But we both know that's not going to happen. Sawyer's the only other lawyer I know we could trust with this."

"You actually trust Sawyer?"

"I trust his arrogance and his professional pride. And . . ." Levi bit his lip. "He'd do it if I asked."

"Because he still has a thing for you," Dominic said flatly.

Levi shrugged and looked away, his cheeks burning. He knew Dominic bore no grudge over his night with Sawyer—they'd been broken up, after all—but that didn't mean Dominic liked being reminded of it.

After a moment of silence, Dominic huffed out a rueful laugh. "I'd ask what it is that makes men who've been with you unable to let go, but I know the answer to that from personal experience." He touched Levi's arm. "If you think I should talk to Sawyer, I will."

"Thank you," Levi said, gripping his fingers.

He wasn't able to arrange that right away, though, because all of his energy was being poured into averting Utopia's murky plans. At Dominic's suggestion, the FBI hadn't let Bishop know they were on to him; instead, they'd put him under twenty-four-hour surveillance, hoping he'd lead them to more concrete evidence.

Between the FBI and the LVMPD, word of the elevated threat level was quietly spread to the city's political and business leadership. Security measures were tightened across the Valley, especially at the potential targets Dominic had remembered from Utopia's murder board.

The difficulty of preparing Las Vegas for an attack was that the entire city was one big juicy target for terrorism. There were shows and special events going on every day of the week, a transient population that was challenging to monitor, and multiple locations where huge numbers of people gathered regularly, like the Strip and the Fremont Street Experience. Without more specific intelligence, they were floundering in the deep end of a pool whose existence they'd only just discovered.

The majority of law enforcement resources were diverted to the threat, which meant that the Seven of Spades investigation had been mostly shelved for the time being. Levi understood the rationale: A potential terrorist plot endangering hundreds if not thousands of lives was a more immediate problem than a serial killer who murdered one person at a time, and had been inactive for over a month besides. It made sense.

But Levi couldn't help being secretly, selfishly resentful that this had to happen *now*.

Sunday rolled around with no real progress made, and Wen insisted that Levi take the day off as scheduled. Over the past few weeks, Levi had fallen into a pattern of training with Adriana on Sundays after brunch at Dominic's mother's house, but there was no way he was letting her come into the city given current events.

Instead, he visited the Andersons' horse farm in Henderson, where they trained in the spacious backyard. Adriana's foster siblings Josh and Rima were eager to join, and Levi watched with amusement as Adriana proudly demonstrated some of the basic techniques she'd already mastered.

He politely declined the Andersons' invitation to join them for dinner afterward. As Adriana was walking him to his car, she said, "So what's the real reason you wanted to train here instead of at Counterstrike?"

"I told you." He hit the remote unlock button on his keys. "I needed to get out of the city, clear my head."

She put her hand on the driver's-side window so he couldn't open the door. "Uh-huh. Has anyone ever told you you're not a great liar?"

Sighing, he turned to meet her eyes.

"You can tell me. I won't freak out, and I won't tell anyone else, I promise."

He looked at her hopeful expression—her obvious longing to be trusted, to be taken seriously—and relented. "Las Vegas is a dangerous place to be right now. We're working hard to contain the situation, but we don't have a full handle on it yet. I want you to be safe. I *need* you to be safe."

Her eyes softened, but then she frowned. "What about you?"

"I'm a cop. Not being safe is kind of what I signed up for."

"I guess," she said reluctantly. "Just be careful, okay?"

After several promises of caution, she let him go. He checked his phone as he was buckling his seat belt to find a text from Dominic.

Stressed out. Going to meeting w/ Judd. Be home around 8. Dominic had followed that up with a couple of kissy-face emojis.

Levi typed a quick reply, hesitated, and added a simple red heart at the end. He felt silly the moment he sent it, but a little discomfort was worth the smile it would put on Dominic's face.

The drive home was uneventful, full of domestic thoughts like whether they had enough coffee in the pantry and what they should eat for dinner. Between the two of them, Dominic was the cook, but he wouldn't be in the mood after a GA meeting.

Postmates, then—Levi's specialty. He was debating options as he jogged up the stairs and headed for their apartment door, keys in hand.

The scuff of shoes on concrete was his only warning. A heavy body slammed into him from behind, driving him toward the door as a thick leather belt wrapped around his throat.

Levi lashed out one leg so his foot instead of his body was driven into the door, then shoved himself off with a mighty kick, pushing his head and shoulders against his attacker's as they reeled backward. He dropped his keys to give the belt one hard yank, just enough for him to twist around inside its grip and knee the guy in the balls. The guy's yelp was followed by a loud grunt as he crashed into the hallway railing.

Two more men closed in on either side. Levi ripped the belt out of the first one's hand and snapped it at the one on the right, cracking the leather against the man's face. As the man crumpled with a shriek, Levi nailed the third with a side kick to keep him at bay, then turned and finished the job with a much more powerful front kick.

Unfortunately for the man, he was standing too close to the stairs. The force of Levi's kick sent him tumbling down the entire flight.

Levi turned back to the remaining men in time to see one drawing a gun. He wrapped the belt around the guy's hand, twisted the gun out of his grip to send it flying, and wrenched the guy's arm up behind his back. Grabbing the guy's hair with a free hand, Levi smashed his face into the metal railing. The man slumped to his knees, groaning and clinging to the bars.

The last man was rising to his feet, one hand clutching his welted cheek and swollen eye while the other fumbled for the gun stuffed into his waistband. Levi kicked him in the stomach, nipping that attempt in the bud, and slipped behind the man to loop the belt around his neck. He crossed the belt at the man's nape and pulled tight before kicking the back of the man's legs to put him on his knees again.

The man thrashed, clawing uselessly at the belt, unable to make a sound. Levi bent down.

"*This* is how you strangle somebody," he hissed.

Levi let go before the man passed out, letting him collapse next to his buddy. He traded the belt for his handcuffs, threading the chain through the slats of the railing and cuffing one of each man's wrists. After he yanked the gun out of the idiot's waistband, a quick pat-down turned up no other weapons on either of the men.

As he straightened, breathing hard and flushed with a triumphant adrenaline high, he realized that Rebel was barking and scrabbling frantically on the other side of the door behind him. Other doors were standing open along the hallway, with frightened neighbors peeking out.

He flashed his badge, although he was sure everyone on this floor knew who he was. "Go inside and call 911, tell them what happened and that we need officers out here." As an afterthought, he softened the command with a "Please."

The doors closed one by one. Though Rebel continued barking, she was safest where she was.

Levi glanced at the bottom of the stairs, but the third attacker was nowhere to be seen. He'd probably fled the second he'd recovered, the coward.

Levi retrieved the first gun from where it'd fallen, emptied both guns of their magazines and chambered bullets, and shoved the ammunition into his pockets before setting the empty guns against the wall for the responding uniforms to deal with. Returning his attention to the two men at his feet, he took in their conditions—one broken-nosed and likely concussed, the other still gulping in air.

"Who sent you?" he asked, although the fact that they were both skinheads glaring at him with unambiguous loathing left little room for doubt.

The men remained silent. Levi crouched down to eye level.

"Let me guess. White, angry, full of hatred?"

"You think you're so smart," one of the men burst out. "But you'll get what's coming to you. We know everything about you."

Levi raised an eyebrow. "If that were true, you would have brought more than three guys."

The other man's mouth pursed, but Levi was familiar with this trick thanks to Lonnie Hale. He jerked aside to avoid the man's spit, then grabbed the guy by the jaw, his fingers digging in cruelly on either side while he struggled against the impulse to do something unforgivable.

He wasn't sure he would have won that struggle if the man's cell phone hadn't chimed at that exact moment. Levi dug through the man's pockets, ignoring the attempts to evade his searching hands, until he pulled the phone free.

An alert of an incoming text was on the screen, but the content of the message wasn't. Levi grabbed the guy's hand and pressed his thumb against the fingerprint reader to unlock the phone.

"Hey! You can't—"

Levi stood up and paced a few steps away. A chill ran down his spine as he read the message, which had come from a contact labeled by a series of numbers rather than a name.

Confirm LA in custody

As he was reading it, another text came in.

??? Need confirmation you have him before 7!

Levi whirled on the two men. "What's happening at seven?"

They shut their mouths, glancing shiftily at each other.

"Let me clarify." Levi took a menacing stride toward them. "What's happening at seven that Utopia was so concerned I'd interfere in that they needed you to kidnap me first?"

"It doesn't matter," said the man he'd belted, an ugly sneer crossing his face. "It's too late now. You wouldn't even be able to get to the Strip on time, let alone stop it."

"Shut up, moron!" the other man growled, kicking his friend's leg.

Levi's chills multiplied exponentially into a cold shock that reverberated through his entire body. They couldn't be serious. The Strip was a tempting target, sure, but it was crawling with private security from every single hotel and casino, not to mention the heightened police presence of the past couple of days. There was no way Utopia could pull off a successful attack there.

Could they?

He scooped his keys off the ground and sprinted down the stairs, already calling Denise. He left her a frantic voice mail as he raced across the parking lot, then threw himself into his car, slammed the bubble light on his roof, and turned on his radio.

"Two Henry five, Dispatch." He rocketed out of his space and toward the entrance of the apartment complex, almost barreling straight through the security gate when it didn't open fast enough.

"Two Henry five, go ahead."

"Credible threat received of a possible 445 on Las Vegas Boulevard, exact location unknown, estimated time of detonation nineteen hundred hours." Swinging a right onto the highway, he hurtled down the center lane. Cars veered out his path. "Activate the city's emergency operations plan and notify the FBI. Mobilize all available units, ambulance, fire department—fuck, send *everybody*."

It took the dispatcher a couple of seconds to respond; when she spoke, her voice was shaky but professional. "Two Henry five, copy. Dispatch to all available units . . ."

He tuned out her request for assistance and glanced at the dashboard clock: 6:43. *Fuck.*

Punching the accelerator, he merged onto I-215 with a squeal of tires. He put a call through to Dominic while he weaved in and out of traffic.

"You know I'm at a—"

"Utopia's going to hit the Strip," Levi interrupted.

"What?"

"They sent some goons after me at our apartment—"

"*What?*"

"And I think they're going to set off a bomb on the Strip at 7 p.m., but I have no idea where or how to stop it."

"Where are you?" When Levi didn't respond, Dominic's voice went dark and flinty. "Levi Abrams, *where the fuck are you?*"

Levi spun the wheel to avoid a collision with a slow-moving SUV. "On my way to the Strip."

The only sound that came over the line was Dominic's heavy breathing. Then he said, "I'll meet you there."

"No!" Levi said, but Dominic had already hung up.

Levi banged a fist against the dashboard. Goddamn it, why had he called Dominic in the first place?

He pretended not to know the answer, but it blazed through the back of his mind: if he was about to die, he'd wanted to hear Dominic's voice first.

He fishtailed onto the Strip, only to hit the brakes as the street's perpetually heavy traffic slowed his progress to a crawl. Even with the bubble light flashing, cars were sluggish to get out of his way.

Did it really matter, though? Now that he was here, he was confronted by the impossibility of his task. The Strip was over four miles long; an explosive device could be hidden in any of the dozens of buildings on either side. Hell, there could be *multiple* bombs, given Dominic's estimates of how much TATP Utopia had manufactured.

Oh God, what if there was one in *Stanton's* hotel?

Up ahead, more flashing lights dotted the Strip. Continuous reports came in over his radio of units responding to his call: cops searching for anything suspicious, a couple of ambulances standing by, a fire truck at the ready, an FBI response team on their way. But none of them knew where to *go*.

Levi should have stayed with those men. He should have made them talk, beaten it out of them—

No. He flexed his fingers on the steering wheel, returning his focus to the current moment as he slalomed between cars. From what he could see of the pedestrians on the walkways, the few who were paying attention to the police presence looked more confused than anything else. Nobody was helpfully skulking around with a bulky package.

He had to think this through more logically. Why 7 p.m. exactly? What was so important about the timing?

An attraction on the Strip, maybe, something that would draw a lot of people. The Fountains at the Bellagio? Unlikely. They'd been going off every half hour since eleven this morning. The Fall of Atlantis at the Forum Shops—no, same thing, it'd been running all day.

Some entitled prick in a Lexus was refusing to move out of the way. Levi rolled down his window to shout, and that was when he heard it—the opening strains of music with a vaguely Polynesian feel, coming from across the street.

From the volcano at the Mirage, which erupted for the first time every night at seven o'clock.

It was 6:59.

Levi slammed on the brakes, causing the vehicle behind to rear-end him. He jumped out of his car, heedless of the blaring horns, and began shouting warnings as he ran across the street toward the crowd that had gathered to watch.

Even in his terror, he was struck by the sureality of yelling, "*Get away from the volcano!*"

People turned to gawk, staying where they were. He was too late. They thought he was crazy, and he was out of time—

The song's drumbeat ramped up, the first flames spouted from the volcano—

And the world blew apart.

White-hot chunks of the volcano slammed into him like snowballs from Hell, throwing him onto his back. Only a decade of muscle memory in learning how to fall safely protected his head from hitting the asphalt as hard as his body.

It knocked the wind out of him, though, and his lungs spasmed as he clawed at the street beneath him. His ears were ringing, a single sharp, clear note that filled his entire head and blotted out any other noise. He knew his eyes were open, but he couldn't make sense of anything he was seeing.

When he finally managed to suck in some air, he coughed violently, choking on the grit that filled his throat. He flopped onto his stomach and retched, bringing up thick gray globs, although at least there was no blood in them. Propping himself on one elbow, he blinked up at the nightmarish vision of a palm tree wreathed in flame.

The Strip was on fire.

He hauled himself into a sitting position and stared. The air was hazy with dust and smoke, but he could see that he was surrounded by overturned cars and broken trees, some of which were burning. Rubble from the exploded volcano was strewn in every direction, along with the twisted metal wreckage of fencing and lampposts. Behind the smoking crater where the volcano used to be, flames had engulfed the entrance to the Mirage.

There were bodies everywhere.

The ringing in his ears began to fade, but he wished it wouldn't, because now he could hear the agonized screams and anguished sobbing all around him. Even worse was the return of his sense of smell, which brought with it the stench of burning flesh.

Gagging, he turned his head. A man lay a few feet away from him, open eyes unseeing in death. Like Levi, the man had been hit by flying debris—but he'd been struck by a piece so large that his chest had caved in. He must have died on impact.

Levi blinked away the tears that sprang to his eyes and did a quick inventory of his own body. He hurt all over, a deep, pervasive ache, but he could breathe okay, and he was pretty sure his ribs weren't broken. He struggled onto both knees, then one, then to his feet, at which point he staggered sideways under a wave of light-headedness that almost took him back to the ground.

Once he was confident of his balance, he started toward the epicenter of the explosion. The fires were worse here, since flaming debris from the volcano had been launched into the thick foliage on all sides. But the volcano was also surrounded by a shallow man-made lagoon, and he could hear the sonorous blare of a fire truck's horn growing steadily closer.

Frantic screaming caught his attention. His head swung toward a woman whose clothes had caught fire; she was slapping uselessly at the flames, clearly panicked, just screaming at the top of her lungs over and over. He ran for her, scooped her into his arms, and jumped into the lagoon, dousing the blaze.

Other people had the same idea, leaping into the water to put out or avoid the fires, helping those who couldn't move themselves. After Levi made sure the woman was all right, he pulled himself out of the lagoon. His arms were throbbing, and he noted with a sort of distant concern that he'd been burned.

Uniformed officers and paramedics were racing through the area, triaging survivors. The fire department had arrived and was working on the hotel and the cars burning in the street. Dozens of uninjured bystanders had rushed into the fray, dragging victims out of the paths of the fires, freeing them from smashed cars, shepherding them to safety.

"Help! Oh God, help me!"

Not far away, a man lay sprawled on the sidewalk. A metal bar—a piece of the destroyed fence—had impaled him through the thigh. He started reaching for it.

"No!" Levi fell to his knees at the man's side, grabbing both the man's hands. "Don't pull that out."

The man stared at Levi, his face chalk white, his eyes enormous with animal fear. Levi showed him his badge, though it didn't seem to make an impact.

"I know it hurts," Levi said. "But you have to leave it in for now, or you might bleed to death."

"No." The man shook his head furiously. "No, it's gotta come out. It's gotta—"

He strained against Levi's hold, trying to get to the bar, crying and cursing. Levi contained the man's struggles as best he could without causing more damage, and glanced around helplessly.

"Officer!" A woman in a cocktail dress and a torn, bloodied sash dropped next to him, pulling off a tiara with a tattered veil attached. "I'm a doctor. I can stay with him. And most of my friends are in the medical field."

She gestured to a group of women who were helping each other to their feet, caked with dust and grime. Some were bleeding, others limping, but all had faces set with grim determination.

"We'll help however we can," the doctor said.

"Thank you." Levi got to his feet and surveyed the scene, overwhelmed by his hellish surroundings. He'd never witnessed devastation like this. It was almost impossible to process.

If only he'd been faster, *smarter*—

"*Levi!*" bellowed a deep voice, loudly enough to be heard over the panicked din.

Levi spun around until he saw a broad form standing head and shoulders above everybody else. "I'm h—" he tried to shout, but had to stop and hack up another lungful of nastiness. "Dominic! I'm over here."

Dominic caught sight of him and rushed over, grasping him by the elbows. "Levi, oh my God, are you hurt? You're burned!" He looked at Levi's forearms, then pressed his fingers to Levi's temple. They came away bloody. "You're *bleeding.*"

Levi hadn't known that. Some of the debris must have hit his face. "I didn't get here in time."

"You son of a bitch." Dominic crushed Levi against his chest, and his voice broke on a sob. "You fucking *asshole.*"

Clutching at the back of Dominic's shirt with both hands, Levi shook uncontrollably.

"Hey, big guy!" said a nearby voice. "We need your muscles."

Levi and Dominic broke apart to face a uniformed officer. Recognition flickered through her eyes when she saw Levi's face, but all she did was gesture to a man on the ground whose legs were trapped by the trunk of a fallen palm tree.

"Think you guys can help me shift this?" she asked.

They nodded and took up places around the tree. As they crouched, the officer's radio squawked. Levi had left his own unit in his car, but he heard Dispatch coming through loud and clear.

"Shots fired, 577 Rivendell Ave. . . ."

That was going to have to wait. Levi gripped the tree and helped heave it off the man, who shrieked and then passed out as the weight of the trunk came off his legs. The bark scored deep cuts into Levi's palms, but that was a drop in the bucket at this point.

The officer's radio went off again. "Shots fired, 21 Weatherstone Drive . . ."

Levi frowned, as did Dominic. The officer knelt to check the man's pulse.

"Shots fired, 2021 Revere Street . . ."

Levi snatched the radio off the officer's belt, ignoring her startled cry, and held it to his ear. The reports came in one after the other.

Shots fired. Shots fired. Shots fired.

All of them from different addresses, coming from every direction in the Valley, and horror turned Levi's muscles to water as he understood.

Dominic's arms closed around Levi before he could collapse. Levi clung to him, gasping, his vision graying out.

"Oh my God," he moaned. "The explosion was just a distraction."

CHAPTER 11

"**C**an't you give him something to calm him down?" Dominic asked the paramedic.

"Not without his consent, unless he's a danger to himself or others."

Dominic gave her an incredulous look as he fought to keep a struggling, ranting Levi on a flimsy cot without grabbing Levi's burned arms. Levi was *always* a danger to himself. Case in point: rushing headlong into a situation he knew had a good chance of blowing him to smithereens.

After they'd heard those reports on the officer's radio, Dominic had needed to forcibly carry Levi away from the scene, all the way to the triage areas being established by the additional EMS units arriving every minute. One glance of recognition had earned Levi immediate medical attention despite his relatively noncritical injuries, but he'd been fighting tooth and nail every second.

"I have to go back!" Levi squirmed beneath Dominic's hands. "I have to help, I need to find out what's going on—"

"You *need* to have your injuries looked at."

"No!" With one quick serpentine movement, Levi freed himself and leapt to his feet.

"*Sit your ass down,*" Dominic barked.

Levi's eyes went wide, his mouth clicked shut, and he sat back on the cot like a docile child. The paramedic raised her eyebrows at Dominic before she moved in to examine Levi.

Dominic rubbed a hand over his face. He was still dizzy with his relief at having found Levi alive; the moment he'd witnessed the explosion from two blocks away would be seared into his memory for the rest of his life.

The full horror of the blast and its implications hadn't sunk in yet. It was like he was watching events unfold in a movie instead of real life, the scope of the disaster so shocking that his brain couldn't comprehend it. He wanted to check in with his family and Carlos and Jasmine, but the cellular networks were probably overloaded, and he didn't have any pressing fears for their safety. They all lived miles away from the Strip, and none of them would have had any reason to be here today.

For now, he had to focus on how he could help in the immediate present. And under no fucking circumstances would he acknowledge the gambling cravings gnawing at his brain like trapped, frantic rats.

He cleaned and disinfected his own cut-up hands while the paramedic gave Levi a quick triage assessment. When she was finished, she put a strip of green tape on Levi's shirt and pulled Dominic aside. "You're Detective Abrams's partner, right? Dominic Russo?"

"Yeah." He was never going to get used to being recognized like this. If it got any worse, it was going to seriously cramp his style as a PI.

"He needs to see a doctor, but his injuries aren't life-threatening. I'd keep an eye on the acute stress reaction he's having, though."

She inclined her head toward Levi, who was sitting motionless on the cot, obviously dissociating—a complete one-eighty from his frenzied state of only minutes before.

"Got it," said Dominic. "Thanks."

After she'd wished him luck and moved on to the next injured victim, he returned to the cot. "Levi."

It took Levi a few seconds to look up. "We need to go back. I have to find out what's happening."

"I can't let you do that, baby," Dominic said as gently as he could. "I'm sorry."

"But it's my fault," Levi whispered.

Dominic wished he'd misheard, but he knew he hadn't. "What?"

Tear tracks streaked through the mess of wet grime on Levi's cheeks. "I was too late. I could have stopped this, and I didn't. I didn't figure it out in time."

"You couldn't have—"

"I could have forced the men who attacked me to tell me what Utopia was planning. I've done it before."

"Yeah, and it was illegal as fuck." Dominic crouched in front of Levi and held his hands, which were bandaged now along with his arms. "There is no universe in which you would have been able to stop what happened here today. You just didn't have enough time. But what you *were* able to do saved lives."

Levi made a face.

"Look." Dominic gestured to the disaster scene, where the chaos was becoming more controlled with each passing minute. "Because you discovered the threat in advance, first responders had already been deployed when the bomb went off. The fire department put out the fires before they could spread to any of the buildings. The paramedics got to people who would have died if they'd been a few minutes later. There were cops here to establish a perimeter right away. None of that would have been possible if you hadn't warned them in time to pre-position those resources."

"I . . ." Levi's brow furrowed as he fell quiet. When he spoke again, he sounded less defeated. "You heard the same reports I did. Shootings all over the Valley, right after the explosion? That wasn't a coincidence. The bomb was planted to divert emergency resources away from whoever Utopia's real targets were." He shifted on the cot, a hint of panic returning to his body language. "I have to know the truth, Dominic. I *have* to."

"Okay." Standing, Dominic scanned their surroundings for anyone he recognized from the LVMPD. He'd decided to just grab any passing cop when he spied Gibbs half carrying an injured woman to safety. "Hey, Gibbs!" he called after the woman had been handed over to the triage team.

Gibbs turned around, frowning, and did a double take before hurrying over. "Russo, what are you doing—" His jaw dropped as he caught sight of Levi. "Holy shit, Detective, are you okay?"

"He's fine," said Dominic. "Do you know if the city's Emergency Operations Center has been activated yet?" After a disaster like this, every agency in Las Vegas would be coordinating via the standardized National Incident Management System, so he was confident of the protocol being followed.

"I'll find out. Give me a minute." Gibbs pulled his radio off his belt and stepped away.

Levi's eyes had glazed over again, and Dominic winced at the sight he made. When Dominic had found Levi, he'd been soaking wet, which Dominic assumed from the scene meant he'd jumped in the lagoon around the volcano at some point. The water hadn't done much to rinse off the dust and dirt caking Levi's skin, though, just kind of turned it into mud. His curls were bedraggled, and his burned, tattered clothing was stiffening in the hot air.

"Hey." When Dominic received no response, he brushed Levi's shoulder, and Levi jerked like he'd been shot. Dominic waited for him to recover before continuing. "We're going to find out what's going on, I promise. But we gotta get you cleaned up first, okay?"

Levi stared at him vacantly, which Dominic chose to interpret as agreement.

Once Gibbs had confirmed the EOC's activation, Dominic walked Levi to where he'd left his truck, and he did what he could with a combination of wet wipes and towels. He left Levi's clothing alone, however, knowing that Levi would rather his colleagues see him in his own messed-up clothes than borrow Dominic's hugely oversized ones.

Levi became more alert and oriented as he was put to rights. But now Dominic was having trouble, his brain skipping from memory to memory like a scratched record—crushed and burned and mangled corpses, wailing survivors, the pounding feet of panicked bystanders running for their lives. Even from two blocks away, he could see the smoke distorting the sunset over the Strip, smell the burned flesh of the victims. Or maybe that last one was just his imagination.

Concentrate on your goddamn mission.

Concrete goals and clarity of purpose had always been Dominic's bulwarks against anxiety. His job was to protect Levi and get him to the EOC. Any thoughts beyond those responsibilities were irrelevant.

The city's EOC was a fair distance from the Strip, and the snarled traffic created by confused, frightened drivers made the trip even more frustrating. Dominic used his native knowledge of Vegas's roads to get them there as efficiently as he could. He deliberately didn't turn on the radio or connect his phone to his mobile hotspot; he couldn't risk Levi freaking out while they were in a moving vehicle.

At Dominic's request, Gibbs had radioed Martine to meet them at the EOC, and she was waiting outside the nondescript building when they walked up.

"Oh my God, Levi." She rushed forward and threw her arms around him, then loosened her hold when he grunted in pain. "You look like shit. Are you okay?"

"I'm fine," he said, returning her hug.

She glanced at Dominic, who was standing behind Levi. Dominic shook his head minutely.

"I'd say I can't believe you'd go rushing into the Strip when you knew a bomb was about to go off, but that's *exactly* the kind of thing you'd do. Thank God you came out alive." Martine handed them both temporary credentials. "I told everyone you were on your way."

A terrorist act meant a complex unified command between the various branches of emergency services, with the FBI taking lead. The EOC was bustling with the staff who'd been called into service, but every person they passed took the time to personally thank Levi for his advance warning. Fortunately, Special Agent in Charge Tisdale took them into a private briefing room before Levi got overwhelmed, along with Martine, Denise, and Arthur Bowen, the deputy chief of the LVMPD's Homeland Security division.

Dominic hung back but kept a careful eye on Levi. He knew—he didn't fear, he *knew*—that if he let his focus waver for one minute, he'd slip out of this building and go straight to the closest place he could gamble, even if it was the video slots at a grocery store.

Tisdale gave them a terse, rapid-fire update. The county manager had declared a local state of emergency. Local law enforcement and public safety agencies had contained the scene at the Mirage, while additional teams from the FBI and LVMPD were combing other buildings on the Strip for any additional explosive devices. Area hospitals were preparing for the influx of patients, and disaster relief organizations had been mobilized. The media was being delicately handled by cooperation between the various agencies' public information officers.

"You said the *county* manager declared the emergency first?" Levi asked. "What about the mayor? The city manager?"

Denise lifted her head from the tablet she'd been working on. "Both shot. Reports are still coming in, but we know the mayor is critically injured, the city manager is dead, and nobody can locate the city's emergency manager. That's only scratching the surface."

"So the shootings reported right after the explosion—they all targeted public officials?"

"We don't have all the facts yet, but it seems like it. Almost a dozen so far, attacked simultaneously in one coordinated wave—at home, out at dinner, even on the road."

Meaning the shooters had known the victims' schedules down to the minute and had unimpeded access to them. The LVMPD wasn't the only organization with a mole problem.

"So I was right." Levi picked fluffy bits of cotton off one of his bandages as he spoke. "The explosion was a distraction, a way to overwhelm our emergency resources so we couldn't handle everything at once. Destabilizing the local government makes responding even more difficult."

"Do you think that's why Utopia came after you too?" Dominic asked. "Besides their personal grudge against you, you're a public figure now."

"Maybe. I'm pretty sure they were trying to kidnap me, though, not kill me, which I can't explain."

"We're doing everything we can to contain the situation," said Bowen. "We've activated our mutual aid agreements with neighboring jurisdictions for more personnel, and we're going to drag in everyone in the Valley who has even the slightest connection to Utopia."

Dominic zoned out during the ensuing discussion of law enforcement tactics, staring at the wall as his gambling fantasies surged to the forefront and sucked him deeper and deeper. There was no way he could handle a strategy-based game like poker in this condition, but slots or roulette could do the trick. The spinning of a roulette wheel could be so hypnotic, almost soothing . . .

"Dominic!" Martine said, with an impatient edge that suggested this wasn't her first attempt at getting his attention.

"What? Yeah. What?" He shook himself.

She inclined her head toward Levi, who'd apparently gotten into an argument with Bowen while Dominic had been distracted.

"But I want to help. You need all hands on deck right now." Levi's arms were crossed over his chest, his eyebrows knitted together.

"You've already done more than enough for one day," Bowen said. "You've been through a hellish experience, and you're injured. Get a good night's rest, have a doctor check you out, and then you can return to work. I'll speak to Captain Birndorf about supplying a security detail in case Utopia tries their luck with you again."

"But—"

"This is not a debate, Detective."

The intercom in the middle of the table buzzed. "Agent Tisdale?" said a woman's voice. "I just received a video you need to see. I'll put it up on the screen in there."

Everyone in the room turned to the large TV mounted on the wall.

"My contact at KTNV forwarded me an email that was sent to every major news network in Nevada," the woman on the intercom said. "It contained a link to this video on some random website."

The video started. On the screen stood three white men wearing plastic Reagan masks, in front of a massive American flag backdrop.

"We are Utopia," said the center man. "We speak for the true Americans, the ones who fight to preserve this once-great nation as it collapses into depravity. No longer will our voices be silenced."

"When has a white man *ever* been silenced?" Martine muttered.

"We claim credit for today's explosion at the Mirage, as well as the attacks on a dozen corrupt public officials. We are doing God's work. And this is only the beginning."

Tension rippled through the briefing room.

"Las Vegas stands as a symbol of everything that is wrong with America," the man continued. "It is a modern-day Sodom and Gomorrah: a cesspool of debauchery, Godlessness, race-mixing, and sodomy. And yet instead of repenting, its people take *pride* in the name 'Sin City.'"

Dominic swallowed against the gorge rising in the back of his throat. The people around him were hardly breathing.

The man in the video moved closer to the camera, his voice thrumming with fanatical zeal. "Like Sodom and Gomorrah, Las Vegas must be destroyed. This is the will of God. We will rain down burning sulfur until this city is cleansed of sin. We cannot be stopped. We cannot be turned aside." He lowered his voice, though his tone only grew more passionate. "And if the demon known as the Seven of Spades seeks to challenge us? *We're ready for you.*"

It took the combined efforts of Dominic, Martine, Denise, and Bowen to force Levi out of the building after that clusterfuck. Martine walked them to Dominic's truck, because Dominic honestly wasn't sure he could get Levi there by himself.

"I'm not going *anywhere*," Levi said as Martine dragged him along by the elbow. "Are you insane? There's going to be follow-up attacks—"

"Not tonight, there's not. An organization puts out a video like that to demoralize a population. If they don't give that terror time to sink in and take root, there's no point."

Levi skipped right to his next argument, which was one he'd already tried inside the EOC. "This is why Utopia wanted to kidnap me. They must think they can leverage me in a challenge against the Seven of Spades to make them the king bad guys of Las Vegas."

"But they failed," said Dominic. "Get in the truck."

"No!"

Martine snapped her fingers in front of Levi's face until he focused on her. "You need to get your head on straight before you come back. I'm not letting you embarrass yourself or the department by losing your cool at a time like this. And do you think I haven't noticed how stiffly you're holding yourself? You're in too much pain to be useful here. Go *home*."

Levi relented—barely—and folded himself into the truck's passenger side with the air of a sulking child. He sat rigidly, not letting his back touch the seat.

Before they left, Dominic connected his phone to the truck's wi-fi and found dozens of texts from worried family and friends who'd been unable to call him with the cellular networks overloaded. There were even a few from Levi's parents, who'd apparently seen the explosion on the news and panicked when they couldn't reach Levi by phone. Of course, Levi's cell had been destroyed by the blast, so he wouldn't have gotten their calls anyway.

Dominic sent a few quick, reassuring texts, then started the slow drive home through clogged streets.

Levi broke his sullen silence a few minutes later. "Once the Seven of Spades sees that video, they're going to slaughter every member of Utopia they can get their hands on."

"Good," Dominic said.

Levi narrowed his eyes. "You don't mean that."

"I do. Those assholes killed a bunch of innocent people and are terrorizing the city I grew up in. If the Seven of Spades wants to wipe them all off the map, I won't stand in the way."

"That's not how we do things."

"That's not how *you* do things. But I can tell you that most American soldiers would have no problem terminating Nazis with extreme prejudice."

Making an exasperated noise, Levi turned his head toward the window. "If we're going to find out what Utopia is planning in time to stop it, we need them alive."

A fair point, but it didn't do much to change Dominic's opinion. The rest of the drive was quiet, and when they got home, Levi didn't say a word as Dominic helped him up the stairs.

The men who'd attacked Levi had long ago been picked up. Dominic unlocked the door to their apartment, where they spent a few minutes soothing a frenzied Rebel. He was still kneeling, stroking her head and speaking to her softly, when he noticed Levi had gone into the living room and was lifting a bottle of Knob Creek bourbon off the sideboard.

"Nope." Dominic joined Levi and snatched the bottle out of his hand. "That's not how we're dealing with this."

"I wasn't going to get *drunk*," Levi said.

"Alcohol shouldn't be used as a coping mechanism. I know you've talked to your therapist about this. Maybe you don't have a problem now, but the more often you self-medicate with alcohol, the more likely you are to develop one." Seeing he wasn't making an impact, Dominic pressed harder. "Or maybe you don't think that's a big deal. We'd be the perfect match, after all—a drunk and a gambler."

Levi recoiled, his nostrils flaring. "How dare—"

"Do you think I haven't been dying to gamble every second since I found you at that blast site?" Dominic slammed the bottle down so hard he was surprised it didn't break. "Do you think I'm not craving the kind of relief that would give me with every cell in my body? I'm hanging by a thread, Levi." He took a shuddering breath, shaking out his hands. "And I—I can't watch you make the same kinds of mistakes I used to. Drowning yourself in alcohol is not the solution for what you're feeling right now. Trust me."

All of the indignation slid off Levi's face. He stepped closer to Dominic and touched his arm. "How can I help?"

"Let me take care of you," Dominic said. "You need that tonight, no matter what you think, and it'll help distract me. Keep me out of my head."

After a brief pause, Levi nodded. Dominic leaned in and kissed him.

"I'm gonna take Rebel for a walk. While I'm doing that, I want you to go take a bath—a *bath*, not a shower—and try not to get your bandages too wet."

With another nod, Levi limped in the direction of the master bedroom. Dominic turned around to find Rebel with her leash in her mouth, wagging her tail enthusiastically.

He double-checked all of the locks and set the alarm before they left. A long walk around their building cleared his head somewhat, and by the time they returned, two uniformed officers had arrived to serve as the first shift of Levi's security detail. After confirming the cops' credentials with the substation, Dominic trusted them to their guard duties while he and Rebel went back inside.

Dominic found Levi in the bathtub as instructed, his legs drawn up and his forehead resting on his knobby knees. Although Levi had regained most of the weight he'd lost in recent months, he was still primarily sharp lines and pointed angles.

Then Dominic circled around and saw Levi's bare back.

"Jesus *Christ*," he gasped. Levi's back was more purple than white, mottled with vicious bruises from shoulders to hips. The bruising wrapped around Levi's rib cage toward his chest, disappearing from Dominic's view. "I know the paramedic said your injuries weren't too serious, but are you sure nothing's broken?"

"Yeah. I know how to fall safely." Levi sighed into his knees. "Hurts, though."

Dominic could see that from Levi's hunched posture and the tense set of his muscles. The more the adrenaline of the attack wore off, the more pain Levi would be in.

Making a split-second decision, Dominic said, "I'll be right back. Rebel, stay with Levi."

He left the bathroom to the sound of Levi's tired laugh as Rebel tried to climb into the tub.

After a quick call to a coworker at Stingray and a heads-up for the security detail, Dominic went back to the bathroom, knelt beside the tub, and helped Levi wash up, gingerly handling Levi's various injuries. He had to wash the blood and dirt out of Levi's hair too, because Levi couldn't do it himself. Once Levi was clean, Dominic dried him off, bundled him into the softest clothes he could find, and changed the bandages on his arms and hands.

As Dominic had expected, his gambling cravings gradually faded to their usual dull roar in the back of his mind. Being useful, being *needed*, was something he could take refuge in. Levi and Rebel needed him to stay with them tonight, so he would stay. End of story.

He settled Levi into bed with Rebel and a mass of pillows to cushion his back, then put together a simple dinner of grilled cheese sandwiches and canned tomato soup. He'd just carried the food into the bedroom on trays when there was a knock on the front door.

Levi startled badly, and Rebel let out a concerned *whuff*. "It's okay, I'm expecting someone," Dominic said. "Rebel, settle."

He hurried to answer the door and greeted Amanda, one of his fellow bartenders at Stingray.

"Got what you asked for," she said, handing him a brown paper bag while side-eyeing the uniforms. They'd withdrawn somewhat for privacy's sake, but Dominic knew they wouldn't interfere regardless.

"Thanks. How much do I owe you?" He reached for his wallet, hoping it wasn't more than the cash he had on him.

"For my favorite coworker and Levi fucking Abrams? No charge."

"Amanda—"

She held up a hand. "I heard what he did today; it's all over the news. Tell him I said thank you, and I hope he feels better soon."

Dominic thanked her again and brought the bag to the bedroom, where Levi was nibbling on a sandwich. "What's that?" Levi asked, watching him pull a small unmarked bottle out of the bag.

"Vicodin."

Levi dropped his sandwich. "That's illegal!"

"Yep."

"For God's sake, Dominic—"

"Any doctor in the world would take one look at your injuries and write you a prescription for this without hesitation," he said. "But given what's happening, we'd never be able to get a doctor to see you tonight." He popped the top off the bottle and tipped out a pill. "This may violate the letter of the law, but not the spirit of it. I think your professional ethics can remain intact."

Levi bit his lip. "The last time I took something like that was after . . ."

"The assault?"

Levi bowed his head.

"Is it a trigger for you?" Dominic hadn't considered the possibility.

"No, but I remember how that stuff makes me feel. It'll sap my energy, dull my reflexes."

"So will pain. And unmanaged pain slows recovery." Dominic sat on the edge of the mattress, set the pill in Levi's palm, and closed Levi's fingers around it. "You wouldn't let *me* get away with that kind of macho bullshit."

Snorting, Levi reached for his water glass.

They watched Netflix while they ate dinner in bed, since Dominic refused to let Levi turn on the news. Dominic could tell when the opiates kicked in, because Levi's head started lolling on his neck and his body went limp in a way Dominic had only previously seen it do after a hard fuck. Dominic moved the trays off the bed and killed the lights.

Levi's floppy hand sought Dominic's on top of the covers. "I don't know what I'd do without you," he slurred.

Dominic smiled and kissed Levi's temple, breathing in the gift of his presence, injured but *alive*. "Same here."

CHAPTER 12

When Levi woke, he was so disoriented that he spent a good ten seconds wondering why Dominic was licking his face until he realized it was Rebel.

"Ugh, stop," he groaned, feebly shoving her away. She bopped him once with her cold nose, as if in reprimand, before settling quietly beside him.

He forced his eyes open and squinted at the room. From the light filtering through the closed blinds, he could tell it was at least midmorning, far later than he usually got up. He was reclining in a half-sitting position on a heap of pillows, but despite the cushioning, his torso was one throbbing ache from shoulders to hips.

Still, he almost preferred pain to the lingering effects of the medication. He'd never understood how people took opiates to get high; they always knocked him right the fuck out and gave him a weird hangover afterward. Even after a full night's sleep, he felt woozy and gross, hating the heaviness in his muscles and the dulled edges of his thoughts.

It reminded him of the months he'd spent recovering in a narcotic haze after being nearly beaten to death in college. He was lucky he'd come away from that without a chemical dependency.

Those unpleasant memories triggered a cascade of worse ones in his jumbled brain: The explosion. The video. *Utopia.*

God, how long had he been asleep? What might have happened to Las Vegas in the meantime?

He tried and failed to sit up, too enervated to coordinate his muscles, and the attempt only made him dizzier. He couldn't defend himself like this—and while Rebel might be here, Dominic wasn't. That left him vulnerable. Helpless. He couldn't *stand* being helpless.

His breathing went shallow, his pulse fluttering madly. He struggled again to push himself upright, a panicked gasp escaping him when he couldn't manage it. He couldn't just lie here like a child; God, he had to get out of this bed—

Rebel climbed halfway into his lap, heavy and solid and *real*, licking his jaw with her rough tongue. Levi sank his hands into her fur and let her presence ground him. He wasn't in any danger. Dominic would never have left him alone in the apartment while he was injured and coming off of strong painkillers.

Even as he thought it, he heard a distant knock on the front door, Dominic's deep bass rumble in response, and the sound of the door opening and closing. A new voice joined the mix—one Levi vaguely recognized but couldn't place.

A few moments later, Dominic rapped on the bedroom door and cracked it open. "Baby, you awake?"

"Yeah."

Dominic swung the door inward and stepped back to let someone else in first. It was a man Levi hadn't seen in at least a year, gray-haired and well-dressed, his posture no less dignified for his slight limp.

Levi blinked, wondering if opiates could make him hallucinate this long after he'd taken them. "Dr. Feinberg? What are you doing here?"

"I'm told you had a close brush with death yesterday." Feinberg's gaze swept the bed, keen and assessing, and Levi scowled.

"I'm fine."

"I'll be the judge of that." Feinberg set his case—an old-fashioned doctor's bag straight out of the 1800s—on the nightstand and waved an imperious hand at the desk chair. Dominic quickly brought it over for him.

Feinberg was a concierge doctor, a private physician to Las Vegas's wealthiest citizens, as renowned for his discretion as for his brusqueness. He'd treated Levi a couple of times when Levi had been living with Stanton.

Dominic caught the look Levi was throwing him. "Stanton asked the doc to pay you a visit."

"You talked to Stanton?" Levi cooperated as Feinberg shooed Rebel back, helped him sit up, and palpated his neck. "How is he?"

"Fine. His hotel is a mile north of the Mirage."

"Why—" Levi grunted when Feinberg, apparently confident that he had no spinal damage, pulled his head around by the chin and shone a penlight into his eyes without warning. "Why would you call him?"

Dominic crossed his arms. "Let me get this straight. It's fine for me to call the one-night stand you don't even like for legal advice, but it's weird for me to call the serious ex you still care about to check in after a terrorist attack?"

Flushing, Levi glanced sideways at Feinberg, but Feinberg just clipped a pulse ox monitor to Levi's finger and began unwrapping his bandages.

"I didn't call Stanton, anyway," Dominic said. "I was planning on it, but he called me first. He was worried when he couldn't get through to you after the cellular networks were restored."

"Oh." Levi ducked his head, watching Feinberg wrap a blood pressure cuff around his upper arm. Fortunately, the burns didn't extend that far.

"I told him about your phone being broken when you were injured. He knew there was almost no chance of you getting to see a doctor today, so he said he'd ask Dr. Feinberg to stop by and take a look at you."

What did that mean? Why wouldn't Levi have been able to see a doctor today?

His heart rate spiked just as Feinberg was inflating the cuff. Feinberg sighed, deflated it, and plucked his stethoscope out of his ears before turning an icy look on Dominic.

"A little privacy, please?"

"Sure." Dominic slapped his thigh to summon Rebel and left the room, closing the door behind them.

Feinberg gave Levi a few minutes to calm down, dressing and rebandaging the burns in the meantime. Still, he shook his head disapprovingly after he took a second reading. "Your blood pressure is far too high for a man your age in otherwise excellent physical shape."

"You say that every time," Levi muttered.

"You need to stop drinking so much coffee."

Levi rolled his eyes.

After a thorough examination, Feinberg agreed with the paramedic's conclusion that Levi's injuries weren't life-threatening, suggested an X-ray to check for cracked ribs, and recommended several days of quiet rest and recovery—though his dry tone during that last part made it clear how likely he thought it was that his advice would be followed. Then he scribbled on his prescription pad and ripped off the top sheet.

"I'm going to pretend I didn't see that bottle on your nightstand and give you this instead," he said. "Remember that you can't work in the field or carry your service weapon while you're taking narcotics."

I can't fire my gun anyway, Levi thought, but all he said was, "Thank you, Doctor."

Dominic showed Feinberg out, then returned to the bedroom. "All good?"

"Yes. You don't have to worry about me; you should go to work."

Dominic hesitated just long enough to set off alarm bells in Levi's head. "I can't."

Levi didn't ask why not. He folded his hands in his lap, resisting the urge to pick at his bandages.

"They've been evacuating the Strip since last night," Dominic said. "The surrounding area's been declared an exclusion zone."

Meaning only official response and recovery vehicles could enter—and McBride's office was a block off the Strip. "They're actually evacuating?" Levi asked faintly. He wasn't sure what he'd expected, but evacuating over a hundred thousand people, most of them tourists with no vehicles of their own, was such a complex undertaking that it boggled the mind. The city wouldn't invest the massive resources necessary unless the situation was desperate.

"Not just the Strip. UNLV, the area around the Fremont Street Experience—basically, anything the governor thinks is an attractive terrorist target. The airport is shut down; schools and most government buildings are closed. It's . . . kind of a clusterfuck out there."

"I want to see the news." When Dominic didn't respond, Levi hardened his tone. "*Dominic.* You can't keep me in the dark forever."

With an exasperated huff, Dominic picked up the remote and clicked on the TV, tuning it to a local news station. The current shot was a live feed being filmed from a helicopter above the city.

A reporter was talking, but none of the words penetrated Levi's brain while he stared at the screen. That was I-15, one of the highways that led out of the Valley, except all the northbound lanes had been converted to southbound. And every single lane was choked with cars and trucks to the point where traffic had come to an absolute standstill.

The view changed to a panning shot of US-93, which cut through Henderson. Same thing here: all of the lanes were so congested that it would be faster to *walk* out of the Valley.

Levi ground his hands into his eyes. "People who aren't supposed to are spontaneously evacuating."

"Exodus-style."

Fuck, that would make things a thousand times worse. The Las Vegas Valley was a genuine *valley*; there were a limited number of routes in and out. Spontaneous evacuations would overwhelm the county's infrastructure and law enforcement resources. People would run out of gas and get stranded on the road, intensifying the problem. There would be multiple fender benders from the stop-and-go traffic. The combination of fear and frustration and desert heat would provoke violence. And emergency vehicles wouldn't be able to get where they needed to go in time.

"Everyone's panicking," Dominic said. "The explosion alone would have been bad enough, but a good chunk of the local government is dead or in critical condition, and Utopia's video went viral long before anyone could stop it. There's no putting *that* genie back in the bottle."

The news station showed an aerial view of the destruction at the Mirage: the decimated volcano at ground zero, surrounded in all directions by ravaged streets, mountains of rubble, and charred landscaping. Wrecked cars had been abandoned half-buried in debris. Behind the volcano, the front of the hotel itself had been burnt out, and its porte cochere lay in ruins.

"Updated estimates confirm at least thirty-five people dead and over two hundred seriously injured in the explosion at the Mirage, including casualties from multiple car accidents which occurred on

Las Vegas Boulevard," said a reporter. "Fortunately, fires at the scene were quickly contained by first responders before they could spread to neighboring buildings."

The shot transitioned to footage of a mobbed grocery store, its shelves swept bare like a swarm of locusts had ripped through it.

"Requests by public officials for people to remain in their homes have largely been ignored. Concerns about potential riots have raised the possibility of the governor mobilizing the National Guard. Local and national law enforcement continue the search for the perpetrators of yesterday's horrifying events, but although many arrests have been made, the FBI has yet to issue a definitive statement."

Levi clenched his fists, heedless of the pain in his bandaged palms. He might not have grown up in Vegas like Dominic, but this was still his city. His *home*. He couldn't watch it tearing itself apart like this.

"We're waiting now on a press conference with FBI Special Agent in Charge Stephen Tisdale—"

"Turn it off," Levi said.

Dominic did. The sudden silence was almost worse.

Levi took one deep breath, in and out. First things first. "I have to call my parents."

"You can use my phone. I called them myself first thing this morning, but I know they're eager to hear from you."

"Thank you." He met Dominic's eyes. "And then I have to go to work."

He braced himself for a fight, readying half a dozen counterarguments to Dominic's most likely objections.

Dominic nodded. "I'll drop you off wherever you need to go. I asked Martine to pick up a new cell phone for you—disposable, for now. Text me the number when you get it."

"And what are you planning on doing?" Levi asked, eyeing him askance.

"After I talk my family and Carlos and Jasmine out of joining all those people on the road? I'm going to help with the legit evacuations. Natasha's on the Community Emergency Response Team, and she told me to meet her at UNLV later."

Dominic's body language was calm yet alert, his speech coolly precise. Levi had seen him this way a handful of times, the most recent being after he'd killed Scott West to protect Levi and an untold number of innocent civilians.

Levi didn't often think about Dominic's military service. It was part of Dominic, an important experience that had shaped his life and helped make him the man Levi loved. Yet beyond the few occasions when Levi had relied on that experience to get them through a harrowing situation, it didn't hold any greater significance to him. That was all in the past.

But looking at Dominic now, Levi was hit with the realization that there was nothing past tense about it. Dominic would always be a soldier, the same way Levi would always be a cop, right down to his bone marrow. That didn't change when you took off the uniform.

A rush of admiration gave Levi the strength to say, "Can you help me up?" with no embarrassment.

Dominic assisted him out of bed and onto his feet, then leaned down to touch their foreheads together.

Last night, Dominic had needed to take control because Levi hadn't been in his right mind. But that had changed, and as they stood there quietly, a moment of understanding passed between them without needing to be spoken aloud: Dominic wouldn't stand in the way of Levi's mission any more than Levi would stand in the way of his.

Once their security detail had been relieved of duty, Levi took half a pain pill—which rendered him fuzzy-headed but not unconscious—and spent the better part of an hour talking down his frantic parents. After hanging up, he got dressed and locked his service weapon in the safe, then hobbled downstairs with Dominic, where he learned that Dominic had borrowed a motorcycle from a neighbor.

Levi remained on the sidewalk, frowning at the hulking black-and-chrome monstrosity. Dominic grabbed a pair of helmets off the bike, took in Levi's expression, and said, "Don't tell me you've never ridden a motorcycle before."

"What about me makes you think I've *ever* been on a motorcycle?"

Dominic snorted and handed him one of the helmets. "Well, we don't have much of a choice. With the roads fucked up, it'd take an hour to go two miles in a car. The bike gives us much better mobility."

He was right, so Levi didn't object further. "You know how to drive one of these things?" Levi asked as he buckled his helmet.

"Yep. No license, but I think the cops have bigger things to worry about today."

The ride was painful, thanks to Levi's injuries, but the meds took the edge off. And because Dominic had no compunctions about zipping in between cars and even driving on the sidewalk when it was clear of pedestrians, they did arrive at the CCDC much faster than they could have hoped to in a car. In fact, after what Levi had seen on their way Downtown, he wasn't sure they'd have made it here in a car at all. The city was in total gridlock.

When Levi had called in this morning, he'd been instructed to report to the CCDC to help process and interrogate the dozens of people who'd been arrested since last night. He said goodbye to Dominic on the curb and watched the bike speed away before he entered the detention center.

Calling the mayhem he found inside a "zoo" would have been an insult to zoos everywhere. Working in tandem, the FBI and LVMPD had been pulling in every person with a connection to Utopia that they could hunt down, and they were still going strong; the holding cells had swelled to capacity. Utopia members were well-coached to request a lawyer immediately, but between their numbers and the city's condition, there simply weren't enough lawyers to go around. Levi also suspected that Utopia's legal defense fund didn't have the supply to meet this level of demand.

Sorting through the arrestees to determine who might be involved in the terrorist plot and who was just human garbage was exhausting, and mostly unproductive. A few hours in, Levi took a break, slumping sideways against the wall of an empty corridor and knocking back the other half of his pill.

"Levi," Leila said behind him.

He turned around—slowly, because he'd learned the hard way this morning that sudden movements made his chest and back shriek in agony. "Leila."

Her eyes darted up and down, but her face was otherwise expressionless. "I heard you were injured."

"Nothing serious." He shifted from foot to foot, painfully aware that this was the first time she'd acknowledged his existence in a week. "What's up?"

"I have Conrad Bishop in an interrogation room. Denise told me you're familiar with him?"

Levi nodded. "Dominic obtained strong evidence that Bishop's been financing Utopia on the down-low."

"I think I can pressure Bishop into striking a deal, but he's dragging his feet. Coming face-to-face with Levi Abrams might be unsettling enough to give him a kick in the ass, especially since you were caught in the explosion yesterday." She cocked her head. "How about it?"

"Of course," he said without hesitation. He would have agreed to just about anything in the interests of eventually earning her forgiveness.

He followed her to the interrogation room in question. She knocked on the door, grasped the handle, and chose that moment to toss out, "By the way, Sawyer is his attorney."

She went inside, leaving him gaping on the threshold. After a couple of seconds, he shook it off and entered behind her.

Bishop was hunched over the table, his shirt stained with sweat, his face drawn and sallow. He was continuously washing his uncuffed hands together, a nervous habit that set Levi's teeth on edge.

Seated beside Bishop, Sawyer blinked at Levi before arching an eyebrow in Leila's direction. "Bringing in the big guns, I see."

She shrugged, the hint of a smirk curving her lips.

What little color remained in Bishop's face had drained out the moment he'd caught sight of Levi. He opened his mouth, then snapped it shut and swallowed convulsively without saying anything.

Levi locked eyes with Bishop as he came forward to sit across the table in silence. A bead of sweat rolled down Bishop's temple.

"This posturing is ridiculous," Sawyer said. "What do you think you have on my client? Photographs of him giving a man money in a public park? That's not illegal."

Leila sauntered over and leaned one hip against the table. "That man's name is Jim Watts, a student at UNLV and a known member of Utopia. He took that money straight to a Utopia safe house which was being used to manufacture IEDs—most likely the same explosives used in the terrorist attack last night."

Though Bishop flinched, Sawyer was unfazed. "You have no proof that my client gave Mr. Watts the money to be used for any such purpose, or that he had any knowledge whatsoever of Mr. Watts's criminal affiliations."

"Sure," Leila drawled. "Maybe he was just paying for the answers to the OChem final."

Throughout Leila and Sawyer's back-and-forth, Levi had been studying Bishop, who seemed unable to look away from him. He saw plenty of fear, unsurprisingly, but what gave him pause was something he identified deeper in Bishop's bloodshot eyes: remorse.

"Do you know who I am?" Levi asked, interrupting the verbal sparring.

Bishop laughed a bit hysterically. Okay, it was a dumb question. Everyone in Las Vegas knew who Levi was—as did most people in the entire country, by now. It was something he still hadn't gotten used to and would probably never stop hating.

"I was at the Mirage when the volcano exploded," he said. "I tried to stop it, but I didn't get there in time. I was injured. Burned." He indicated his bandaged forearms.

Sawyer didn't cut Levi off as he'd expected, just listened with a small frown. Bishop chewed his lower lip, but that wasn't enough of a reaction. Levi needed to push harder.

What had Dominic said? Bishop's ex-wife had been angling for sole custody of their children. And Dominic had spied on Bishop while he'd been playing with his kids in the park.

Levi leaned forward, never breaking eye contact. "Still, I got off easier than the people who died, or were maimed. Or the people who lost loved ones: Spouses. Parents." He paused. "Children."

Bishop blanched, curling in on himself. Sawyer put a hand on his shoulder and said, "I think that's enough."

"Tell me, Mr. Bishop, do you think I deserve to die because I'm Jewish?" Levi asked.

"Oh, come on, Detective," Sawyer snapped.

Bishop's head jerked up, his eyes wide as a spooked horse's. "God, no, of course not."

"How about because I'm gay?"

"Detective!"

"*No.*" Bishop dragged both hands down his damp face. "I would never want anyone to die, let alone in such a horrible way. I didn't know what they were going to do—"

Sawyer's hand clamped around Bishop's wrist, but it was too late. Levi smiled; above him, Leila's grin was positively sharklike.

"So you do admit to some knowledge of Watts's affiliation with Utopia," she said.

"Don't answer that." Sawyer's voice was clipped.

"It's fine." Bishop pulled his arm out of Sawyer's grasp. "I want to make a deal. I never would have given them money if I'd known they were going to use it to hurt innocent people."

Levi scoffed. "What *did* you think Nazis were going to use your money for?"

"They aren't Nazis," Bishop said, though the words rang hollow. There was a good chance he'd believed that before—after all, Utopia self-identified as an "alt-right" militia, not a neo-Nazi organization. But their actions yesterday left no doubt as to their true nature. "That money was supposed to go to lobbying, political organization. They told me they were trying to take Utopia in a new direction, that they were setting up a PAC to campaign for conservative candidates and ballot initiatives." He looked down at his hands. "I—I knew they had an unsavory reputation, so I didn't want my donations to be public record in case my ex-wife tried to use that against me. But I had no idea that they were planning any kind of attack, I swear."

"What are you offering?" Leila asked as she settled into the chair beside Levi.

"I know the location of several Utopia meeting places. Identities of a few of their other donors. I'll give you everything I can think of if it'll keep me out of prison—my ex would never let me see my kids again."

"Hmm." Leila tapped her pen against her lips, affecting doubt. "I'm not sure that's enough. After all, Mr. Bishop, you funded a terrorist organization."

Sawyer opened his mouth, but his objection was preempted by Bishop's nauseated moan.

"I—I know who founded Utopia. The man who's in charge, the one who makes all the decisions. He's the person who must have organized the attack."

Leila dropped her pen on the table, and she and Levi frowned at each other.

"Utopia doesn't have one central leader," Levi said. Did Bishop think they were stupid? "It's run by committee."

"It's not. But the man behind it can't have his name tied to it." Inexplicably, Bishop shot an anxious sideways glance at Sawyer, who looked as perplexed as Levi felt.

"All right," said Leila. "Who is this boogeyman who's been pulling Utopia's strings behind the scenes?"

Sawyer held out his hand. "Don't tell them anything until you have a deal in writing."

"I won't *offer* him a deal unless I know his information is worthwhile," Leila snapped.

"Who do you think I am, some kind of public defender fresh out of—"

"It's Oliver Hatfield," Bishop said—whispered, really, but it shut Sawyer and Leila up as effectively as a shout. Sawyer paled, his face going slack; Leila's mouth fell open.

"Oliver Hatfield?" Levi asked in a daze. "As in Hatfield, Park, and McKenzie?"

Bishop nodded miserably. This time, the grimace he gave Sawyer was more apologetic than nervous.

Levi was still processing the implications. "When Milo Radich helped Utopia sabotage Vegas's other gangs, he did everything he could to pin it on the Parks. And the fallout from that case *did* devastate the family."

Scooping her pen off the table, Leila clicked the end with a flourish. "I think we can work something out."

In short order, they possessed a treasure trove of new intelligence. Law enforcement teams were dispatched to raid the safe houses and bring in everyone Bishop had named who hadn't already been arrested, including Hatfield. Levi returned to work, a bit more optimistic than he'd been earlier.

It was early evening when Denise called him on the phone Martine had provided him this morning. "I'm at one of the addresses Bishop gave us," she said. Her voice was strained, with none of its usual pep. "The one in North Las Vegas. I think you should come up here."

"I'm not working in the field today."

"Make an exception."

He tensed, reversing direction toward the lobby. He'd need to scrounge up some form of transportation. "What's going on? Did you find any Utopia members at the house?"

Denise cleared her throat. "We did—but the Seven of Spades found them first."

CHAPTER 13

"**B**ecause it's *dangerous*, Ma," Dominic said for the fiftieth time as he watched his mother whirl around her bedroom like determined tornado. "If you haven't been told to evacuate, you should stay put."

Rita tossed another armful of clothes into her overflowing, haphazardly packed suitcase. "I'm not sitting around waiting for those crazies to blow us to kingdom come."

"Utopia's not gonna target a majority white, suburban neighborhood in North Las Vegas." Dominic scrubbed a hand over his face. His mother's fierce stubbornness was a quality he usually adored, but at the moment, it was a huge pain in the ass.

"You a mind reader now?"

"Nonna," Dominic appealed to his grandmother, who was standing in the doorway. He knew she was on his side.

"Listen to the boy, Rita." Despite her age and small stature, Silvia was no less a force of nature than her daughter-in-law, and her voice rang with authority. "You saw the news. The roads are a mess."

"So we'll go around." Rita kicked a pile of discarded clothes out of the way as she strode to her closet.

"This is a valley. There *is* no 'around.'"

"What would you do if you ran out of gas on the highway in this heat, with no water and no air-conditioning?" Dominic asked. When he saw the shot hit home, he dialed it up a notch. "Or if some idiot got all fired up and grabbed his shotgun out of his car to move traffic along the old-fashioned way?"

"So we're just supposed to hunker down in the house and pretend there aren't terrorists running rampant around the city?"

"Yes. This isn't like a wildfire; in situations like this, spontaneous evacuation does more harm than good. And think about it: what could be more tempting to terrorists than a bunch of panicked civilians getting stuck while trying to escape?"

That was the clincher. Rita sighed and threw her arms up in a gesture of defeat. "Fine. But I don't like it."

"I know." Dominic crossed the room to pull her into a hug. "Maybe you should have everyone come stay here, call it a big family slumber party. That might make it less scary for the kids."

Unlike Dominic, his four siblings and their families all lived in this general area. The traffic wasn't as bad in these northern suburbs as it was on the outskirts and in the heart of the city, so they should be able to make it to their mother's house safely long before dark.

"I'll call Angela," Rita said, pulling away and dialing her cell.

Dominic turned to Silvia. "You have enough supplies for a few days? Flashlights, batteries, clean water?"

"We have everything we need." She tilted her head, looking up at him with shrewd eyes. "And you? Will you be staying here with us?"

"I can't. I'm volunteering to help the evacuation efforts."

"Of course you are," she said with dry amusement. "But even if you weren't, you wouldn't leave the city, would you? Not when Levi has to stay there."

There was no trace of resentment in her tone. Dominic's entire family had been fond of Levi before the breakup; after the reconciliation, they'd become his biggest fans. They credited him with Dominic's return to recovery—which was true, though not in the way Dominic was sure they imagined.

"No," Dominic admitted. "I need to be wherever he is."

Silvia smiled and waved for him to bend down. When he did, she kissed his cheek and then gave it two hard pats. "Take care of that boy. If Utopia hates him half as much as you love him, he's in big trouble."

Once assured of his family's safety, Dominic returned to the city, heading for Carlos and Jasmine's building. He felt a pang of nostalgia as he glanced at his own former apartment right next door.

That nostalgia was quickly buried under an avalanche of exasperation as he ended up in the same argument with Carlos and Jasmine that he'd had with his mother—only worse, because they lived so close to the UNLV campus, which *was* being evacuated. Jasmine was determined to go to her parents' farm, even though it would be a nightmare to reach Henderson, which lay in the direct path of one of the city's major arteries.

It took him a good half hour and all his powers of persuasion to talk them around, and he only succeeded by convincing them to stay with him instead. His and Levi's apartment was closer than the Andersons' house, while still a healthy distance from both the college campus and the Strip.

Of course, that meant he had to drive them over one by one on the bike, which ate up a big chunk of his afternoon. After he had Carlos and Jasmine settled, he hauled his ass back over to UNLV much later than he'd planned to report for his volunteer duties.

He passed the same handful of casino billboards multiple times, but felt not the slightest stirring of his gambling cravings. He'd strapped them down last night, and this was the most quiescent they'd been since—well, since he'd been in the Army. No surprise there. The discipline and focus of a life-or-death mission had kept him gambling-free for eight years back then, and he was in a similar mental state today.

He hooked up with Natasha in the parking lot of the South Residential Complex, although it took him a few minutes to find her in the chaos. The lot and the adjoining walkways were swarmed with hundreds of college students as the police, Red Cross, and CERT struggled to organize them into groups to load onto the waiting vehicles for evacuation.

They were facing the same challenge here that had come up on the Strip: most of the people being evacuated didn't have their own cars. High-capacity vehicles were being recruited from all over the county, especially school buses, and a good number had been lent by local businesses as well. Dominic caught sight of a shuttle bus emblazoned with the Barclay Las Vegas logo, and tried to ignore a frisson of annoyance that was rooted in nothing but silly jealousy.

He took the crowd's pulse as he moved through it, and was unsurprised to find the mood wildly inconsistent. For every student who was crying or white-faced with fear, there were just as many in high spirits, joking around like it was the first day of spring break. A few scattered groups were passing flasks and blunts with spectacular indiscretion.

"There you are," Natasha said when he located her outside a Red Cross tent.

"Sorry I'm so late. You got my text?"

"Yeah, don't worry about it. We need all the help we can get." She offered him a bright orange vest.

Dominic took one look at it and said, "That's not going to fit me."

"I know, but it's the biggest size we have."

He sighed and pulled on the vest. It strained uncomfortably across the breadth of his shoulders and didn't come close to meeting in the front. "Mind breaking down the situation for me?"

"Sure." She hooked her thumb over her shoulder. "Campus security and administration are responsible for loading the kids into the buses and tracking who goes where. Cops are here to make sure nobody gets too rowdy." She pointed to a row of coolers and bags at the edge of the tent. "We've got water and snacks for the kids while they're waiting, and first aid if they need it. But I thought you'd do best with the team clearing the dorms to root out any stragglers."

"Sounds good. Where—"

Shouts rang out behind him. He whirled around to see two boys scuffling, the kind of angry playground wrestling that spoke of strong emotions but little experience. The people around them had formed a rough circle, cheering the boys on and filming the fight with their phones.

Dominic glanced beyond the group. The nearest cop was hurrying over, his face tense, his hand hovering over his gun holster. Though Dominic doubted the guy would shoot into a crowd of college students, cops could do stupid things when they were nervous. He might decide to fire a warning shot into the air.

With fuses short and fear running high, a single shot could turn this entire area into a lethal stampede.

As Dominic cast around for another solution, his gaze snagged on one of the coolers behind Natasha. It only had a few water bottles left in it; the rest was half-melted ice.

Moving quickly, he tossed out the remaining bottles and hefted the cooler into his arms. Then he shoved his way through the circle, tipped the cooler sideways, and flung the ice water onto the tussling boys.

They broke apart, yelping and spluttering like hosed-down cats. The other kids fell silent for a couple of seconds before bursting into laughter.

The boys turned on Dominic, scowling, but he was having none of that. "You think you're the only people here who are scared?" he asked as he lowered the cooler. "Keep your shit together. Or do you *want* to be the guys known for making this worse for everyone else?"

After a bit of shuffling and mumbling, both boys sheepishly shook their heads. The cop beyond the circle relaxed; a few volunteers came over to separate the boys and disperse the crowd. Dominic returned to Natasha and set the cooler down.

"Sorry," he said. "That's probably not a social worker–approved technique."

She grinned. "Stopping violence without adding to it? I think any social worker could get on board."

She directed him to the campus security officer who was organizing the dormitory sweeps, and he spent the next couple of hours going from room to room to make sure they were empty. A fair number of reluctant, frightened, or flat-out hostile lingerers had to be escorted out of the buildings and to the parking lot, along with a memorable couple who'd decided today was a great day to trip balls on shrooms.

Dominic kept his ears open while he worked, eavesdropping on every conversation and drawing out every student who was in a chatty mood—because although his desire to help was genuine, it was no accident that he'd ended up on this campus today.

Utopia had been recruiting here. If he could figure out how, and through whom, it might provide a fresh source of intel on the militia's plans.

College students weren't a population renowned for their discretion, so it was far from the most challenging task of his career. One name that cropped up over and over again was "Americans United," a so-called alt-right student organization that most of the kids spoke of with disgust.

When he stole a private moment to look up the group's official listing on his phone, he learned that it was a young organization. It hadn't been formed until the prior academic year—which, interestingly, was long before Utopia had made a name for itself. The organization's mission statement was brief and carefully worded, but reading between the lines, it was clear that "Americans United" meant "White People United."

The only other information in the listing was a phone number. No names, no website, no meeting places or times.

Try as he might, he couldn't get any further relevant information out of the evacuees. Either nobody here belonged to Americans United, or they had enough sense to keep their lips zipped.

The sun was beginning to set when Dominic stumbled across a young woman so frightened that she was curled up in bed, sobbing. It took him a while, but he managed to coax her out of the dorm and toward the parking lot. She kept crying inconsolably, however, so instead of having her join the now-dwindling line, he brought her straight to Natasha.

Natasha pulled the young woman aside, handed her tissues and a bottle of water, and spoke to her softly. Within ten seconds, the woman's tears were reduced to sniffles; ten more, and she was nodding with a tentative smile.

Dominic shook his head in admiration and started back toward the dorms. Each floor had been locked down after being cleared, and there was only one left.

He'd been giving every room a cursory search as he worked, but had yet to find anything incriminating—unless he wanted to rat out Sally Student in 5E for her illicit hot plate. A few rooms into the final hall, however, a piece of paper half buried on a messy desk caught his eye.

He tugged it out of the pile. It was a flyer, nothing fancy, but the aggressive typeface was what had grabbed his attention—a belligerent combination of bolded, underlined, and all-capitalized words, along with way more question marks and exclamations points than were necessary.

Worried about the FUTURE of our COUNTRY??? the flyer read. *Want to make AMERICA GREAT AGAIN?? Ready to FIGHT for your RIGHTS but don't know how?!? Join AMERICANS UNITED and BE HEARD!!!*

At the bottom of the page, the reader was instructed to call a Bianca Olsen, at a phone number different from the one in the organization's official listing.

"Jesus Christ," Dominic muttered. His skin crawled just touching this trash, but he folded it up and slipped it into his pocket.

As he was doing so, his phone vibrated. Seeing the number of Levi's temporary cell on the screen, he said, "Hey, everything okay?"

"Can you pick me up in North Las Vegas?" Levi's voice was toneless.

Dominic's heart made a valiant attempt at leaping up his throat. "What are you doing in North Las Vegas?" God, if there'd been an attack there, after he'd told his family they'd be safe—

"What do you think I'm doing here?" Levi snapped. "What could possibly drag me out to another department's jurisdiction in the middle of a terrorist crisis?"

Dominic remained silent.

Levi took an audibly deep breath, then said, "I'm sorry. That was uncalled for."

"Apology accepted. I'm guessing the Seven of Spades has returned from hiatus?"

"Yes. It's bad. Can you please come get me?" Levi paused. "I . . . I'm in a lot of pain."

Dominic knew how difficult it must have been for Levi to admit that, and any remaining irritation dissipated. "Of course. Give me the address, and I'll leave right now."

He explained the situation to Natasha, who was as understanding as always, before taking off on the borrowed bike again. He was going to have to write their neighbor a check for all the mileage he was putting on this thing. Or more accurately, *Levi* would have to write the guy a check, which was kind of an uncomfortable thought.

The approach of nightfall had created a strange dichotomy in the city: the streets were still choked with hundreds of cars trying to flee, but the sidewalks were deserted. During the drive from UNLV to North Las Vegas, he didn't see a single person outside who wasn't in a vehicle. Smart, because the cops' concerns about looting and rioting hadn't been idle. Darkness made scared, angry people both bolder and more stupid.

The empty sidewalks made the bustling activity around the crime scene seem more ominous than usual. The smallish, two-story suburban house was surrounded by flashing lights, yellow tape, and grim-faced personnel from various government agencies. Masses of reporters—part of the horde that had descended on Las Vegas after the explosion and assassinations—thronged the perimeter and spilled into the neighbors' yards.

Levi wasn't waiting outside, but given the media presence, that wasn't surprising. Dominic parked the bike down the street and skirted the reporters as best he could on the walk to the tape, intending to ask someone to find Levi and bring him out.

The cop maintaining the crime scene log was the same one who'd been at the burial site in the desert. "Mr. Russo," she said, smiling. "Consulting again?"

"Yep," he said without missing a beat.

She signed him in and gave him gloves and booties. He mounted the porch and walked through the open front door, entering a tiny vestibule with a flight of stairs straight ahead and an archway to the left.

The stench of blood and death was overpowering. He grimaced, giving himself a few seconds to adjust before he walked deeper into the house.

He'd only taken a few steps when he stopped short, his jaw dropping. The house's small size and open floor plan made it possible for him to view the entire main living area at once, and *unbelievable* wasn't a strong enough word for what he was seeing.

In the living room, four bodies were slumped on the couch and armchairs, their heads lolling above their slashed throats. Two of them were still holding Xbox controllers; a third had his hand loosely wrapped around a beer bottle, which had tipped over and spilled onto the carpet.

The fourth was Roger Carson, a bag of chips tucked between his leg and his chair. Each victim had a seven of spades card in their laps.

Beyond that was a narrow galley-style kitchen. Maggie Spencer lay with her chest and cheek on the breakfast bar as if she'd fallen asleep on her stool, except the blood from her slit throat had soaked her half-eaten sandwich, and a playing card was carefully propped up against the crusts. Another dead man was crumpled on the kitchen floor, the card dropped near his body. Three more corpses were sprawled in chairs at the dining table. Although Dominic couldn't see their cards from this distance, he was sure they were there.

This whole house was a graveyard.

Yet there wasn't a single sign of struggle or resistance anywhere, which should have been impossible. No way the Seven of Spades could have drugged this many people with ketamine at once.

Levi was standing with his back to Dominic, his arms crossed, staring at a spray-painted wall between the living room and kitchen. He didn't turn around as Dominic approached, but the slight relaxation of his shoulders was proof that he knew who was behind him.

"How?" was all Dominic asked.

Levi shrugged. "From what we can tell, the Seven of Spades sealed the house's vents and pumped it full of carbon monoxide until everyone inside passed out. Then they just walked through the house and slit everyone's throat one by one."

Christ. Dominic had the sense he wasn't seeing the full extent of the carnage, either. "How many altogether?"

"Fifteen. There are more in the bedrooms."

They'd found fewer bodies buried in the desert. The Seven of Spades had murdered more people here in one fell swoop than in the first several years of their evolution. That was a pretty decisive response to the threat in Utopia's video.

"Damn," said Dominic. "Challenge accepted, I guess."

"Yeah. I can't tell if this message is for Utopia or me." Levi nodded to the words spray-painted on the wall:

YOUR MOVE

"Why not both? The Seven of Spades has always been efficient."

Levi finally turned toward him, eyes narrowed. "This doesn't even bother you, does it?"

Dominic knew that tone; he'd have to step carefully. "I find it incredibly disturbing that a human being could casually slaughter this many people at once. But I don't care that these particular people are dead, no."

Huffing, Levi looked away.

"Levi, these people surrendered their right to life when they decided to blow up a city."

"Maybe." Levi squared his shoulders. "But that doesn't mean the Seven of Spades had a right to kill them."

A strong argument, so Dominic let it lie. "Let's get out of here, okay? I'm sure the FBI has a handle on this for now."

Levi agreed without protest, which was a good sign of how much pain he was in. As they headed for the door, he glanced over his shoulder one more time. "I know Utopia provoked the Seven of Spades first, but this kind of response is exactly what I was worried about. It's only going to make things worse for everybody."

Looping an arm around Levi's waist, Dominic said, "How much worse could things get?"

He should have known better.

CHAPTER 14

Due to its location on the Strip, Levi's substation had been shut down, its personnel temporarily relocated to other substations throughout the Valley. When Dominic brought Levi to work—walking him in like a parent bringing a kid to school—Levi found that he and Martine had been crammed into one shared, makeshift desk in the corner of the overcrowded bullpen.

"You okay?" she asked. This was the first they'd spoken since the discovery of the Seven of Spades's house of horrors.

"My bruises hurt less today," he said, although that was in no way what she'd meant. "How are the girls?"

Martine gave him a pointed look, but allowed herself to be redirected. "Scared. They *begged* me not to come to work, and I almost gave in. I feel like I abandoned them."

"You can do more to protect them here than you could at home."

"Sure, but they don't *want* to be protected. They want their mom to not get hurt." A brief shadow crossed her face, and then she shook it off. "Anyway, we've been reassigned to intelligence analysis, so the most dangerous threat we're probably facing is eye strain. What about you, Dom?"

"Recon." Dominic pulled out Levi's chair, blithely ignoring Levi's irritation at the coddling. "I was at UNLV yesterday, digging around to see how Utopia might have been recruiting the students there. I thought all I'd gotten was a name and a couple of phone numbers, but after comparing notes with Levi, I realized I had a lot more than that."

"Yeah?"

"There's a student organization there called Americans United that we can now be pretty sure is a Utopia front, because it's run by a young woman named Bianca Olsen—who, it turns out, is Oliver Hatfield's granddaughter."

Martine perked up. "No shit. You think she knows where he is?"

After Bishop had thrown Hatfield under the bus, every attempt had been made to locate and arrest him, but Hatfield was long gone. It wasn't surprising, given the man's immense economic resources.

"That's what I'm gonna find out." Dominic kissed Levi's cheek. "See you guys later. I'll let you know if I get any good leads."

As Dominic walked away, Levi called out, "Don't do anything illegal!"

Dominic turned around, continuing to walk backward while he grinned. "Baby, I think that ship has sailed."

Intelligence analysis was a lot like Levi's job in reverse: anticipating crimes that hadn't happened yet, rather than responding to ones that had already been committed. It was the kind of detail-oriented work he could lose himself in, and he committed every ounce of his focus to it.

The clock was ticking. Utopia had wanted to give the city time to panic, but they couldn't wait *too* long. If they were planning a second wave of attacks, it would be soon.

After a couple of hours, he lifted his head from his laptop and stretched his stiff, sore back. He needed to move around a little, or his bruises would hurt worse later. "You want another coffee?" he asked Martine.

"Sure, thanks."

"Excuse me, Detectives?"

Startled, Levi and Martine both turned toward Dr. Paquin. She was dressed to travel, an overnight bag slung over one shoulder, and was holding a few thin folders in her hands.

"This seems nonessential under the circumstances," she said, "but my university is insisting I evacuate, and I wanted to make sure you had these before I leave."

"What are they?" Levi asked as she handed him the folders.

"The IDs of three J. Does—the first one who was tortured, and two of the more recent victims whose fingerprints we were able to rehydrate."

Levi's fingers spasmed around the folders. Next to him, Martine exhaled with a loud *whoosh*.

Paquin gave them a rueful smile. "I would have emailed the information to you, but we were instructed not to use the LVMPD servers for anything unrelated to the current crisis."

"Of course. Thank you for bringing it by." Levi strove to remain professional, when all he wanted was to rip the folders open and devour everything that lay inside. The key to the Seven of Spades's identity could be in there. He could be holding it *in his hands*.

"Once the situation here is under control, I'll return with my team and resume work on the remaining J. Does." Paquin shook both their hands, wished them luck, and headed off.

Levi looked at Martine pleadingly, clutching the folders so hard they crumpled beneath his grip. This wasn't what they were supposed to be working on. What he *should* do was set these folders aside and come back to them later, when the city was no longer under threat of an imminent terrorist attack.

There was absolutely no fucking way he could do that.

"Oh, what am I gonna say, you should ignore those?" Martine made a beckoning gesture with one hand. "Gimme."

He handed her the folders of the two fingerprinted victims, keeping the tortured victim himself. As Paquin had expected, she'd managed to ID the guy from the fixation plates in his arm. Levi scanned the thin sheet of demographic information she'd included.

Theodore Hollis. The name rang a bell, albeit distantly. Levi frowned and kept reading.

Date of birth indicated that Hollis had been in his midforties when he was murdered. Former occupation as a vice president in a wealth management firm. Last known address in Santa Monica—

"Theodore Hollis!" Levi exclaimed, as he remembered where he'd heard that before. "Motherfucking Ted Hollis."

Martine looked puzzled, obviously trying to place the name the same way he had, and then her eyes widened. "That rich asshole who got off a few years ago for beating that sex worker?"

"Yeah."

Levi recalled the scandal clearly now; the story had been all over the local news for weeks. On one of Hollis's many weekend trips to Vegas, he'd physically and sexually assaulted an escort he'd hired. There'd been a divisive, controversial trial, and things had only gotten worse when he'd been acquitted. But the story hadn't ended there—he'd disappeared shortly after the trial, by all reports unable to handle the social and professional fallout.

"Everyone thought Hollis took off because he couldn't stand the heat," Levi said. "There was never any suspicion of foul play, because—"

"Because he liquidated all of his assets and drained his bank accounts before chartering a plane to the Maldives," Martine finished.

They stared at each other. The kind of information someone would need to get their hands on all of Hollis's money and book a plane in his name was exactly the kind of information Hollis would surrender if, say, he was being tortured by a psychotic serial killer.

Levi felt faint. "Well, I guess we know how the Seven of Spades funds all of their elaborate setups. What've you got?"

"Nothing that interesting. Two local guys with criminal records, pretty standard Seven of Spades victim profile."

They dove deeper into their respective research, branching out from the basics Paquin's team had provided. Levi pulled up a bunch of old stories about Hollis's arrest, trial, and acquittal, needing to refresh his memory on the details and hoping something would strike a spark.

He found what he needed within five minutes. "*Whoa.* The judge on Hollis's trial was Cameron Harding." The Seven of Spades had killed Harding only a couple of months ago—no way was that a coincidence.

Martine's head popped up. "Seriously? Who else was involved?"

Levi clicked through the news stories, his mouth hanging open. "Prosecuting attorney, DDA Loretta Kane." Another of the Seven of Spades's victims, one who'd been posthumously revealed as corrupt. "Lead attorney for the defense, Maria Dekovic. Second chair for the defense . . ."

He blinked. Closed his eyes, opened them again. The name was still there. He swallowed hard.

"Jay Sawyer."

Martine went still. For a long, breathless moment, neither of them spoke.

"Okay," she said. "Okay. That's weird, but not *too* weird. Hollis's case was a huge one for Sawyer's firm. This would have been before he'd made a real name for himself. It makes sense that he would angle to get himself assigned to such a prominent trial."

"Uh-huh." Levi folded his hands together, suppressing the small tremor that had started up. "Out of curiosity, who represented the other two victims in their court cases?"

"Not Sawyer. I would have noticed that right away."

"The firms?"

"Um . . ." Martine fussed with her laptop. "Kerry Milner, Emily Park of Hatfield, Park, and McKenzie. Rodrigo Cortez, Erik Johansen of . . . Hatfield, Park, and McKenzie."

"What about Seth Fowler? Do we have a record of who his attorney was before his charges were dropped?"

They did. Both times that Fowler had been accused of criminal negligence, he'd run straight to Hatfield, Park, and McKenzie, and the charges had been dismissed within days.

"This has to be a fluke," Levi said through numb lips. "We checked all of this information for every single one of the Seven of Spades's victims who'd had contact with the criminal justice system, right from the beginning with Billy Campbell. There were *no* patterns. Not even in the bailiffs or court stenographers. We *checked*."

"The Seven of Spades intended for those bodies to be found. They would have made sure there was no connection to their own identity." She glanced around the busy substation, and although no one was close enough to hear them, she lowered her voice. "But these bodies? They were buried in the desert. They were never supposed to be found and identified, so it wouldn't have mattered if there was a connection. That might even be *why* the Seven of Spades buried them in the first place."

"We've discussed the possibility of the Seven of Spades being a defense attorney before, and we decided it was unlikely. Rohan himself said the killer's black-and-white concept of justice would prevent the kind of compartmentalization and moral flexibility defense attorneys need to do their jobs."

"And that's a logical argument—unless we've had the cause and effect backward this whole time. Maybe the Seven of Spades's obsession with old-school justice didn't influence their choice of profession. What if the disillusionment of a particular profession *created* the Seven of Spades?"

Levi rocked back.

"If there's any job in the world that would make you so disgusted with people you'd want to slit their throats, it's being a criminal defense lawyer," Martine said.

Even before Rohan's profile, the Seven of Spades's insider information and flawlessly executed crime scenes had made it obvious that they were involved with the criminal justice system in some way. The assumption had always been that the killer was attracted to such a career for the same reasons they'd ended up becoming a vigilante. Rohan's theory that the killer had been the victim of a violent crime only solidified that belief—because as Montoya had pointed out, trauma often motivated people to take jobs in criminal justice. It was why Levi had become a cop himself.

But what if Martine was right, and they'd been approaching it from the wrong angle? A person with the potential to become a vigilante serial killer could be pushed over the edge by a job that shoved human weakness and corruption in their face every day.

Plus, a traumatic event didn't have to be experienced first-hand to wreak havoc on a person's psyche. Secondary trauma from listening to victims' stories burned out cops and people in helping professions all the time. Levi had experienced it himself, to an extent; the sense of helpless rage it created could be overwhelming. Defense attorneys must hear similar stories all the time too, with the added stress of helping the perpetrators avoid punishment for their crimes.

"Levi." Martine clapped her hands softly in front of his face.

He jumped, realizing he'd been zoned out for a while. "What?"

"What does your gut say? Do you think Sawyer could be the Seven of Spades?"

His brain shied away from the idea so violently that he cringed. "I don't know. How am I supposed to answer a question like that?

We don't have any evidence besides a suspicious connection to a few of the killer's early victims."

"Maybe not," Martine said slowly. Levi knew that tone, that expression; she was arriving at several rapid-fire conclusions, none of which he wanted to hear. "But Sawyer's always had kind of a thing for you, hasn't he? He's smart as hell and he knows the system inside out. He's got the Seven of Spades's arrogance, but he's still more than charming enough to set people at ease while he drugs their drinks. He could easily have the connections to hire a contract killer and keep tabs on the criminal underworld."

Levi wanted to slap his hands over his ears like a child. *La la la, I can't hear you!*

"Also, he was supposed to meet you at the substation for your hearing the day Carolyn Royce was murdered, and he was over an hour late."

"He blew out a tire."

"Can he prove that?"

Levi closed his eyes in an attempt to retain his slipping equilibrium, but the darkness only served to drag several previously unexamined thoughts to light.

Such as how Sawyer had always found their most antagonistic interactions amusing at worst.

Or how Sawyer had come to Levi's rescue when he'd been interrogated by IA, offered to represent him pro bono, lied about how he'd learned of Levi's suspension, and never provided the real explanation.

How the very next night, Sawyer had magically shown up at the bar where Levi was drinking alone.

How Sawyer almost never called Levi by his first name, and the Seven of Spades had done so only once, at the close of a particularly stressful encounter.

How the Seven of Spades had chosen Sawyer to deliver a message to Levi about Sergei Volkov's poker tournament—a message that had been left on the dashboard of Sawyer's locked car in a gated parking garage.

The day Stanton had been kidnapped, the Seven of Spades had sent Dominic several ambiguous text messages, trying to capture his interest. When Dominic had ignored them, their final text had read *Don't say I didn't warn you.*

Levi remembered the night Sawyer had given him the invitation to Volkov's tournament. Levi had made it clear that he intended to go in alone, and now he heard Sawyer's response again, said with a smirk as Sawyer melted backward into the darkness of the parking lot.

"Don't say I didn't warn you."

"Oh my God," Levi whispered. He leapt out of his chair and bolted for the bathroom.

Martine called his name, and people gave him startled looks as he rushed through the substation, but he barely noticed. He reached the bathroom in the nick of time, collapsing on his knees in front of a toilet only a moment before his lurching stomach turned inside out.

He clenched the sides of the bowl, his body convulsing under the force with which he expelled what felt like everything he'd ever eaten. It was agonizing for his bruised chest and back, and tears of strain sprang to his eyes.

Behind him, he heard cries of alarm, concerned inquiries that didn't quite sink in, and then several indignant exclamations at the tap of high heels on linoleum.

"Oh, get over it," said Martine. "Levi, you okay?"

From the sound of her voice, he could tell she was outside the stall, facing away from him. Her near-phobia of vomiting was so intense that he was surprised she'd followed him into the bathroom. She probably wouldn't have done it for anyone else besides her husband and kids.

He coughed once more, spat into the bowl, and flushed. Then he grabbed a wad of toilet paper to wipe his mouth and slumped against the metal partition, shaking and drenched in sweat. "I'm okay."

She tentatively peeked into the stall and grimaced. "Jesus, no, you're not. Hang on." She walked away, returning with a handful of damp paper towels for him to sponge his face. "What the hell *was* that? I know it was kind of a shock, but isn't it better for it to be Sawyer than someone else? You don't even like him."

Levi tipped his head back against the stall divider. His whole upper body ached abominably, and his stomach was still cramping. "I had sex with him."

For a few long moments, Martine was utterly silent. "*When?*" she finally asked, in a high-pitched squeak he'd never heard from her before.

"The night before Stanton was kidnapped."

"Oh." Comprehension dawned on her face. "The night after you outed Dom's addiction and then punched Gibbs in the face?"

"Yeah. Not my finest hour." Levi paused, reconsidering. "Not my finest weekend, really."

"Does Dominic know?"

"Of course!"

"Okay. Shit. I . . . I don't even know what to say."

"I do," Levi said bitterly. "I had sex with a serial killer. Sawyer's murdered dozens of people and has been torturing me for months, and I let him *fuck* me."

He retched again, doubling over the toilet, but he had nothing else to bring up. Martine crouched by his side and put a hand on his shoulder.

"We don't know it's Sawyer. All of our conclusions are based on circumstantial evidence."

"It's him. It's him, Martine. God, I'm so *stupid—*"

"All right." She rubbed his back soothingly, like he was one of her kids. "We'll turn this over to Leila, okay? We don't have enough to arrest Sawyer, but she can bring him in for questioning, hold him as long as she can, and put a police detail on him after he's released. We'll get to the bottom of this. Everything's going to be fine."

No, Levi thought. Nothing was ever going to be fine again.

Dominic didn't like the word *bitch*. He rarely used it in reference to a woman, especially one as young as Bianca Olsen.

But after a morning immersed in her various social media feeds, there was no getting around it: Bianca was a spoiled, racist little bitch.

The rising ubiquity of social media was a blessing to bounty hunters and PIs everywhere; it was truly astonishing how much personal information people were willing to reveal on the internet.

Dominic could credit more than one collar to an ill-advised Facebook check-in, Snapchat geofilter, or nostalgic Instagram post.

Bianca had a presence on every social media platform known to mankind, each updated with such regularity and thoroughness that managing them must have been a full-time job. That made Dominic's task much easier, and as a PI, he was grateful for the wealth of open-source intelligence.

As a human being, it made him want to drink bleach. There were only so many xenophobic rants about immigrants and breathtakingly ignorant comments on poverty that a guy could be expected to endure.

Bianca and her entire family, sans her missing grandfather, were on vacation in Lake Tahoe—they'd left the day before the explosion at the Mirage, which wasn't suspicious at all. Assured by her comprehensive documentation of the trip that nobody was home in Las Vegas, Dominic broke into the Olsens' Summerlin house and turned it over room by room. With no need to rush, his search was meticulous, and would leave no evidence of his passing.

He continued monitoring Bianca's social media while he worked. Isaiah, McBride's tech guru, had whipped up a cool app for the firm that collated and tracked an individual's social media activity with minimum effort on the investigator's part. Dominic had never appreciated it more, even if he was interrupted every few minutes by a notification about a new Instagram post of Bianca's latte or whatever.

So far, his search hadn't been as productive as he'd hoped. The house was spotless, not to mention organized in a near-obsessive way he'd only seen in magazines before, so he was pretty confident that he wasn't missing anything. There simply weren't any indications of where Hatfield had gone.

He'd reached the home office of Vanessa Olsen, *née* Hatfield, and was investigating the contents of her desk when his phone dinged.

Bianca had updated her Facebook with a selfie of her in a bikini, relaxing by the pool at the family's rented house in Lake Tahoe. In the mere seconds it took Dominic to absorb the picture, likes were already pouring in from her literal thousands of followers. Then a comment popped up from a woman named Hailey, whom Dominic knew from his background work was one of Bianca's closest friends.

Can't believe that slut Roxy came with you!!

Bianca responded a moment later. *I kno rite?!? Grandpa should have sent her somewhere else. Look at her rolls in that bikini!!!* That was followed by the barfing-face emoji.

Frowning, Dominic studied the picture more closely. There was another woman in the background of the shot, a stunning redhead partially out of frame. She was so beautiful that Dominic had no trouble remembering that he'd seen her in multiple pictures while researching Bianca this morning. She was about Bianca's age, maybe a little older, so he'd assumed they were friends.

Hailey's and Bianca's comments made him rethink that assumption. He abandoned his search of Ms. Olsen's desk and returned to Bianca's social media feeds, particularly Facebook and Instagram.

The redhead, Roxy, did pop up in Bianca's photos here and there. Now that Dominic was paying more attention to her than Bianca, though, he noticed that she was never the subject of the photos; she was always in the background, as if her presence in the picture was unintentional. And Bianca never tagged her or mentioned her by name.

Dominic set down his phone and resumed searching the desk, this time with a specific goal. He found what he was looking for within seconds: an old-school, leather-bound address book.

The entries had been made with pristine handwriting. He skimmed the pages, flipping through the book until he saw it. *Roxanne Calhoun.*

He looked up the address included beneath her name and was surprised to find it located at the Whitby, a luxury condominium high-rise Downtown. Further research informed him that Roxy was currently unemployed, but several years ago, she'd been a paralegal at the firm of Hatfield, Park, and McKenzie.

He slammed the address book shut triumphantly. Roxy wasn't Bianca's friend at all. She was Hatfield's *mistress.*

As far as he knew, the police and FBI were unaware of her existence, which meant they hadn't searched her place. This was where he should probably stop and turn over the lead. No way could he break into a high-rise condo with the same ease he'd had breaking into this house.

His phone dinged again, and he picked it up, bracing himself for Bianca's next scintillating update.

But the notification wasn't from his monitoring app. It was his long-standing Google alert on the Seven of Spades.

RENOWNED LOCAL DEFENSE ATTORNEY NAMED PERSON OF INTEREST IN SEVEN OF SPADES CASE

His stomach bottoming out, Dominic clicked through to the news story. He'd read no further than the first sentence before he leapt to his feet and sprinted out of the room.

As Levi stood with Martine, watching Sawyer through the two-way glass, he concluded that this was the most flustered he'd ever seen the man—and Sawyer's "flustered" looked like most people's "mildly discomfited." He was beautifully dressed in a designer three-piece suit, not a hair out of place, and seemed more irritated by the inconvenience than anything else.

"This is so ridiculous it barely merits a response," Sawyer said to Leila, who was alone in the interrogation room with him. "If you were going to arrest me, you would have done so. You know I'm not going to speak without an attorney present, and all my attorney will say is that you have no real grounds on which to hold me, so keeping me here is a waste of everyone's time."

"Really?" Instead of sitting at the table with Sawyer, Leila was standing a couple of feet back from it, as she often preferred to do while questioning people. "So you have *nothing* to say to accusations that you're one of the modern era's most prolific serial killers?"

Sawyer leaned back in his chair, folded his arms, and raised his eyebrows.

"I get it. Nobody knows to keep their mouth shut in a room like this better than a lawyer." Leila bent over, resting her hands on the edge of the table. "I just thought you might make an exception, considering the effect this whole thing is having on Levi."

Sawyer stiffened.

"I mean, if you want to leave him in the messed-up state he's in now, be my guest. He probably won't jump off a building or anything—just take a few hundred Silkwood showers, maybe never have sex again."

"Oh my God," Levi muttered.

Giving Leila the side-eye, Sawyer straightened up. "He told you—"

"That you fucked him? Sure did." She shrugged. "I'm only surprised that *you* didn't start crowing about it the very next day. From everything I've heard, you've been gagging to tap that narrow ass for years."

Levi choked. A snort burst out of Martine; when he glared at her, she hastily rearranged her expression into a disapproving frown and patted his arm.

He understood that Leila was trying to knock Sawyer off-balance so he'd be easier to manipulate, but really? *Really?*

At least she seemed to have had some success. Sawyer was contemplating his hands, his brow furrowed.

"You know, Levi threw up after he figured it out," Leila added.

"I—" Sawyer closed his mouth with a frustrated exhalation, his body as tense as an angry cat's. He was quiet for a few seconds. "I'm willing to speak to Detective Abrams, *alone*, under several conditions."

She gestured for him to continue. Behind the glass, Levi shook his head—he didn't *want* to speak to Sawyer, today or ever again.

"There will be nobody else present in the room besides Detective Abrams and myself, nor anybody observing from the viewing room." Sawyer gestured toward the mirror, and Levi shrank back despite himself. "The conversation will not be recorded in any format. And nothing either Detective Abrams or I say during the conversation will be admissible in any court proceeding, nor used as the basis for requesting any form of court order."

"Deal," said Leila, heading for the door.

"I'll have that in writing, Ms. Rashid," Sawyer said icily.

Half an hour later, Levi was psyching himself up outside the interrogation room. Everything in him recoiled at the idea of facing Sawyer, but if he was the only person Sawyer would talk to, he had no choice. He had a responsibility to protect the public safety, and it wasn't the public's fault he'd slept with a serial killer. He'd made his bed, literally; now he had to lie in it once more.

He opened the door and stepped inside.

Sawyer watched him intently, but didn't move as Levi shut the door behind himself, slowly approached the table, and took a seat. Levi's eyes flicked toward the camera in the corner, turned off as agreed. The viewing room next door was empty, and Martine was standing guard to ensure it stayed that way.

He and Sawyer were truly alone.

Forcing himself to meet Sawyer's eyes, Levi remained silent. Sleeping with Sawyer had been a mistake, for several reasons, but it hadn't been *wrong*. Sawyer was the one who should be ashamed, not Levi.

After an uncomfortably long staring contest, Sawyer broke first. "I'm not the Seven of Spades."

"Oh, okay," said Levi. "I guess we'll just let you go, then."

Sawyer exhaled heavily through his nose. "I don't understand what made you think this was even a possibility."

"When Carolyn Royce was murdered, the Seven of Spades livestreamed it to the substation. They knew I would be there. You were supposed to meet me there at the same time, but you were over an hour late. Where were you?"

"You already know the answer to that. I had a flat tire."

"Pretty convenient, don't you think?"

"Actually, it was a massive *in*convenience."

"Did you request roadside assistance?" Levi asked. It would be an easy way to verify Sawyer's story. "Call for a tow truck?"

"I changed the tire myself."

That seemed so unlikely that Levi laughed aloud. "And it took you an hour?"

Sawyer threw his head back with a loud groan. "The lug nuts were rusted; it took forever to get them off."

"In other words, you have no solid alibi for Royce's murder." Levi changed subjects abruptly, aiming to put Sawyer in a position where he'd have to struggle to keep up. "Let's talk about the time the Seven of Spades used *you* to deliver my invitation to Volkov's poker tournament. They leave me messages all the time without needing a go-between. Why break from their pattern?"

"Without context, would you have known what that invitation meant?" When Levi didn't answer, Sawyer added, "And is there anyone else in your life who could have explained it to you?"

Dominic, technically, but the less said about that the better. "Any ideas how the invitation ended up in your locked car in your firm's secured parking garage?"

"Do *you* have any thoughts? After all, I sent you the security footage—of my own initiative, I might add."

"And we went through it with a fine-toothed comb, vetted every vehicle in and out. They all had legitimate reasons to be there. What's interesting is that once your car was parked, it was no longer within the sightlines of any cameras."

"Because those cameras are positioned to watch the gates."

"Again, convenient. How did you find out about my IA hearing?"

"*What*?" Sawyer said, scowling. Levi's ploy seemed to be working; Sawyer was vibrating with frustration, and he looked about ready to flip the table.

Levi took a moment to savor Sawyer's irritation. "After Quintana was murdered, you found out about my suspension and Internal Affairs investigation almost as soon as I did. At the time, you said Leila called you, but she told me later that wasn't true. Who really told you, and why did you lie about it?"

Releasing a long breath, Sawyer rubbed his eyes. "I lied to protect the person who actually called me. They would face serious consequences for it."

"Not within the parameters you've set for this conversation, they won't."

Sawyer chewed that over, then nodded. "It was Detective Montoya."

Okay, *that* was unexpected. Levi blinked and sat back.

"She called me as soon as she was assigned to your investigation," Sawyer continued. "She believed you were being railroaded and thought I could help. She could lose her badge for that, Detective."

True. And it wasn't outside the realm of possibility that Montoya would act to protect Levi behind the scenes, not when it came to the

Seven of Spades case. "If I ask Montoya about this, will she tell me the same story?"

"Depends on how badly she wants to cover her ass, I guess." Sawyer leaned forward, propping his elbows on the table. "Do you really believe the Seven of Spades would have sex with you, after everything else they've done to you? That would be fucked-up beyond measure."

"The Seven of Spades has always had a weird fixation on me," Levi said. "So have you."

"You..." Sawyer's mouth worked open and shut, his head shaking blankly. "You must be joking. Are you really that full of yourself?"

"You can't deny you've spent years trying to get me in bed, no matter how many times I rejected you."

"There's this phenomenon called sexual attraction, you know. It's possible for it to exist without obsession. Sure, I've always thought you had a great ass, and I wondered what it would be like to fuck someone so intense. The way you'd get all worked up when I hit on you only made the idea more intriguing. But that was the extent of my interest."

Levi flushed, grateful that nobody else would ever hear this conversation.

"All of the things you've brought up so far are things you already knew." Sawyer tilted his head. "You can't expect me to believe you just put them together this way out of nowhere. What was the trigger? What *really* made you think I might be the Seven of Spades?"

There was no point in keeping it from him. The truth might even knock something loose.

"We've identified several of the bodies from the desert burial site. One of them was a former client of yours—Ted Hollis."

"Hollis? He wasn't murdered. He fled the country because he couldn't handle the public scrutiny after his trial."

"Oh no, he was definitely murdered," said Levi. "Tortured, too. Our working theory is that the Seven of Spades forced him to liquidate his assets before they killed him. They've always been suspiciously well funded."

"Okay, so one of their early victims had been my client." Sawyer spread his hands. "So what? I've worked on hundreds of cases over the years. I wasn't even the lead attorney on Hollis's."

"True. But we ID'd *four* of those early victims, and every single one had contact with the criminal justice system in which Hatfield, Park, and McKenzie represented them. That's not a coincidence. That's a pattern."

Frowning, Sawyer sat back. "What were the others' names?"

There was no need for Levi to check his notes. "Dr. Seth Fowler. Kerry Milner. Rodrigo Cortez."

Sawyer's frown deepened as Levi spoke, and he remained silent. Then he blinked hard, just once, his jaw tightening and his face going pale under his spray tan. Levi shifted to the edge of his seat, sensing an imminent breakthrough.

"I—" Sawyer cleared his throat and shook himself. "I have nothing more to say."

"Really?" Levi asked, narrowing his eyes. "That's not what it looks like."

"I'll see my attorney now, please."

Levi didn't move yet. He studied Sawyer, who wouldn't meet his eyes—something he couldn't remember Sawyer having ever done before.

Forget flustered. Now Sawyer was unnerved, his body tense and his expression shuttered. Those names had struck a chord, but Levi wasn't sure what he was seeing. Guilt? Fear? Had Sawyer realized he'd left incriminating evidence on one of those corpses?

"All right." Levi stood. "But you know we'll keep digging."

Sawyer didn't respond; he didn't even look up.

"What do you think?" Martine asked when Levi emerged from the interrogation room. She was standing with Leila, and between her fierce glare and Leila's cool disdain, they were doing a good job of keeping any nosy cops at bay. "Is Sawyer the Seven of Spades?"

"I don't know," Levi said honestly. "There's something going on there, but I'm too close to this. It's too personal for me to be objective *or* trust my gut."

"His lawyer will have him out of here in a couple of hours, maybe less," said Leila.

Levi waved a hand. "That's fine. We'll put a police detail on him and keep him under a microscope while we firm up our case. Besides, since the news already broke, he won't be able to go anywhere public without being mobbed by reporters and angry citizens."

Martine began leading the way back to the bullpen. "I don't know if it's feasible to put a 24/7 detail on Sawyer in the middle of all this Utopia shit. Our resources are strained as it is."

"I know, but we don't have a choice." Levi scanned the noisy, overcrowded bullpen, searching for Sergeant Wen. "Sawyer could take advantage of the chaos to bolt. I'm kind of surprised he didn't make a break for it after we found the bodies in the desert."

Leila snorted as she scrolled through her cell phone. "The Seven of Spades is too egotistical to think they'll be caught. If the shoe fits . . ."

Wasn't that the truth. Levi caught sight of Wen, gestured to get his attention, and headed over. Halfway across the room, however, someone called his name. He turned to see Dominic hurrying toward him, a visitor's badge pinned to his shirt and worry etched all over his face.

They hadn't planned to meet up again until tonight. Why—

God, Dominic must have heard about Sawyer. Of *course* he'd rush right over here.

Dominic reached Levi, touched his arm, and opened his mouth— but before he could speak, a uniformed officer near them shouted, "Guys!"

They only heard her because they were standing so close; for most of the people in the bullpen, her voice was lost in the roar of dozens of people talking over each other. Almost nobody noticed.

"Guys!" she tried again, to the same effect. Then she groaned, cast around, and snatched a megaphone off her coworker's desk. "*Hey, everybody!*"

All over the bullpen, people jerked, flinched, and jumped. After a few initial exclamations of surprise, everyone fell silent and gave her their attention.

Blushing, she set the megaphone aside. "I just got a hit on the media alerts we set up. Another Utopia video went live a couple of minutes ago."

Levi sucked in a breath as people sprang into action, scurrying back and forth. Would it be another warning? Maybe Utopia would indicate concrete potential targets. Or would it just be taunting news of an attack that would happen any moment, sent out to demoralize law enforcement with the realization that they could do nothing to stop it?

In short order, a large mobile monitor was queued up with the internet video, and everyone gathered around it in a rough semicircle. Levi easily pushed his way to the front of the crowd, Dominic close at his shoulder. Martine joined them a second later.

The video started.

It was the same American flag backdrop, the same Reagan masks, except this time, there were only two men. They'd added a table, on which ten metal briefcases were stacked in a wide pyramid.

"The devil known as the Seven of Spades has slaughtered fifteen of our people," said the man in front. His voice was recognizable as the one who'd spoken in the last video. "That's fifteen God-fearing patriots who were struck down for defending their country. They're martyrs, all of them, and they will not be forgotten."

Next to Levi, Martine whispered, "I can never tell if freaks like this actually believe the crap they're spouting, or if they're just using it as an excuse to be terrible people."

"But this act of war cannot go unanswered," the man said. "This is our response."

He gestured to the second man, who popped open the pyramid's top briefcase, revealing that it was stuffed to the brim with banded stacks of hundred-dollar bills.

Gasps sounded all around Levi. Dominic gripped his elbow.

Though the mask hid the man's expression, Levi could tell from his tone of voice that he was smirking. "Utopia will give ten million dollars cash to anyone who brings Detective Levi Abrams to us alive."

CHAPTER 15

The man in the video was still speaking, but Dominic was no longer listening. His mind was working five steps ahead, mapping out strategies and planning contingencies.

Shocked whispers rippled through the packed bullpen, and although everyone was looking at Levi, nobody moved. That made Wen's rapid approach as he shouldered through the crowd all the more conspicuous.

"Get him out of here *now*," Wen hissed at Martine.

"How?" Her face was tense, her mouth set in a thin line, but she spoke calmly. "All of the roads out of the city are backed up for miles."

"Helicopter," said Dominic.

Wen startled and met his eyes, then nodded. "I think the closest helipad is at Desert Springs Medical Center; it's about two miles from here. Go now and I'll have a chopper meet you there." He stepped away, pulling out his cell phone.

Dominic and Martine turned to Levi, who hadn't reacted to any part of the conversation; he was just gazing blankly at the monitor.

All around them, Dominic sensed the atmosphere taking a dangerous turn. People had withdrawn from them, clustering into small groups, muttering amongst themselves and shooting furtive glances Levi's way. Every second Levi remained here, he was at greater risk.

The promise of ten million dollars cash could make a lot of people willing to do very bad things.

Pressing her keys into Dominic's hand, Martine said, "Put him in my car. I'm going to round up some uniforms to escort us."

"Got it." Dominic grabbed Levi's elbow and tugged, leading him out of the substation. Though Dominic was ready to knock out anyone who stood in their way, nobody tried to stop them.

Levi followed along obediently until they reached the parking lot, at which point he seemed to realize what was happening. He dug in his heels and wrenched his arm out of Dominic's grip. "Wait! This is crazy; I can't just *leave*."

"You have to."

"In the middle of a terrorist crisis? When we've just identified the probable Seven of Spades? No way."

Dominic was all too familiar with the mulish frown on Levi's face. Levi would never privilege his own safety above the greater good, so using the threat to his life as the basis for an argument would be pointless.

"People are going to come for you," Dominic said. "Think about the ways that could go down. People fighting each other to be the one who gets to you first. Cops forced to fire on civilians to protect you. Rioting mobs. If you stay in the city, you'll create a huge public safety problem, and the fact that Vegas is dealing with an ongoing terrorist threat only makes it *more* important for you to avoid making things worse."

Levi cursed under his breath. "Fine. Let's go."

They hustled to Martine's car, where Levi ducked into the back seat with his head lowered. Dominic, who was over a foot taller than Martine, had to slide the driver's seat all the way back before he could get in as well. He locked the doors and started the ignition; they'd wait for Martine, but if any hostiles preempted her, they needed to be able to move at a moment's notice.

"Where am I supposed to go?" Levi asked.

"I think we should leave the state altogether. Go to California, maybe, to the limits of the chopper's range. Then we can hunker down in a motel somewhere without anyone knowing where we are."

"What do you mean 'we'? You're not coming with me."

Dominic twisted around in his seat. "Like hell I'm not."

"*Dominic.*" Levi's voice was low and intense. "You can't just walk away from your hometown while it's in crisis. And what about everyone you'd be leaving behind? Rebel needs you. Your family needs you."

"*You're* my goddamn family!"

Levi blinked; his eyes warmed, and he reached out to brush his fingers against Dominic's hand.

"You're not going anywhere alone," Dominic said more evenly. "The rest of my family is safe where they are, and me being physically present won't make that any more true. Rebel is with Carlos and Jasmine. They'll take good care of her until this is resolved."

"Okay." Levi gave him a small, soft smile.

From the corner of his eye, Dominic saw Martine jogging toward them. He popped the locks so she could jump into the front passenger's seat.

"A couple of patrol cars are going to follow us to the medical center," she said. "I told them not to run lights or sirens. We may need the backup, but we don't want to draw attention to ourselves."

Nodding, Dominic pulled out of the parking space and turned left on East Harmon. Two silent patrol cars fell in behind them as they sped down the street.

Martine drew her gun and held it in her lap. "Are you armed?" she asked Dominic.

"Heavily."

Levi made a disgruntled noise. "I don't want anyone to get hurt because of me."

"If anyone gets hurt, it'll be because of Utopia, not you," she said.

Fortunately, enough time had passed since the initial attacks that the city's core streets were no longer as congested as those on the outskirts; the official evacuations had been completed, and most people who'd decided to spontaneously evacuate were already on their way out of town. Their other advantage was that the route from the substation to the medical center was a straight shot down one broad roadway. Dominic was easily able to weave around the other cars, driving as fast as he could without attracting notice.

The helipad in question was at ground-level, in the center of a cluster of medical buildings. It was surrounded by a parking lot and further enclosed by a low chain-link fence. Within five minutes of leaving the substation, Dominic barreled into the lot and pulled right up to the gap in fence, the squad cars flanking him on either side.

The chopper was waiting for them, its rotors whirling. Dominic saw no threats in the surrounding area, but they couldn't be more exposed here—there was no landscaping anywhere around the helipad, obviously, and the chain-link fence was useless. The only cover was their own cars.

They'd just have to move fast, then.

Dominic drew his gun and silently checked in with Levi and Martine. In unison, they jumped out of the car and sprinted for the chopper.

The four cops from the squad cars closed ranks as a rear guard, and Dominic was unsurprised to see Jonah Gibbs and Kelly Marin among the group, both stone-faced and determined. Their feet pounded along the ground as an FBI agent leaned out of the helicopter and beckoned them frantically.

Sudden panic on the agent's face and the squeal of multiple tires were the only warnings they got before a hail of bullets chewed through the cement in front of them. Dominic recoiled, crouched down, and scrambled backward along with everyone else, instinctively yanking Levi behind him.

They'd been betrayed.

It could have been anyone; there'd been too many people around when they made their plan, too many potential leaks. *Goddamn it.*

More bullets sprayed the helicopter, ripping through the FBI agent. Staying low, Dominic spun around to see that two large SUVs had pulled up beyond their own cars, past the fence. Men were hanging out of the open windows, firing semiautomatic rifles.

Firing *around* their group, not directly *at* them—cutting off their means of escape and herding them backward.

They need Levi alive.

"Back to the cars!" Dominic shouted. Yes, it was where their attackers wanted them, but they had no other choice. They'd be shot down if they tried to run in any other direction, and at least the cars would offer minimal coverage and the slim chance of escape. But they needed to get there before these men decided to risk harming Levi in order to take out his guards.

They raced toward the edge of the helipad, opening fire as soon as they were within a feasible range for their handguns. Several of the enemy ducked into their cars or behind the open doors, but the rest continued shooting. Their firepower was far superior, and the only thing that kept Dominic and his group from being wiped out in seconds was Utopia's demand that Levi be brought in alive.

Kelly cried out as she was winged, but shook it off and ran even faster. Seconds from the cars, one of the other cops took a bullet to the leg and went down screaming. Gibbs grabbed him under the arms and dragged him the last few feet.

They were all still alive when they hunkered behind the makeshift barrier of their three cars and persisted in returning fire. As Dominic changed out his magazine, he remembered that Levi wasn't armed.

Dominic drew the small Glock from his ankle holster and pressed it into Levi's hand, asking the question with his eyes: *Can you handle this?*

Levi firmed his grip on the gun, popped up, and fired, his eyes cool and clear as he brought down one of the men.

Of course. Levi might not be able to use a gun to defend his own life, but he'd never had a problem using one to defend others.

The cops were aiming for center mass, as they were trained to— but now that Dominic was stationary and within range, he went straight for headshots. He took out the driver of the nearest car first, shattering the windshield, then got a guy who made the mistake of turning to his dead buddy in shock.

Minor successes aside, this wasn't sustainable. They were outgunned and outnumbered, with a limited supply of ammo. Enemy reinforcements could show up long before a law enforcement response. Or a rival group could come along and turn this into a three-way nightmare.

Their one small hope was to flee in Martine's car before it took too much damage. Dominic swiveled, intending to tell Levi to get in the car—just in time to see one of the cops abruptly turn his gun on Martine.

Levi leapt for the guy, but Gibbs was much closer. "No!" Gibbs yelled, shoving himself between the cop and Martine and wrestling for the gun.

The gun went off, right up against Gibbs's chest. Gibbs's eyes flew wide, he gurgled wetly, and then his body went limp and he collapsed to the pavement.

Without hesitation, Martine put three bullets in the other cop's chest. The guy dropped like a stone.

Levi fell to his knees beside Gibbs; Kelly did the same with the traitor. She grabbed his gun away even as she set her fingers against his neck. Seconds later, she looked up at Martine and shook her head.

Martine blinked rapidly, her throat working. Dominic knew that was her first confirmed kill, and for it to be a fellow cop . . . He trusted her to compartmentalize it for now, though.

Levi had his hand on Gibbs's throat, his lips pressed into a thin line. He gently brushed his fingers over Gibbs's eyes to close them, then rested his hand on Gibbs's face for a moment. "We have to get out of here."

Agreed. The enemy was closing in, emboldened by the temporary lack of return fire, and now they were down two people. "Get in the car," said Dominic. "It's our only chance."

Although Kelly's face was bloodless, she said, "Go. We'll cover you." The only other remaining cop—the one who'd been shot in the leg—nodded grimly.

Dominic, Levi, and Martine piled into the car from one side, keeping their heads low. Dominic buckled his seat belt one-handed while he jammed the key into the ignition. As soon as he stomped on the accelerator, he could tell a couple of the tires were blown—but the car was running, and that was all that mattered.

He gunned the engine, blasting across the helipad and smashing right through the chain-link fence on the other side. As they bounced and jostled through the parking lot beyond, the car's wheels grinding against the asphalt, his mind worked feverishly to plot an escape route.

This car wasn't going to last much longer, and their enemies would be in hot pursuit. They had to get somewhere safe. Not a police station—there was no telling who else might sell them out.

His usual strategy, getting lost in the crowd at a busy public place, wouldn't work. There *weren't* any busy public places in Vegas right now, and Levi couldn't blend in anywhere.

He growled low in his throat as he emerged onto the road past the parking lot, intending to hook a right and cut through the medical center to the street on the other side.

"Look out!" Martine screamed—too late.

A speeding SUV hurtled into the driver's side of their car with a tremendous, earth-shattering *crash*. Agony exploded through Dominic's skull in the seconds before he blacked out.

Levi coughed, wavering in and out of consciousness before his brain sputtered fully back online. He wrinkled his nose, which was full of the smell of blood and burnt rubber, and opened his eyes.

Still woozy from the collision, it took him a second to understand what he was seeing: the car was upside down, and he was hanging from his seat belt. His body was all over pain, but he pushed that into the corner of his mind and ignored it.

Dominic and Martine were dangling from their seat belts too. Though Martine was stirring with twitches and groans, Dominic wasn't moving at all.

"Dominic!" Levi said. Animal panic clawed at him when Dominic didn't respond. "*Dominic!*"

"He's alive," Martine rasped. "He's breathing."

Levi exhaled a shuddering breath. "Are you okay?"

"I'll live. You?"

"Same." For how much longer, though?

He heard approaching footsteps and men shouting back and forth to each other outside the car. Bracing one hand against the roof, heedless of the chunks of safety glass, he unbuckled his seat belt and slowly lowered himself flat. The gun Dominic had given him lay on the roof as well; he picked it up before squirming toward the broken window. On the other side of the car, Martine was doing the same.

A pair of legs appeared in Levi's field of vision. He fired, kneecapping the guy, and smiled viciously as the asshole crumpled to the ground with a shriek.

There were only a few rounds left in the mag, so he kept firing as he crawled out of the window, more to keep the men at bay than anything else. He knew there was no escape from this.

Once freed from the car, he dragged himself to his feet, glaring at the men who were gathering in a wary semicircle around him. He was sure he didn't look at all intimidating, banged-up and leaning against a flipped car for support, but if these fuckers wanted him alive, they were going to have a hell of a fight on their hands.

A loud cry sounded behind him, and he whirled around so fast that he stumbled and had to catch himself on the car. His heart seized.

Martine had been disarmed, and two men stood on either side of her—one restraining her arms, the other pressing a gun to her temple.

"Don't!" Levi dropped his gun and kicked it away without looking at it. "Please don't hurt her. I'll do whatever you want."

Martine shook her head, her eyes shining with tears. "Levi—"

The man ground the gun harder against her temple. She flinched and squeezed her eyes shut.

"Please," Levi said, more desperately. "She has children. I'll come with you; you don't have to hurt anyone."

"You'll cooperate?" asked the man with the gun.

"Yes. Just leave everyone else alone."

The man nodded to someone behind Levi. Remaining still while an enemy approached his unprotected back made Levi's nerves shriek in protest, but he held Martine's gaze, clinging to the knowledge that she would make it through this, and she'd take care of Dominic as well. That was enough for him.

Tears were spilling down Martine's cheeks now. *I'll find you*, she mouthed.

A hood was pulled over Levi's head, he felt a sting at his neck, and all was darkness.

Dominic heard the wail of sirens like it was coming down a long tunnel. He tried to move, but found his body strangely uncooperative; his limbs were floppy, his neck immobilized.

Fighting an onslaught of pain and nausea, he opened his eyes, squinting at the blurry image of a woman hovering over him. When he struggled again to get up, she placed a hand on his chest and said, "Don't move. You're in an ambulance; we're taking you to the hospital."

Ambulance? Hospital? *What?*

Something stiff covered half his face, making it difficult for him to speak. He clumsily batted the thing aside, and it became ten times harder for him to breathe.

"Levi," he croaked. That one word used all of the remaining oxygen in his lungs.

The woman resettled the mask on his face, her lips pursed and her eyes shadowed. "Just relax. We're almost there."

Where was Levi?

He wanted to ask again, but he passed out instead.

The next time he regained consciousness, it was with a sense of rapid movement, the hard surface beneath him vibrating uncomfortably. He opened his eyes and hissed at the blinding lights rushing by overhead. There were people all around him, their voices running into each other, so that he caught only garbled snippets of what they were saying.

"—stable airway—"

"—diminished breath sounds—"

"—normal saline—"

"Levi," Dominic said, but that fucking mask was still on his face. He reached for it.

Someone caught his hand halfway to his mouth. "Sir, please don't touch that," said a woman who leaned over to look in his eyes. "Can you hear me?"

He threw off her hand and knocked the mask aside. "Levi." He gasped, sucking in an agonizing, labored breath. "Levi."

"Sir, you have to stay still—"

Marshaling his strength, he tried to heave himself upright, though he was stymied by the same problems as before. The sense of motion stopped abruptly, and multiple pairs of hands grabbed him all over his body.

He shook them off, only for an even greater number of hands to grip his arms and legs. Loosing a strangled roar, he fought harder, flailing from side to side.

"For God's sake, keep him still!"

"*How?*"

"His spine—"

More people surrounded him on every side, laying the lengths of their bodies across his legs, his hips, his chest. *They were trying to keep him from Levi.*

He went berserk, shouting incoherently, thrashing against the restraining bodies with all his might. He had to get to Levi. Nobody was going to stop him.

"Get me 10 mgs of haloperidol *stat*."

Dominic kept fighting, but soon faltered as the energy drained from his limbs and his brain went fuzzy. He moaned in protest.

He had to get to Levi. He had to . . . He had . . . He . . .

Levi had no idea where he was or how much time had passed since he'd been taken, but there were a few things he knew for certain.

First, these men were not worried about him seeing their faces. They'd removed the hood before he'd woken up, and there were half a dozen of them in the windowless, featureless room where he was being kept. They were sitting around a couple of folding tables by the door, drinking beer and chewing tobacco while they played cards.

Second, Utopia had learned their lesson about underestimating him. He was zip-tied to a sturdy, armless chair, his wrists bound together behind its back—which was torture for his burned forearms and bruised muscles—and his ankles bound separately to the chair's front legs. The chair itself was set near the wall farthest from the door, though not close enough for the wall to be used as leverage. Two surveillance cameras mounted in opposite corners were monitoring the room.

Third, he was completely and royally *fucked*.

He couldn't allow himself to wonder if his kidnappers had kept their promise about not hurting Martine, or if Dominic had made it out of the car alive. The only way he wouldn't lose his shit was to maintain focus exclusively on the present moment.

He pretended to phase in and out of consciousness for a while, taking stock of the situation without tempting any of the men to interact with him. The gambit paid off, because these guys were talkers.

Levi's capture wasn't the only reason they were in high spirits. They were excited, almost giddy, about something going down later tonight, something that would "change everything" and "make our voices heard." A couple of the guys bemoaned not being able to join the riots—*what* riots?—while others gleefully theorized about how the city would react to another explosion. Their conversation was peppered with self-righteous zealotry and smug anticipation.

Levi didn't need to be a detective to piece together Utopia's plan for tonight. They were repeating the success they'd had in using a distraction to interfere with the response to their main threat, except this time, they'd be inciting riots as a diversion from a second bomb. From what he could tell, this explosion would be far worse than the one at the Mirage.

He absorbed as much information as possible, but he could only remain motionless for so long. Eventually, the misery of his bonds forced him to shift, searching in vain for a less excruciating position.

The movement caught the attention of one of his captors, who swung around toward him. "Look who's awake."

These men were the same Nazi prick template copy-and-pasted onto bodies of various heights and builds, with little to distinguish them from one another. The one who'd noticed Levi's return to consciousness had a giant tattoo covering his upper left arm, a glaring bald eagle perched on a Christian cross. *Tasteful.*

Tattoo approached Levi's chair, accompanied by two buddies—one with a wispy goatee and another who'd been recently sunburned. The rest of the men remained at the folding tables.

Levi abandoned all pretense of unconsciousness and lifted his chin, staring straight ahead.

"Nothing to say?" said Tattoo.

Levi met the man's eyes but kept his mouth shut.

Goatee stepped closer. "There's a bet going about who's going to be the one to kill you, you know. Hatfield wants the whole thing filmed, but he hasn't decided who gets the honors."

Clenching his jaw, Levi rode out the surge of panic that coursed through his body. "Is that why you've been trying to take me alive?" he asked when he could speak without inflection. "Seems like a bad idea."

He'd rather provoke them into killing him here and now than have his murder put on the internet for Dominic, Martine, and his *parents* to see.

Goatee snorted. "Worked pretty well. Nobody knows where you are, and nobody's gonna find out. Except maybe the Seven of Spades—but we're counting on that."

Levi frowned as the men snickered and exchanged self-congratulatory looks. "You're . . . using me as *bait*?" He couldn't keep the incredulity out of his voice, though it shouldn't have been much of a surprise. Utopia had always had a hard-on for being the ones to take out the Seven of Spades. They believed—not without merit—that doing so would vault them to the highest levels of status and intimidation.

"We heard the Seven of Spades is that pretty-boy defense lawyer. Everyone knows he'll try to find you. And if he manages it . . . well." Sunburn mimed firing a gun with his fingers. "We'll be ready."

"I'm sure your friends in North Las Vegas thought the same thing."

Goatee lunged forward and backhanded Levi across the face, whipping his head to the side and splitting his lip.

Worth it.

He ran his tongue over his bloodied lip and smirked as he raised his head. "The Seven of Spades has slaughtered more than fifty people by this point, and you want to lure him right to you? How stupid can you be?"

"Watch your mouth, cocksucker." Goatee gripped both sides of Levi's jaw, yanking his head up; the other two assholes crowded closer.

"He's going to kill you all," Levi said, with far more bravado than he felt. There were too many variables. *If* Sawyer was the Seven of Spades, *if* enough time had passed for him to be released from custody, *if* he cared enough about Levi to risk himself, *if* he was able to slip his police detail, *if* he could locate this safe house . . .

Goatee gave Levi's head a hard shake. "You wanna be gagged, is that it?"

Taking a page out of Utopia's playbook, Levi spat in his face. Goatee jerked backward, crying out, and scrubbed at his face way more frantically than was necessary—probably desperate to fend off those gay Jew cooties.

Tattoo replaced him, grabbing Levi's throat instead and squeezing until Levi grunted. He tipped Levi's head back and eyed him speculatively. "Maybe we should give him something better to do with his mouth."

Levi didn't understand what he meant until Sunburn shot him a disgusted look and said, "You queer now too?"

The ice-cold realization made Levi jerk back instinctively, but Tattoo only tightened his clutch on Levi's throat. Levi breathed shallowly through his nose.

They couldn't be serious. Neo-Nazis were too homophobic to even consider sexually assaulting a male captive.

Weren't they?

"Hell, no," said Tattoo, in answer to his friend's taunt. "But how different can one mouth be from another?"

Sunburn's disgust didn't fade, but Goatee narrowed his eyes. "You seen that giant animal he gets on his knees for? Bet he learned real quick not to choke on a horse-cock like that guy's probably got."

"That true, bitch?" Tattoo put more pressure on Levi's throat. "Pervert like you must love sucking cock, huh? Don't even matter whose it is."

Levi shuddered, swallowing a whimper that wanted to escape. He'd never felt this brand of sick terror. Even when he'd been attacked in college, those men hadn't threatened him with sexual violence.

He felt a healthy amount of fear when his life was in danger—he wasn't crazy—but that fear was always tempered by experience, by confidence in his abilities, by the knowledge of how much damage he could take and keep going. This, though? This was a different monster entirely, and he had no defenses against it.

"Stop fucking around," Sunburn said. "He'd bite your dick off before he'd suck it."

"I don't think so. Not if he knew we'd go get our kicks with his pretty piece of jailbait in Henderson instead."

"No," Levi choked out, squirming in Tattoo's grip. The thought of these depraved pigs putting their hands on Adriana . . . No fucking way. He'd suck every cock in this room and beg for more if that's what it took to keep her safe.

"Would you morons cut that gay shit out?" yelled one of the men near the door. "You know you're not supposed to be that close to him. We're not even supposed to talk to him!"

There were a few terrifying moments in which the men debated their options, before Tattoo released Levi's throat with a huff and all three of them retreated.

Levi dropped his head, taking shaky breaths and concentrating on calming his roiling stomach. All of his muscles were watery, and his skin was crawling from head to foot.

After that, the men mostly ignored him, and were far more circumspect in their conversations amongst themselves. They rotated in and out of the room as time passed; at one point, Levi was offered bottled water through a straw.

His pain worsened, clouding his mind with a red haze, until it was the only thing he could think about. So when the lights went out, he thought he was losing consciousness.

But the other men in the room were exclaiming in confusion, their radios squawking with static. "Hey!" one of them shouted into his unit. "We lost the lights up here."

"Us too," responded a crackling voice. "Power's out to the whole warehouse."

"What—"

There was an ominous moan of clanging metal, and then the sprinkler system went off, showering the room with cold water. Levi flinched, spitting out his accidental mouthful, and turned his face aside, squeezing his eyes shut against the sudden downpour.

The men spluttered, yelling back and forth to each other as they scrambled around the room, trying to figure out how to stop the sprinklers. Levi heard the door slam open and shut.

Rat-tat-tat-tat.

Levi stiffened at the distant burst of automatic gunfire—but it was drowned out when the warehouse's speaker system erupted with a deafening cacophony that couldn't really be called music. It sounded like two screechy heavy metal tracks being played over one another.

He squinted through the gloom and pouring water, watching his captors hold their hands over their ears the way he wished he could. Their mouths were moving, but he couldn't hear them over the din; he doubted they could hear each other either. Another one darted out of the room, leaving only three behind with Levi.

Law enforcement wouldn't use these tactics. Cutting the power, sure. Setting off the sprinkler system and blasting the warehouse with what could have been the soundtrack to Hell itself? No. They would have used smoke grenades and flashbangs.

This was the Seven of Spades.

Levi's stomach churned as he experienced two wildly divergent reactions simultaneously: relief and bone-deep terror. He wasn't sure which one he was supposed to feel. *Was* there an appropriate emotional reaction to being rescued from certain death by a serial killer?

The music cut off abruptly, leaving his ears ringing. The other men tentatively lowered their hands.

"Looks like you got what you wanted," Levi called over the patter of the still-falling water. "He's here."

The men exchanged frightened glances. More gunfire sounded, closer this time—and now, in between Utopia's rifles, Levi could make out the report of a single, powerful handgun. It fired much less frequently, indicating that the shooter was privileging quality over quantity. And every time that gun went off, somebody screamed.

Levi grinned. "Sounds like he's *pissed*."

The sprinklers shut off with a strained creak, but the lights were still out.

"Stay here," one of the men said to Goatee.

"Wait—"

His two buddies charged out of the room, guns drawn. Goatee was the only one who remained with Levi.

The "music" started again, even louder this time. Unable to shield his ears, Levi could only grimace and ride it out. Seconds later, the lights began flickering rapidly, like a strobe light in a nightclub; the music cut in and out erratically, switching tracks and sliding up and down in volume at random. The resulting disorientation was nauseating.

In between bursts of music, the gunshots and screaming drew ever closer, and more unintelligible shouts and groans and curses came over Goatee's radio. Goatee paced back and forth, his gun shaking in his hand.

Just one guy. Even injured, Levi could so easily take one guy. If only he weren't bound and helpless—

Well, he wasn't gagged, was he? There had to be some way he could drive Goatee into a frothing panic, maybe enough to make the guy run. But his power, his strength, was all in his body—not his words.

Okay. So what would Dominic do?

The next time the music stopped, Levi said, "All of your friends are dying out there, you know."

Goatee whirled on him. "Shut up!"

"You thought your little cult was something special?" Levi scoffed. "The Seven of Spades will massacre you all and never even break stride."

Goatee stomped over, raising his gun threateningly. "I said shut your mouth!"

"He's coming for me," Levi said, holding the man's gaze. "He'll be here any second. *And he's going to kill you.*"

The lights came back on.

Goatee blinked, shaking his head, and groaned in pure animal terror. He turned and ran for the door—but he didn't have time to reach it before it flew open.

Natasha shot him point-blank.

CHAPTER 16

"I'm a social worker, Levi. I'll always be in victim advocacy."

2011

Natasha rapped on the back door of a run-down house, her gaze raking the disused toys littering the yard and the dead flowers in the window box. The occupants of this house hadn't spent time outside in weeks.

The door opened a crack, and a suspicious eye peered out.

"I'm alone, Crystal," said Natasha.

The door swung open the rest of the way, revealing a skinny white woman whose face, throat, and arms bore the mottled yellow remnants of old bruises. "I need money," she said without preamble.

Natasha gave her Smile #3, *Patient and Understanding*. "Why don't I come inside so we can discuss some community resources?"

Crystal Merritt stepped aside to let Natasha into the kitchen. It was scrupulously clean, which only drew more attention to the cracked linoleum and peeling wallpaper. Crude crayon drawings were tacked up on the refrigerator, and a handful of scraggly daisies were wilting in a vase on the counter.

"Are the girls at school?" Natasha asked, though she already knew the answer.

"They . . ." Crystal's eyes darted shiftily to her left. "They stayed home sick."

Natasha nodded. "According to their principal, they've been sick a lot recently."

This wasn't really part of Natasha's job. She was Crystal's victim advocate, assigned to help Crystal through the process of prosecuting her husband for aggravated assault. But all of the other social service agencies involved with the family had taken a step back, turned off by Crystal's pattern of aggressive behavior intermixed with tearful self-pity, which had left Natasha in a sort of case-manager role.

Natasha didn't mind. One irritating person was more or less the same as the next.

"I'm afraid to let them go to school." Crystal walked to the kitchen table, snatched a pack of cigarettes, and tipped one into her palm. "Eugene would grab them there and take them away just to spite me. You know he would."

"We can discuss measures with the school to make sure that doesn't happen."

Crystal's hand shook as she lit her cigarette and took a long drag. Natasha kept her reaction off her face with the ease born of a lifetime of practice. So Crystal needed money, but she had enough to indulge an expensive habit that would slowly kill her and her two children?

Natasha would never say that aloud, of course. It wasn't an empathetic response. It wasn't something a social worker would say.

"I don't trust the school," Crystal said. "They're on his side. Everybody is."

Coaxing Crystal to sit at the table with her, Natasha asked, "What makes you say that?"

Crystal launched into her usual litany of complaints, which Natasha could safely tune out. They were always the same, from one person to the next: *Blah blah blah, my life is so hard, nobody understands me, blah blah blah.* Boring.

At one point, the two young girls ran into the kitchen, only to shrink back when they realized their mother wasn't alone. They were quiet, big-eyed waifs, traumatized by years of watching their father beat their mother. Natasha drew them out a bit, got them smiling, and handed them a couple of small toys from the supply she brought on every home visit.

She liked children; for the most part, they hadn't learned to be terrible yet. Ezra had been dropping hints lately about trying for a child of their own, and that might not be a bad idea. It was what a normal person would do.

The girls were playing happily on the kitchen floor when the conversation came back around to money. "I don't know how anyone expects me to be able to take care of my kids *and* get all these work hours in," Crystal said. She tapped her cigarette ash into a glass. "It's impossible without any help."

"Well, there are some local resources available for low-income single mothers—"

Bang bang bang!

Crystal and her daughters jumped and shrieked at the sudden violent hammering on the back door. Natasha, who'd never had a startle response, faked the same reaction a half second later.

"Crystal!" a man bellowed from outside. "Let me in! I know you've got a guy in there."

White-faced, Crystal dropped her cigarette and scrambled to her feet. Natasha stood as well, pulling out her phone to call 911.

She never got the chance. The door slammed, shook, and then cracked, the wood splintering around the flimsy lock. Crystal screamed as her husband charged inside.

Merritt was a big, burly guy, with the stench of whiskey billowing off him in waves. He swept Natasha out of his path, knocking her into the kitchen table. Her phone fell out of her hand and slid beneath the oven.

"Where is he?" Merritt grabbed Crystal by the throat. "Whose car is that outside, slut?"

She gasped, scrabbling at his hand. "Nobody's! It's just the social worker's!"

"Don't lie to me!" He drove Crystal into the far wall, lifting her onto the balls of her feet.

Natasha judged the distance between him and the place her phone had disappeared. He was far stronger than her, and if he saw her trying to call the police, he might turn on her instead. She couldn't put herself in the vulnerable position of lying on the floor to retrieve her phone, but she didn't know where Crystal kept her own cell, and the house had no landline.

Crystal met Natasha's gaze over Merritt's shoulder, her eyes wide and pleading. She looked deliberately at her sobbing children, then back at Natasha. Her entreaty couldn't have been more clear.

Natasha swept up both girls and ran.

She'd been in this house once before. It was small, all on one story, with two bedrooms in the back. She raced to the farthest one, kicked the door shut behind her, and stuffed the girls into the closet, ignoring their hysterical wails. Then she shoved a chair underneath the doorknob so the closet couldn't be opened from the inside.

A racket of crashes, thuds, and bangs sounded from the kitchen, accompanied by Merritt's deep shouts and Crystal's higher-pitched screams. As Natasha approached the bedroom door, debating her options, there came a single ear-piercing shriek, followed by an abrupt silence.

Wary, she opened the door and slipped into the hallway. She crept back toward the kitchen, and when she got closer, she heard the sound of a man crying.

Natasha rounded the kitchen doorway. Crystal was sprawled in a pool of her own blood on the linoleum, her open, sightless eyes turned in Natasha's direction. Merritt was crouching by her side, his back to Natasha; there was a bloody kitchen knife on the floor a few feet behind him, as if it'd been thrown.

"Crystal!" Merritt shook her shoulders. "Come on, baby, wake up. You know I didn't mean it. Stop playing around."

Crystal didn't respond. But then, dead people so rarely did.

With an angry roar, Merritt slapped her face. "Stop fucking with me, bitch!" That didn't work either, of course, and he broke down in sobs.

Natasha padded into the kitchen, staring at the mess of what had been a living, breathing woman only a few minutes ago. Besides the funeral of a great-aunt, Natasha had never been in the presence of a dead body before. Merritt must have stabbed something vital for Crystal to bleed out so quickly.

She scooped the knife off the floor. It was lightweight in her grip, still dripping red.

Merritt spun around on his knees and saw Natasha. His hands and clothes were soaked with blood.

"I didn't mean to," he said. "You gotta—you gotta tell the cops that." Struggling to his feet, he swiped at his puffy eyes, which only smeared the blood over his face. "She just made me so crazy, you know? But I didn't mean to kill her."

"She was your wife," Natasha said quietly. "Your children's mother."

"I know." Merritt glanced at Crystal over his shoulder. "I didn't mean to, I swear. If she'd just—"

Natasha drove the knife into his stomach.

He didn't scream. Instead, he made a sort of liquid burble, his eyes going round and shocked as he looked down at the knife in his guts and then up at her face.

She twisted the blade—just a little, just to see what would happen. He choked, jerking and swaying on his feet.

When she pulled out the knife, he collapsed to his knees, clutching his abdomen with both hands. That did little to stem the tide of blood that poured from his ravaged organs.

"Why?" he whispered, before he toppled over onto his side.

She hadn't planned to stab him, but watching him writhe on the floor, she felt something click into place that she hadn't even known was missing.

This was *right*. This was the way things were supposed to be.

Merritt tried to pull his cell phone out of his pocket, but it slipped from his blood-slicked hand. She kicked it away and then stepped out of his reach—she wasn't stupid.

"Please," he said through foam-flecked lips. "You could still call 911. I won't tell anyone. Please."

"Why would I do that?" She walked around him, cocking her head. "You deserve this. You understand that, don't you?"

He shook his head.

"You vowed to love Crystal, to protect her, and then you beat her for years until you took her life. How long would it have been before you did the same to your children, or another woman?" Knife in hand, Natasha squatted by his side. "Now you'll never hurt anyone again. The world will be a better place without you."

And *she'd* been the one to ensure that. She was the reason Merritt's life was draining away on the same floor where he'd slaughtered his wife. Merritt had ended Crystal's life, so Natasha had ended his. It was a far more appropriate fate than the one that would have been handed to him by the so-called "justice" system.

This—this was true justice.

The rush of it was sharp, electric, like the free-fall of a roller coaster. Her eyelids fluttered, and she flexed her tingling hand around the knife handle.

Merritt tried to speak again, but all he could manage was a raspy grunt. He looked at her with those big dumb eyes, crying like the woman-beating coward he was.

Ugh, he was ruining it. She grasped his chin and turned his face in the opposite direction.

Better.

It didn't take long. The flow of blood became sluggish; his breathing slowed, stuttered, and stopped. Soon, he was no longer moving at all. She rested the fingers of her free hand against his pulse.

Dead.

A shudder coursed through her body. For the first time in her life, she felt whole.

The wail of police sirens broke through her reverie, and she lifted her head. One of the neighbors must have heard the commotion and called 911. She was lucky nobody had tried to enter the house.

Scanning the kitchen, she assessed the situation. Nobody would suspect the truth of what had happened here; she could sell Merritt's death as self-defense, no problem.

Well . . . one problem.

She considered her pale, unmarked hands and arms, then shrugged and raised the knife. Good thing she'd seen so many defensive wounds in her career.

The knife stung as it bit a random pattern of slashes and cuts into her skin, but the adrenaline high rendered the pain negligible. She was more concerned by the possibility that Crystal or Merritt might have had a blood-borne illness, though that couldn't be helped at this point.

When she finished, she looked like she'd struggled with Merritt for the knife before being forced to use it to defend herself. She dropped the knife on the floor, smeared the blood over her clothes, and ran her sticky hands over her face and into her hair for good measure. Then she returned to the bedroom where she'd left the children.

They were still trapped in the closet, crying at the tops of their lungs. She moved the chair to its original position, sat on the floor, and leaned against the closet door just as she heard a shout of "Police!" from the other side of the house.

She'd need a reason she hadn't called 911 herself— Ah, of course.

Having often been in the presence of traumatic dissociation, she could fake a reasonable approximation of catatonia. She let her limbs go slack, blanked her expression, and unfocused her eyes, staring into space.

The sound of running footsteps was followed by a man's loud and creative cursing. Natasha didn't bother trying to attract the cop's attention; the girls' hysterical crying would draw him right to them.

He appeared in the doorway a few seconds later—a wiry, uniformed cop with curly black hair and cheekbones like the edge of a cliff. When he saw Natasha, he cleared the rest of the room before holstering his gun and crouching in front of her.

"Ma'am? Can you hear me?"

He touched her face gently, then laid his fingers against her pulse. She didn't respond.

"How badly are you hurt?" As he examined her bloodied arms, studying what seemed to be a tell-tale pattern of defensive wounds, fury flashed across his face—not too unusual. Most cops would be angered by finding an injured woman at a crime scene.

Then his brow furrowed, and he glanced over his shoulder as if recalling what he'd seen in the kitchen. Natasha imagined it from his perspective: a bruised woman stabbed to death, a large man lying dead beside her, and a second woman hiding in a back room, traumatized and covered in cuts.

As she'd intended, there was only one realistic conclusion that could be drawn. And that's when she saw it.

He smiled.

It was brief but unmistakable—a swift, vicious twist of his lips, there and then gone. For one moment, however fleeting, he'd been *glad* she killed Merritt.

Interesting.

His attention returned to the din the girls were making in the closet. "Are there kids in there?" he asked Natasha, though he didn't wait for a response. "I need to move you so I can get them out, okay? I'm not going to hurt you."

He lifted her with astonishing strength for such a thin man, moved her over a few feet, and set her carefully back down. When he opened the closet door, he stayed low to the ground, speaking to the girls inside in quiet, soothing tones.

Things happened quickly after that. The cop took the girls out of the house, and shortly afterward, paramedics arrived to attend to Natasha. She decided to continue the ruse of dissociation for now, as it prevented anyone from asking her questions and made it easier for her to keep tabs on the situation.

Eventually, the paramedics brought her outside, sitting her on the back edge of an ambulance while the cops took photographs of her arms and hands. The house was surrounded by police cars and yellow tape, and the entire neighborhood was out in force, clustered as close to the scene as they could get while they whispered to each other excitedly.

The responding officer was among the cops maintaining the perimeter. He was more successful than most, because one icy glare from him was enough to dampen the enthusiasm of the nosiest busybody. Intrigued, Natasha watched him prowling the edges of the crime scene like an angry panther.

She'd become a social worker to better understand human behavior, and that had been after decades of surviving on her own self-taught observations. This man was hypervigilant in a way she'd rarely seen, not to mention so tense that he looked like his spine would snap if he moved too abruptly. She would bet her degree that he'd experienced something terrible—something he'd pretended to recover from, but that had left deep scars on his psyche.

Yet he'd been so gentle with Natasha and the little girls. When Crystal's sister ran up to the tape, screaming and sobbing, he was the one who held her as she collapsed in hysterics. And as the paramedics were loading Natasha into the ambulance for transport, he came over to ask them how she was doing.

He was a bundle of contradictions. Natasha had always enjoyed puzzles.

The cop was turning away. "Wait," Natasha said, her voice small and meek. When he turned back, looking surprised, she added, "I don't want to be alone. Will you come with me? Please?"

"Sure," he said without hesitation. He jumped into the back of the ambulance with her and one of the paramedics. "What's your name?"

"Natasha."

He smiled. "Nice to meet you, Natasha. I'm Levi."

CHAPTER  17

Present

Natasha touched a small device in her left ear. "I've got him, Carmen." She stepped into the room and shut the door. "Can you keep an eye on the rest of the building for me? Thanks."

Levi stared at her. "Natasha, what are you doing here? You're going to get hurt."

She blinked several times, looked at the dead man at her feet, and glanced over her shoulder at the closed door. Then she turned back to him and raised her eyebrows.

"No." He laughed at the pure ridiculousness of it all, shaking his head. "No. No."

Her gaze remained steady on his.

"*No*," he said, his voice cracking. "No." He could barely draw his next breath. "No!"

"I'm sorry. I didn't want you to find out this way, but I couldn't trust anyone else to come get you, not with that bounty on your head."

Water splashed onto his lips, which were already damp from the sprinkler system. He licked it away and distantly noticed how much saltier it was now. And when had it gotten so cold in here?

"No," he said again, because that was the only word he could remember.

Then Natasha started toward him, and suddenly he remembered a *lot* more words.

"Don't fucking touch me!" He lurched violently backward, tipping his chair onto its rear legs. It hit the wall and slammed back down, jarring his bound body.

"Okay." Natasha raised her hands, one of which was still holding the gun. "Okay."

God, it was *freezing* in here; his teeth were chattering. "I want to hear you say it."

She frowned, then bit her lip as comprehension dawned. "Levi..."

"*I want to hear you fucking say it!*"

Her eyes fell briefly shut. When she opened them, she nodded and squared her shoulders. "I'm the Seven of Spades."

A low, agonized moan scraped the skin off Levi's throat as he crumpled in on himself. He dropped his forehead to his knees, heedless of the strain it put on his back and arms, twisting his spine like he could evade the truth if he just contorted his body the right way.

Something terrible was writhing in his gut, a spiny, many-legged insect shredding his insides as it fought to claw its way out of him. Noxious, oily rage filled his mouth and coated his throat, so thick he choked on it. Still hunched over, he rocked fitfully back and forth.

"Levi." Natasha's footsteps sounded on the floor, drawing closer. "We can't stay here. Utopia will send reinforcements."

He sensed her reaching for him and jerked his head up, snarling like a feral animal. "Don't untie me."

"But we—"

"If my hands are free, I *will* kill you."

She snatched her own hands back and retreated a few steps. After a moment of silence, she said, "I appreciate your honesty. There's only so long we can wait, though. Carmen has control of the warehouse's security system, but we'll have to move eventually, or we'll get pinned down here."

He forced himself to look at her straight-on. What he wanted to see was a stranger, a monster wearing Natasha's face, speaking with her voice. Someone unrecognizable beyond the surface level who'd managed to fool him all this time.

All he saw was the Natasha he'd known for years—the same calm demeanor, the same gently concerned expression. The only unfamiliar thing about her was the gun she was holding. In every other way, she was the woman who'd become his trusted confidante. The friend whose house he'd visited countless times. The peer counselor he'd leaned on for support in his darkest hours.

The serial killer with one of the highest body counts in modern history. The nightmare who'd stalked and harassed and tormented him. The psycho who'd forced Dominic to murder an unconscious man.

He groaned and shook his head frantically. The sick fury inside him was tearing at his stomach lining, ripping him apart, about to burst free any moment. It would turn him inside out, and if that happened, he would lose himself forever.

Tilting his head back, he took several shaky breaths. These circumstances were far more dire than his own emotional reactions, however profound. The city needed him—*him*, Detective Levi Abrams, not whatever shadow of himself he'd become if he flew into a homicidal rage or surrendered to despair. He had to stay in control.

When he focused on Natasha again, she was watching him warily. He decided to try a few simple, factual questions, hoping a rational approach would help stabilize him.

"Does Carmen know who you are?" he asked.

"Yes. I told her the truth after I extracted her from police custody."

Levi didn't bother asking for Carmen's location; wherever she was would be far beyond his reach. Instead, he remembered a conversation he'd had with Natasha after he killed Dale Slater, in which she'd empathized with him over an experience they'd ostensibly had in common. "When you killed Merritt, was it really self-defense?"

"No," she said quietly. "He did kill Crystal, but he never tried to kill me. I took him by surprise and watched him die. Then I inflicted my own defensive wounds."

So even their very first meeting had been based on a lie. Levi cracked his neck and tried to control his voice when he spoke again. "Was he the first person you killed?"

"Yes."

She didn't seem to plan on saying anything more, but he glowered at her in silence until she gave in. Sighing, she dragged over one of his dead captors' chairs, sat in front of him, and crossed her legs, resting her gun on her top knee.

"I didn't think I'd do it again, you know. It was supposed to be a one-time thing, a perfect storm of circumstances that couldn't be repeated. But once I knew what it felt like . . ." She paused, gazing into the distance. "I couldn't forget. It gnawed at me all the time, and the more I tried to ignore it, the worse it got. I *had* to capture that feeling again."

"The feeling of power over life and death?" Levi said in disgust.

She made a face. "No. The feeling of seeing true justice done."

"Vigilante murder isn't justice."

"And what *is* justice? A violent man escaping punishment altogether thanks to an expensive lawyer, or a mistake by the officer who arrested him? A rapist serving a handful of years in prison before being released for *good behavior*? Every day, people ruin others' lives with little to no consequences. Being the one to set that right, to balance the scales—it was a satisfaction I'd never known."

He'd had this argument with the Seven of Spades more than once. It was bizarre to hear the other side in Natasha's melodic voice, rather than the grating electronic tones of her voice-changer.

"So you kept doing it." He sorted the timeline in his head now that he knew the truth. "You found people who you believed deserved to die, killed them, and buried them in the desert. At first you stabbed them, the same way you'd killed Merritt, but when you realized you could use ketamine to immobilize your victims, it made it possible for you to slit their throats instead, which you found more gratifying. How am I doing?"

She inclined her head. "Accurate so far."

"Now, here's the problem, Natasha." He leaned forward. "If all you really cared about was enacting old-school, biblical justice, you would have just kept secretly burying your victims in the desert. Or you would have made their deaths look like suicides, accidents, random acts of violence—anything that would prevent suspicion from interfering with your crusade. You wouldn't have started dropping playing cards on their corpses like a *motherfucking psycho*!"

Though his voice had risen to a shout, Natasha was unfazed. She waited with an indulgent air while he reined himself back in.

"The only reason you would do that was if killing alone wasn't enough anymore," he said. "You needed people to know what you were doing. You wanted *credit* for it."

"Is it so unusual for a person to want their hard work acknowledged?" she asked, shrugging one shoulder.

"When that 'hard work' is slitting throats? Yeah, it's a little out there." He scoffed, deep and contemptuous. "I've said this before, and I'll say it again: there is a sickness inside you that's driven you to escalate things every single step of the way. Every murder had to be more dramatic than the one before. Every contact with the public or law enforcement had to be showier, more outrageous."

Natasha was scowling at him now, but that only spurred him on.

"It wasn't enough for you to be a killer. You had to be *immortalized*: a boogeyman, a national sensation, a living legend. The *Seven of Spades*." With a shake of his head, he sat back in his chair. "That's the kind of personality disorder that would take years to unpack. I doubt you truly care at all what your victims have done."

"That is *not* true." For the first time, irritation sparked in Natasha's voice, and her posture stiffened. "I've never killed an innocent person. I wouldn't."

"Would Keith Chapman agree with that?"

She recoiled like he'd shoved her, her nostrils flaring. "I didn't kill Keith."

"You framed him for your own crimes. You were his counselor. He trusted you, and you poisoned him—with the baked goods you bring to the office, I'm assuming?" Levi saw her subtle flinch and nodded. "You pumped him full of drugs, gaslighted him, and brainwashed him into believing he was a serial killer. He committed suicide, but you may as well have pulled that trigger yourself."

Natasha leapt from her chair, agitated, and paced behind it.

"You betrayed him." Levi wanted to rend and wound with every word. "Aren't you guilty of the very sin you punish in others?"

She whirled around. "Keith was weak. He was supposed to be a temporary diversion, a smokescreen. The case against him would have fallen apart in days, and he would have been fine. I couldn't have known he'd give up so easily."

"What about me, Natasha?" Levi's fury was receding, retreating to the deep well at his core where it always lived. Left in its place was nothing but a crushing hurt. "What did I do to deserve the pain you've caused me?"

"Levi . . ." The anger drained from Natasha's body, and she looked at him with sorrow in her eyes. "Everything I've ever done has been to help you."

His mouth fell slack. That wasn't a line she was spouting, or a game she was playing: she believed it. He could hear the sincerity ringing in her voice.

As he searched for a response, she jerked and turned her head to the side, touching her ear.

"How many?" she asked. "All right. Yes, thank you." Turning to Levi, she said, "We have to move. A van full of Utopia foot soldiers is approaching from the west."

He clenched his jaw.

"I know Utopia is planning something tonight, something big. The police can't be trusted, and by extension, neither can the FBI. But I know that both you and I would give everything to stop Utopia. So it's time for you to decide: Do you want to kill me more than you want to save Las Vegas?"

"No," he said. "Let's get out of here."

She holstered her gun on her hip, pulled a folding knife from her pants pocket, and sawed through his zip ties. He grunted at the burning pain in his shoulders as he brought his arms in front of his chest and stretched his spasming muscles.

"You should take the guard's gun," she said while she checked the magazine of her own.

"I can't trust that I would fire it." He stood, steadied himself, and shook out his limbs. "You've never used a gun before."

"I always have one on me, just in case. I've never needed to use it until today, but even with Carmen's help, I couldn't take on a warehouse full of armed gunmen with a knife." Natasha unzipped her military-style jacket, reached inside, and came out with a stun gun, which she handed to Levi. "Here. At least we know you won't hesitate to use this."

His pulse roared in his ears as he contemplated the stun gun. The knife with which she'd cut his zip ties couldn't have been the murder weapon that had slit so many people's throats—it wasn't nearly big enough.

But this? Odds were, this was the very stun gun Natasha had used to incapacitate Milo Radich when she'd taken him by surprise. The one she'd used to torture a confession out of Grant Sheppard in Philadelphia before stabbing him to death.

In that split second, there was nothing Levi wanted more than to jam the prongs into Natasha's neck and fire.

His hand flexed on the grip. When he looked up, she was watching him with an expression that said she knew exactly what he was thinking—but then, she'd always been good at that.

"Can you handle this?" she asked.

He swallowed. There was no place in his brain for vengeance right now. He only had two goals—protect the city, and get to Dominic. Everything else would have to wait.

"I'm good," he said.

Natasha led the way to the door, readied her gun, and rested her other hand on the doorknob. "All right, Carmen. We're ready for that exit."

When Dominic regained consciousness, he wasn't confused. He absorbed the antiseptic brightness of the hospital room, the scratchy sheets against his skin, the nauseating pain throbbing through his head. None of it mattered.

"Levi," he said.

Someone rested a hand on his arm. As he was turning his head—slowly, carefully—he realized that Rebel was draped over his legs at the foot of the narrow bed, and blinked. That was weird.

His mother's worried face peered down at him. "Oh, thank God, you're awake."

"Where's Levi?"

Rita exchanged a glance with someone on Dominic's other side. He did another painful turn, this time to the left, to see Carlos perched in a chair next to the bed.

"I'm gonna call Martine," Carlos said. "She wanted me to let her know the second you woke up."

He patted Dominic's shoulder and hurried out of the room, leaving silence in his wake. Rebel wriggled up the bed to lick Dominic's fingertips.

Dominic fixed his gaze on the ceiling. "If he's dead, just tell me," he said, the words ringing hollowly in his ears.

"He's not. At least, not as far as we know." Rita leaned over, stroking Dominic's forehead the way she had when he'd been sick as a child, though she avoided the part of his skull that hurt the worst. "Do you remember the car crash?"

"Yes." Oh, he remembered the crash, all right. He remembered that it had been his fault. He hadn't been paying attention, hadn't reacted to Martine's warning fast enough—

"Levi was taken from the scene. We haven't heard anything since then, good or bad."

"How long has it been?"

"About seven hours."

Dominic closed his eyes. Tears leaked from the corners and trickled down his temples.

"In this case, no news is probably good news." Rita rustled through her purse, then dabbed his face with a tissue. "The police issued a public statement claiming that Levi managed to escape the attack and leave the state, so very few people know the truth. After Utopia made such a fuss about wanting him alive, if they'd killed him—"

"They'd have splashed the news of their victory all over the city?" Dominic's voice was dull, lifeless.

She sighed. "Yes. But they've been quiet since the video this morning."

Rebel pushed her entire face into Dominic's hand, licking aggressively until he took a more active role and scratched under her chin. He opened his eyes and gave her a weak smile.

His mother was right. She *had* to be. If Utopia had killed Levi after they'd gotten their hands on him, they would have shouted it from the rooftops. Until that happened, he could operate under the safe assumption that Levi was still alive.

And he was *not* going to think about what they might be doing to Levi in the meantime.

"How'd you get Rebel in here?" he asked to distract himself.

"Jasmine convinced the staff that Rebel's an emotional support dog trained for combat veterans with PTSD. She had them all believing you might fly into some sort of violent flashback if you woke up without Rebel here."

He managed a faint chuckle. Though Rebel was trained for personal protection, not emotional support, in truth she fulfilled many of the same functions—even if PTSD wasn't one of his personal demons.

While he stroked Rebel's head, he took stock of his physical condition. His entire body ached deep into his bones, like—well, like he'd been in a bad car accident—but none of the pain was sharp or stabbing. The worst of it was in his head, mostly on the left side. The nausea and fatigue were significant yet manageable.

His unoccupied hand had an IV line taped to the back. He raised it to feel out the edges of the bandages on his head. "How badly am I hurt?"

"Nothing life-threatening, by the grace of God. The head injury is the worst of it. You have a concussion, and between that wound and some other lacerations, you lost a lot of blood. They gave you a transfusion."

"Broken bones? Internal bleeding?"

"No."

A vague memory of entering the hospital flashed through his mind. "Is there anything wrong with my spine?" He doubted it, since he could move all his extremities, but he had to ask.

Though Rita choked up when she spoke again, she was holding it together pretty well. "We were afraid there might be, but the doctors said everything looks fine."

Dominic took away one thing from this assessment: *mobile*. He eased himself into a sitting position, fought through the brief dizzy spell and surge of nausea, and reached for the IV line.

"Hey!" She grabbed his hand. "What do you think you're doing?"

He met her eyes. "I'm not going to sit on my ass in a hospital bed while Levi's being held prisoner by Nazis."

"I never thought you would," she said tartly. "You think I don't know my own son? But there's no need to go ripping out your IV and charging out of the hospital like some kind of barbarian."

He ducked his head, shamed in a way that only his mother could manage.

"They can't keep you here against your will. You'll sign the paperwork to leave against medical advice, treat the staff with respect, and be discharged properly like a grown man."

"Okay. I'm sorry."

She ran her fingers through his hair on the uninjured side of his head, a wistful smile crossing her face. "You're so much like your father. He'd be proud of you."

Dominic cleared his swelling throat. Rita patted his cheek, much more gently than she normally did, before standing.

"I'll go down to the nurses' station. You don't leave this bed until I get back, you hear?"

"Yeah. Thanks, Ma."

After she left, he raised the top half of his bed and slumped against it, grimacing. This concussion was even worse than the one he'd gotten when he'd been pistol-whipped protecting Levi last year. At this rate, the hospital should give him a punch card—your fifth concussion and your CAT scan is free.

Alone in the room save for Rebel, there was nothing to keep his mind off Levi, so he didn't try. As much as he hated to admit it, Levi's greatest hope right now rested with the Seven of Spades. Dominic couldn't believe the Seven of Spades would take this provocation lying down, and between their underworld connections and Carmen Rivera's technical assistance, they could find Levi faster than anyone else.

But if Sawyer really was the killer, he might still be stuck in police custody. Or, if he'd been released, he might have trouble slipping the tail the police would be sure to put on him. Once Dominic left the hospital, his best plan might be to track Sawyer down and lend his aid. He wouldn't hesitate to ally with the Seven of Spades if that's what it took to rescue Levi.

He was mulling that over, absently petting Rebel's head, when a shrill ringing drove spikes of pain through his skull. Glancing around, he saw his cell phone in a tray on the bedside table, snatched it, and immediately silenced the ringer.

The phone was scratched and dinged from the accident, with a nasty crack across the screen, but it obviously worked. He squinted at it before he answered, not recognizing the number. "Hello?"

"Dominic?" said an anxious voice. "Hi, it's Ezra Stone."

"Ezra? Um . . . hi." Dominic was taken aback by the call until he remembered his mother saying the police had lied about Levi's capture. Chances were, Ezra had no idea that Levi had been kidnapped or that Dominic was in the hospital.

"I'm sorry to bother you, but I've been calling everyone I know. Natasha never came home from her volunteer assignment today, and she hasn't been answering her phone. Nobody seems to know where she is. With everything going on in the city, I'm worried something terrible may have happened to her, and I know how good you are at finding people."

Ezra's voice became faster and more panicked with every word, aggravating Dominic's headache. "Whoa, slow down," Dominic said. "When was the last time you spoke to her?"

"This morning."

"Okay. She probably just got caught up in her volunteer work. Her phone may have run out of battery, or the service may be spotty where she is. You know it's been going in and out."

Dominic liked Natasha, but with Levi missing, he didn't have the mental energy to worry about anyone else. Natasha was smart and resourceful; she could take care of herself.

"I talked to her CERT supervisor. She checked in this morning and then vanished; nobody's seen her since. It's not like her at all. I *know* something terrible happened." Ezra's voice cracked like he was on the verge of tears. "These past few days have been a nightmare. Levi barely making it out of the city alive, and *Sawyer* being accused of being the Seven of Spades, I mean, *Jesus*—"

"Do you know Sawyer?" Dominic asked in bewilderment, because Ezra's tone implied a sense of personal betrayal.

"Yeah. We went to law school together—we used to be good friends, actually."

Dominic went absolutely still.

"We've drifted apart over the past few years, but I still find it hard to believe he could be a serial killer. I guess you never really know people the way you think you do." Ezra sighed. "After we graduated, we used to give each other crap about how we'd both gone into defense law, but for such different reasons. He'd call me a bleeding heart, and I'd say he'd sold his soul to the devil. Thinking back on it seems gruesome now."

"So . . ." Dominic's throat was bone dry; he licked his lips, swallowed, and tried again. "So after you graduated law school, you stayed in touch for a while? Discussed your cases?"

"Well, nothing that would break privilege. But we traded war stories, yeah. There was always something crazy going on at his firm."

Dominic clutched the bed rail with his free hand. Rebel sat upright, reflecting his tension in the stiff lines of her body.

"You said Natasha's been MIA since this morning?" Dominic asked, striving for a normal tone of voice.

"Yes. I have no idea where she could have gone."

Dominic wished he didn't, either. "This is going to sound weird, but it's important. Did you and Natasha go away for Christmas this past December?"

"Uh . . ." Though clearly puzzled, Ezra didn't question him. "No, we stayed in Vegas. It didn't make sense for us to travel for Christmas, because Natasha had to fly out for a social work convention in Chicago the day after."

The Seven of Spades had murdered Grant Sheppard in Philadelphia on December 27.

Dominic shut his eyes tightly; his stomach pitched and rolled, and it had nothing to do with his concussion. "I'll look for her," he heard himself say, his mouth speaking independently of his horrified brain.

"You will?" The bright hope that rang through Ezra's words twisted Dominic's heart inside out.

"I'll do everything I can to find her. I promise."

"Thank you so much, Dominic. I can't tell you how much I appreciate that."

Don't thank me yet, you poor son of a bitch.

Shell-shocked, Dominic ended the call, dropped the phone on the table, and stared at nothing. He was wrong. He *had* to be. It didn't make any sense.

Except he wasn't—and it did.

"Dom?"

He jerked his head up to see Martine in the doorway. Whatever expression was on his face made her snap to attention and take several quick steps into the room.

"What is it?" she asked.

He shook his head mutely, unable to speak the words aloud, and then winced as his dented skull reminded him what a bad idea that was.

She came closer to his bed. "I asked your mother and Carlos to wait outside for a minute so you and I could speak privately. They said you're leaving the hospital?"

"Yeah."

"I won't try to stop you, but . . ." Her lower lip quivered, and she made a helpless gesture with her hands, more defeated than he'd ever seen her. "I don't know what to do next. We've been combing the Valley for Levi all day; there's no trace of him anywhere. Then again, we have no way of knowing which of our own people might be working against us, or who can be trusted."

Struck by the horrific irony of her statement, he made a quiet, pained noise—one she misinterpreted as grief, judging by the way she reached out a comforting hand.

"We thought Sawyer might be our best bet, so we released him from custody this morning and kept his tail as discreet as possible, hoping he'd track Levi down on his own. But he just went back to his apartment and hasn't budged all day."

"Sawyer's not the Seven of Spades," Dominic said.

"What?"

"And we don't need to find Levi. All we need to do is find Natasha."

"Why Natasha?"

He still couldn't say it, so he looked at Martine, waiting for her to connect the dots on her own.

"Oh, come on," she said with a snorting laugh. "You can't be serious." When he didn't respond, the incredulous smile slid off her face like melting candle wax. "You're serious?"

"I need to get out of here." Dominic hit the call button for the nurse. "And I need a gun."

CHAPTER 18 ♠

Natasha had ditched her phone, maybe destroyed it, but she'd used her own car—either because she hadn't considered its GPS, or because she hadn't been able to get another ride before pursuing Levi. Dominic tracked it down in the time it took Martine to requisition their needed supplies.

They didn't tell anyone what they were doing or where they were going. Dominic hadn't wanted to risk returning to his own apartment, which ended up not being a big deal, because Martine was able to gear them both up with a minimum of explanation.

In fact, the substation was in such disarray that she could probably have just grabbed the stuff and walked out. The precarious balance of the past few days was crumbling, the city sliding into the chaos they'd feared since Utopia's first video. Across Las Vegas, vandalism, petty theft, and bar fights were escalating into Molotov cocktails, looting, and all-out street brawls.

Listening to the news on the radio, Dominic heard the same word repeated by one stunned reporter after another: *riots*.

Since Martine's car had been totaled in the accident, the LVMPD had assigned her an unmarked sedan from the motor pool. Dominic, who was in no shape to drive, inspected their weapons in the front passenger's seat, calmed by the familiar task of breaking down and reassembling a gun.

From the moment they'd left the hospital, he'd known that Martine was only humoring him. She didn't believe him about Natasha, and she was going along with him solely because she was out of other options.

He didn't blame her. If it wouldn't mean losing his best chance of finding Levi, he'd *want* to be wrong.

But he wasn't.

They found Natasha's car by the side of the road outside an industrial office complex in North Las Vegas. The area was deserted, which it might have been at this time of night even if the city weren't in a state of emergency. When Dominic, Martine, and Rebel got out to investigate, they saw no signs of life in any direction. The creepy twilit silence crawled across Dominic's skin, making his hands twitch around the grip of his gun.

Then they heard a spate of gunfire from deep within the complex. Dominic bolted in that direction, ignoring the jarring pain that reverberated through his neck and skull. Martine and Rebel kept pace with him on either side, slowing themselves down for his sorry injured ass.

Past several buildings, well out of sight of the road, was a two-story warehouse with a group of empty SUVs parked outside. A couple of the cars' doors stood open; three dead men lay crumpled on the sidewalk, their guns inches from their limp bodies.

Martine crouched by the nearest man and felt for his pulse, though there was no way any of these guys were still alive. She frowned as she looked over the others. "These men were all shot. No evidence of knife wounds."

"Even the Seven of Spades couldn't survive bringing a knife to this gunfight," Dominic pointed out.

As they quickly yet cautiously rounded the building, passing a few more dead men on their way, Dominic caught bright muzzle flashes through the second-story windows, along with the sound of more gunshots and shouting. God, if Levi was in there—

They were approaching the warehouse's rear door when it flew open and a terrified man ran out, sprinting like the hounds of hell were snapping at his heels. Before either Dominic or Martine could react, a bullet to the back took him down.

Natasha emerged from the warehouse, cool as a glacier, and lowered her gun with a small smile on her face.

Although Dominic had *known* he was right, he dropped his own gun to his side, swaying on his feet. Martine clutched his arm and exhaled an uneven moan like she'd been the one shot.

Another man sailed backward out the door, either kicked or thrown, and sprawled on the asphalt. Natasha spun around to shoot him too, but Levi darted out of the warehouse and shoved her gun arm aside.

The shot missed. Levi kicked the guy in the face, knocking him unconscious, and whirled on Natasha with an expression of utter fury. Then he saw Dominic and Martine and froze.

Heedless of the danger, Dominic rushed across the thirty feet that separated them. Levi did the same, meeting him halfway, where they clutched each other simultaneously.

"God, Dominic, your *head*," Levi said with horror. Angling the stun gun he held in one hand away from Dominic, he grazed the fingers of his other hand along the side of Dominic's face. "You should be in the hospital!"

"I'm fine." Dominic patted Levi down, searching for new injuries. "Did they hurt you?"

"No."

Dominic looked past Natasha, who was hanging back guardedly at the open door with her pistol still in hand. "Anyone else gonna come out of there?"

Levi shook his head. "They're all . . ." He glanced at Natasha. "Well, they're not going to be doing any more fighting today."

Now assured of Levi's safety, Dominic focused all of his attention on Natasha, pulling Levi slightly behind him. He felt Martine's presence at his shoulder, although she was deathly silent.

Natasha approached them, making no attempt to escape or hide the truth. "Did you find us through my car's GPS?" she asked. When Dominic nodded, she sighed. "I knew that might be a problem, but I didn't have time to find another solution."

Levi looked back and forth between them, his brow furrowing, before he stopped on Dominic. "You already . . . know? How?"

"Ezra called me, worried sick, because his wife hadn't been heard from all day." Dominic didn't take his eyes off Natasha as he spoke. "Then he told me an interesting story about how he and Jay Sawyer used to be law school classmates and good friends."

Stiffening, Levi turned back to Natasha.

"I'm assuming that's how you chose your earliest victims?" Dominic asked.

She gave a noncommittal shrug.

Rebel was huddled against Dominic's legs, hiding behind him with her ears pinned back, regarding Natasha fearfully. He'd only ever seen her afraid one time before.

"That's why Rebel wouldn't come out of our room the day we moved into our apartment. She's scared of you—you traumatized her when you wrecked my place." He stepped closer to Natasha, his anger growing. "What did you *do* to her?"

"Nothing!" Natasha appeared genuinely offended. "I would never hurt a dog."

Dominic snorted. "Right, of course. Because that would be crazy."

Martine, who had yet to say a word this entire time, lunged forward without warning and punched Natasha square in the face. There was so much force behind the blow that Natasha's head whipped to the side and she stumbled, barely catching herself on one knee.

"That's for giving my baby girls nightmares." Martine shook out her hand. There were tears in her eyes, but her voice was steady.

Natasha got back to her feet, stretching her jaw and gingerly touching her bloodied mouth. "Fair enough."

"You sure you're okay?" Martine asked Levi.

"Yeah. But we don't have much time."

"Until what?"

"Until Utopia makes good on their threat to rain down fire and sulfur," said Natasha.

Levi shot her a glare before addressing Dominic and Martine. "While Utopia had me, I overheard some of their plans for tonight. There's going to be a second bomb, bigger than the first, but I don't know where or when it'll go off. They're also planning to incite riots across the city beforehand to spread resources thin."

Fuck. "The riots have already started," Dominic said, and then addressed Natasha. "You always know more than we do. You really have no idea where the bomb is?"

"No. I've been getting all kinds of conflicting intel, nothing solid." She smoothed a stray lock of hair off her forehead. "Does anyone else know you're here?"

Though Dominic was fairly sure she wouldn't use this opportunity to try to kill them all and head for the hills, he hesitated before he said no.

"We couldn't trust anyone else not to betray Levi," Martine added, every word dripping a venom that didn't seem to affect Natasha at all.

"We still can't." Dominic rubbed Levi's back; he hadn't stopped touching Levi since they'd reunited. "Most of the city thinks you escaped this morning. We need to keep it that way."

Levi raised his eyebrows. "Well, I know you wouldn't say we should just walk away from this situation, so what *are* you saying? That we should take on an entire militia by ourselves?"

"How much choice do we have? We've gotta to do something to stop this, but we know for a fact that Utopia has agents inside the LVMPD and local government. There's a good chance the FBI is compromised as well. One word to the wrong person and it could be game over."

Martine had been glowering at Natasha since punching her in the face. "I think the wrong person's already standing here."

"At the very least, you must believe that I'd do anything to stop Utopia from launching another attack." Natasha spread her hands. "Who do you know who's hurt their organization more than I have?"

"Nobody, but then, I don't know anyone else willing to commit mass murder."

"They were Nazis," Natasha said dismissively. "Does that even count?"

Martine sucked in a breath, but Levi stepped between them before the situation could devolve further.

"Stop! We can't do this right now." He appealed to Martine. "I know how you're feeling, believe me. But if we can't trust the police or the FBI, Natasha is best positioned to help us. I just don't know what the four of us . . ." He looked down at Rebel, still cowering behind Dominic's legs. "The five of us can hope to accomplish on our own. We don't even know the full scope of Utopia's plan."

"Then we stop them from putting the plan into action at all," Natasha said.

"How?" Dominic's fingers flexed around his gun. He wasn't holstering his until she holstered hers.

"Cut off the head of the snake. Hatfield never left Las Vegas. Carmen found him hiding out at—"

"His mistress's condo Downtown?" Dominic said dryly.

Natasha did a double take. "Yeah. Damn, you *are* good. Anyway, if we kill Hatfield, it'll throw Utopia into chaos, demoralize them, disrupt their chain of command."

All three of them gaped at her.

She rolled her eyes. "Oh, what, you're shocked?"

"You are not killing anybody else today," Levi snapped. "In fact, we're trading weapons. Give me that gun."

They faced off for a few tense moments before Natasha made an exasperated noise and shoved the pistol into Levi's hand. He gave her the stun gun he was holding.

Natasha stowed the stun gun inside her jacket. "I hate guns anyway. They're a coward's weapon."

"As opposed to drugging someone's drink and slitting their throat from behind?" Dominic couldn't help saying.

While Natasha bristled, Levi rested a hand on Dominic's chest. "Dominic, stop. Please."

Seeing the profound hurt in Levi's eyes, Dominic shut his mouth. However betrayed he felt, it couldn't compare to the devastation that must be crushing Levi, and he wouldn't do anything to make this ordeal harder on Levi than it already was. He remained silent as he slipped an arm around Levi's waist to hold him close.

"It would be counterproductive to kill Hatfield, anyway," Martine said. "He'd have to know where the bomb is, right? If we could isolate him, interrogate him—"

"We might be able to stop it," Levi finished.

Natasha frowned. "Maybe. But that would mean infiltrating a neo-Nazi stronghold full of armed whack-jobs."

Shaking off the bizarreness of hearing sweet, socially conscious Natasha use such a contemptuous insult, Dominic said, "We're not equipped for that kind of operation."

"I could take care of that," she said. "But I'd need access to my storage unit, and the key is at my house. I can't go back there." She gestured to Dominic. "*You* could, though. Ezra asked you to look for me, right? He knows I have the unit; if you tell him you need to get in there, he'll give you the key, no problem."

Dominic scoffed at the mere idea. "I'm not leaving you alone with Levi and Martine."

"I wouldn't do anything to hurt them," she said impatiently.

Levi barked out a harsh laugh that sounded like glass going through a garbage disposal. It was a terrible noise, and Dominic tightened his arm around Levi in response, wishing he could draw out Levi's pain and take it on himself.

For the first time, remorse flickered across Natasha's face. She cleared her throat and bit her lip, briefly averting her eyes.

Rohan had been right. Natasha wasn't a true psychopath, at least not in a classic sense. If she could feel bad about what she'd done to Levi, that meant she could empathize with him to some extent—which meant she wasn't totally soulless. She was just super fucking messed up.

She recovered herself and said, "Fine. But Levi can't go, for obvious reasons. Martine?"

"It would risk someone picking up my trail and following me. Especially if Ezra told anyone why I stopped by, which I wouldn't be able to warn him not to do."

"Then we need somebody else," said Dominic.

"There *isn't* anybody else. Even the people we could almost definitely trust not to betray Levi, like Denise or Wen, would never be okay with an extra-legal operation, let alone *this*." Martine flapped a hand in Natasha's direction. "Or they could be followed right to us. What we need is a person Levi's enemies wouldn't think to track, who'd keep Levi's confidence, would be willing to operate outside the bounds of the law, wouldn't be fazed by working with a serial killer, and could handle themselves if things go sideways. We don't know anyone like that."

Dominic and Levi both blinked, looking at each other as they came to the same conclusion.

Levi's lips quirked. "Yes, we do."

Despite the tight fit, all five of them squeezed into Natasha's car. Martine sat in the front passenger seat, her gun aimed unambiguously at Natasha while the latter drove. Dominic sat in the middle of the back—not ideal, given his dimensions, but he needed to be close to both Levi and Rebel.

Although Natasha's storage unit wasn't far from the warehouse, the drive was interminable. Martine was seething with a quiet fury that poured off her in waves, her expression so forbidding that Dominic worried she might just shoot Natasha and be done with it. Levi, on the other hand, was slumped against the door, gazing dully out the window like all the life had been sucked out of him.

Dominic could only tolerate that miserable silence for so long before he had to break it. "The Seven of Spades texted me while you and I were having a conversation," he said to Natasha. "How'd you pull that off?"

"Carmen was the one who texted you."

Fuck. Of course.

Natasha's eyes met his in the rearview mirror. "I'd just found out that Stanton had been kidnapped, and it was only a matter of time before the mercenaries would contact Levi. I knew he'd go charging off after Stanton, and if he didn't have you to rely on, he'd go alone. So I needed you two to reconcile quickly. I didn't think either of you suspected me, but I figured I might as well use the opportunity for misdirection anyway."

"You sought me out at the casino and gave me that whole pep talk just so I'd go to Levi before he found out about Stanton?"

"Yes."

Dominic rocked back, his hand stilling in the act of stroking Rebel's head. She whined in protest and pushed her face against his fingers.

It wasn't an exaggeration to say that conversation with Natasha had changed the course of his life. It was what had broken him out of the denial of his relapse, what had driven him in search of Levi so they could hash things out once and for all. To know that entire situation had been engineered with an ulterior motive . . .

Dominic glanced sideways. Levi had his eyes shut now, and Dominic might have thought he was sleeping, if not for the fact that his body was more tense than before.

"There's something else, something that's been bothering me for a year." Dominic rubbed Rebel's silky ear to keep himself calm. "Matthew Goodwin had skipped bail and was on the run. How could you possibly have earned his trust enough for him to bring you back to his hideout and give you a chance to drug his beer?"

Only half of Natasha's face was visible from Dominic's vantage point, but that was enough for him to see the cruel smile that curved her lips.

"Here's the thing about rapists like Goodwin," she said. "They don't view women as real people, not the way they view themselves. To them, women are two-dimensional objects, no more than projections of their own desires. So if a pretty redhead were to bump into a man like that at a gas station, and giggle and flirt and be *so* impressed by his bullshit story about being on the run from a dangerous gang he pissed off with his badassery—well, he'd take her right back to his safe house to milk that for all it was worth. He could never even fathom that she might be any kind of threat to him. *Idiot.*"

That last word was said with a rich satisfaction that bordered on glee. Levi flinched against the door.

Dominic settled his free hand on Levi's thigh, deciding to endure the silence after all. But only moments later, Levi opened his eyes and spoke.

"How'd you get into our apartments?"

Natasha scoffed. "It's pretty easy to break into an apartment if you have the right tools. We're not talking Fort Knox."

"You know I don't mean last summer when you planted those surveillance devices." Straightening up, Levi laced his fingers through Dominic's and gripped tightly. "I mean after we installed extra locks and wireless security systems, and you *still* managed to get in without problems. How'd you do it?"

Natasha didn't answer. Dominic could see her knuckles whitening around the steering wheel.

"An explanation is the least of what you owe him," said Martine, low and threatening.

With a jerky nod, Natasha asked, "Do you remember that night you got so drunk at Stingray that Dominic called me to take you home?"

"I . . ." Levi shifted in his seat. "I remember that it happened. The night itself, not so much."

Dominic's memory of it was crystal clear. That had been months ago—before they'd broken up, while Rohan Chaudhary was in town. Levi had been in a dark place, angry and frustrated over the Seven of

Spades investigation, and his drinking had gotten out of control when he'd visited Dominic at work. With Martine busy, Natasha had been the next best option to handle him. Or so Dominic had thought.

"You had to tell me the alarm code for us to get into your apartment." The car sped up, as if it were absorbing Natasha's unease. "We were joking around about Dominic having set it for sixty-nine squared, and when I asked you if he used the same one, you said no—and told me the code he *did* use."

Levi palmed his face.

"Then I saw your keys and his together on your key ring, and I knew I'd never get a better chance. So . . . I put ketamine in your water."

"You did *what*?" Levi gasped, dropping his hand. Rebel's ears twitched anxiously back and forth.

"It knocked you out, which gave me enough time to run the keys down to the nearest shop and get them copied. You never knew I was gone."

"So that's why my hangover was so bad the next day? Because you fucking *drugged* me?"

"It was just a small amount!" Natasha shot back. "If you hadn't already been drunk, it wouldn't even have been enough to get you high. You weren't in any danger."

"You *psychotic*—"

"Okay." Dominic squeezed Levi's hand, dragging Levi's attention back to himself. "Remember what you said earlier about this not being productive? I'm sorry I started us down this road to begin with. I thought it might help to get some things out in the open, but I was wrong."

It makes everything way worse.

Levi subsided, but the air around him was crackling with angry tension rather than the melancholy he'd been wrapped up in earlier. Dominic found the change oddly heartening; under these circumstances, angry Levi would be stronger and more resilient than sad Levi.

Nobody spoke again until they reached Natasha's self-storage complex. Dominic understood why she'd chosen it—the building was in an isolated spot, out on the eastern fringes of North Las Vegas, and the area around it was mostly undeveloped. Large, empty lots on either side buffered the complex from its neighbors; the entire swath of land across the street was desert scrub that extended at least a quarter mile. The parking lot lacked any kind of security system or surveillance cameras.

Natasha parked in the corner, though there was nobody else in sight. The main office was locked up, a Closed sign hanging in the window.

As they got out of the car, Levi pulled Dominic aside, leaving Martine to keep an eagle eye on Natasha. He lifted a hand to the bandages on Dominic's head.

"What happened?" he asked, quietly enough that the others wouldn't be able to hear.

"A concussion from the car accident. It's not a big deal."

"Yes, it is." Levi lowered his hand to Dominic's chest, spreading his fingers wide over Dominic's heart. "You shouldn't be doing this; it's not safe in your condition. If anything happens to you . . ."

Dominic covered Levi's hand with his own. "Would you let *me* go into a situation like this without *you*?"

At first, Levi looked set to argue, but then he relented with a sigh. "No."

"Then don't expect that from me. I'll be fine—I know my own limits." Dominic turned Levi's arm over, scanning the bandages that covered Levi's burned forearms and remembering the bruises on his back, which could only have been worsened by the crash. "Besides, you're injured too."

"Yeah, but at least my head is fine."

Softly, Dominic asked, "Is it?"

Levi's eyes flicked toward Natasha, who was standing awkwardly with Martine about twenty feet away. Then he looked back at Dominic and gave a defeated shrug.

His heart breaking, Dominic bent down and kissed Levi. "Let's just get through this, okay? I've got your back."

As he began to move away, Levi caught his elbow. "I won't let you get hurt again because of me," Levi said, his voice fierce. "Not ever."

Dominic blinked, taken aback by Levi's forcefulness and unsure of how to respond, but Levi just let go and rejoined the women.

"We good?" Martine asked.

Levi nodded.

"While we're waiting for the key, we might as well get the lay of the land." Natasha's fingers slid over a tablet she'd retrieved from her car; moments later, she turned the tablet around so the rest of them could see Carmen's face on the screen.

Without so much as a cursory greeting, Carmen said, "As Dominic surmised, Hatfield's been staying at the condo he bought for his mistress in a luxury high-rise Downtown. He's holed up in there with some other guys for security, but most of the residents have evacuated. As far as I can tell, the majority of the units are unoccupied."

"Well, at least that'll minimize possible collateral damage," said Martine.

Dominic frowned. "If Utopia's about to set off another bomb, why is Hatfield sticking around in the heart of the city?"

"The communications I intercepted indicated that he's expecting a helicopter at 11 p.m. The building has its own helipad."

Levi hummed, crossing his arms. "So we can probably operate on the assumption that detonation isn't scheduled until after Hatfield would expect to be free and clear."

"I agree," Natasha said. "That gives us a bit of breathing room."

"Any way you could obtain floor plans of Hatfield's unit, and maybe of the building itself?" Dominic asked Carmen.

"No problem. I'm worming my way into the security system too. It's a 'smart' building, so almost everything in it is automated—great protection against physical assaults, but it leaves the units extra vulnerable to hackers."

"All right. So after we get the equipment we need, we make our way Downtown and bust into the building, then get to Hatfield before he leaves . . ."

They discussed and compared various approaches, which they refined further when Carmen dug up the relevant blueprints and sent them to Natasha's tablet. Hatfield's condo was on the twenty-first floor, and though Dominic wouldn't normally risk the elevator during a mission like this—no matter how daunting the climb—it was different when a teammate had control of the building's infrastructure.

"In the end, the best way in will come down to whichever entrance is less guarded," he said after a lengthy debate.

Carmen's face reappeared on the screen. "I can lead you through the path of least resistance and distract or lure the guards away as much as possible. But I can't guarantee you won't run into enemies on the way up. Plus, Hatfield *definitely* won't be the only person in the condo itself."

"And how exactly are we going to handle those enemies?" Natasha cast a pointed glance at Levi, who grimaced.

"Don't you think you've killed enough people today?"

"It's naïve to think we can accomplish this without fatalities," she said. "This isn't a TV show, Levi. We can't take these guys out by kneecapping them or shooting them with some mythical tranq gun."

Dominic blew out a breath. "I hate to say this—and I mean, I *really* hate to say it—but Natasha has a point. If a SWAT team were infiltrating this building, they'd have the go-ahead to use lethal force."

"I can't emphasize enough how much we're *not* a legally sanctioned SWAT team," Martine said, holding up her hands.

"It doesn't matter. We're not talking about penny-ante drug dealers or thieves or street punks. These people are *terrorists*. What Utopia's done, and what they're planning to do, are deliberate acts of war. That changes the rules. We have every right to defend our home, and a *responsibility* to protect the defenseless. If that means enemy fatalities—well, that's the price they pay for starting this war in the first place."

Martine cocked her head, then nodded. "Okay, yeah, that changes my perspective."

Raking a hand through his hair, Levi said, "It's not just legality I'm worried about—"

He was interrupted by the roar of a motorcycle engine. A Kawasaki Ninja zoomed into their corner of the parking lot, far sleeker and more graceful than the stout Harley Dominic had borrowed from his neighbor. Its single rider turned the bike off, dismounted, and removed her helmet, straightening her low ponytail.

"What the *hell* is going on?" Leila demanded.

She was staring at Levi, her face screwed up with confusion and a healthy amount of suspicion. Levi looked at Dominic, who shrugged and turned to Martine. Though Martine had been the one to enlist Leila's help, with a brief pretense for why she needed Natasha's key, it was clear from the ensuing uncomfortable silence that none of them had considered how to explain the real situation.

"I thought you made it out of Nevada hours ago," Leila said to Levi. Her eyes roved over Natasha, narrowed, and came to rest on Martine. "And *you* told me that Natasha was missing. Ezra's having a nervous breakdown. Why haven't you told him—"

She froze. Dominic followed the direction of her gaze to the tablet Natasha was holding—the tablet on which Carmen's face was still visible.

Leila lurched a single step backward, her face wiped clean of expression. For a moment, she seemed to be in a state of suspended animation. Then she shook herself, blinked a few times, and said, "You crafty bitch."

Natasha snorted, at which Martine made an exasperated noise.

"I'm sorry I couldn't tell you the truth over the phone," Martine said.

"No, I get it." Leila strode forward, joining them without any sign of reluctance. "But I'm here now, so seriously—*what the hell is going on?*"

"Levi can fill you in on the way to my unit." Natasha extended her hand. "Can I have the key, please?"

Leila passed it over, and Natasha headed deeper into the complex at a rapid clip. Martine stayed on her ass, still covering her with a gun, while Dominic hung back with Rebel, listening to Levi summing up the events of the day for Leila.

Natasha's unit was in the back corner of the complex, as far from the entrance as possible. Dominic had been wondering why she couldn't just break into the unit, if she'd found it so easy to enter their apartments, but he understood as soon as he saw the lock securing the garage-style door. It looked more like a shapeless hunk of metal than a padlock. The shaft wasn't visible, which would make it practically impossible to cut through, and only a world-class thief would have any hope of picking it.

She popped the lock open, rolled the door up, and disappeared inside. Martine followed her, but Dominic hovered at the threshold as Levi wrapped things up with Leila.

"Jesus," Leila said. "So Nazis are about to bomb the city again, the police are compromised by double agents, and one of your closest friends is the serial killer you've been hunting for a year?"

"Could you make it sound *more* depressing?" Levi said wryly.

"You were right. The Seven of Spades *is* someone you trusted. I don't even . . ." She rested a hand on Levi's arm, her eyes soft with something Dominic was tempted to label sympathy, though he'd never seen her exhibit that before. "I'm sorry I reacted the way I did when you suspected me."

Levi shook his head. "Don't be. I'm sorry I hurt you. That was never my intention."

Satisfied by their reconciliation, Dominic entered the unit to give them a moment of privacy.

The unit was a surprisingly large cement cube, lit by a single bare bulb overhead. As he and Rebel wove between haphazard piles of old furniture, cardboard boxes, and plastic storage bins, he scanned some of the labels: *Baby clothes. Textbooks. Halloween decorations.*

Despite every appearance of normalcy, he kept his guard up. This place reminded him uncomfortably of the murder room Natasha had trapped him and Levi in last month, and there was always a chance that this was a trap as well.

Natasha and Martine had stopped at the unit's back wall, in front of a column of bins that were all labeled *Christmas.* Natasha was shoving other boxes aside to create more space.

"We need to get these down," she said when Dominic approached. "Can you grab one of those chairs?"

He followed her pointing finger to several dining chairs that had been stacked atop each other. Fetching one down, he brought it over and held it steady while she climbed on and reached for the top Christmas bin. By the time she'd brought down all of the bins and laid them out side by side, Levi and Leila had rejoined the group.

"First things first." Natasha opened the leftmost container, revealing a mass of boxed tree ornaments. "We need to be able to stay in communication with each other and Carmen, without everyone relying on me as a go-between."

She felt along the insides of the container with both hands, then lifted out a dividing tray on which the ornament boxes were sitting. As she set it aside, Dominic leaned forward to peer into the container.

The bottom half of the bin was full of neatly sorted tech—everything from concealable cameras to bugs to a cell phone interceptor. He recognized the same brand and quality of equipment that she'd used to spy on them last summer.

"Whoa," said Leila. "Creepy much?"

Shooting Leila an irritated look, Natasha picked up a handful of plastic-packaged devices. When she tossed one to Dominic, he realized it was identical to the earpiece she was wearing.

"Carmen will key us all into the same encrypted channel. We won't have to worry about the LVMPD or FBI picking up on it."

Natasha passed them to Levi and Martine as well, then hesitated as Leila raised her eyebrows.

"Leila, you've done more than enough," Levi said. "You don't have to come with us."

"Like fuck." Leila held out her hand.

As the four of them ripped into their packages and extracted their earbuds, Natasha moved on to the next storage bin, which was crammed with garlands of red and green tinsel.

"Dominic, Martine, and Rebel already have body armor," she said, "but the rest of us need some protection. It's a good thing we're not drastically different sizes."

Beneath the garlands were layers of bulletproof vests, along with a heap of black gloves, jackets, and ski masks. After grabbing vests for herself, Leila, and Levi, Natasha dug up a black hoodie and offered it to Levi.

"You should hide your face as much as you can. If word gets out that you're still in the city, it'll cause big problems."

Levi nodded, accepted both garments, and strapped himself into the vest before zipping the hoodie over it. Both were a little short on him, but circumference-wise, they fit fine.

"Now, for the squeamish among us . . ." Natasha moved on to the remaining containers. "I have some less-lethal weapon options that may be more palatable."

She opened the rest and removed their top halves. Dominic's jaw fell open further with each one.

They were chock-full of weaponry: A truly staggering array of knives; multiple guns and piles of ammo; Tasers, stun guns, and what looked like a goddamn *cattle prod*; even flashbang grenades and tear gas. It was a collection that would have put the most paranoid doomsday prepper to shame. Packing all of those instruments of death and mayhem with cheerful Christmas decorations made for a macabre contrast.

Martine's eyebrows had almost reached her hairline, and her gun hung by her side. "Where did you *get* all of this?"

"I've been collecting these for five years." Natasha knelt and rummaged through one of the bins. "I like to be prepared for every contingency. You have to admit, it's worked out well for me so far."

"Do you really think reminding us of all the psycho stunts you've pulled is a good idea right now?" Leila asked.

Glancing up, Natasha said, "I thought you didn't care about the people I've killed."

Leila shrugged. "I don't. If that was all you'd done, we wouldn't have a problem. It's what you've done to Levi and Dominic that makes me want to punch you in the throat."

Dominic snickered, and even Levi's lips twitched.

Ignoring that comment, Natasha found a pair of MMA gloves in the bin and gave them to Levi. "Do you want—"

"No."

"Take a stun gun, at least, since you gave me the one you were using earlier."

Levi conceded, and Natasha turned back to Leila.

"I'm good." Leila unzipped her leather bomber jacket and patted a black rod stashed in an inner pocket. Dominic knew from Levi that it was two expandable batons screwed together.

Natasha threw her a can of mace. "For backup. How about you, Dominic? Need anything?"

He had three guns on him—two in his shoulder rig and one on his ankle—but there was no such thing as overprepared. "I could use some extra ammo, if you've got any for a Glock."

"Help yourself." She pointed him to the relevant bin, then moved to the last one in the row and withdrew a double-barreled shotgun.

This she handed to Martine, along with a sidesaddle and belt pouch both full of shells.

Martine held the shotgun like it was dripping with sewage. "Uh . . ."

"Those are beanbag rounds," Natasha said in her usual patient tone—so bizarre to hear now that Dominic knew the truth. "You've trained with them, right?"

"A few times." Now seeming intrigued, Martine cracked the gun open to load it.

While they continued gearing up, Dominic took a couple of the flashbangs, as did Levi and Martine. The tear gas, unfortunately, was out of the question. Even if Natasha had enough gas masks for the five of them, there would be no way to protect Rebel from the fumes.

A few minutes later, they were all set, but Dominic was still troubled. "This is a good start, but chances are, we're gonna be way outnumbered. We need a more decisive form of crowd control."

Natasha frowned, fiddling with the buttons on her jacket pockets, then perked up. She waved him over to a wooden trunk in the corner, the kind of toy chest with a flip-top lid that had existed pre-safety standards.

"Do you remember the distraction I created the night of the assault on Volkov's compound?"

"Yeah . . ."

"Well, when I was buying those supplies, I went way overboard. There's a bunch of stuff I ended up not using." She opened the lid, pulled out a pile of blankets, and stepped aside so he could see into the trunk.

"Holy shit." Despite the dire situation, a grin broke across Dominic's face. "Yeah, this'll work. This'll work just fine."

CHAPTER 19

Hatfield's building, the Whitby, was a straight shot about six miles southwest from the storage complex. Levi sat in the back seat of Natasha's car with Rebel, who was less frightened now but refused to take her eyes off Natasha for a single moment. Martine had gone with Leila on the bike, so Dominic sat up front to watch Natasha as she drove.

Levi removed his earpiece, dialed Dominic's phone, and listened to it ring.

"Mr. Russo?" Stanton answered, his voice tense. "What's wrong? Did something happen to Levi?"

"No, it's me. I mean, it's Levi. My own phones keep getting, uh ... messed up."

Stanton's relieved sigh came across loud and clear. "Levi, thank God. I've been so worried since I heard about the bounty Utopia put on you, but then I saw on the news that you'd managed to get out of Nevada. You're safe now?"

Levi glanced out the window. This was a working-class area, a far cry from the glitz of the city center. They were speeding down a desolate highway, passing gas stations, fast-food joints, half-empty RV parks, and one dreary strip mall after another. Even those businesses meant to be open twenty-four hours were closed and dark, and everyone with any sense had retreated to their homes.

"I'll be fine," he said. "I was actually calling you for the same reason. I know it's late, but I wanted to make sure you're not in Vegas."

"I'm not. When the Strip was evacuated, I came out to Mother's property in Newport Beach."

Levi closed his eyes, a bit of the tightness in his chest easing. "Good. That's good."

After a long beat, Stanton said, "There's something you're not telling me."

"What? No, there's not."

"*Levi—*"

A sudden rustling sounded on the other end of the line, followed by an indistinct murmur. Stanton responded, his own voice muffled as if he were covering the phone with his hand.

Startled, Levi asked, "Is there someone else there?"

"Um . . ."

The second person spoke again, still too low for Levi to make out the words, but they were undoubtedly male—and annoyed.

"Well, yes," Stanton said. "It's Caleb. He's my, ah, occupational therapist. You know, to help me adjust to having monocular vision."

Levi would have thought he was lying—it wasn't like Stanton to be dishonest, but what would his occupational therapist be doing with him at this time of night in Newport Beach? Before Levi could call him out, though, Caleb's distant voice said, "*Former.*"

"Yes, all right." Stanton cleared his throat. "Former occupational therapist, I should say. I had to start seeing a different one, because . . ."

Levi heard the familiar blush in Stanton's tone, and his lips twitched. "Because you and Caleb started dating?"

"Yes." There was a soft whisper and more rustling on Stanton's end. Then Stanton yelped and hissed, "*Stop it,*" sounding incredibly flustered.

Levi's smile broke free. This was the first truly good news he'd had in—well, he couldn't remember how long. "That's great. I'll let you go, then. I just wanted to make sure you were somewhere safe."

"I can still tell you're hiding something." When Levi didn't answer, Stanton chuckled. "But knowing you, it's for a good reason. Stay safe yourself."

"Thanks. And Stanton?"

"Yeah?"

"I'm really happy for you." Levi infused the words with warmth, needing Stanton to understand how much he meant them.

He ended the call and returned Dominic's phone before popping his earpiece in. But without the distraction, his relief at knowing Stanton was happy and safe faded quickly, his thoughts drawn inexorably back to what they were about to do.

He stroked his restless fingers through Rebel's fur, his heart heavy with dread. He didn't doubt the justness of their plan. They had to take action, and they couldn't trust anyone else—for God's sake, trusting the wrong cop had gotten Gibbs killed this morning. With an entire city at risk, he would do what needed to be done, and worry about the personal consequences later.

No, it was *himself* he doubted. A battle like the one they were facing would bring out the parts of himself he feared the most: his savage delight in violence, his exhilarated bloodlust. He'd lost himself in that darkness before. What if he did the same—but couldn't find his way back this time?

He caught Dominic watching him, mustered a weak smile, and turned away. Dominic probably knew what he was thinking, and he didn't want to see his worries reflected on Dominic's face.

As they transitioned to a better-kept neighborhood—indicated by the gradual proliferation of parks, small museums, and more attractive landscaping—Carmen spoke through their earpieces.

"Bad news, guys. The riots in the city are spreading, and you're heading right for them. The Fremont Street Experience is swarmed with looters."

Shit. One of the FSE's entrances was a block from the Whitby.

"Things are deteriorating by the minute," Carmen said. "The law enforcement response is going to be massive."

Martine's voice crackled over the connection. "That's what Utopia wants. The more the cops and FBI are distracted by the riots, the less prepared they'll be for the bomb."

"I'll try to steer you around the worst of it, but the streets are such a mess that you may have to go the last bit on foot. Leila's bike might be able to get through, though."

The neon skyline of Downtown Las Vegas came into sharper view as they approached the freeway exchange. For the first time, there were other cars on the road—all heading in the opposite direction, gunning it out of the city, tires squealing as they fishtailed onto the freeway's entrance ramps like birds fleeing a forest fire.

"Well, that's comforting," said Dominic.

Deferring to the rush of oncoming traffic, Natasha slowed down beneath the overpass. When they emerged, something smashed onto the roof with the sound of shattering glass.

Levi and Dominic both shouted, and even Rebel yelped, but Natasha just grimaced and said, "What the fuck was that?"

Twisting to look out the rear window, Levi saw a rowdy group of people clustered by the railing of the overpass, whooping as they flung bottles, rocks, and other detritus at the cars below. As he watched, one flung another bottle in the direction of Leila's bike. She veered neatly out of the way, and the bottle crashed into the asphalt instead.

He turned back and leaned forward, judging the road ahead. Past the approaching intersection, rapidly heading in their direction, a car was trapped behind an SUV and a minivan that apparently weren't moving fast enough; it swung back and forth between lanes, trying in vain to edge past them.

The minivan accelerated, opening a small gap to its left. The car darted toward it, but at the same moment, the SUV sped up to keep them out. With a thunderous *crash*, the car slammed into the SUV, propelling it over the median and flipping it onto its side—right in the path of Natasha's car.

Natasha stomped the brakes as Levi instinctively grabbed Rebel. The rear of their car swung around in a wide circle, rubber and metal screeching, and slid to a halt inches from the SUV. Levi lurched forward against his seat belt and rebounded hard, making his bruised back flare with pain.

"Everyone okay?" Natasha sounded more irritated than shaken.

"Yeah." Levi released his death grip on Rebel's K-9 vest, which had kept her from being tossed off the seat. Dominic echoed him.

Behind them, Leila had detoured safely onto the sidewalk and stopped her bike, with Martine secure on the back. But the cars on the other side of the road weren't so lucky. Reacting too slowly to the wreck, they crashed into each other one after the next, skidding onto the sidewalk and colliding with the palm trees in the median. The pile-up was six cars deep before anyone braked in time to avoid it.

The SUV's driver struggled free of his vehicle, limping, but intact enough to run screaming at the car that had hit him. The other driver jumped out as well, shouting back, until the first hauled off and punched him in the face.

"Get out of the car," Levi said. "*Now.*"

Without the car's insulating effect, the noise was deafening. The angry shouts and curses of the people involved in the accident were overlaid by the blaring horns of the cars stuck behind it. One woman shoved another, sending her sprawling onto the street; a man pounded his fist violently on the roof of his car as he bellowed at the driver behind him.

Levi knew rage, and the air here *thrummed* with it—the mindless, panicked rage of terrified people whose lives had been upended, lashing out at each other like frenzied animals. Few things could be more dangerous. Pulling up his hood, he retreated to the sidewalk where Leila and Martine were waiting, and the others followed suit.

"What happened?" Carmen asked.

"Major car accident," said Natasha. "It blocked both sides of the road. I can't drive around it."

"I can," Leila said. "What should I do?"

Levi glanced south. The Whitby was a few blocks away, easily visible from where they were standing. "You and Martine keep going. We'll meet you there."

She nodded, revved the bike, and took off.

The angry confrontations around the wrecked cars were escalating into an all-out brawl. "We gotta get moving," Dominic said. He hefted the large duffel bag he was carrying more securely onto his shoulder.

They raced down the sidewalk, past uprooted street signs and trampled landscaping. Trash littered the road from overturned garbage cans.

The farther they ran, the more Levi felt like he'd been transported to an upside-down nightmare version of the city he loved. The neon signs and bright windows that normally blazed against the night sky were at half-strength, as a random scattering of buildings stood in absolute darkness. Shrieking car alarms competed with screams, breaking glass, and the wail of police sirens. People tore through the streets, hollering in a crazed mix of fear and manic excitement, destroying everything in their path with no seeming motivation other than to cause havoc.

A block away from the FSE, Levi stumbled to a halt at the intersection and gaped.

What had started as a swarm of looters had devolved into an angry mob in an unchecked free-for-all. The violence spilled from the FSE's entrance into the surrounding streets as people pummeled each other with fists and improvised weapons. Some darted in and out of the busted-open shops with their spoils, only to be taken down by others who fought them for the goods. One of the buildings was on *fire*.

The police were out in force, clad in full riot gear, but they weren't doing much to turn the tide. As Levi and the others absorbed the chaos, a car that was weaving its way through the horde swerved to avoid two people who ran in front of it and smashed head-on into a fire hydrant, which erupted in a geyser of water.

"At this rate, there may not *be* a city left to save," Natasha said.

Levi leapt back from the water now gushing down the street. The sound of sirens escalated, and he looked up to see a wall of flickering red and blue lights moving toward them—police reinforcements, and no doubt the FBI. It was only a matter of time before the National Guard was called in too.

"Go the long way around the building," said Carmen. "It's not a clear route, but it'll keep you out of the worst of the mess."

Following her instructions, they turned left at the intersection and crossed the street to the base of the Whitby. The building's ground floor was all restaurants and retail shops; there were looters here as well, jumping in and out of the broken windows and clogging the sidewalk. The cars parked along the curb had been flipped over and smashed.

As they ran along the length of the building, dodging rioters and the debris strewn across the sidewalk, a man dashed out of a restaurant with his arms full of liquor bottles. He collided with Levi, reeled backward, and dropped his haul all over the concrete.

"Watch it, asshole!" he yelled, winding up for a wild punch.

Levi blocked the punch, smashed the heel of his hand into the guy's nose, and shoved him aside impatiently before continuing on. Rebel sprinted ahead of them, clearing the way with loud barks that convinced people to scamper out of their path. They rounded a couple of corners unmolested, then reached the building's parking garage and ran up the entry ramp.

There was no security guard in sight, and Carmen had already lifted the gate. Leila and Martine were standing right inside, next to the bike, with their helmets off. Martine was cradling her shotgun, while Leila had both batons extended and at the ready.

The thick concrete walls provided a welcome deadening effect to the mayhem outside. Gathering in a rough circle, everyone checked in with Carmen.

"Keep your voices down," she warned. "There's a couple of guys hanging out by the elevator bank. It's a good distance from your position, so you should be fine as long as you stay quiet."

"Do you have access to all the cameras?" Levi asked.

"Yep. The only places I can't see are inside the units themselves."

"What's the situation?"

"Three armed guards outside the door to Hatfield's condo, three more by the elevator bank, and another two by the stairwell on the other end of the floor. Then you've got a few teams of two to three guards roaming around the other floors. They're fairly scattered, so we should be able to proceed as planned."

Martine adjusted her grip on the shotgun. "What about the residents? There have to be some who haven't left. We don't want them to get caught in the crossfire."

"I told you, this is a smart building. All the door locks are electronic. I can literally lock everyone into their units for the duration. Hopefully, they'll have enough sense to stay to the rear of the condos so they don't get clipped by stray bullets going through walls."

"Do that." Levi looked around the circle. "We good to go?"

Everyone nodded. Rebel wagged her tail.

"The guys by the elevator are carrying radios," Carmen said briskly, "so make sure you take them out before they can contact the others. The last thing you want is every guard in this building converging on your position while you're exposed."

"How?" Dominic asked. "From the layout of the garage you showed us, the approach to the elevator bank is wide open. Without some kind of distraction, they'll see us coming way before we can disable them, but a distraction that's too loud will alert the other guards anyway."

Natasha smiled, her eyes glinting with malice. "I have an idea."

"I just don't know what we're going to do," Natasha said into her cell phone as she approached the elevator bank. Her jacket was draped over her left arm, leaving her in a tank top that bared her shoulders and collarbone. "It's like a war zone out there. I barely made it home. And what if those looters try to get into the building?"

From Levi's vantage point, crouched behind a line of parked cars with Leila, he watched the two Utopia guards hanging out by the elevators. They had their guns tucked into their waistbands beneath loose shirts—probably not noticeable to the average civilian—and one was drinking from an insulated mug. When they saw Natasha, they straightened up and gave her their full attention, though they didn't seem too concerned.

She saw them as well and did a double take, stopping a few feet away. "Hang on a minute, Jen." Lowering the phone, she heaved a sigh and addressed the guards. "Don't tell me the elevators aren't working, on top of everything else?"

The men exchanged a glance. "Uh . . . no, they're working fine," said one.

"Thank God." She lifted the phone again and said, "Tell Dylan that Mommy will be up soon. We'll figure something out." Then she slid the phone into her pants pocket.

The men were now completely at ease: shoulders relaxed, expressions friendly. Levi nodded to Leila, and the two of them began creeping down the aisle behind the cars. They needed to get as close to the elevators as they could before they ran out of cover.

On the other side of the elevator bank, Dominic, Martine, and Rebel were doing the same, though all Levi could see of them were furtive movements in the shadows.

"Have you seen how crazy it is outside?" Natasha stepped between the guards, into the middle of the elevator bank, obliging them both to turn around and face her. "My husband's out of town, and our babysitter's been all alone with our son. There's no way that poor girl will be able to get home now."

One of the men nodded. "Probably best if you all stay put. This building's pretty safe."

Ensuring his breathing was slow and silent, Levi emerged from the parked cars and padded toward the men's turned backs. Leila kept pace with him and readied the baton in her right hand.

"Thanks in part to you, I'm sure," said Natasha, flashing the men a sweet smile. "That's what you two are doing down here, right? Keeping watch to make sure nobody gets in who isn't supposed to?"

The men's chests puffed up. The one on Natasha's left said, "We'll do what we can, ma'am."

"What gentlemen," she said, and zapped him with the stun gun she'd been hiding beneath her draped jacket.

As the man collapsed, gasping and spasming, the other guard stumbled backward and scrabbled for his gun. With an aggressive lunge, Leila whacked him in the back of the head with her baton. The man reeled, half turning, and Levi punched him hard in the face. One more good smack from Leila sent him to the ground, unconscious.

Levi flexed his hand, grateful for the MMA gloves, and looked up. Dominic was crouching by the stunned guard, stripping the man of his weapons and radio while Martine and Rebel covered him. Two down—God knew how many to go.

Once they'd confiscated the unconscious guard's belongings as well, they dragged both men out of sight around the corner, zip-tied their wrists and ankles, and gagged them with duct tape.

"Can you give me the radio frequency Utopia is using so I can tap into it?" Carmen asked. "It'd be nice to have eyes *and* ears on them, and this way you guys won't have to lug one of the radios around with you."

While Dominic gave her the information she needed, Levi returned to the elevator bank. Natasha, who'd put her body armor and jacket back on, was bending down to retrieve the one guard's fallen mug. She unscrewed the cap and sniffed the steam that wafted forth.

"Time for a coffee break?" Levi said snidely.

She just smiled and screwed the cap back on.

With the guards secured, their group piled into the freight elevator, which stood across from two regular elevators in the central bank. It was huge, with padded walls, designed for use by residents moving in and out of the building.

"How do things look up there, Carmen?" Martine asked.

Carmen broke down the situation for them. Besides the guards stationed on the same floor as Hatfield's condo, there were several teams of two or three men patrolling the nearby floors in regular patterns, as well as a team in the lobby.

After hearing the specifics, Leila whistled. "That's . . . a lot of guards."

"Thirteen against six?" Dominic shrugged. "Those odds aren't too bad."

"*Twenty-one* against six," said Levi. "There's eight more on Hatfield's floor."

Shaking his head, Dominic said, "They won't break position and leave the condo undefended."

"Okay, guys." A burst of rapid typing came from Carmen's end of their shared link. "I think the eighteenth floor is your best bet. I'll send you up so you get there right after the patrol team has left. It'll give you enough time to get in position, and put you as close to a halfway point between the various enemy teams as I can get you."

Martine readied her shotgun, tossing her hair out of her eyes. "They won't be able to tell the elevator is moving?"

"I can prevent the panels on the other floors from lighting up. I've locked down the other elevators too, as well as the individual units. But you need to move fast, because any residents still in the building will definitely call 911 when you get started, and I can't guarantee that the cops are too overwhelmed by the riots to respond."

"Understood."

"Everyone ready?"

After a chorus of confirmations, the elevator lurched and began its slow ascent. The ride was silent and tense—but it was an anticipatory tension, the dangerous intoxication of impending battle. Levi's blood buzzed with it; he saw the same charge reflected on the faces around him, even Rebel's.

When they arrived on the eighteenth floor, they moved swiftly toward the east stairwell. Levi grabbed the fire extinguisher from its box on the wall in passing.

"Wait!" Carmen said sharply as Natasha reached for the door. "The team upstairs is lingering . . . Okay, go. *Quietly.*"

Natasha eased the door open, poked her head through, and then slipped into the stairwell. The rest of them followed, making as little noise as possible—in this tunnel of concrete and metal, every sound would echo like crazy.

On the landing beside the door, Dominic set down the duffel bag and eased the zipper open. The first thing he pulled out was a bundle of fireworks which so authentically resembled sticks of dynamite that Levi hadn't been able to tell the difference at first. Dominic handed it to Natasha along with a fuse kit, and she darted up the stairs like a ghost.

Being outnumbered, their strategy was to create choke points that would funnel their enemies through a limited number of routes they controlled. A stairwell could be perfect—except for the fact that Utopia could enter the stairs from any floor along the height of the building. Fire safety measures made it impossible for the doors to be locked on the residential side.

Nasty-looking traps on the nineteenth- and sixteenth-floor landings should scare Utopia off and force them to enter the stairwell only through floors seventeen and eighteen. But if that didn't work, the fireworks would detonate anyway. Though they weren't real dynamite, they packed a hell of a kick.

Dominic passed Levi and Leila each a roll of firecrackers, took another dynamite trap kit for himself, and went down to the sixteenth floor. Martine scooped up the bag and established their base position: the wide landing on the other side of the stairwell, at the midpoint between floors seventeen and eighteen. There, they'd have the wall to their rear, and a clear vantage point from which to monitor both doors and the two lengths of stairs connected to the landing.

Levi and Leila split up, unrolling their 16,000-count strips of firecrackers along the stairs leading down from seventeen and up from eighteen, then lit the delayed-ignition fuses. Levi kept the fire extinguisher at hand—none of the materials in the stairwell were flammable, so he doubted there'd be any lasting fire, but accidentally burning down the building would throw a pretty big wrench in the works.

With all measures in place, everyone retreated to the landing, hunkered down, and covered their ears. Dominic tucked Rebel's head between his arm and chest.

For a few endless moments, they crouched in place, barely breathing.

Crack. Crack. Crack crack crackcrackCRACKCRACKCRACK—

The strung-together firecrackers ignited each other like toppling dominoes, erupting in showers of sparks and puffs of smoke, filling the air with their violent reports. The acoustics of the stairwell amplified every explosion, bouncing the noises back and forth off the walls and layering them over each other, so that the cacophony grew ever faster and louder.

To people on the other side of the door, it would sound a lot like automatic gunfire.

A few seconds later, Levi heard the tinny, panicked shouts of distant voices. He was confused until he realized they were coming from Carmen's tap into Utopia's radio frequency, audible through his earpiece.

"Report! What the hell is going on down there?"

"It must be the FBI!"

"Where is that gunfire coming from?"

"I don't—"

"The stairs!"

"Hold position," Carmen said, her voice tight. "Three guards entering on nineteen."

Just as the noise from the last firecrackers died away, a door above them opened with a creak. "What the fuck?" said a voice that floated down the stairwell.

Multiple footsteps sounded on concrete, and someone let out a strangled gasp.

"Back, get back! There's explosives in the stairway!"

"I think I saw people down—"

The door slammed shut.

"Worked like a charm," Dominic said, grinning. He released Rebel and met her eyes. "*Enemies.*"

Her lips pulled back from her teeth in a menacing growl.

"They're making a beeline for the west stairwell," Carmen said. "Two more about to come through the door on seventeen."

Levi stood, pulled the pin on the fire extinguisher, and hurried halfway down the steps. As expected, the firecrackers had burned scorch marks into the stairs, but nothing had caught flame. That meant this extinguisher could serve a different purpose.

While the rest of the team prepared themselves to engage as well, Carmen continued her sitrep. "The guards on twenty-one are maintaining their positions, but everyone else is moving in your direction. You're gonna get hit hard and fast."

The door below Levi swung open. A man ventured into the stairwell, gun drawn, only to come to a stunned halt when he saw the six of them arrayed on the stairs.

Levi sprayed him in the face.

The guy flailed backward, stumbling, and collided with the man entering behind him. Levi jumped down the remaining steps, slammed the end of the fire extinguisher into the guy's foam-soaked face, then adjusted his grip and whacked the guy in the head like he was wielding a baseball bat.

That took the first man decisively out of the running, but the second had already recovered and was aiming his gun point-blank at Levi's face. Levi wouldn't be able to react in time—

With a blood-curdling snarl, Rebel leapt from the landing and crashed feetfirst into the man's chest, bringing him to the ground with her entire weight. His screams rent the air as she clamped her jaws around his gun arm and savaged it without mercy.

On the staircase above him, Levi heard several gunshots, the *bang* of Martine's shotgun and the rapid-fire *thwacks* of Leila's batons, and answering screams and curses. Levi craned his neck in time to see a man tottering halfway down the stairs, a tell-tale red stripe across his dazed face, trying to steady his gun arm.

Two steps down, Natasha threw hot coffee in his face, seized his jacket, and yanked him casually down the rest of the stairs. The man landed at Dominic's feet, shrieking, and dropped his gun to claw at his burned skin with both hands.

"Two more about to come through eighteen," Carmen reported. "The other teams have gotten a little more cautious."

That gave Levi some breathing room. He gathered the guns from the men at his feet, then told Rebel to release her hapless victim. The guy curled up around his ravaged arm, groaning, as Rebel backed off with a blood-streaked muzzle.

The door on eighteen flew open. Dominic—who, as their best ranged combatant, was positioned on the landing to cover both staircases—fired off a shot. The bullet went wide, embedding itself in the doorframe, and the Utopia guards retreated hastily.

There was no way Dominic would miss a shot at this distance. He'd aimed to deter rather than kill, which could only have been for Levi's sake. The sole difference between Dominic's and Natasha's willingness to kill under these circumstances was that Dominic wouldn't take pleasure in it.

Dominic gave Levi a quick, tight smile. Levi mimed tying someone up, and Dominic tossed him a bundle of zip ties from the open duffel bag.

Confident that the rest of the team had the men upstairs under control, Levi focused on binding his own two opponents. He dragged them both in front of the door, side by side, so they'd serve as an obstacle to anyone coming through, then sprayed more fire-suppressant foam on the floor for good measure.

When he finished, the latest aggressors had been dealt with, leaving five disabled Utopia guards sprawled over the stairs and landings above him. Most were unconscious and seriously injured, but he didn't think any were dead. By his count, there were six guards remaining, not including the ones stationed on Hatfield's floor or in the condo itself.

They all turned toward the doors, panting, ready for the next wave. Dominic and Martine reloaded their weapons. Leila swiped impatiently at her bleeding mouth.

Nothing happened.

"Um . . . Carmen?" Natasha said.

"I know. They're just . . . hanging back. Three on eighteen, three on seventeen. They're whispering among themselves, so I can't— Oh, here we go."

Utopia's radio crackled over Levi's earpiece. "Baker, you copy?"

"Yeah."

"We're gonna rush 'em all at once, hit 'em with everything we got. Don't hold back. Shoot to kill."

"Got it."

Natasha turned to Levi. "*Now* is it okay if I kill them?"

He glared, but before he could respond, Carmen called, "Incoming!"

The foam in the fire extinguisher was spent, but it still made an excellent blunt weapon. He snatched it up again and positioned himself behind the door—which swung inward when entering the stairwell, another disadvantage for their enemies.

This time, he heard the men running toward him, their feet pounding along the carpeted hallway on the other side. Levi braced himself, and when the first guard charged through the door, leading with his gun arm, Levi threw his entire body weight forward.

The door slammed closed on the man's elbow, pinning it against the jamb. The man screamed, then shrieked even louder when Levi smashed the fire extinguisher into his hand until he dropped his gun.

Though the element of surprise had been in Levi's favor, he couldn't hold the door shut against three people by himself. They combined forces and burst through, knocking him backward. He stumbled over the men lying on the ground, but hopped away and managed to regain his footing on the part of the landing that wasn't slick with foam.

The guard with the mangled hand wasn't so lucky. Already disoriented by pain, he tripped over his prone comrades, slipped in the foam, and went tumbling down the stairs, landing perilously close to the "dynamite" trap below.

The other two guards caught themselves before they suffered the same fate. Rebel launched herself at the nearest man—who was clearly unprepared to face an enraged hundred-pound dog—and tussled with him in the foam, her four legs giving her more confidence on the slippery surface.

Levi redirected the second guard's gun arm a split-second before the guy pulled the trigger. It was such a close call that he felt the heat of the bullet as it whizzed past his cheek, and the sheer volume of the gunshot battered his eardrums.

He gripped the slide with his free hand, intending to disarm the man, but a vicious kick to the stomach caught him off-guard. Reeling backward, he collided hard with the railing at the edge of the landing. Lightning shocks of agony radiated through muscles that had already been beaten and bruised to the limits of his endurance.

Momentarily paralyzed, Levi struggled to regain control of his spasming limbs. More shots were ringing out above, interspersed with the shouts and cries of the bloody confrontation engaging the rest of his team. Rebel was thoroughly focused on her own opponent. Nobody had noticed Levi's predicament.

The Utopia guard grinned, jumped over his friends' bodies, and raised his gun. Staring death in the eye, Levi did the only thing he could do—he pulled down his hood, exposing his face.

The guard faltered as his jaw dropped.

That was the opening Levi needed. Gritting his teeth, he rocked back onto the railing, drew his knees to his chest, and uncoiled with explosive power, driving both feet into the man's chest. The force of the double kick sent the man flying into the opposite wall, where he hit his head with a nasty *thud* and slumped to the floor, moaning weakly.

Levi strode forward, wrenched the gun out of the man's hand, and pistol-whipped him.

Rebel's guy was on his hands and knees, trying to crawl away from her, only for her to snag his ankle and drag him back. Levi called her off, pushed the man down flat, and pinned him there with one knee while reaching for the zip ties.

"Levi!" Dominic shouted. His gun fired in the same breath.

Flinching, Levi spun to his right, staying atop the man beneath his knee. The guard who'd fallen down the stairs earlier had recovered without Levi noticing. He must have had another gun on him, because his hand was wrapped around the grip as he lay in a crumpled heap halfway up the stairs—mere feet from where Levi had been oblivious to his approach.

Death had found the guard instead. Blood streamed from the neat hole Dominic had put in his skull.

Levi looked up at Dominic, whose face was soft with understanding but no apology. "I had to," Dominic said.

"I know—"

Levi was interrupted by a shout from above. Leila was whaling on a guard—the last one standing, Levi saw—and driving him aggressively down the stairs toward Dominic's landing. The guy was trying to evade her and get a shot off with his gun, but he couldn't hold his ground against the fluid barrage of attacks. The brutal grace with which she wielded her batons was mesmerizing.

Near the bottom of the stairs, she spun on the step and delivered a blow that knocked the guard clear across the landing. He banged hard into the metal rail, taking the edge right to the solar plexus, and hunched over it as he wheezed.

Natasha grabbed his legs and flipped him over the railing.

The terrified, primal scream the man unleashed as he plummeted eighteen stories raised all the hair on Levi's neck and arms. It echoed through the stairwell, then was cut off by a sickening *crash*.

Silence ensued as they all stared at Natasha, who was gazing at the central well with a faint, almost dreamy smile.

Leila hopped down the last couple of steps, peered over the railing, and grimaced. "That's gonna be a bitch to clean up."

The man beneath Levi began thrashing, yelling obscenities, and it took all of Levi's strength to keep him restrained. That spurred everyone else to action as well, breaking the surreal moment.

As they bound and gagged the guards—the living ones, anyway—several of the walkies chirped. "Baker? Roth? Come in! What the fuck is going on down there? Baker!"

"I took the radio channel off your earpieces so it wouldn't distract you guys," Carmen said, answering Levi's question before he could ask it. "The guards on twenty-one are staying in position, but they're going nuts. They've been arguing non-stop with the guards inside the condo. Extrapolating from those conversations, I'd estimate about a dozen guys in there besides Hatfield. Oh, and they called for reinforcements, although the state of the city is proving to be an obstacle."

Dominic ejected the mag from his Glock, popped in a fresh one, and racked the slide. "That'll complicate exfiltration."

Licking blood off her lip, Leila said, "Any other good news you want to share with us?"

"The LVMPD dispatched a pair of officers to the Whitby. They've got their hands more than full with the riots, but they can't ignore multiple 911 calls about shots fired in a building with so many wealthy residents."

"One problem at a time." Levi turned to Martine, studying her as she gagged the last of the guards.

Of everyone on their team, she was the one he was most concerned about. Not physically—she could hold her own—but emotionally.

Leila, like Levi himself, thrilled to the endorphin rush of violence and victory. Even now, she was bright-eyed, all but humming as she skipped down the steps to retrieve the booby trap. Dominic had fought in literal wars. Natasha killed people for fun.

Martine was . . . a normal person, if such a thing existed. This had to be hitting her hard, without the balancing effect of Dominic's experience, Natasha's sadism, or whatever the hell it was that made Levi and Leila love to fight.

She caught him looking when she straightened up. Her face was grim, the strain showing around her eyes and mouth, but she seemed as calm and self-possessed as ever.

"Any injuries?" he asked.

"Took a couple of hits. Nothing too serious." She cocked her head. "How's your back?"

"I'm pretty much running on pure adrenaline right now. I don't even want to think about how I'm going to feel once it wears off."

She chuckled, and he cracked a smile, reassured by the genuine amusement in the sound.

With all of the patrolling guards disabled, secured, and no longer a threat, their team re-entered the eighteenth floor and crossed to the west stairwell. Carmen, who'd continued keeping Utopia's radio channel off their earpieces in the interests of focus, updated them as they ran up to twenty-one.

"These guys are scared shitless. They're holding their ground, but it's freaking them out that they haven't heard from the others and don't know where you are. One wrong move, and they'd probably all shoot each other."

Dominic was in the lead as they arrived on the landing outside the door to the twenty-first floor, close to Hatfield's condo in the west corner. The floors in this building were in a rough U-shape, with a stairwell on each of the short sides and the elevator bank in the middle of the long north hallway. So although there were three teams of Utopia guards on this floor, monitoring each point of ingress, none of them were in sight of each other.

"Like we discussed," Dominic whispered as he set down the duffel bag. "Leila, Natasha, and Rebel will keep the other two teams at bay while the rest of us deal with the ones on the door. The important thing is to prevent them from being able to gang up on us all at once. Carmen will keep the condo locked so the ones inside can't come out to help."

He took a flashbang grenade off his belt. The rest of them stayed back.

"Whenever you're ready," said Carmen.

Dominic pulled the pin, yanked the door open, and spun into the hallway just long enough to lob the grenade toward the condo before he darted back into the stairwell and slammed the door shut.

BANG.

The ensuing screams were their signal to move. They burst into the hallway en masse.

To the left, the three guards on the door were staggering around, disoriented by the combination of blinding light, deafening volume, and concussive force. To the right came the sound of answering shouts and running feet.

Leila and Natasha raced in that direction, each tossing another of Natasha's party favors. The two balls hit the ground and exploded into billowing plumes of thick, colorful smoke, one blue and one red, blending into purple where they met in the middle of the hall.

As the incoming guards let out startled cries, Levi left them to the women's not-so-tender mercies and headed for the stunned men. Sprinting at top speed, he launched himself into a scissor kick; his foot connected with the underside of his target's chin, snapped the guy's head back, and sent him to the floor. Levi dropped onto the man's chest and whipped an elbow across his face to finish the job.

Next to them, the second guard took Martine's beanbag round to the thigh and collapsed with a pained shriek. He wouldn't be using that leg again for a while.

Dominic was on the third guy, and he didn't bother using his gun. He just swung his massive fist in the kind of wild haymaker that only worked on a person too dazed to see it coming. Blood and teeth sprayed across the hallway as the guy went down.

A spate of furious barking sounded behind them. Levi jumped to his feet and whirled around to see a guard struggle through the smoke, only to take Leila's baton to his face and Natasha's stun gun to his neck. Rebel darted into the smoke, forcibly dragged another man out of it, and wrestled him to the ground. Natasha stomped on his face.

The smoke was beginning to clear—those balls were special effects, not genuine smoke bombs. As Levi ran down the hallway, he could make out the shape of a gun-toting guard through the remaining haze.

"Get down!" Dominic called out.

Levi flattened himself along one wall, and both Leila and Natasha ducked without hesitation. Dominic fired a couple of shots into center mass.

"Last two guards approaching along the north hallway," Carmen said. "They're sticking to the near wall."

Leila pressed her back to the adjoining wall right at the corner, one baton held vertically in front of her. Understanding what she intended, Levi stood at the ready by her side.

"*Now*," said Carmen.

Leila snapped her baton out to the side, clotheslining the first guard. His feet went out from underneath him, and he crashed onto his back, choking and clutching at his throat.

The second guy had to veer to the side, away from the protection of the wall, to avoid tripping over his friend. Levi swung around Leila to confront him and ended up face-to-face with a raised gun and a pair of furious eyes.

In a single movement, Levi redirected the gun with one hand and punched the guy in the face with the other; when the gun went off, the bullet cracked harmlessly into the wall. Levi grabbed the gun and twisted it, breaking the guy's grip, and then gave the guy an almighty shove so that he stumbled out into the open. Martine took him down with the shotgun.

That accounted for all the guards on the floor, but more were hammering on the other side of the door to Hatfield's unit, shouting among themselves about being unable to unlock it. Levi and his team moved as swiftly as possible to secure the fallen guards before regrouping by the condo.

"There's no cameras inside, so you'll be going in blind from here on out," Carmen said. "At least you're familiar with the floor plan."

Dominic considered the door, which the Utopia guards were battering with so much force that it was shaking on its hinges. "I don't think the flashbang trick is gonna work a second time. If they're all right on the other side, we wouldn't be able to shut the door again."

"So what do we do?" Martine asked. "We can't just charge in."

As Levi scanned the hallway, he noticed the same kind of fire extinguisher box he'd raided downstairs. There were two on each residential floor of this building.

"The trick with the flashbang might not work twice." He jogged over to the box, opened it up, and pulled out the fire extinguisher. "*This* will."

Everyone clustered on either side of the door, with only Levi standing in front of it. He prepped the extinguisher and chambered one leg for a kick.

"Ready, Carmen?"

"Just say when."

Levi listened carefully to the men on the other side, waiting for the right moment. "Go!"

Carmen unlocked the door exactly as the men were yanking on it. They cried out as it gave way unexpectedly and swung into them, helped along by the robust front push kick Levi delivered.

While the men were still off-balance, Levi sprang forward and unleashed the fire extinguisher, sweeping it back and forth to douse them liberally with foam. The guards recoiled, coughing and spluttering; the few panicked shots they let loose didn't come anywhere near him.

The rest of Levi's team poured through the door behind him, falling on the guards in a whirlwind of snarls, gunshots, blunt force trauma, and electric *zaps*. In short order, four unconscious men lay in a heap at their feet.

One of the condo's features that worked in their favor was that it didn't have a foyer: the entryway inside the door had just enough room to provide access to a bedroom on the left and a narrow hallway around a corner to the right. Dominic jerked his head toward the bedroom, indicating for Martine to clear it while he took point at the corner.

Natasha eased the front door shut and murmured to Carmen to lock it again. That would keep out any Utopia reinforcements—or cops—who arrived while they were busy in here.

Levi heard urgent voices deeper in the condo, along with multiple footsteps on the hardwood floors. Dominic leaned around the corner, then jerked back as a bullet sailed down the hallway. When he returned fire, the footsteps hurriedly withdrew, and the voices grew fainter.

Their team proceeded cautiously along the hallway in the same formation, Dominic covering their front as the rest cleared the bedrooms and bathrooms they passed. All were empty, and by the time they reached the end of the hall, Utopia had yet to engage them again. In fact, the condo was eerily quiet.

Straight ahead was the kitchen, a sideways U of gleaming marble counters and dark cabinetry around a central island. Around another corner to the right lay the condo's main living and dining area—a large, wide-open space where the only cover would come from whatever furniture Hatfield's mistress had put in.

Dominic snuck a brief look and shook his head. "Empty," he said, his voice pitched low. "Whoever's left must be in the master suite."

"Or on the balconies," said Levi. Because this was a corner unit, the condo had two, both of which were entered via the living room.

"Open space, minimal cover—we'll have to split up and clear all three doors at once, or there's too good a chance they'll take us by surprise."

Through a discussion based mostly on eye contact and hand signals, they did just that. Dominic and Leila headed for the balcony behind the dining table, Martine and Natasha to the door of the master suite at the midpoint along the opposite wall, and Levi and Rebel through the living room to the second balcony on the far side.

They were halfway to their targets when all three doors flew open and Utopia guards surged into the room with guns drawn.

Levi dropped to a crouch behind the sofa, narrowly avoiding a bullet to the chest. Rebel bolted from his side toward the two men who'd emerged from the balcony, her bloody teeth bared. One of the men froze; the other shrieked, darted back onto the balcony, and slammed the door shut, abandoning his comrade to Rebel's attack.

Checking on the others, Levi saw that Dominic and Leila were handily dispatching their opponents, but Martine and Natasha were facing off against four men. Martine had shot one and was tussling with a second, using her shotgun as a club. Another advanced on Natasha and managed to knock her stun gun out of her hand before raising his gun.

"Hey!" Levi shouted, popping up from the sofa. "Recognize me?"

The man spun toward Levi, his eyes going wide before his face screwed up with hatred. Instead of taking aim as Levi expected, he charged at Levi like an enraged bull.

Too startled to dodge, Levi planted his foot in the man's stomach just as the man tackled him. He let the momentum take them to the ground and continued backward, using his foot to shove the man up and over his head. Completing the somersault brought him to a sitting position on the man's chest.

Unfortunately, the man was barely fazed, and Levi was *not* good at groundfighting. He blocked the man's punch and had his own punch blocked in turn before he pushed himself off the man's chest and onto his feet. Capitalizing on the seconds it took for the man to rise, Levi vaulted the couch and then the coffee table, heading for a paneled media center holding an enormous flat-screen TV.

The man scrambled after Levi and grabbed him from behind. Levi donkey-kicked the guy in the balls, then twisted out of his grip, punched him in the face, and swept his legs out from underneath him. When the man fell to the floor, Levi tipped the TV out of the media center. It landed on the man with a bright cascade of sparks.

Panting, Levi rested his hands on his thighs and looked around the room. Dominic and Leila's last opponent had jumped onto

Dominic's back, trying to get an arm around his neck. Dominic rolled his shoulders like an irritated horse shrugging off a fly and flipped the man onto the dining table. A vase crashed to the floor, spilling water and red roses everywhere.

Rebel had joined Martine to take down the last remaining guard. Natasha had gotten out of their way, letting them do their thing, and was backing up toward the other balcony.

Wait. Wasn't there a guy—

Levi had no chance to shout a warning before the guard who'd fled Rebel darted back inside. Natasha whirled toward the man, and he seized her by the throat with both hands.

For all her brutality, Natasha was of average strength for a woman her size, and she wasn't trained in hand-to-hand combat. Yet instead of frantically clawing at the man's hands and face like most people would while being strangled, she remained calm. She unzipped her jacket, plunged a hand inside, and withdrew a long, wicked knife.

No, Levi realized. Not *a* knife. *The* knife.

She stabbed the man in the guts.

He released her immediately, swaying on his feet and staring at the knife until she pulled it out. Then he fell to his knees and one hand, the other hand clutching the wound.

Natasha casually walked behind him, gripped his hair, and yanked his head back. With one clean stroke, she slit his throat from ear to ear.

Levi had watched her kill Carolyn Royce on camera, but he hadn't been able to see her face then. And even when she'd killed people earlier today, she hadn't looked like this.

Her face was tipped up toward the ceiling, her eyes half-lidded and her lips gently curved in an expression of utter bliss. She looked . . . *reverent*. Like this was a spiritual experience for her.

She released the man, who toppled face-first onto the floor in a pool of his own blood. Taking a deep breath, she opened her eyes and met Levi's gaze across the room.

He retreated several steps without a conscious thought, his lizard brain reacting instinctively to the alien, eldritch predator lurking behind her eyes. He couldn't even describe what had changed. He was just overcome by the sense that he was looking at something *wrong*.

Then Natasha blinked, and the sensation dissipated.

An insistent pounding made Levi jump and tore his attention away from Natasha. Dominic was thumping the door to the master suite, which someone had apparently shut and locked from the other side during the melee. Behind him, Martine and Leila were binding the downed guards.

"Hatfield!" Dominic banged his fist against the door. "We know you're in there. Don't make this harder than it needs to be."

Leila snapped her last zip tie into place and jogged over to Levi, taking in the sight of the man beneath the fallen television with raised eyebrows. "Everything o—"

She spotted the dead man and went silent, her throat bobbing once. Her eyes flicked toward Levi's.

He gave his head a slight shake: *Leave it*. "Help me check on this guy?" he asked, gesturing to the man he'd dropped the TV on.

The man was breathing normally, his pulse steady, but he was cut up and unconscious, with a nasty head wound. Levi didn't bother binding him; that would just be adding insult to injury at this point.

Dominic rattled the door again, then took a step back. "Fuck this." He shot off the lock and barged inside.

Though the master bedroom was empty, Levi found Hatfield in seconds, cowering in the lavish en suite bathroom. The man was shaking so badly he could hardly hold his gun, let alone fire it.

Levi felt weird about punching a guy in his seventies—but then, Hatfield had started a Nazi militia, so he got over it quick. He disarmed Hatfield without effort, dragged the man out to the bedroom, and shoved him into the chair Martine had pulled away from a desk.

Hatfield was in good shape, not a hint of frailty about him despite his fear. He had a full head of thick salt-and-pepper hair, and his canny eyes were blazing with hatred as he glowered at each of them in turn.

"Bad news," Leila said, dropping the duffel bag on the plush carpet. "We're out of zip ties."

"That's all right." Dominic stood behind the chair, clamped his hands on Hatfield's shoulders, and bent down to speak in Hatfield's ear. "He's not going anywhere. Are you, Mr. Hatfield?"

Dominic nodded to the door between the bedroom and living room. Rebel sat on the threshold, ears perked up, her happy expression at startling odds with the blood matting the fur of her muzzle and throat.

Hatfield stiffened, wetting his dry lips with a nervous flick of his tongue. His apprehensive gaze lingered on Rebel for a moment longer before he focused on Levi.

"I knew you would come." Hatfield's vicious sneer saturated every word with contempt. "My men at the warehouse warned me you'd escaped. You shouldn't have left them alive."

"*You* should have taught your men not to discuss their plans in front of a prisoner." Levi stood in front of Hatfield, forcing Hatfield to crane his neck to maintain eye contact. "They were running their mouths the whole time they had me. We know Utopia started these riots. We know it's a diversion, a way to spread resources thin before a bomb goes off."

Levi leaned over and braced his hands on the arms of Hatfield's chair.

"You're going to tell us where the bomb is."

Hatfield grinned, a sick expression of such pure malice that Levi faltered. "Certainly, Detective. Which one?"

CHAPTER 20

Levi backed away, staring at Hatfield. "What do you mean, 'Which one?'"

Hatfield tried to shrug, though he was restricted by Dominic's grip on his shoulders. "Just that. I'm happy to tell you whatever you'd like, but you'll need to be more specific. Do you mean the bomb in city hall? The one at LVMPD headquarters? Or maybe the one in the Stratosphere Tower?"

The room was silent as Hatfield continued smirking. Levi exchanged glances with Dominic over Hatfield's head; Dominic's face was ashen, his mouth slack.

"How—" Levi cleared his throat. "How many bombs are there?"

"Six."

Levi's eyes fell shut. Beside him, Martine made a soft noise of distress.

"He's bluffing," said Leila, prompting Levi to open his eyes. "He has to be. How could Utopia get that many bombs into such well-secured areas, with the city on high alert?"

"What do you think we are? Furtive thugs sneaking around under cover of night?" Hatfield snorted. "Every one of those bombs was *walked* in by someone who had every reason to be there. You have no idea how far our reach extends. How many people are sympathetic to our cause."

Levi couldn't speak. He thought Natasha would say something, at least, but she hadn't spoken since she'd killed that guard. And she was standing directly behind Levi, so he couldn't see her expression.

The lack of interruption gave Hatfield more confidence. "You believe that Utopia is just gangbangers in the city and gun-toting rednecks in the desert, but we're so much more. Even before Milo Radich helped us make a name for ourselves, I'd cultivated allies everywhere: government, law enforcement, public works. All of them patriots who understand the natural order of things and want to see that order restored."

Remembering Utopia's videos, Levi said, "You think this is what God wants? For you to raze a city to the ground?"

Hatfield made a face. "Please. I don't believe in God. That's just the easiest way to rile up the cannon fodder." He exhaled, shaking his head. "I've lived in Las Vegas all my life. I've watched the city be overrun by immigrants, seen freaks like *you* flaunt their perversion in public with more audacity each year. I've stood by while my city, like the rest of the country, fell under the control of the weak-minded, simpering bleeding hearts who want to destroy the American way of life. But Las Vegas was a great city once. With a fresh start, it can be again."

Levi's stomach churned, his chest heaving with the effort it took for him to remain still. He had to clench both fists until they ached to stop from launching himself at Hatfield and beating the bastard unconscious.

"You know, I keep waiting for one of these fuckers to say something that's not completely batshit insane," said Martine. "But nope."

Hatfield tossed her a scowl before looking back at Levi. "Like I said, Detective, I have no problem telling you the location of every bomb. They'll be detonating in . . ." He made a show of looking at the Rolex on his wrist. "About fifty minutes. Even if the city weren't in chaos, even if you could trust the LVMPD and the FBI to help, you wouldn't be able to reach and disarm them all in time."

"The bombs are all going off at the same time?" Dominic said thoughtfully.

Beneath Dominic's hands, Hatfield tensed. His furrowed brow made it clear that he knew he'd slipped up but didn't quite understand how.

Leila swung one of her batons idly back and forth. "That requires a lot of coordination. And white supremacists aren't the type to use suicide bombers."

"They can't just be on automatic timers, though," Levi said. "What if something went wrong, and one or more needed to be deactivated? With such secure targets, it'd be risky to send someone back in."

Martine picked up their train of thought. "So you'd want the capability to control and detonate the explosives remotely. But six different triggermen? That would mean trusting six people to not get caught, to not lose their nerve or have second thoughts."

"I don't think Hatfield would trust that many people with something so important." Watching Hatfield's face closely, Levi moved toward the chair. "The bombs are all controlled by one central device, aren't they?"

Hatfield's nostrils flared, and a muscle jumped in his jaw. But a moment later, he scoffed and said, "What does it matter? You still can't stop it."

"We can if you tell us where to find it." Levi cracked his knuckles, flexing his hands in their MMA gloves. "Of course, we're on a tight deadline, so we'll need that information quickly."

"How gullible do you think I am?" Hatfield shot back. "You have a few screws loose, no doubt about it, but you're still a cop. You wouldn't torture or kill an old man." His gaze shifted to Martine. "Neither would your partner. Or a decorated veteran. Or a deputy district attorney. You can't frighten me with empty threats. None of you have what it takes to do what needs to be done."

Hatfield's smugness infuriated Levi, prodded at that dark, angry place deep inside. This piece of shit thought he could murder innocent people, destroy a city, and *get away with it*? He believed there'd be no consequences for his evil?

Levi took a single step to the side. "Have you met my friend Natasha?"

Puzzlement flashed across Hatfield's face. Natasha remained quiet, still holding her gory knife. Blood had dripped all over the carpet at her feet.

Now it was Levi's turn to be smug. "Of course, you know her better as the Seven of Spades."

Hatfield laughed. "This kindergarten teacher? You'll have to do better than that."

Natasha tilted her head to one side and smiled. She was standing with her legs slightly apart, her arms at her sides, the knife hanging loosely from her right hand. A single drop of blood welled at the tip, hung suspended for a moment, and splashed to the ground.

There was still a hint of a smirk on Hatfield's face when he met Natasha's eyes. But slowly, the smirk melted away, and the color drained from his skin as his breathing sped up. Levi would have wondered at the source of Hatfield's dawning terror when Natasha was just standing there, smiling, if he hadn't experienced it himself a few minutes ago.

Hatfield was seeing the parts of Natasha that were broken. She wasn't crazy, Levi knew that, but her soul was fractured in a way it was never meant to be. That was a ghastly thing to behold in the eyes of a human being.

"Oh my God," Hatfield breathed.

Natasha took a single step in his direction, and Hatfield tried to launch himself out of the chair. Dominic slammed him back down before he'd risen more than a couple of inches. Rebel's growl reverberated from the doorway.

Panting, Hatfield shrank into his chair while Natasha sauntered toward him, leaving a trail of blood droplets in her wake.

"You know, I've only tortured three people," she said conversationally. "It was necessary, but I didn't enjoy it. Now, *killing* people—that, I enjoy. And I've learned that the worse the person is, the more satisfying it is to kill them."

She stopped in front of Hatfield's chair. He gazed up at her, his pulse pounding so madly that Levi could see his throat fluttering from five feet away.

"You may be just about the worst person I've ever met," said Natasha.

Hatfield groaned. "I—"

"Shh. I'll tell you when it's your turn to talk." Natasha crouched in front of him, the way she did when speaking with children. "Before you, that honor belonged to five human traffickers from the Slavic Collective. They bought and sold children for sex, and they weren't above sampling the product themselves. After I killed them, I lost control a little. Mutilated them. Cut out their tongues, gouged out their eyes, chopped off their hands—well, I'm sure you read about it at the time."

She said that with a self-deprecating smile. Hatfield was breathing harshly through his open mouth, his skin corpse gray and his entire body trembling. Levi was half concerned that the guy might just drop dead of a heart attack before they got what they needed.

Natasha shifted onto her knees. "There was one thing I didn't do to those men, though. Something I *should* have done, maybe, since it would have been more thematic. But it wasn't something that appealed to me."

When she rested the edge of her knife against Hatfield's knee, he all but levitated off the seat in his desperation to escape. The adrenaline of unadulterated fear lent him so much strength that Dominic had to expend visible effort to wrestle him back down and hold him still.

Unfazed, Natasha traced her knife along the inseam of Hatfield's trousers, then rested the point on his zipper. "After all," she said, "castration is *such* an intimate form of mutilation."

Hatfield's strangled sob caught in his throat. There was a flutter of movement in Levi's peripheral vision, and he glanced over to see that Martine had turned her back to them, her posture hunched and tense. He wasn't sure if she was more upset by Hatfield's terror, or by watching her erstwhile friend torment a person so gleefully.

"But I'm a social worker." Natasha's knife toyed with the placket of Hatfield's trousers. "I'm always counseling people to broaden their comfort zones and try new things. And who knows? Maybe mutilating you will be more fun if you're alive to feel it."

"Jesus Christ," Hatfield gasped. He shot Levi a frantic, pleading look. "This is insane. Call her off, for God's sake!"

Levi spread his hands. "What about the past year makes you think I have any control over what the Seven of Spades does?"

With one flick of her knife, Natasha popped the button off Hatfield's trousers.

Hatfield screamed—a piercing, high-pitched note. Everyone flinched except Natasha.

"The college!" Sweat poured down Hatfield's face as he tried to curl in on himself. "The control device for the explosives is at UNLV. The Facilities Management building. Please don't. *Please.*"

"Are you telling me the truth?" Natasha asked sweetly.

"Yes! I swear. *Please* stop."

"If you're lying, I'm going to come back for you. Let me tell you what I'll do then."

Rising to her feet, Natasha leaned over to whisper in Hatfield's ear. As she spoke, Hatfield began shaking even harder, then gagged and cringed away.

Natasha took a few steps back. "Do you understand me?"

Hatfield nodded speechlessly.

"There's no way we can get from here to UNLV before the bombs are scheduled to detonate," Dominic said. He released Hatfield's sweat-drenched shoulders, grimaced, and wiped his hands on his pants. "We don't even have a car anymore."

"I could make it on my bike," said Leila.

"You'd only be able to take one person with you."

"Uh, guys?" Carmen said over their earpieces. "I hate to interrupt, but you've got Utopia reinforcements arriving in the parking garage. And the cops are closing in as well. You need to get out of there."

Natasha turned to face Levi. "We could—"

With an animal shriek, Hatfield hurled himself at Natasha and wrested the knife from her loose grip. Holding the knife to her throat, he grabbed her jacket and dragged her backward as Dominic and Martine aimed their guns at him.

"I'll kill her," Hatfield snarled. "I'll kill this psycho bitch."

Levi's vision blurred. Instead of a knife in Hatfield's hand, it was a gun. Hatfield's face shifted rapidly to Dale Slater's, to Keith Chapman's, to Raul Acosta's. And it was no longer Natasha he held—it was a six-year-old boy. A rookie cop. *Stanton.*

Rage seized Levi's body and exploded. Springing forward, he charged Hatfield with no regard for risk, for strategy, for morality. There was only the blinding fury.

And it wanted blood.

He crashed into Hatfield at full speed, bringing them both to the ground. Natasha rolled away, and Levi knocked the knife out of Hatfield's hand with crazed aggression instead of finesse. Then he punched Hatfield in the face. Punched him again. And again. And when that wasn't enough, he grabbed Hatfield's throat and slammed his head against the floor.

He drew back his fist for another blow. A hand caught his wrist.

"Levi," Dominic said—quietly, not shouting. "If you keep going, you'll kill him."

Levi blinked at the man he was straddling. Hatfield's face was a shattered, bloody mess, his head lolling insensate on the carpet. His wet breaths gurgled in his throat.

Recoiling with a cry of dismay, Levi scooted backward on Hatfield's chest. Dominic released his wrist, and his arm fell limply to his side.

"You should kill him," Natasha said as she approached from the left. "Think of everything he's done. Everything he *planned* to do."

Levi was transfixed by the mess he'd made of Hatfield: Nazi. Murderer. Mastermind of a plot to level a city and slaughter tens of thousands.

Natasha was suddenly right beside him, murmuring into his ear. "Nobody has to know you were the one who killed him. You can even say it was me. The only people who'll know the truth are the ones in this room."

Levi's hands shook.

"Kill him, Levi." Natasha's voice was quiet and relentless, an undercurrent of excitement charging her words. "You know you want to. He deserves to die."

Deserves?

Did Hatfield deserve to die? Who the hell was *Levi* to judge that? Who was he to take matters of life and death into his own hands, to decide when it was time for another human being to draw their last breath?

Hatfield had been an immediate threat when Levi attacked him. Now he was just a broken old man. Levi didn't *want* to kill him.

"No," Levi said, shaking his head. Then, more firmly, "*No*." He rose to his feet. "Hatfield's down; he's not a threat to anyone anymore. I have no right to kill him. He belongs in jail."

Levi stepped aside, moving away from Hatfield's prone body. Dominic gripped Levi's shoulder, meeting his eyes for a single heavy moment before he let go and knelt to administer to Hatfield. Martine came to assist him, squeezing Levi's arm as she passed.

Watching them work on Hatfield, Levi had to retreat farther, ashamed of his loss of control. Leila was standing by the door with her trademark stoicism, stroking Rebel's head.

She raised a single eyebrow in Levi's direction: *You okay?* He nodded, and that seemed to satisfy her.

"I was wrong," Natasha said behind him.

He turned around. "What?"

"I was wrong." Her dumbfounded expression was echoed by the faintness of her tone. "I've always thought that you and I were the same—that you were repressing that side of you, locking it away because you were afraid of it. But your anger is only a product of your unhealed wounds. There's nothing deeper driving it. You . . . you aren't a killer."

"I've killed people," he said, bewildered.

"You've taken life. That doesn't make you a killer." She shrugged. "I misjudged you. I'm sorry."

His mouth fell open as he struggled to find words. "You're . . . sorry?" Hysterical laughter bubbled in his throat, drawing the others' attention. "You're *sorry*? Are you fucking kidding me?"

"I—"

"What do you think is happening here?" The macabre humor of the situation fled, and Levi was left drowning in a sea of adrenaline, rage, and grief. "Do you think this little adventure to save the city will somehow make up for everything you've done? Do you think it'll make me forget—not only the people you've murdered, but the ways you hurt Keith, Adriana, *Dominic*?"

Natasha clenched her jaw. Behind her, Dominic had stood, eyeing their confrontation but hanging back.

"There's no forgetting," said Levi. "Once this is over, you're going to jail just like Hatfield, and you're going to rot there until the day you die. Maybe then God will forgive you, Natasha." He swallowed hard, blinking back tears. "But I never will."

He stalked out of the room.

When the rest of the team joined Levi by the condo's front door, nobody commented on his rant. Utopia's reinforcements had arrived, but since Carmen still controlled the elevators, they were forced to climb twenty-one flights of stairs. All Levi and the others had to do was slip onto the freight elevator when Carmen unlocked it, then ride it to the first level of the parking garage while she disguised their descent.

Utopia hadn't stationed new guards in the garage, so they discussed their plan—or rather, the lack thereof—as they retrieved Leila's bike and headed for the exit ramp. The closer they got to the sidewalk, the louder the screams, sirens, and bedlam of the riots became.

"We still have the same problem," Dominic said. "A tight deadline to travel six miles across a city in chaos, with no form of transportation other than a single motorcycle." He gestured to the bike, which Leila was walking down the ramp with effortless control.

Martine, who'd used all her beanbag rounds, had her shotgun tucked beneath one arm. "We could call Denise now, tell her what's going on. The FBI could get to UNLV before us."

"And if the wrong person overhears and warns the triggerman to change locations?"

"Look," Leila said impatiently, "if one of you knows how to drive a bike, you and Levi can just take it and go."

Levi's stomach turned over at the mere suggestion. "I'm not leaving Natasha alone with you two."

"Whoa, hold up." Martine hurried in front of him, extending a hand to stop him in his tracks. "You don't trust me to keep her in custody?"

"I don't trust *her* not to kill you."

Natasha's glare dripped venom, but she said nothing. Martine hesitated, glancing back and forth between them, then dropped her hand without further argument.

Leila threw her head back with a dramatic groan. "Fine. Then Levi can go with Natasha."

"No," said Dominic.

As they approached the sidewalk, one of the sirens seemed far closer than the rest—and for good reason. "Those cops who were dispatched to the Whitby are about to be right on your ass," Carmen said. "Time to make a decision."

"We— Hey, what's in your mouth?" Dominic said to Rebel, who'd been trotting at his side. "Oh gross, is that *skin*?" He holstered his gun, knelt, and pried her jaw open.

Martine stepped onto the sidewalk beside them. "This is like that riddle about crossing the lake—"

Screeeech.

An SUV fishtailed up to the curb, all of its doors flying open at once, and men poured out of it with guns blazing.

Natasha was closest to the garage, and she ducked back around the corner. But Leila flinched and lost her grip on the motorcycle, which toppled over onto her leg. Martine, dropping her shotgun to draw her Glock, scrambled toward her.

And Dominic—Dominic was caught on his knees and without a weapon, completely unprepared.

With the odd, slow-motion tunnel vision of impending doom, Levi saw a man aim for Dominic's head. Behind him, a shot rang out, and Martine screamed.

Levi spun sideways and flung himself over Dominic.

A bullet slammed into his back.

CHAPTER 21

Levi's body collapsed on top of Dominic, heavy and inert.

Dead weight, Dominic's brain supplied.

As Dominic rotated on his knees, he caught Levi with one arm and drew his gun with the other. The man who'd shot Levi took a bullet to the brain before he could fire a second time. A second gunman went down under a hundred snarling pounds of muscle and teeth.

To his left, Natasha darted out from cover to drag an injured Leila to safety. Martine laid down suppressive fire as she went with them, her left arm bleeding profusely from a nasty bullet wound.

Dominic continued returning fire as well, causing the Utopia bastards to take refuge behind the open doors of their SUV. But there was no chance he'd get himself and Levi to safety before they were gunned down. They were too exposed, too outnumbered, too far from any source of cover.

He'd just have to take as many of these fuckers with him as he could.

A police car skidded around the corner, barreling toward them with lights flashing and sirens wailing. Spitting curses, the remaining able-bodied Utopia soldiers piled into the SUV and fled, abandoning their dead and injured comrades as they rocketed in the opposite direction.

Instead of chasing the SUV, the cop car braked in front of the garage. Two uniformed officers emerged, guns at the ready.

"Everybody freeze!" one bellowed as their feet pounded along the pavement. "Drop your weapons!"

Dominic did drop his gun, but only so he could lay Levi out on the sidewalk. He tore off Levi's hoodie, ripping it in his haste, and unstrapped one side of Levi's vest so he could plunge his hand in to search Levi's back.

All of the air left his lungs in one noisy gust. No blood, no wound. The bullet hadn't fully penetrated the vest.

"I said hands on your head!" One of the cops leveled his gun at Dominic from a few feet away. Rebel growled at Dominic's side, her hackles rising.

"*Settle.*" Dominic gently released Levi and raised his hands in the air.

The cop glanced at Levi, then did a double take. His aggressive stance wavered.

"Detective Abrams?" he said, at the same time a second voice from the garage exclaimed, "Detective Valcourt?"

"Stand down, Officers," came Martine's weary voice.

The cop covering Dominic lowered his gun but didn't holster it. He jerked his chin toward Levi. "Is he . . ."

As if those were the magic words, Levi coughed, drew a labored breath, and groaned. "Ugh, *fuck*, oh my God." His eyes fluttered open. "Yeah, that's exactly what my back needed."

With a laugh that was more than half sob, Dominic cradled Levi's face and kissed him. "You absolute fucking bastard," he mumbled against Levi's mouth, then kissed him again, until Rebel whined and tried to get in on the action.

Levi smiled when Dominic pulled back, his breathing still pained. Though he didn't move, his gaze traveled from Dominic to Rebel to the cop standing over them, and Dominic could see him processing the implications. "Martine—she screamed—"

Dominic checked on Martine, who was speaking to the other officer where the garage's exit ramp met the sidewalk. She was cradling her left arm, which was bound up with Leila's jacket, but she was managing to stay on her feet. Beside her, Leila was leaning on Natasha to keep the weight off her hurt leg.

"Martine took a bullet to the arm, but it looks like she's got the bleeding under control for now," Dominic said. "I think she'll be okay."

The cop finally jammed his gun into his holster. "What the hell is going on? We got a flood of 911 calls about shots fired at this address."

"That was us fighting Utopia." Levi's fingers snagged Dominic's sleeve. "Help me up."

Dominic eased Levi into a sitting position, at which point Levi's face whited out and he clutched Dominic's arm with a trembling hand. They paused for a moment so Levi could breathe through the pain before Dominic brought him slowly to his feet.

"I thought you weren't in Las Vegas anymore," the cop said.

Levi made an impatient gesture with his hand, like he was pushing the remark aside. "There's no time to explain. We need your car."

He received nothing but a blank stare in return. The others heard him as well, and the second cop turned toward them with a frown.

Understanding Levi's intention, Dominic added, "Please." A little courtesy never did any harm.

"Call for backup," said Levi. "Get these men into custody and get medical attention for Detective Valcourt and DDA Rashid. The rest of us have to go, *now*, and we need that car to do it."

He held out his hand, severe and commanding despite being stooped over in obvious pain. The cop hesitated.

"That's an order, Officer," Martine said, steel all the way through.

Relenting, the cop dropped the keys into Levi's hand.

"Thank you." Levi closed his fingers around the keys and looked at Martine. "Get in touch with Denise. Let her know what's going on but make sure she doesn't tell anyone else. If I don't think we'll make it in time, Carmen will notify you."

Martine gave a brisk nod. "Good luck." Her jaw worked, like she wanted to say more, but she left it at that.

Dominic whistled for Rebel and followed as Levi limped to the car. Natasha transferred Leila to one of the cops before doing the same.

Levi stopped at the driver's-side door, bit his lip, and said, "I don't think I can drive."

"Neither can I." Dominic gestured to his bandaged head. "Concussion."

They turned as one to Natasha. After a moment, Levi sighed and gave her the keys.

Natasha grinned. "I've always wanted to drive one of these things."

"We can't stop any bombs if we die in a car crash," Dominic said through gritted teeth, clinging to the door handle for dear life.

Natasha laughed, cutting the wheel to the left to swing around a car and narrowly avoiding a collision with an oncoming vehicle. She slid back into the right lane and blew through a red light at eighty miles an hour.

Dominic winced and tightened his grip.

There were plenty of cars on the road—it seemed that everyone who hadn't spontaneously evacuated earlier in the week was now fleeing the riots, which were spreading throughout Downtown and along the length of the Strip. The cop car's lights and sirens convinced most drivers to get out of the way, and Natasha's audition for the Fast and the Furious franchise took care of the rest.

Dominic risked a glance over his shoulder to check on Levi and Rebel. Levi had his eyes shut; his jaw was clenched so tightly that the tendons in his neck were popping out, though that could be as much from the cumulative pain of his injuries as from a reaction to Natasha's insane driving.

It was disconcerting to watch Levi through the mesh grating. Had Levi ever been in the back of a police car before? Probably not, unless it had been part of some academy exercise. Or hazing ritual.

Natasha whipped around a turn at such vicious speed that the car tilted onto two wheels, then dropped back to all four with a jolt.

"*Fuck*." Deciding Levi had the right idea, Dominic closed his eyes.

After years of jogging through the UNLV campus, Dominic was familiar enough with the grounds to direct Natasha to the right area. As they approached, traffic thinned out and Natasha slowed down—slightly—so Dominic dared to open his eyes again.

The evacuated campus was an eerie sight, like one of those abandoned ghost towns. Nobody had bothered to riot here. Made sense: Utopia had instigated the riots in the first place, and they wouldn't have wanted that pandemonium anywhere near the device controlling their bombs.

Levi leaned forward, resting one hand on the grate while stroking Rebel's head with the other. "Kill the lights and siren."

Natasha complied, plunging the car into an abrupt, unnerving silence that grew exponentially more uncomfortable with each passing second.

Carmen spoke first, her voice coming through crystal-clear on their earpieces. "Martine and Leila are safe, so I took them offline."

"Thank you," Dominic said. He hadn't really thought Martine and Leila would face any more danger, but it was nice to have one less thing to worry about.

A block south of the Facilities Management building, Natasha turned off the headlights as well and coasted near-silently into an empty parking lot. "We're here, Carmen."

"All right. Remember, I won't be able to help you here the way I did at the Whitby. This building has no cameras, no security system at all. And I don't have access to whatever form of communication the people inside are using, either. The most I can do is unlock the fire exit and deactivate its alarm."

"That's all we need," said Levi. "What time is it?"

"You have ten minutes."

No time to be cute or clever about how they handled this. They got out of the car and closed the rest of the distance on foot with as much stealth as possible, taking cover wherever they could. Dominic kept an eye on Levi, but although Levi was moving stiffly, he wasn't letting it slow him down.

Several armed guards were patrolling the perimeter on high alert. After a pause to observe the guards' patterns, the four of them timed their final sprint to the building just right, slipping through the fire exit moments before a pair of guards turned the far corner.

Once inside, they crept through the halls in search of the triggerman. This wasn't a huge building, and it only had one floor—but there were a lot of rooms, and they didn't know where to even start looking.

Dominic wished he were wearing a watch. "Maybe we should split—"

"Guys, get over here!" a voice shouted in the distance.

Dominic and the others froze in place.

"What is it?" another voice shouted back.

"The alarm went off! Someone's in the building."

Alarm? Dominic exchanged a confused glance with Levi. There was no . . .

Scanning the hallway, he saw it—a subtle white box mounted low on the wall of the corner they'd turned seconds earlier. A motion detector, silent and passive, transmitting a signal only when it was triggered.

Just like the one you tripped at Roger Carson's house, you unbelievable moron.

Multiple pairs of feet started running in their direction. Natasha was already trying the nearby doors; finding one unlocked, she pushed it open and waved them all inside.

It was a utilitarian office, on the small side, dark save for what moonlight filtered through the one tiny window. Dominic shut the door without sound and held his breath as the guards arrived in the hallway.

"There's nobody here," said one.

"Don't be an idiot. You know what happened at the Whitby, and who was responsible. Simmons said he wasn't sure Lawson's bullet killed Abrams. If that cocksucker is still alive and that alarm just went off, you bet your ass he's in here somewhere. Spread out and search the building."

Among the murmurs of assent, someone asked, "Should we relocate the device?"

"No. It's too late. Text everyone—and I mean *everyone*. Tell them to drop whatever they're doing and get their asses over here *now*. Let's see Abrams try to fight his way through a goddamn army."

The group outside broke up, their footsteps and voices heading in different directions. Levi reached out to lock the door, but Dominic stopped him and shook his head.

A second later, the door to the next room over—which Dominic knew was locked from watching Natasha try it—rattled in its frame. Then a gun fired as the guard shot the lock off.

They couldn't stop the guy from coming in here, but if the door was unlocked, he'd be less suspicious. Best to take him unawares.

While Dominic backed into the corner beside the door, he indicated for the others to hide. Bringing Rebel with them, Levi and Natasha hunkered down behind the desk against the far wall. It wasn't an ideal hiding spot, but their options were limited, and it only needed to work for a few seconds.

The door swung open. A man crossed the threshold, aiming a gun with one hand and fumbling for the light switch with the other.

Dominic stepped up behind the guy, caught him in a carotid choke, and squeezed, putting pressure on both of the arteries in the man's neck. Instinctively dropping his gun to claw at Dominic's arms, the man thrashed against the choke, but he couldn't make any noise. With all of the blood flow to his brain cut off, the man passed out in seconds.

Releasing the choke before it could do permanent damage, Dominic laid the man on the floor and quietly closed the door again. The others emerged from behind the desk.

"We still have time to find the triggerman and stop the bombs," Levi said, hushed yet urgent.

"Well, yeah," said Carmen. "But you heard that guy. If every member of Utopia in Las Vegas is about to head straight for your position, that building is gonna be swarmed. They could start arriving any minute. Which means anyone who doesn't leave that building *now* is never coming back out."

They were silent as the implication of her words sank in, crystallizing into a horrible realization.

If they stayed here to continue pursuing the triggerman, they would die. But they couldn't leave. Those bombs had to be stopped, no matter the cost.

Levi nodded and inhaled deeply, his face resolute in the dim light. "It won't take all of us to finish this," he said to Dominic. "Take Rebel and go."

God, sometimes Dominic wanted to *punch* him. "If you think for one fucking minute—"

Zap.

Levi choked, his body spasming as Natasha's stun gun emptied its voltage into his nervous system. Then he lost all muscle control, and Dominic had to dive to catch him before he hit the floor.

With Levi safe in his arms, Dominic turned an incredulous glare on Natasha, unable to believe she'd chosen *now* to betray them. Rebel growled, waiting for the signal to attack.

"You should have done me too if you wanted to make a break for it," he said. He'd kill Natasha before he let her get away with this.

She tucked the stun gun back into her jacket, regarding him calmly.

What the fuck was she . . . Oh. *Oh.*

Levi was right: stopping the bombs didn't require three people. Under the right circumstances, it would only require one.

Despite the way Levi had torn into Natasha at Hatfield's condo, he would never let her take on a suicide mission alone while he fled for safety. But *Dominic* would if it meant saving Levi's life. And she knew that.

"Can you run fast enough to get out of here if you have to carry him?" she asked, handing Dominic the keys to the cop car.

"Yes."

"No," Levi slurred.

Natasha retrieved the unconscious guard's gun, checked the mag, and smacked it back in.

"You really think you can pull this off by yourself?" Dominic could help asking.

Natasha's only response was a cruel smirk. Dominic fought the urge to recoil at the sadistic anticipation on her face.

"Take care of him," she said with a nod to Levi.

"No." Levi struggled weakly, his limbs as floppy as an infant's. "Don't . . ."

Dominic slung Levi over his shoulders in the fireman's carry he'd used with wounded buddies in Afghanistan, one arm wrapped around Levi's thigh and the other around Levi's arm. Levi tried to kick him, but only managed a useless jerk of his leg.

"What are you guys doing?" Carmen asked, though the anxiety in her voice made it clear she'd figured it out on her own.

"With me," Dominic said to Rebel, who huffed acknowledgment.

Standing next to the door, Dominic and Natasha looked at each other. She arched an eyebrow, and he inclined his head.

Natasha threw the door open. Dominic and Rebel bolted back toward the fire exit while Natasha raced in the opposite direction.

His heartbeat thundering in his ears, Dominic flew out the door, startling a pair of Utopia soldiers posted there. They took a few wild shots, but he kept sprinting, never looking back, running the fastest he ever had in his life.

Over his earpiece, he heard the screams and gunfire of Natasha tearing through the building without mercy. When the men behind him stopped shooting at him, he knew they'd prioritized her assault over his escape.

By the time he reached the car—unscathed, but wheezing with every breath and seriously cramping—Levi was beginning to regain motor control. That was bad news for Dominic, because even injured and recovering from electrocution, Levi was a challenge to subdue. And Levi's fear and rage would only increase his strength.

Dominic tossed Levi into the back of the cop car and slammed the door shut.

Levi kicked the window impotently. "Dominic!"

Ignoring him, Dominic opened the front door so Rebel could leap inside, then hopped into the driver's seat. He sucked a gasping breath into his burning lungs and shook black spots out of his vision as he started the car.

"Dominic, you motherfucker—"

With the screech of burning rubber, Dominic peeled out of the parking lot and gunned the accelerator, blasting past several cars speeding toward the building.

A louder, higher-pitched scream came through his earpiece—definitely Natasha.

"What happened?" Carmen demanded.

"Got shot," Natasha said tightly. "I'm fine."

"Dominic, stop!" Levi banged his fist against the divider between the front and back seats. "We can't just leave her there. We have to go back. *Dominic!*"

When Dominic refused to respond, Levi shifted backward and drove both feet into the grating with a powerful kick. Then he did it again, and again.

Dominic flinched as the divider creaked and groaned, and Rebel growled anxiously. There was more than one reason criminals were handcuffed before being put in the car.

All he could do was keep driving, heading away from both the campus and the known locations of the bombs, listening to Natasha's progress with horrified fascination.

"What the—" said a new male voice.

There was a gunshot, a scream, and the slam of a door. Levi went still in the back seat.

"Stay there or I'll shoot the other knee," Natasha snapped. She was breathing hard, her voice strained. "Carmen, I found the device that controls the bombs."

"Tell me what you're looking at."

"It's like a laptop inside a metal briefcase. A small keyboard and a screen with a bunch of stuff I don't understand."

A stab of pain throbbed through Dominic's head; his vision swam, and the car swerved onto the shoulder before he righted it. Yeah, he really should *not* be driving.

"Is there a field for a disarm code?" Carmen asked.

"Uh . . ." Natasha paused. "Yes."

"That's good. All you have to do is input the right code to stop the timer. Then the bombs won't go off unless the code to arm them is entered again."

Levi's feet slammed into the grate again, but the kick was weaker this time. Dominic could hear him trying to catch his breath.

"Tell me the code," Natasha said.

"Fuck you, b—" The triggerman's voice cut off in a wail of pain.

Crisply enunciating every word, she said, "Tell me the code, or I'm going to start slicing body parts off one by one and making you eat them."

"Christ—all right, fuck!"

The man rattled off a sequence of numbers and letters. Moments later, there was a soft beep, and Natasha's satisfied grunt echoed down the line. "Got it. Bombs are disarmed."

Dominic exhaled, his shoulders relaxing. But his relief was short lived, because the next thing he heard were multiple loud shouts and a door banging—then a gunshot.

There was a strange note in Natasha's voice when she spoke again. "Carmen, take me to a different channel, please."

Her and Carmen's voices vanished from Dominic's and Levi's earpieces.

"What's happening?" Levi said. "Carmen? Answer me!"

There was no response. With renewed vigor, Levi started kicking the grate again.

The noise and vibration were like nails being driven through Dominic's skull, making it impossible for him to concentrate on driving any longer. He pulled to the side of the road, got out with Rebel right on his heels, and opened the back door.

Levi half fell out of the car, shoving Dominic away when Dominic tried to help. He lurched upright and staggered a few steps back the way they'd come.

"There's no point," Dominic said. "We're miles away."

Levi spun around, lost his balance, and reeled against the trunk. "You just *left* her there!"

"It was her choice."

"She'll die!"

Dominic sighed. "Someone had to. Better her than you."

With an inarticulate shout, Levi lunged at Dominic and threw a wild punch. Dominic barely had to move to dodge it before grabbing Levi from behind and wrapping him up in a tight rear bear hug.

Levi knew how to get out of a hold like this, even pitted against someone Dominic's size. But all he did was sag in Dominic's arms, his breath catching on a sob. Rebel watched them from a few feet away with her ears pinned back and her tail held stiffly.

Dominic didn't say he was sorry. He'd promised not to lie to Levi anymore.

"Levi?" Natasha's voice crackled over their earpieces again.

Levi went rigid. "Natasha! You can still get out—"

"I can't."

Listening closely, Dominic heard the wet, sucking breaths underlying her words and pressed his lips together. He recognized the sound of someone whose lungs were filling with blood.

If Levi heard it too, he gave no sign. "Yes, you can. Don't tell me that after all of the crazy shit you've pulled, you can't escape a fucking one-story building."

Her laugh turned into a thick, burbling cough. "I've barricaded myself in a room, so I'm safe for now. But I'm out of ammo, I'm too injured to move, and more members of Utopia are showing up every minute."

"You—"

"And what if I did survive somehow? What then, Levi? Would you let me go?"

Levi fell silent. Dominic still had him in the bear hug, afraid to loosen his grip for a second.

"Of course not," said Natasha. "But I won't go to prison. And you—you'd spend the rest of your life hunting me until it drove you insane."

"I wouldn't," Levi said, but all three of them knew it was a lie.

"It doesn't matter. In a few minutes, I'm going to bleed out."

As Levi stifled a sob, Dominic rested his forehead on Levi's hair and gave him a gentle squeeze.

"Just listen, okay? If Utopia gets in here after I die, they can take the device off my body and re-arm the bombs. But the room I'm in? It's full of explosives."

"What?" Dominic and Levi said at the same time.

"I saw it when I was searching for the triggerman. Utopia's been stockpiling explosives here, tons of them. Whatever their plans are, Las Vegas is only the beginning." She paused to take a couple of ragged breaths, then chuckled. "They shouldn't have stored the detonation equipment in the same room."

"Holy shit," Dominic breathed.

"*No*," Levi said. "Natasha, don't."

"When this place goes up, it'll destroy the explosives, the device, and every member of Utopia in and around the building. I can end them, here and now."

"Don't you fucking dare." Levi's voice was shaking as hard as his muscles; Dominic could do nothing but hold on, supporting Levi's body with his own. "Don't you *dare* pretend you're doing this for any reason other than your need for a dramatic grand finale. This is your swan song, isn't it? The perfect ending to the legend of the Seven of Spades."

"Two birds," said Natasha. "One Stone." There was a hint of wistfulness to her words when she said, "Maybe someday you can explain things to my son. I don't want him to hate me."

"Then don't *do* this!"

"It's already done. I know it's not worth much to you, Levi, but I meant what I said before." Natasha's voice was much weaker now, the pauses between wet inhalations longer and more pronounced. "I'm not sorry for the things I've done. But I *am* sorry for what those things did to you." One more drawn-out, agonized rattle. "Goodbye."

"Wait!" Levi jerked forward, as if Natasha were right in front of him rather than miles away. "Wait, please— Natasha—"

BOOM.

Even from this distance, the explosion lit up the night sky, a massive fireball splashing red and orange and yellow against the black. Thick clouds of smoke bloomed in every direction.

Levi collapsed, crying freely, and Dominic went with him. Kneeling on the side of the deserted road, Levi clung to Dominic and wept onto his shoulder, his entire body racked with the force of his sobs. Rebel huddled against them and nuzzled Levi's face.

As Dominic comforted Levi, holding him close, he watched the fiery sky that marked the place where Utopia burned—and the Seven of Spades burned with them.

CHAPTER 22

Levi draped his tie around his neck and paused, considering his reflection in the hotel bathroom mirror. Sluggishly, as if moving through water, he crossed the wide part of the tie over and pulled it back underneath.

"You ready?" Dominic appeared behind him, dressed in a somber dark suit.

"This uniform is so ugly," Levi said, still transfixed by the image in the mirror. Halfway through tying the tie, he realized the proportions were way off and started again.

"It looks fine to me."

"Did you know the LVMPD won a 'best-dressed police department' award a few years ago? Whoever made that decision must have been high." Nobody in their right mind could believe that the combination of an olive-green shirt with tan pants was flattering to any human being in history.

Dominic came closer and rested his hands on Levi's shoulders. "We don't have to go," he said gently.

"Gibbs died saving Martine's life. We're going." Levi pulled the knot in his tie too tight, winced, and loosened it up. "Besides, we haven't left this hotel in weeks."

"Okay. My mom should be here in a few minutes. I'll go make sure your parents are ready."

With a light squeeze to Levi's shoulders, Dominic left the bathroom. A few seconds later, Levi heard the main door open and shut.

He pinned on the LVMPD-issue tie tack, then smoothed out the lines of the department's dress uniform. It was ugly, sure, but there was no question of wearing anything else to Jonah Gibbs's long-delayed funeral.

His badge was the last element, placed on the left breast. He'd already shrouded it; a half-inch stripe of black tape ran diagonally across the face of the badge, a symbol of mourning for a fallen officer.

No more stalling. He grabbed his dress hat and said goodbye to Rebel before leaving the hotel room.

His parents, who were staying in a room several doors down, were waiting in the hallway. "Oy," Nancy said as she took in Levi's uniform.

"I know, it's the worst."

"I think you look sharp," said Saul.

"Thanks, Dad."

"You're always handsome." Nancy reached up to fuss with his hair. "But you need a haircut."

"Dominic likes it longer," Levi said irritably, twisting away. "Speaking of which, where is he?"

"Meeting Rita in the lobby." Nancy pinched Levi's chin and tipped his face down, her eyes narrowing. "Have you eaten today?"

"When are you guys going back to New Jersey, again?" Levi snapped.

She arched an eyebrow. Deflating all at once, he pressed his face into her shoulder, and she hugged him tightly. His father rubbed his back.

His parents had arrived in Las Vegas the day McCarran Airport reopened, and he knew they wouldn't leave until they were sure he was okay, no matter how long that took. He and Dominic couldn't have gotten through the past few weeks without the unwavering support of their families.

Once Levi had composed himself, they traveled down to the lobby, where Dominic was standing off to the side with his mother. Rita brightened when she saw them approaching.

"Oh, what a gorgeous dress!" Nancy exclaimed, rushing forward to embrace her.

"And you!" said Rita. "Where did you get these earrings? They're stunning!"

They fell into an animated discussion. Dominic grinned at Levi over their heads, and Levi couldn't help smiling in return. Recognizing a kindred spirit within seconds of meeting, Nancy and Rita had formed an instant bond that had quickly cemented into a steadfast friendship.

While the two women continued talking, Saul put a hand on Levi's arm and spoke so only he could hear. "I know today is going to be difficult for you."

"I'll be okay. It's not like Gibbs and I were close."

"I don't just mean the funeral. I mean . . . going outside. Being seen."

Levi swallowed and glanced at the hotel's large glass doors. He hadn't walked through them since he and Dominic had checked in under pseudonyms, and he was no more eager to do so now. For one thing, the press hadn't found them here yet. Neither had any remaining Utopia members seeking revenge for the utter destruction of their organization.

The immediate aftermath of the explosion at UNLV was a blur of hospitals and FBI debriefings, but everything after that was clear as day: The exhaustive investigation. The shockwave that had rocked the country when the truth of that night—and the Seven of Spades's identity—hit the news and blew up into an overnight sensation. The constant hounding from reporters and the occasional threats of retribution that had driven Levi and Dominic from one makeshift safe house to the next while they tried to recover.

Even Dominic's relatives had reporters camping outside their houses—a barrier to their resolute, self-determined mission of bringing Levi and Dominic as many home-cooked meals as possible. But none of them had uttered a word of complaint. Like Dominic, his mother and siblings all had a keen sense of adventure; they relished the challenge of shaking their pursuers, to the point of making it a competition among themselves.

The moment Levi stepped outside, though, everyone would know who he was. There probably wasn't a single person in America who wouldn't recognize his face. Even now, whispered conversations were springing up across the lobby as the other guests noticed him. Everyone knew who he was and what had happened the night of the riots.

Everyone knew the Seven of Spades had turned out to be one of his closest friends.

Leery wasn't a strong enough word for how Levi felt about going out in public. *Terrified* would be more accurate.

Realizing that his father was still waiting for a response, Levi forced a smile. "It needs to be done. I can't hide forever."

Saul nodded, clapped Levi's shoulder, and left it at that.

An unmarked FBI SUV was parked outside the hotel along with a second escort vehicle, both manned by two armed special agents. Levi had protested the security detail, but Denise had brooked no argument. Although Utopia as a whole had been decimated—many of its members killed in Natasha's explosion, most of the rest rounded up by law enforcement over the following weeks—there were stragglers out there bearing a serious grudge. And even people who meant Levi and Dominic no harm could cause damage through sheer enthusiasm and curiosity.

Gibbs was having a graveside service, so they drove straight to the cemetery. Through the tinted windows of the back seat, Levi took in the city's staunch rebuilding efforts, which he'd only watched on television until now. The city had been dealt a catastrophic blow, but with time and effort, it would bounce back.

Las Vegas always did.

A horde of news vans, cameras, and reporters ten deep was thronging the cemetery gates, held back by stone-faced cops and not a few FBI agents. As the SUV inched through the mob to be allowed inside, Levi instinctively reached for Dominic's hand, turning his face away from the window even though he knew nobody could see through the glass.

The parking lot, while packed, was less chaotic. Stepping out of the car, Levi spotted several members of the LVMPD's permanent Honor Guard heading inside a small building. Each man looked exhausted, and little wonder; Gibbs was far from the only cop who'd died the day of the riots.

In fact, Gibbs's funeral had been delayed more than most—not just because of the sheer number of deaths the city was processing, but due to the need to verify the circumstances of his murder. His heroism now confirmed, he was receiving a line-of-duty funeral with full honors.

Whispers and stares broke out across the lot as people caught on to Levi and Dominic's arrival. Levi jammed his cap on his head and pulled the brim down low, but even with his parents and Rita falling in around him, it was too late. Besides, there was simply no hiding Dominic.

A bright-eyed young officer was the first to approach, bounding over with a wide smile and an outstretched hand. Before he could reach Levi, he was intercepted by a striking figure in a black pantsuit.

"Keep moving, buddy," Leila said crisply.

The officer cringed, mumbled an apology, and scurried away. Levi felt a little bad for the kid, since he'd clearly had good intentions. Then again, this wasn't the time or place.

Leila turned to Levi. "Thought you might not show."

"I thought *you'd* be too busy on your press tour," Levi retorted, a smile tugging at his mouth.

She grinned. Of the four of them, Leila was the least perturbed by their newfound fame, and the most willing to take advantage of its benefits.

For his part, Levi had ignored the flood of appearance offers, honors, and awards that had come his way over the past weeks, as had Dominic. The only one that meant anything to him was the LVMPD's Medal of Valor, which both he and Martine were slated to receive.

With Leila on one side, Dominic on the other, and his parents and Rita behind, Levi walked along the cemetery's pleasant footpaths. The sun blazed overhead, bathing them in radiant afternoon light.

But it was difficult for Levi to focus on the cemetery's beauty when he was distracted by the murmurs of everyone around them, by the stares burning into his skin from every direction. He'd read secondhand accounts of that night online; like most stories, their group's actions had been blown way out of proportion, layer after layer of hyperbole elevating it to the stuff of legend. He knew that he and the others were being hailed as heroes by most.

The awe and admiration in people's eyes would have made Levi uncomfortable no matter the circumstances, but that wasn't what made him want to break into a sprint and disappear over the horizon.

No, that would be the *pity*.

It was different for the others. Leila had barely known Natasha; Dominic and Martine had been friends with her, but not the way Levi had. And it was Levi whom Natasha had focused on, called out, thrust into the public spotlight against his will. He was the one who'd been a notorious hot mess even before the truth was revealed.

These people might see Levi as a hero—but a fragile one, broken by betrayal, ready to shatter at the slightest touch.

Damaged goods.

They arrived at the sturdy white folding chairs arranged at Gibbs's gravesite, and Levi shoved his self-pitying thoughts deep down when he saw Martine. She was accompanied by Antoine and wearing the same dress uniform as Levi, the only difference being the sling supporting her left arm.

He hugged her, careful not to jostle the healing injury. "Beautiful day."

"Yeah," she said, then smiled fondly. "Gibbs would be complaining nonstop about how hot it is."

Levi saw other people he knew: Sergeant Wen, sitting in the front row; Kelly, already crying quietly; even Montoya and Freeman, who'd been instrumental in ferreting out Utopia's mole network. He wasn't up for conversation, though, so he avoided eye contact and took his seat.

Sitting at the end of a row, with Dominic's large body blocking the sight of him from most, gave Levi a temporary reprieve. This day wasn't supposed to be about him; he shouldn't be the center of attention.

The funeral began shortly afterward. Gibbs's casket was escorted to the grave with full ceremony by the Honor Guard, and his childhood pastor gave a solemn, touching service. A few LVMPD and government officials who'd barely known Gibbs made some bland remarks—and then, as Gibbs's mother had requested, Martine rose to eulogize him.

"Jonah Gibbs and I didn't get along," she said. There was a smattering of chuckles from those in the crowd who'd witnessed their interactions firsthand. "We disagreed on a lot of things. We argued almost every time we crossed paths. He was a passionate man—dedicated to his job, steadfast and unapologetic in his beliefs. He never backed down from a fight. When someone or something was important to him, he went to the mat for them, every time."

She paused, choking up. Levi's throat ached in sympathy.

"Jonah fought for me. He took a bullet that was meant for me, and he did it without a moment's hesitation or concern for his own safety. It's because of his courage, his fire, that I'm standing here today. Because of his sacrifice, my children didn't lose their mother."

She had to stop again and close her eyes. Dominic rested a hand on Levi's thigh; Levi covered Dominic's hand with his own and leaned against him.

"I'll never forget what Jonah did for me," Martine said, opening her eyes. Though there were tears on her cheeks, her voice was steady. "As a department, as a community, we'll never forget that he went down fighting for the life of a fellow officer. His life ended too soon, but his legacy lives on in those he inspired." She turned to the flower-heaped casket gleaming in the sunlight. "Rest in peace, Jonah. And thank you."

Martine stepped down. The service continued, but Levi tuned it out, bowing his head to silently mouth the words of Psalm 16. *Preserve me, O God, for in you I take refuge . . .*

The psalm was often recited at the *shiva*. Gibbs hadn't been Jewish, of course, but the God Levi believed in wouldn't care.

After the final ceremonies, the mourners began to disperse, most planning to move on to Gibbs's wake at a nearby bar. Levi stayed in his seat, surrounded by his family, until they were the only ones remaining at the gravesite.

Martine and Antoine stopped by his chair. She knew what Levi had to do next, so Antoine probably did too.

"Will we see you at the wake?" she asked.

"I'll be there."

She kissed his cheek and left, bringing Leila along. Levi's parents and Rita departed as well, promising they'd wait in the parking lot, and then Levi and Dominic were alone.

The two of them headed in the opposite direction and slipped out the cemetery's back gate a few minutes later. Maintaining a low profile, they walked two blocks north to another cemetery—owned by the same company as Gibbs's, but much larger and more heavily wooded.

This cemetery wasn't hosting a famous funeral, so the gates stood open and unguarded. Jasmine, Carlos, and Adriana were waiting outside.

Adriana's eyes were bloodshot, her nose swollen and red. Levi extended his arms, and she rushed into them with a sob, burying her face in his chest. He rested his cheek on the top of her head and held her silently while she cried.

It didn't take long for Adriana to pull herself together. She released Levi, sniffling, and scrubbed her hands over her cheeks. Jasmine fished a pack of tissues out of her hemp messenger bag.

"Thanks for meeting us," Levi said to Jasmine and Carlos.

"Of course. We'll be right here when you're done."

Dominic kissed Levi, then moved to stand with his friends. Levi took Adriana's hand.

"Ready?" he asked.

With another loud sniff, she nodded grimly, her other hand clutching the tissues. They walked into the cemetery together.

Natasha's remains—what little had been left after the explosion—were buried in the far northeast corner. The flat, simple grave marker bore no name, only dates of birth and death. In the interests of preventing defacement, misplaced hero worship, and hordes of the morbidly curious, the grave's location was a closely guarded secret. Even Ezra had declined to know where it was.

God, poor Ezra. At least Levi hadn't been the one to break that news. After learning the truth, Ezra'd had to be placed on a psychiatric hold in the hospital to stop him from committing suicide.

The last Levi had heard, Ezra and Jack had left the state to stay with family. If they wanted any hope of a normal life, they'd have to change their names and start completely fresh so they wouldn't be forever identified as the husband and son of America's most prolific serial killer.

Just two more people Natasha had fucked over.

Levi and Adriana stood at the foot of the grave, gazing at it in silence. Adriana was no longer crying.

"I hate her," Adriana said after a few minutes.

"Me too," said Levi.

"I just don't get it. Natasha *helped* me. I mean she really, truly helped me, and she didn't have to. It wasn't part of her job; nobody was paying her. So why did she bother? Was it all a game to her?"

"No. Natasha helped you because she wanted to."

"She also tricked me, though. She called me as the Seven of Spades and manipulated me into spilling my guts so she could use my voice against you. How could she do both?"

Levi removed his cap and raked a hand through his hair, fluffing up the curls. "Some people believe that the ends justify the means. But usually those people have something in their brain that stops them from taking that belief to its extreme, that warns them when they're going too far. Natasha . . . didn't have that. She didn't think there was anything wrong with tricking you, because she believed she was doing it for a good reason, and that made it okay. The part of her brain that should have told her it was wrong—the part that should have stopped her from doing the things she did—it was missing."

Fiddling with the tissues, Adriana continued scowling at the grave. "You can't know that for sure. You don't know she actually cared about me. She could have been laughing at me the whole time."

"I *do* know that for sure." Steeling himself, Levi turned to face Adriana instead of the grave. "There's something I need to tell you."

She gave him the side-eye.

"Last week, your former foster father was murdered."

Adriana's jaw dropped.

"It was an apparent home invasion," Levi said. "He was the only one in the house at the time. There aren't any suspects, and the only lead is a neighbor's report that they saw strangers with hornet tattoos outside the house around the time of the break-in."

"Los Avispones," she whispered.

"Yes."

"They don't have territory in Reno." Her eyes were wide and shocked. "There's no way they would have been there unless . . ."

She clearly understood, but Levi had to say it anyway. "The working theory is that Natasha put measures in place to order his murder in the event of her death or capture. The Seven of Spades told you that they couldn't kill him because it would reveal a connection to you. Now that she's dead, that's no longer a concern."

Adriana looked back at the grave, blinking rapidly, her face twisted with confusion. "I . . ." She darted a glance at Levi that was full of shame.

"It's okay," he said, putting a hand on her shoulder. "It's okay if you're glad he's dead, and even if you're grateful to Natasha for arranging it. You don't have to feel guilty."

"How can I hate her for everything she did, but then be happy about this one thing that's personal to me? That's so hypocritical. It's—it's not fair."

"Is there a reason it should be?"

Adriana paused, considering, and then shook her head. "I guess not."

"Human beings like to pretend we're rational." Levi shrugged. "We aren't. It would be easier if we could write Natasha off as completely evil—if we could say that everything good she ever did was a lie or a trick, and then cut her out of our hearts like she never existed. If we could deny that some of the terrible things she did ended up having positive consequences."

He put an arm around Adriana's shoulders. She slipped her own arm around his waist and leaned against him.

"But people don't work that way," he said quietly. "It'll never be simple. It'll never be easy. We just have to learn to live with that."

In the aftermath of Natasha's Pyrrhic victory, some people were hailing her as a hero, as if one grand gesture repaid the years of murder and torture. Levi knew better. Natasha's final sacrifice, like every action before it, had been motivated by selfishness. There had been nothing heroic about her.

But she hadn't been evil, either. This wasn't a comic book, and the Seven of Spades hadn't been some genius villainous mastermind. She'd been nothing more or less than a broken human being who'd wreaked untold grief and destruction in her quest to feel whole.

Standing at her grave, Levi was no longer angry. All he felt was sorrow.

In a lifetime of being othered, Levi had never felt more keenly out of place than he did at Gibbs's wake.

The rowdy bar was packed past capacity with people honoring Gibbs by getting uproariously drunk, just like he would have wanted. The atmosphere was lighter than it'd been at the funeral—celebrating Gibbs's life, rather than mourning his death.

But Levi, without meaning to be, was a total buzzkill. People didn't know whether it was okay to approach him, and those who decided against it gave him the kind of wide berth they'd give a man who hadn't showered in a month. The ones who stopped to chat had no idea what to say, bumbling through a blend of gratitude, sympathy, and determined cheerfulness that resulted in one painfully awkward encounter after another. Dominic did his best to smooth things over, but even his legendary charm was no match for Levi's unintentional downer aura.

Half an hour in, Dominic returned to the bar for a second round of drinks—though only after asking Levi a dozen times if he'd be okay by himself. Levi tamped down his instinct to snap an acerbic response. He truly appreciated Dominic's concern; he wouldn't imply otherwise by lashing out.

Alone at their table, Levi studied the half-melted ice in his glass to avoid looking at anyone's face. How the hell was he ever going to work with these people again?

Of course, that was assuming he returned to work at all. Like Martine, he was currently on paid leave—but unlike Martine, he'd be required to undergo a thorough psychiatric evaluation before the LVMPD restored him to active status. The way things stood now, any halfway decent psychiatrist who spent five minutes with Levi would deem him unfit to be a crossing guard, let alone a homicide detective.

He didn't know how he was supposed to get better when he couldn't trust anyone, living in this pressure cooker of nosy reporters, pitying colleagues, and constant reminders of Natasha's betrayal. And who said that all of Utopia's moles had been found? That network had existed long before the attacks; Freeman and Montoya could have missed someone. Even if they hadn't, there was no guarantee that the FBI or the local government had cleaned house.

For fuck's sake, he couldn't even go back to his own apartment. He loved Las Vegas, but he couldn't *breathe* here.

Slumping in his seat, Levi made the mistake of looking up, only to see Sawyer heading straight for him. He clutched his glass more tightly, wondering if it was too late to crawl under the table.

"Detective," Sawyer said, stopping at the table's edge. He was wearing an elegant black suit, perfectly tailored to flatter his body, and was holding a glass of red wine.

"Sawyer. What are you doing here?" Levi hadn't seen Sawyer at the funeral. Then again, if Sawyer had arrived after Levi and sat behind him, there was no reason he would have. It wasn't like he'd been monitoring the crowd.

"At the wake of one of the city's new heroes? Someone from the firm had to make an appearance." Sawyer's lips quirked. "Especially after the debacle with Mr. Hatfield."

A thrill of savage triumph ran through Levi. Hatfield, along with the rest of his cronies from the Whitby, was being held in the CCDC without bail. With the terrorism charges he was facing, all the money in the world wouldn't save Hatfield from spending the remainder of his life in prison.

"Look," Levi said, biting the bullet, "I'm sorry about—"

Sawyer held up his free hand. "Don't apologize. You were doing your job. You were *wrong*, but that happens to everyone. Or so I'm told."

Levi rolled his eyes, though he was relieved that Sawyer didn't seem set on holding a grudge.

"Besides, now I'm known all over the country as the dashing lawyer who was wrongfully accused. There are worse forms of publicity. And the combined downfalls of Park and Hatfield have created a serious power vacuum at the firm."

"A problem I'm sure you're all too happy to solve."

Shrugging one shoulder, Sawyer sipped his wine with obvious relish.

Since Sawyer wasn't here to tell him off, Levi asked the question that had been gnawing at his mind for weeks. "You figured out Natasha was the Seven of Spades while I was interrogating you, didn't you? When I told you the names of those early victims, you realized you'd discussed all of those cases with Ezra, and that it had to be her."

Sawyer twirled the stem of his wineglass. "Yes."

"Why didn't you say something?"

"I didn't think there was any way you'd believe me."

Fair enough. Levi sighed, set down his own glass, and pushed it away.

"I just came over to express my condolences," Sawyer said. "Learning the truth must have been devastating, and for her to die so soon afterward—well, I can't imagine. Nobody should have to experience that kind of pain."

Sawyer spoke frankly and with compassion, but not an ounce of pity. A lump formed in Levi's throat as he realized that, while many people had told him they were sorry Natasha had been the Seven of Spades, not one had said they were sorry she'd died.

Maybe he wasn't supposed to mourn her, to miss her even as he despised her, but he did. And it meant a lot for somebody to acknowledge that.

He had to clear his throat to manage a gruff, "Thank you."

Sawyer nodded, then glanced to his right. "I'd better make myself scarce before that studly boyfriend of yours comes back. Be well, Detective."

Without giving Levi a chance to respond, Sawyer vanished into the crowd. Seconds later, Dominic returned and placed two fresh drinks on the table.

"Was that Sawyer?" he asked.

"Yeah." Levi picked up the Boulevardier, held it to his lips, and set it back down without taking a sip. "I think we should go. I'm obviously making everyone uncomfortable."

Dominic didn't look put out or grumble about how he'd just gotten new drinks. "Okay. Let me hit the bathroom first, though. No telling what traffic's gonna be like."

Suddenly overwhelmed by his love for this man, Levi gripped Dominic's tie and pulled him in for a kiss. When they separated, Dominic grazed his thumb along Levi's cheekbone before he left the table again. Levi got out his phone to text his parents, whom he'd lost in the crowd within the first couple of minutes, so they'd meet him outside.

And then what? Back to the hotel room that had become a cage? Back to having nothing to do all day except relive every mistake he'd ever made and obsess over what he could have done differently?

"Excuse me, Detective Abrams?"

Levi lifted his head to see a conservatively dressed woman standing where Sawyer had been minutes earlier. He didn't recognize her, and she definitely wasn't a cop.

"No comment," he said automatically.

She blinked, then shook her head with a chuckle. "Oh no, I'm not a reporter. But if I could have a minute of your time, I think you'd be very interested in what I have to say."

Walking as if in a daze, Levi met Dominic on the sidewalk outside the bar a few minutes later. Dominic took one look at him and asked, "What's wrong?"

"Do you think McBride would let you extend your sabbatical?"

Dominic snorted. "After the flood of positive press and big-ticket clients my new and improved reputation has brought the firm? I'm pretty sure she'd give me her firstborn if I asked. Why?"

"Because I just agreed to sell the rights to my life story for half a million dollars," Levi said. "Let's go on vacation."

CHAPTER 23

Dominic loved rising without an alarm.

He and Levi never drew the curtains in the bedroom, so every day, he woke naturally and by degrees to the sunlight slanting across their bed. Because the tree-shaded lake house had southwestern exposure, that usually happened midmorning.

Today, Dominic woke before Levi. He spent a few lazy minutes luxuriating in the pleasure of not being on a schedule, then got out of bed and motioned to Rebel. She yawned and hopped down to follow him.

He moved as quietly as he could; the hardwood flooring tended to creak, especially on the stairs. The house was an interesting juxtaposition of woodsy and modern, with pine-paneled walls, natural stone fireplaces, and rustic furniture contrasted against giant flat-screen TVs and the kitchen's top-of-the-line steel appliances. There was no need to turn on the lights, as wide picture windows flooded the house with a warm, sunny glow.

His first stop was the kitchen, where he grabbed a cranberry muffin from the batch he'd baked yesterday. Then he went out to the backyard with Rebel so she could do her business. While she frisked around the towering trees, he ate his muffin and gazed at the shimmering waters of Lake Kawaguesaga—the shore of which was only fifty feet from their back door.

They'd rented this house in Minocqua, Wisconsin, for the entire summer. It was exactly what they'd needed: a secluded, tranquil retreat from the rest of the world. Although there were other houses in the area, the combination of the dense woods, the curve of the shoreline, and the sheer size of the lake meant that they couldn't even be heard by the neighbors, much less seen.

After he finished his muffin, he and Rebel returned to the master suite. She got back in bed with Levi, but Dominic had other plans. He showered, shaved, and dressed; when he was done, Levi was still fast asleep.

Dominic leaned over the side of the bed to speak softly in Levi's ear. "Baby, I'm going to the farmers' market, okay?"

Levi didn't open his eyes. "Mmm."

"Anything you want me to get?"

"Coffee," Levi mumbled.

"We brought enough coffee with us to last a year."

Levi just grumbled drowsily, flung an arm over Rebel, and buried his face in her neck. She happily squirmed closer.

Grinning, Dominic kissed them both in turn and left the room.

When they'd first arrived, Dominic had been worried about how much time Levi spent sleeping. Levi had been an early riser since childhood, but he'd been sleeping late all summer—often later than Dominic, who was notorious for sleeping in.

After that first week, though, Dominic had realized that this wasn't the kind of oversleeping that accompanied depression. It was more like Levi was catching up on years of accumulated sleep debt.

Logically, Dominic knew that sleep didn't work that way. But there was no denying the evidence: Levi was alert and refreshed during the day. He relaxed more with each passing week; there was color in his cheeks and no dark circles under his eyes. Most tellingly, he hadn't had a nightmare in a month.

Dominic retrieved the envelope of cash Levi had set out in the kitchen last night. They rarely left the lake house, so they hadn't needed a lot of cash on hand, but Levi did have a supply hidden somewhere. He doled it out as needed for Dominic's shopping expeditions.

Dominic hadn't been tempted to search for the stash. There was nowhere to gamble out here anyway; they'd even shut off the house's wi-fi. This was the closest thing to rehab he'd ever experienced.

He got in his pickup and started the five-minute drive into town, leaving the windows open to enjoy the cool, fresh air and the smell of trees. Summer in Wisconsin was so different from summer in Las Vegas that they could have been on different planets.

Here, it would have been a lot more comfortable to wear a jacket to cover his shoulder holster, but he didn't need to. He'd stopped carrying a gun on him, even though Wisconsin had reciprocity with Nevada for concealed carry licenses. The loss of that extra weight had been an adjustment, after he'd gotten used to being perpetually armed during the last few months before Natasha's death.

He did keep a gun locked in his glove compartment, though.

The twice-weekly farmers' market was in full swing when he arrived. He grabbed his tote bags and hopped out of his truck to begin perusing the stalls.

Their vacation had provided him with the opportunity to stretch his culinary skills in ways he'd never had time to before. He'd been setting challenges for himself all summer: making pasta, bread, and baked goods from scratch; nailing the perfect risotto; experimenting with shellfish-free paella recipes. His plan today was to make a healthy, flavorful meal that he could cook entirely on the backyard grill.

He hadn't missed a single market since his first, so he'd gotten to know the vendors pretty well. He chatted and joked around with them while he filled his bags with vibrant tomatoes and corn, mouthwatering berries, and the biggest watermelon he'd ever seen.

Though he was certain that at least some of the area's residents had recognized him right away, they'd been respectful enough to pretend otherwise, and treated him like any other friendly tourist. He and Levi hadn't been harassed at all.

Once his bags were bulging with produce, he visited his favorite vendor, a young woman who sold gourmet homemade dog treats. He stocked up for Rebel and couldn't resist a few minutes playing with the vendor's adorable schnauzer.

The truck was low on gas, so before heading home, he stopped at a food mart down the road. Because he only had cash, he had to go inside to pay.

Unfortunately, there was a huge display of scratch-off lottery tickets right next to the registers.

He tried not to look at them, but his gaze was dragged back every few seconds. Those tickets were designed to catch the eye and lure people in, with their vivid, dynamic illustrations and peppy fonts screaming things like *One Million Now* and *Big Money*. There was no ignoring them.

He rubbed his fingertips together, reliving the sense memory of scraping a coin against the foil. The edge of anticipation as the image beneath was slowly revealed, the thrill of victory when his choice resulted in a winning combination . . .

God, it had been so long. He had thirty bucks left; that was enough for a handful of tickets, if he stuck to the lower-priced ones. The truck could go without gas a little longer, and it wasn't like the farmers' market provided receipts he had to furnish as proof of what he'd spent the money on. Levi would never have to know.

That thought was like a sudden electric shock. It gave Dominic just enough self-control to pay for the gas and jog back to his truck, sweat popping out on his forehead. *Christ*, that had been too close.

By the time he returned to the house, he'd reined in the worst of the craving, though he was still shaken and queasy. Levi, now up and dressed, came out to help bring in the tote bags.

Dominic tried to behave normally, but as they were unpacking the groceries in the kitchen, Levi narrowed his eyes and said, "Are you okay?"

"Yeah." Dominic opened the refrigerator with a package of wild strawberries in hand. He hesitated, then shut the door with a *thump* and turned back, still holding the berries. "Actually, no, I'm not."

Levi gave Dominic his full attention. "What's wrong?"

"I gassed up the truck on the way back from the market, and I . . ." It was difficult for Dominic to force the words past his fear that Levi would be ashamed of him, or disgusted by his inability to do something as simple as go into a gas station without losing his shit. "I almost spent the last of the cash on lotto scratch-offs."

"But you didn't," Levi said, tilting his head.

"No."

Levi relieved Dominic of the strawberries, set them on the counter, and smoothed his hands over Dominic's shoulders. "That must have taken a lot of strength."

Dominic's scoff was thick with self-loathing. "Doesn't feel that way."

"Well, it looks that way to me." Levi cradled Dominic's jaw with one hand. "How are you feeling now?"

"Better." It *was* comforting to share the dark turn his morning had taken, and to have Levi respond with calm understanding. His nausea receded.

"Good. Let me know if it gets worse." Levi kissed him, then met his eyes again. "Thank you for telling me."

The words rang with sincerity. Dominic pulled him into another, longer kiss, loving every part of him.

They returned to unpacking the bags, falling back into their usual, easy groove. Dominic's anxiety faded into nothingness.

He would suffer the cravings again, worse than this morning. There was a good chance he'd relapse again at some point. But there was no reason to fear what the future held.

With Levi by his side, he could survive anything.

Levi was reclined on a deck chair in the backyard, reading a book while Dominic and Rebel played in the lake under the afternoon sun. The book was engaging, but he kept being distracted by Dominic's laughter and Rebel's joyous barks as they chased each other in and out of the water.

He felt at peace here. The time and privacy to reconnect with nature, Dominic, and his own soul was having a healing effect, stitching up his psychological wounds one by one.

Though he'd worried that he would second-guess his decision to sell his life story rights, he hadn't felt a moment of regret. No matter what he did, there would be unauthorized books and Lifetime movies made about his relationship with the Seven of Spades. Now there would be at least one version of the story out there created with his endorsement, as one of the contract stipulations gave him final right of approval on every element of production.

Darla, the agent who'd approached him with the offer—a lesbian herself—had also made a passionate case for him and Dominic being positive gay role models who needed their story told the right way. That had hit home with Levi, who remembered thinking as a kid that a gay man could never be a detective. So, no, he didn't regret his decision.

After all, that money had made this summer possible.

Rebel, soaking wet, bounded over to Levi's chair with the stick she and Dominic had been tussling over. Seeing the glint in her eyes, Levi hastily cast his book aside and held up his hands.

"Oh no, no, no—"

She shook with extreme gusto, showering him with lake water. As he wiped off his face, she dropped the stick by his chair and gave him a doggy grin, her body swaying with the force of her wagging tail.

Levi threw the stick back toward the lake. Rebel raced after it as Dominic jogged up to the chair, wearing nothing but a pair of drenched swim trunks.

There were few sights Levi enjoyed more than a wet, half-naked Dominic: the glistening sheen of his tanned skin, the water beading along the curves of his thick muscles, and especially the way those trunks left very little to the imagination. He could have been an ancient Roman deity who'd just risen from the lake.

"Your dog got me wet," Levi said with mock indignation.

"What a shame." Dominic leaned down, dripping more water all over Levi. "I think she missed a spot."

He kissed Levi thoroughly, dragging his wet hands up and down Levi's T-shirt before delving beneath to grope Levi's bare skin. Levi arched into the touch, tangling a hand in Dominic's hair and moaning into his mouth.

When Dominic broke the kiss, he cocked his head and gave Levi a considering look. "Nope, that's not gonna do it."

He had the same mischievous air about him that Rebel'd had, and Levi pushed him away. "Don't even think about—"

Dominic scooped Levi out of the chair and began charging toward the pier. Levi put up a token struggle, his shouts of protest broken by his helpless laughter.

With Levi in his arms, Dominic sprinted down the length of the pier and cannonballed into the lake. He released Levi when they hit the water.

Levi shot to the surface, spluttering, and tossed his hair out of his face. "Asshole!" he said, though he was still laughing.

"Hey, you were already wet—"

Levi braced his hands on Dominic's shoulders and tried to dunk him. Dominic retaliated in kind, and they wrestled with each other, each striving to gain the upper hand but never succeeding for more than a couple of seconds. Inevitably, their scuffling turned into kissing—tricky, because the lake was so deep here that even Dominic's feet didn't touch the bottom. Kissing while treading water wasn't easy.

Then Rebel soared off the end of the pier, landing with an enormous splash that doused them both.

They chased Rebel around in a three-way game of tag, then raced each other to the lake's swim raft, where they played a no-holds-barred game of King of the Mountain until they were both panting and lightly bruised. After swimming back to shore, Dominic retrieved a dog toy that shot tennis balls like a gun, and they took turns shooting the balls for Rebel to fetch.

An hour later, all three of them were exhausted. Rebel sacked out on the pier, dozing in a patch of sunshine, while Levi and Dominic stretched out on the sandy shore. The house's southwestern exposure allowed them to bask in the glow of the afternoon sun, and they were close enough to the lake for the water to lap at their feet.

Levi had shed his T-shirt earlier, leaving him in swim trunks. As he caught his breath, he closed his eyes and focused on the moment's concrete details: the sunlight sinking into his bones, the cool breeze drying the water on his skin, the grit of sand beneath his back, the sounds of Dominic's heavy breathing and the lake sloshing against the pier supports.

This was as close to perfect as his life had ever come.

Rolling onto his side, he slung a leg over Dominic's thigh and brushed his lips against Dominic's chest. Dominic let out a contented sigh, so Levi continued trailing kisses along Dominic's collarbone and sternum, wriggling down the length of Dominic's leg as he went.

When he reached Dominic's groin, he tugged at the trunks to free Dominic's cock, which was beginning to stir. He buried his face into the hollow of Dominic's hip and inhaled deeply, groaning at the arousal triggered by the scent.

Still straddling Dominic's leg, Levi nudged his nose against Dominic's balls, bathed them with his tongue, and caressed the swelling shaft with his cheek before taking Dominic into his mouth.

Without a full erection, Dominic's cock was much easier to handle. Levi proceeded gently, mindful of the suction and generous with the use of his tongue. As Dominic stiffened in his mouth, he sucked harder, relaxing his jaw to welcome Dominic into his throat.

Dominic cupped the back of Levi's head with one hand—not pushing or pulling the way he liked Levi to do when their positions were reversed, but simply creating another point of connection. Levi moaned, rocking his hips to rub himself off on Dominic's leg while blowing him hungrily.

Levi didn't stop until his jaw was aching and Dominic's cock was straining fit to burst. He pulled off, scrubbed a hand over his mouth, and moved to straddle Dominic's hips instead so he could seize a kiss. Dominic responded eagerly, plunging both hands down the back of Levi's trunks to squeeze his ass.

The strength in those grasping, kneading hands drove Levi crazy. He bit Dominic's neck; Dominic gasped and bucked underneath him.

"Take these off before I rip them off you," Dominic growled, yanking at Levi's trunks.

Levi shifted to the side and stripped out of them. Dominic did the same, kicking his trunks into the edge of the lake, and Levi climbed back on top.

This time, he lay flat and undulated against Dominic, kissing and nipping and raking his fingers over Dominic's skin. Dominic's hands eagerly roved Levi's body, sweeping up and down his sides, grabbing his ass, carding through his hair.

When Dominic's fingers slid between Levi's cheeks to massage his hole, Levi canted his hips, spreading his thighs wider and pushing back into the touch with shameless need.

"Yeah?" Dominic asked.

Levi nodded. "Stay here."

Because there was no risk of being seen or heard in the secluded backyard, they'd been having sex out here so often that they'd started keeping the lube next to the sunscreen. Levi retrieved it and hurried back to resume his position.

He cried out at the first press of Dominic's slick fingers inside him. Dropping his forehead onto Dominic's chest, he lifted his ass in the air to open himself up.

The frantic desire for penetration grew exponentially. He fucked himself on Dominic's fingers while they stretched him, his deep groans gusting over Dominic's skin, which made Dominic shiver and moan in turn. Sand scraped his knees and shifted between his grasping fingers.

"Come on," he said desperately. "Come on, I need it." He sank his teeth into Dominic's shoulder.

"*Fuck*." Dominic curled his fingers, found Levi's prostate, and tapped it fast and hard until Levi was writhing atop him.

"Ungh, God, I'm good, that's— *Ah*!" Levi reached back to shove Dominic's tormenting hand away. "Give it to me."

Once Dominic's cock was lubed, Levi adjusted his position, spreading his knees to give himself a stable base. He held Dominic's cock with one hand, braced the other on Dominic's heaving chest, and lowered himself onto that thick erection.

Dominic groaned something incoherent, the only word of which Levi understood was *tight*. Levi eased himself through the initial entry, savoring the pleasure of Dominic slowly filling him up, relaxing his body so he could get what he wanted. When he no longer needed the aid of his hand, he was able to lean forward and push himself harder until he bottomed out.

Levi swiveled his hips, then rocked back and forth, his breath stuttering as he dragged his prostate against Dominic's cock. Dominic clutched Levi's thighs, his fingers digging into Levi's flesh while he watched with rapt attention.

Within moments, Levi's hole was rippling around Dominic's shaft, eager for more. Levi slid up the entire length, deliberate and unhurried, and dropped himself back down all at once. He and Dominic both cried out.

Levi repeated the movement a few more times, but as much as he enjoyed teasing Dominic, this was a tease for himself as well. He could only tolerate it for so long before he gave in to his body's demands for speed and depth, ramping things up until he was bouncing so briskly on Dominic's cock that his own erection slapped against his stomach.

"Yeah, fuck." Dominic bent his knees and planted his feet in the sand, counterbalancing Levi's thrusts. "Love it when you ride me, baby."

"Nnn." Hanging his head back, Levi impaled himself more savagely. He wanted every inch of Dominic as deep as he could get it.

The lake water had long since dried on his skin; now he was dripping sweat, sand sticking to him in random patches. He moaned without restraint as he reveled in the pleasure zinging through his veins, building in his balls and the base of his spine.

Dominic began moving underneath him, matching his rhythm, and Levi gasped at the sudden extra pressure right where he needed it. He fell forward, one hand landing on the ground beside Dominic's chest, the other grabbing his own cock to jerk himself off.

"God, *yes*." Levi bit his lip as he vigorously worked himself over.

"You like that?" Dominic asked between heavy grunts.

"Yeah. Harder."

Their bodies surged together, almost violent in the urgency and intensity of their lust. Bliss raced up Levi's spine, making him twist and shudder. Loud, staccato cries escaped him every time his ass slammed against Dominic's hips.

"I know you want to scream for me, Levi." Dominic pounded up into him, hands bruisingly tight on Levi's hips. "Come on. Let me hear it."

His thighs burning, Levi tilted his hips at a shallower angle that drove Dominic's cock relentlessly against his prostate. Two thrusts like that, and a scream *did* burst out of him, along with a stream of pre-come.

Once Levi started screaming during sex, it was impossible for him to stop—his carnal point of no return. His cries rang out across the lake, his hand flying on his cock as he surrendered to the rising tide of inexorable pleasure. It carried him higher and higher until it finally pushed him over the edge, into a euphoric free-fall that shattered him from the inside out.

He painted Dominic's chest with thick pulses of come, a release that seemed to go on forever. Even after he was wrung dry, shaking with overstimulation, he didn't stop fucking himself on Dominic's cock, still greedy for it. His screams devolved into sobbing gasps, his body writhing through multiple aftershocks.

"God, Levi, you're so . . ." But Dominic didn't finish his thought. He heaved up onto one elbow, anchored his other arm around Levi's waist, and snapped his hips in a blur of speed as he hurtled toward his own climax.

Levi swayed, almost losing consciousness, but caught himself on Dominic's shoulders. Wrapping one hand around the nape of Dominic's neck, he touched their foreheads together, drinking in the beauty of Dominic's eyes and the magnificent soul behind them.

His *bashert*.

"I love you," he said breathlessly. "I love you, I love you, come inside me—"

With a guttural shout, Dominic yanked Levi's ass flush to his hips and arched against him, grinding his cock deep inside Levi as he came. His hips slowed gradually, in time with his harsh breathing, but he was still thrusting a little when he captured Levi's mouth in a kiss.

They were both too winded to kiss for long. Dominic flopped back onto the sand; Levi collapsed on top of him, keeping him inside. Levi's own come smeared wet and warm between their chests, but they were so soaked with sweat that it barely registered.

Panting, Levi kissed Dominic's Hebrew tattoo, then turned his head to rest his cheek on it so he could listen to the fast, strong beat of Dominic's heart. Dominic draped one arm loosely over Levi's back.

They lay joined together in the warm sand, with the summer sun beaming down on them and the lake washing softly onto the shore at their feet.

Levi did what he could to help Dominic with dinner, but he was limited to tasks with no chance of ruining the food, like setting the table and opening the wine. After the delicious meal Dominic grilled, they sat by the firepit in the backyard to eat dessert while they watched the sun set over the lake.

Dominic had found the perfect compromise between his sweet tooth and Levi's lack thereof: he'd made grilled fruit skewers for them both, and paired his own with vanilla ice cream. They chatted about his morning at the farmers' market for a bit, but the sunset was so gorgeous that they soon lapsed into silence.

Even after everything that had brought them here, this was the happiest Levi had been in his entire life. He'd never felt this *whole*, this capable of welcoming the future instead of dreading it. And those feelings weren't just the product of privacy, or time to relax, or the natural beauty of their surroundings.

They were thanks in large part to the man sitting beside him.

Levi glanced at Dominic, who was in deep communion with his dessert bowl. The possibility that had been tugging at Levi's brain for a few days abruptly coalesced into a certainty. No—a *necessity*.

"I've been thinking," he said.

Dominic shifted his attention to Levi, swallowing his mouthful of ice cream and fruit.

"About what'll happen when we go back to Las Vegas."

"That's still a long way off." His forehead creasing, Dominic set his bowl aside. "You don't have to—"

"I do. We can't pretend that this—" Levi waved a hand to encompass the woods and lake. "—is going to last forever, as much as we might like it to. The problems we left behind in Las Vegas will still be waiting for us when we go back. The notoriety, the media attention, the fallout from Natasha's betrayal—none of it will have gone away."

Though Dominic's frown deepened, he didn't speak.

"I know you're worried about me, and for good reason. I didn't exactly handle the past year well."

Dominic scooted to the edge of his chair and leaned forward intently. "Nobody could have handled the past year better than you did. What Natasha put you through would have wrecked anyone else."

"It wrecked *me*," said Levi. "Which might have been okay, except I was already a wreck. I've been a hot mess for a long time. I can't cope with stress; I run away from uncomfortable emotions; I don't trust people. All of that made me an easier target for her—because I've defined my entire adult life by the pain I've endured."

With a startled blink, Dominic sat back.

Levi spoke slowly, searching for the right words to articulate the realizations he'd made during weeks of self-reflection. "When I was attacked in college, I let it take me over. It filled me with an anger I'd never had before, drove me across the country, changed my personality. And when the Seven— When Natasha started up, it was the same pattern. The way I let my suffering define me, it's like I'm saying that those painful events are the most important things that've happened to me."

Dominic reached out to hold Levi's hand.

"But they aren't. Or at least, I don't want them to be." Levi intertwined their fingers. "If my life is going to be defined by anything, I want it to be defined by love. And the most important thing that's ever happened to me is falling in love with you."

"Levi," Dominic said softly. In the darkening twilight, the radiance of the fire played in golden flickers across his face, setting him aglow.

"Even during the worst year of my life, you found ways to make me smile and laugh." There was a time when it would have been difficult for Levi to speak like this, but now the words poured forth without effort. "You've seen me at my worst, and you didn't flinch. You give me strength and courage and joy, and that's why I'm not afraid to go back to Vegas. There's nothing I can't face if we're together. There's no pain that's more powerful than my love for you."

"*Levi.*" Dominic's throat bobbed. His eyes were wide, his hand tight around Levi's own. "You know I feel the same way."

"I do. You make me happy, Dominic." Levi's heart thumped as anxiety finally set in. "And I want to make you happy for the rest of our lives."

He drew one deep breath, then slid to his knees in the sand.

Dominic's mouth fell open. "What . . ."

"I don't really know how to do this," Levi admitted. "It's probably not as romantic as you would've made it, and I don't have a ring or anything—I don't know if I'm even supposed to—"

Okay, he was getting off track. All he had to do was say how he felt.

Levi took Dominic's other hand and looked up at him. "My soul's been searching for yours my entire life. I want to spend the rest of that life with you."

There was a long pause during which Levi could taste his pulse in the back of his throat. Eventually, Dominic raised his eyebrows and said, "Are you asking me to marry you?"

"Of course!"

A smile broke across Dominic's face. "You realize you didn't actually *ask*, right?"

Levi glared at him. With a joyful laugh, Dominic dropped to his knees as well and flung his arms around Levi, crushing Levi to his chest.

"Yes," he whispered into Levi's ear. "Of course I'll marry you, Levi. There's nothing I want more."

Levi kissed him, melting into the warmth and love of Dominic's embrace.

Going home wouldn't be easy. *Life* would never be easy. This was a world full of pain, and it would do its best to crush Levi under its heel again and again.

Now, though, he was ready to face those threats head-on, knowing that he and Dominic were in this together. So let the world take its best shot.

He was ready.

Explore more of the *Seven of Spades* series:
riptidepublishing.com/collections/seven-spades

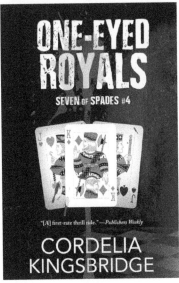

Dear Reader,

Thank you for reading Cordelia Kingsbridge's *A Chip and a Chair*!

We know your time is precious and you have many, many entertainment options, so it means a lot that you've chosen to spend your time reading. We really hope you enjoyed it.

We'd be honored if you'd consider posting a review—good or bad—on sites like **Amazon, Barnes & Noble, Kobo, Goodreads, Twitter, Facebook, Tumblr,** and your blog or website. We'd also be honored if you told your friends and family about this book. Word of mouth is a book's lifeblood!

For more information on upcoming releases, author interviews, blog tours, contests, giveaways, and more, please sign up for our weekly, spam-free newsletter and visit us around the web:

Newsletter: riptidepublishing.com/newsletter
Twitter: twitter.com/RiptideBooks
Facebook: facebook.com/RiptidePublishing
Goodreads: tinyurl.com/RiptideOnGoodreads
Tumblr: riptidepublishing.tumblr.com

Thank you so much for Reading the Rainbow!

RiptidePublishing.com

ACKNOWLEDGMENTS

♠

With special thanks to the following readers for their generosity and support: Arouet, Chiara Allegra, Chika Setrance, I-Db, Karley Beck, Kassandra Girard, Minijdk, Sarah, and Zarknark.

ALSO BY CORDELIA KINGSBRIDGE

Seven of Spades series
Kill Game
Trick Roller
Cash Plays
One-Eyed Royals

Can't Hide From Me

ABOUT THE AUTHOR

Cordelia Kingsbridge has a master's degree in social work from the University of Pittsburgh, but quickly discovered that direct practice in the field was not for her. Having written novels as a hobby throughout graduate school, she decided to turn her focus to writing as a full-time career. Now she explores her fascination with human behavior, motivation, and psychopathology through fiction. Her weaknesses include opposites-attract pairings and snarky banter.

Away from her desk, Cordelia is a fitness fanatic, and can be found strength training, cycling, and practicing Krav Maga. She lives in South Florida but spends most of her time indoors with the air conditioning on full blast!

Connect with Cordelia:
Tumblr: ckingsbridge.tumblr.com
Twitter: @c_kingsbridge
Facebook: facebook.com/Cordelia.Kingsbridge

Enjoy more stories like
A Chip and a Chair
at RiptidePublishing.com!

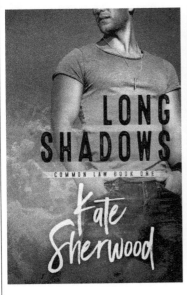

Long Shadows

Sometimes a bad decision is so much better than a good one.

ISBN: 978-1-62649-526-5

Risky Behavior

When inexperience is paired with difficult, things start heating up.

ISBN: 978-1-62649-632-3

CPSIA information can be obtained
at www.ICGtesting.com
Printed in the USA
LVHW092021290819

629406LV00005B/626/P